D0533276

The Cornish Girls series:

Betty Walker lives in Cornwall with her large family, where she enjoys gardening and coastal walks. She loves discovering curious historical facts, and devotes much time to investigating her family tree. She also writes bestselling contemporary thrillers as Jane Holland.

A Wedding for the Cornish Girls is the fifth novel in Betty Walker's heart-warming series.

BETTY WALKER

A Wedding for the
Cornish
Girls

avon.

Published by AVON
A division of HarperCollins*Publishers* Ltd
1 London Bridge Street
London SE1 9GF

www.harpercollins.co.uk

HarperCollins*Publishers*
Macken House
39/40 Mayor Street Upper
Dublin 1
D01 C9W8
Ireland

A Paperback Original 2023

1

First published in Great Britain by HarperCollins*Publishers* 2023

Copyright © Jane Holland 2023

Jane Holland asserts the moral right to be identified as the author of this work.

A catalogue copy of this book is available from the British Library.

ISBN: 978-0-00-861581-9

Typeset in Minion Pro by Palimpsest Book Production Limited,
Falkirk, Stirlingshire

Printed and Bound in the UK using 100% Renewable Electricity
at CPI Group (UK) Ltd

This book is produced from independently certified FSC™ paper
to ensure responsible forest management.

For more information visit: www.harpercollins.co.uk/green

For Becki and Gary, whose love knows no bounds

CHAPTER ONE

Porthcurno, West Cornwall, September 1943

It was a glorious September day and the rolling hills of West Cornwall lay basking lazily in the afternoon heat, the weather still teetering on the tail end of summer. And into this deep, idyllic silence came the unexpected sound of a car engine. Intrigued, Alice put down the novel she'd been reading and rolled over in the straw to peer through a knot hole in the barn wall, still munching on her sandwich.

A large black car was chugging up the steep track towards the farmhouse, sunlight glinting off its windscreen, the whole vehicle bouncing uncomfortably up and down over dried mud ruts.

Alice watched its slow progress with interest, frowning as she finished her mouthful. 'Hello, who on earth can this be?'

She was supposed to be mucking out the chickens. But it was lunchtime, and besides, that wasn't her real job.

Her real job was helping to teach youngsters to read

and write at the school in Penzance. But it was the weekend, so she was stuck home on Uncle Joe's farm in Porthcurno instead, miles from bustling Penzance. Weekends ought to be her free time, of course. But instead of reading all weekend as she'd hoped, Aunt Violet had given her a stack of jobs as long as both her arms, and her only respite was to find hiding places about the farm. The top of the hay barn was her favourite hideout. People often wandered into the barn below, hunting for her, but they never thought to look in the hayloft. So, she would climb up here on a Sunday afternoon, library book in one hand, sandwich in the other, and relax for a few hours, far from the demands of her loved ones.

As the car pulled into the farmyard at last, swerving to avoid two or three utterly unconcerned chickens, Alice recognised the man behind the wheel.

George Cotterill.

Alice sat up, surprised and instantly on the alert. George Cotterill practically ran Eastern House, the secret government listening station in Porthcurno, and had been her aunt's first boss here in Cornwall. That had been in the early days though, when they'd first moved here from London, evacuated because of the bombs in Dagenham, and her aunt had been desperate for work. Only George Cotterill had broken his leg, and Aunty Vi had fallen foul of his replacement and lost her job.

Things had looked grim for a while after that. But Joe Postbridge had proposed marriage to Aunty Violet, and they had all moved in with Joe on his farm. The two were head over heels in love, which made Alice rather uncomfortable at times. She was eighteen now, of course, and knew how the world worked. But that didn't mean she enjoyed the sight of them smooching away on the settle when she was trying to read in the evenings.

Thankfully, there was her eccentric gran to talk to, and the Land Girls who worked on the farm too: Selina, Caroline and Penny, or 'Pickles' as everyone called her. It wasn't always sensible conversation, granted. But there was a war on, and beggars couldn't be choosers.

'Whatever is George doing here, of all people?'

Alice finished her sandwich in a few hasty bites. Then, grabbing her novel, she skimmed down the ladder and hurried out of the hay barn, picking straw from her hair as she went.

George was not alone. He walked around to open the back door for his wife Hazel, who climbed out holding their young child in her arms. Hazel's first husband had been killed on active service earlier in the war, leaving Hazel expecting a baby. Rather heroically to Alice's mind, George Cotterill had asked Hazel to marry him and was raising the girl as his own.

Before Alice could say a word, the back door to the farmhouse was flung open and Violet charged out, wearing a floury apron and with her hair hidden under a scarf. 'Hazel!' she cried, running to embrace her old friend.

Luckily, George extricated the baby before any damage could be done and stood watching as the two women hugged each other with loud exclamations of pleasure, a grin on his face.

'How lovely to see you!' Violet gushed, turning as Gran also came out of the farmhouse, followed by her admirer old Arnold Newton, who seemed to spend more time at the farm these days than in his shop down in the village. 'Look who it is, Mum . . . Hazel and George have come to visit us.'

Gran shook her head in amazement. 'Hello, strangers,' she said to them, and took pity on George, removing the baby from his arms. 'Oh, ain't she gorgeous? Look at this sweetheart, Arnie. What a dainty little thing!'

The child had been named for Alice's older sister, Lily, since it was she who'd brought the baby into the world after Hazel's labour came on unexpectedly during an air raid. Lily had later shifted from nursing to become a midwife and seemed much happier now.

Barely glancing at the baby, Arnie gave a grunt of agreement. He exchanged nods with George Cotterill. 'How do, George?'

'Very well, thank you, Arnold. How's business in the shop these days?' George asked, shaking the old man's hand.

'Ah, you know . . . can't complain.'

'Though he always does,' Gran threw in slyly.

Arnold grinned before adding, 'Supplies are hard to come by. But there is a war on, so that's no surprise.' He gave a throaty chuckle. 'Unless you want a turnip for your Cornish pasty. Plenty of them hereabouts.'

Both men laughed, but nobody else seemed to find that funny.

'My goodness,' Violet said, her fair hair glinting in the sunlight as she cooed over the baby, 'how Baby Lily's grown since we last saw her. I wish Joe were here. But he's out tramping the fields with the dogs somewhere. Hazel, I hope you'll stay long enough for him to say hello to you and George.' She gave her old friend a cheery wink.

'Meanwhile, how about a nice cuppa and a slice of Cornish hevva cake? I tried that recipe you gave me and it turned out smashin'.'

'I'd like that, Vi, sounds proper tasty,' Hazel agreed, beaming with pleasure.

Hazel was wearing her hair longer than was fashionable these days. Not that Alice paid much attention to fashion. But the soft rolls of glossy dark hair that hung past Hazel's shoulders gave her a more relaxed look than when they'd worked together as cleaners at Eastern House. And her face was full of joy too, no longer frowning with constant worries. It was obvious that married life – or perhaps motherhood – suited her.

'Hello,' Alice said loudly, though nobody was paying her much attention.

Still, George had noticed her, and gave her a friendly nod. 'How do you do, Alice?' He removed his hat, turning it in his hands as he looked her up and down. His dark hair was already silvering, though she'd never thought of him as old, exactly, for he and Hazel were both in their thirties. 'You look well.'

'Fit as a fiddle,' Alice agreed, wondering why he sounded so awkward. 'I see you didn't bring Charlie with you. Has he gone away?'

Charlie was Hazel's son by her first husband, and had made friends with Alice and her older sister Lily when they'd all been forced to share Hazel's tiny cottage two years before. Aunty Vi had found them new digs soon enough, but Alice still remembered those days fondly, even if Charlie had caused more than his fair share of trouble as a lad.

'Yes, Charlie's busy with his war work. Seems to be enjoying it too. Talking of which . . .' Again, George looked fidgety. 'I thought maybe you and I could have a little chat.'

Alice was astonished. 'You want to talk to *me*?'

Violet had caught some of this conversation and was frowning. ''Ere, what's that? You're not offering her a job at Eastern House, are you, George?' Her Dagenham accent sharpened as she added, 'I mean, I'm sure we're very grateful to you. But Alice has a steady job now, working at the school in Penzance. She's a bright girl. She don't need to be mopping up after soldiers – you can be sure of that.'

George cleared his throat. 'It's confidential business, I'm afraid,' he told them, shooting Violet an apologetic look. 'I need to talk to Alice on her own, if you don't mind.'

Alice said nothing but her heart began to thump. Confidential business? What on earth could he mean?

'On her own?' Aunty Violet was staring.

'Let's go inside,' Gran said diplomatically, still cradling the baby in her arms, and shepherded Violet and Hazel into the kitchen. 'We was about to make a few loaves of bread,' she told Hazel with a smile. 'But I can manage on me own. And Arnie here can look after the baby.'

'Eh?' Arnold began to protest.

Gran ignored her beau though, as she usually did. 'You and Vi can have a good ol' natter in the snug. We'll be fine.'

Throwing a confused backwards glance at Alice, Violet nonetheless allowed herself to be dragged inside by her friend Hazel, the promise of a cosy catch-up chat no doubt too enticing to resist.

Left alone with George Cotterill, Alice felt unaccountably

nervous. Equally though, she couldn't wait to hear what he had to say. She tucked her book under her arm and nodded towards the gate that led into the pasture. It was a nice day and perfectly fine for walking.

'How about a stroll?'

Replacing his hat, George smiled. 'Lead on,' he agreed easily.

The September sunshine was warm on her back. So warm it could almost have been midsummer still. The fields were thrumming with bees and painted butterflies, a skylark singing so high above their heads it was a mere speck in the blue sky. Joe's farm being situated near the coast meant the sea was a constant whisper in their ears, though its shining strip was invisible at that point. She loved this wild piece of land, but Joe had sadly admitted it would probably need to make way for crops soon, to help with the war effort.

They walked as far as the cluster of bent, gnarled trees near the centre, dominating the sloping Cornish landscape.

There, Alice stopped and looked round at their unexpected visitor.

'Well?' she asked, rather abruptly, unable to contain her curiosity any longer. 'What's this all about?'

'I have to ask you a difficult question.' George studied her from under the shady brim of his hat. He was no longer smiling, a sombre look in his eyes instead. 'I need you to think carefully before you answer.'

She felt again that quick thump of her heart. 'Go on, I'm listening.'

'Would you be willing to serve your country, Alice Fisher,' George said slowly, his gaze fixed steadily on her face, 'even if it was dangerous, if it meant you might lose your life?'

She took a moment to consider that carefully, as he had requested, though there was no real need. She already knew the answer. Many people risked their lives every day for the sake of England's freedom. It would be a poor show if she couldn't find the same courage.

'Yes.'

He took a deep breath and then nodded. 'Good.' Then he reached inside his jacket and withdrew a folded sheet of paper before handing it to her. 'This came to me at Eastern House. I expect they weren't sure of your current address, what with you working in Penzance these days. But they had your aunt's details on file from when she used to work for us.' He cleared his throat. 'Anyway, I don't need to tell you to keep your mouth shut about this.'

Alice took the document he was holding out. 'What's this?'

'Don't open it yet. Wait until I've gone.' George checked over his shoulder, and she looked too. Just visible in the distance, Uncle Joe was heading home with his dogs. The farmer called out and raised a hand, and they both waved back. 'Pop it in your pocket. Then we can talk.'

Obediently, she folded the letter and pushed it into the deep pocket of her skirt.

Watching this, George nodded in satisfaction. 'You're eighteen now, Alice, so it won't be any surprise to hear you've been drafted.'

Her jaw dropped. She was surprised, in fact. She'd assumed her work at the school would protect her from being called up to work in some northern factory.

'Drafted? But where? And to do what?'

'Specialist war work. I can't say much more, I'm afraid. But you're to report to the address in that document within seven days.'

Alice blinked, taking that in. 'Please, can't you tell me where, at least?' She was shocked at the thought of leaving her family.

'Bude,' he said quietly, once more glancing over his shoulder. But Uncle Joe and his dogs were no longer in sight, and the countryside lay peaceful and still. 'You'll be paid weekly,' he went on, 'with accommodation already arranged for you. The details are all in the letter.'

Alice had studied maps of Cornwall and knew that Bude was a seaside resort on the north coast, close to the border with Devon and a good day's journey from remote Porthcurno. Her overactive imagination conjured up all sorts of possibilities, mostly culled from Saturday matinee war films at the cinema in Penzance. The sort of inspirational movies that depicted courageous women working away from home for the good of Britain and her allies.

'Bude? But that's miles away . . .' She chewed on her lip, a little unnerved by the thought of leaving behind everyone she knew and loved to work among strangers at the north end of Cornwall. 'Why all the secrecy? What kind of work will I be doing?'

But George merely tapped the side of his nose. 'Mum's the word. And you're not to mention this to anyone except your aunt and gran, all right?' He gave her one of his rare smiles. 'I know *they* can be trusted to keep it under their hats.'

Alice regarded him, frowning. 'Yes, but other people are

going to wonder where I'm going and why. What should I tell them?'

He shrugged. 'You'll think of something. Smart girl like you.' He looked up at the blue skies over the sea and expelled a long breath. 'Phew, it's lovely up here. I can see why you and Violet like it.' He glanced at her sharply. 'But your skills will be put to better use elsewhere. You know that, don't you?'

It was a question that didn't seem to need an answer.

Alice and George walked back to the farmhouse together without saying much, both lost in thought. A cloud scudded in front of the sun, casting a dark shadow over the landscape, and a slight breeze whipped up off the sea. Alice shivered, hair flying, skirt ruffled, and hugged herself. *Would you be willing to serve your country, even if it was dangerous, if it meant you might lose your life?* What on earth had possessed her to say yes? Exactly what had she let herself in for?

They trod carefully across the farmyard, avoiding the chickens who were always left to run loose about the place. 'You all right, Alice?' George asked as they came to the side door into the kitchen. He studied her, a frown in his eyes. 'Look, it's a big step, I know. And you can always say no if you get to Bude and it feels wrong.' He paused. 'But I hope you'll make a go of it. Someone's obviously pulled a few strings to get you this opportunity. Not many girls get to do this kind of training.'

She stared at him. *This kind of training? Mum's the word?* It sounded like top-secret work to her, for sure.

'I'll do my best,' she said, though she felt rattled.

'That's the spirit,' George said with an encouraging wink,

and disappeared inside the farmhouse to join his wife and baby daughter.

As soon as he'd gone, Alice ran for the hay barn and pulled the door shut behind her, standing in the dusty straw to read the document he'd given her. She knew she'd not get a moment to herself for hours once she went into the farmhouse.

But she was soon disappointed. For the letter, which had been addressed to *Miss Alice Fisher, courtesy of George Cotterill, Eastern House, Porthcurno*, gave almost as little away as George had done.

Her mouth quirked as she studied the sheet. Perhaps he couldn't say more because he didn't *know* more.

TOP SECRET was written in bold red capitals at the top of the sheet. That instantly got her excited. But the rest was mundane.

She was to report with her identity papers to Belle Vue Printers, Belle Vue Road, Bude, in seven days' time. Her accommodation would be half-board, with her ration book to be handed over to a Mrs F. Pritchard, Proprietor at Ocean View Guest House, Downs View Road, Bude.

The war work in the description line was merely noted as 'Intelligence Training'. No uniform would be given, with trainees instructed to wear 'civvies' instead, everyday clothing. Remuneration was set at an impressive thirty shillings a week, but since nearly half that was assigned to cover food and accommodation, she had to admit it wasn't much higher than her current wages as a lowly class assistant. Though a thousand times more exciting, she felt sure.

No further details were given.

Intelligence Training.

For some minutes, she stood motionless in the hay barn, rereading those words, her heart thumping like a drum in her chest.

Someone's obviously pulled a few strings to get you this opportunity.

She thought instantly of her father, but she couldn't ever ask if this training had come through him. Dad was dead. Or was supposed to be. Her German-born father, Ernest Fisher, was in fact still very much alive, and working undercover in his native country as a British spy.

For a long time after their mother had died in the Blitz, she and her sister had thought their father dead too, the government having declared him 'missing in action' early in the war. But to their amazement, Ernest Fisher had turned up in Cornwall earlier that summer, making himself known to Lily first, who had recently married and was living in St Ives with her husband Tristan. His visit had been fleeting though, and he'd returned to Germany within days, warning the family not to let anyone know he was still alive. It was safer for people to think their father was dead, he'd told his two daughters, so he could continue his work behind enemy lines without being compromised.

Alice had thought her father ever so brave to be working undercover in such a dangerous situation, and both she and Lily had promised faithfully to keep his secret. Now this letter had arrived via Eastern House, the government's top-secret listening base, and it was hard not to suspect her father was behind it.

During his recent visit, she'd told her dad how much she admired him, and also how she loved reading spy stories and imagining she was reading about him.

'Sometimes I watch strangers walking about Penzance, and try to figure out who they are and what they're doing in town, just for the fun of it,' she'd admitted bashfully.

'Ah, my little Alice,' Dad had said with a fond smile, his strong arm about her shoulders, 'you're a born spy.'

Now this.

Was it possible her absent dad had put in a good word to get her this placement? Not that it mattered. She was just glad to be doing something important at last.

Excitement flooded her as she stood there, her heart racing, and the hand that held the letter began to tremble. Not out of fear, she realised, but with a flush of enthusiastic energy. She couldn't wait to pack her bags and travel to Bude, to get started on this new challenge . . .

Her heart sank though. She didn't want to leave the farm and everyone she loved best in the world. But she couldn't be in two places at once. And she'd already said yes to going, so that was that.

Alice studied the letter again, suddenly uneasy. Aunty Violet would be bound to put her oar in, demanding to know why she was leaving the farm and her comfy job as a teaching assistant. She could hardly tell them the truth, could she? Her close family knew about Dad's secret identity, but George had made it clear she couldn't share her special news with them.

Besides, the letter had TOP SECRET in bold red letters across the top. Hardly an invitation to blurt it all out over dinner.

Like George had said, she needed to come up with a cover story. And it had better be a bloomin' good one, to get past her Aunty Vi's bloodhound nose for fibs.

Belle Vue Printers.

Perhaps she could say she was being drafted to Bude to print wartime information pamphlets for the Ministry of Food or Information. That would make sense. Everyone knew she was keen on books and reading.

Besides, government pamphlets were often delivered with the post, and dozens of posters were sent to the school every month to be pinned up for display to parents and staff. Bright, illustrated posters urging people to dig for victory or make-do-and-mend or how best to cook for a family of four on rations. Someone had to print those pamphlets and posters for distribution, and it would certainly be considered 'war work'. Yes, that would keep any awkward questions at bay for now . . .

Slowly, she shouldered her way out of the barn and into the September sunshine, still clutching the letter in a daze.

'Penny for them,' a voice called out cheerfully.

It was Penny herself, or rather 'Pickles' as they always called her, one of the three Land Girls who'd been working on Joe's farm for almost two years now. A comfortably built girl with ample hips and a friendly smile, clad in the breeches and green jersey allotted to the Land Girls – Alice had always liked her best of the three. Perhaps that was because Penny reminded her of Lily, her older sister, who was a similar age and equally kind and easy to be around. Penny didn't mind spending time with Alice either, despite the age difference between them, for Alice was only eighteen to her twenty-two. She'd been brought up very differently to the Fishers though, coming from a posh family somewhere in the Home Counties. But she never gave herself airs and graces, unlike the other two Land

Girls, who were forever mocking Gran's Dagenham accent behind her back.

No, Penny was a good 'un. And now she'd spotted the letter.

'What's that?' Penny asked innocently, tipping the brim of her floppy hat back to peer down at it. 'Has your sister Lily written to you again? How's she getting along with married life?'

'Oh, no, it's . . .' Hurriedly, Alice folded the sheet again and shoved it into her generous skirt pocket. 'I've been drafted, if you must know. War work.'

'Goodness!'

'It's not too bad. A government-run printing press up in Bude.' Alice smiled as the cover story came easily to her lips, relieved to hear how natural it sounded. 'Though I'll have to leave fairly soon. They don't give you much notice.'

'Bude?' Pickles looked blank. 'Where on earth is that?'

'On the north coast of Cornwall. Up near the border with Devon.' Walking back towards the farmhouse with her, Alice struggled to remember her geography classes. 'They've got some good beaches there. And, erm, fishing. And the town is popular with holidaymakers. Before the war, anyway.'

'Sounds heavenly. Porthcurno is beautiful but . . .' Pickles bit her lip, her large blue eyes wistful. 'Well, there aren't many people here, are there? Or places to go for company. There's only Mr Newton's shop in the village, and the pub, and the church . . . Otherwise it's a bit dead. And it's such a long trek into Penzance for the pictures or a dance.'

'I suppose so. But you're in a for a treat today.' Alice flashed her a quick grin, hoping Penny would take the hint and leave her to mull over her news alone. 'Aunty Vi's friend Hazel has come to visit, with her husband and baby. You could have a chat with them, if you hurry.'

Uncle Joe's sheepdogs were lying in the shade by the kitchen door, panting. So he must have come home while she and George were talking.

The other two Land Girls were walking down the track from the upper fields, chatting and laughing together, their hats pushed back and held in place by knotted strings. Whatever job they'd been doing, Joe must have released them early. But he was always doing that, soft-hearted soul that he was, and too generous for his own good, as Gran was forever complaining.

Penny shot her co-workers a resentful look and folded her arms across her chest. Rather belatedly, Alice noticed the girl's flushed cheeks. Penny must have had a row with Selina and Caroline again. Last year, the Land Girls had been thick as thieves, going everywhere together as an inseparable trio. Now it was obvious that allegiances had shifted and Penny was being given the cold shoulder by the other two.

'You lot had another barney, then?' Alice asked her friend bluntly. She liked the word, 'barney'. It was what her gran used instead of 'argument'.

Penny hesitated, then muttered, 'Selly and Caro aren't being very nice to me, that's all I'm saying,' and dragged one of her long fair plaits into her mouth. 'You're lucky, Alice, being able to get out of here,' she said indistinctly, chewing on the end of her plait as she eyed her fellow workers with unhappiness. 'I wish to goodness I was going with you.'

'Watch out Gran don't see you chewing your hair,' Alice warned her automatically. 'She'll read you the Riot Act.'

Gran saw it as her duty to look after the Land Girls in the absence of their mothers, often advising them on matters such as boyfriends and nail-chewing. Alice suspected the girls paid her little attention, but it didn't stop Gran trying.

Penny spat out the soggy plait end with a grin. 'Bad habit, I know. I'll be growing a hairball in my stomach if I keep on doing it, your gran always says.' But she hesitated, her hand on the side door handle. Inside the kitchen, they could both hear the baby crying and the sound of women laughing and cooing over the child. 'I've been checking the bulletins lately. To see if I can get war work somewhere else,' she admitted in a whisper.

Shocked, Alice stared at her. 'You're thinking of leaving the farm?'

'I don't know. I can't decide.' Penny pushed the door and they trailed into the kitchen together, the Land Girl carefully removing her mucky outdoor shoes and slipping on the clogs that Violet asked them to wear about the farmhouse. She turned to Alice, her voice low. 'You won't say a word to Joe, will you? I've not made up my mind yet. And maybe I won't be able to find anywhere else. Or the Land Girls' coordinator might refuse permission for me to move.'

'Mum's the word,' Alice promised her, borrowing George's phrase.

But her brain was still fizzing with excitement over the

letter. Soon, she'd have to tell Violet and Joe and Gran about her imminent departure, and blimey, they'd kick up such a fuss. But that could wait until after dinner, when George and Hazel had left, the Land Girls had gone up to their bunks and Newton back to his rooms behind the village shop, and the farmhouse was quiet again.

Caroline and Selina wandered in, still chattering noisily about boys, and kicked off their shoes before heading over to the sink to wash their hands.

'Oh, Alice, love, come and see Baby Lily,' her aunt urged her fondly, holding out the plump, rosy-cheeked child, who looked nothing like her blonde namesake. 'Mind she's not sick on you though. She just chucked up on our Joe.'

And everybody laughed, apparently finding this amusing. Even Uncle Joe, who was wiping his shirt with a damp cloth.

Alice looked round at them all and felt a real pang in her heart. She would miss them.

But that wouldn't stop her leaving.

CHAPTER TWO

With the blackout curtain pulled firmly down and the bedside lamp on, Penny leant on her elbow in bed, peering at the Cornish newspaper with little hope of finding fresh war work advertised there, not least because it was three weeks out of date, having been rescued from the fireside pile where it was waiting to be turned into screws for lighting the logs. In the narrow bed opposite, Caroline lay flicking through a women's magazine, and Selina lay above her in the upper bunk, snoring gently.

She'd never felt so alone and unhappy in all her born days. But it wasn't her fault that she and Caro had argued.

Jack, one of the young soldiers who manned the barbed-wire barriers in the village, part of the security precautions around Eastern House, had smiled at her last Wednesday, and that incident had caused an absolute humdinger of a row.

It had been their half-day off, and she, Caro and Selina had wandered down into Porthcurno village for something to do, there being no time to take the bus into Penzance to look at the shops as usual or enjoy a spot of paddling on the seafront, which was strictly *verboten* in Porthcurno, the sandy beach there having been mined to kingdom come. They'd stopped for a chat with the guardsmen on the main entrance to the military camp, and Caroline had flirted and tried to catch Jack's eye as usual. He was her favourite, of course, being what she called 'flaxen-haired' and therefore a god among men, apparently.

Only he'd turned to smile at Penny instead and offered her a cigarette.

Penny had refused at once, panicking at the look in Caro's eyes, and hurried away. She still had no idea what had possessed him to do such an unexpected thing, when Caroline was by far the prettier of them all, and he had never looked twice at Penny before.

But Caro had not let up the entire walk back to the farm, furiously claiming that Penny had 'made eyes' at Jack and was trying to 'steal' her chosen boy. All nonsense, but even Selina's common-sense responses had not convinced Caro, and ever since that day, they'd been at daggers drawn.

After nearly a week of this icy treatment, she'd given up and apologised at breakfast that morning, even though she hadn't done anything wrong.

'You're right, Caro,' Penny had stumbled over the lie, never terribly good at subterfuge. 'I . . . I probably did talk to Jack a bit longer than I ought, and I'm very sorry. I hope you'll forgive me.'

But Caro had not forgiven her, her eyes spitting fire over the home-made jam and pot of weak tea that barely did for one, let alone three people. 'Don't you dare speak to me again, Pickles,' she'd declared, gesticulating wildly with her cutlery. 'I thought you were nice. But you're a thief and a bad girl, I see that now.' Her lips had thinned. 'Jack is mine, so keep your blasted mitts off him, do you hear me?'

Joe had come ambling downstairs at that moment, pulling up his braces, with sleep still in his eyes, and caught the tail end of this spat. He hadn't said a word but looked at them both in amazed reproof. Then they'd trudged out to till the fields. Thanks to the farmer working alongside them all day, no more had been said. But Caro's face had been a picture of disdain.

They'd had rows before, but nothing on this scale. And Selina was wrapped up in her own love life, with a boyfriend in the armed forces who wrote to her almost every week, so she hadn't bothered trying to soothe Caroline's temper as usual.

That was why Penny simply had to escape Postbridge Farm, so long as it wouldn't get her into trouble with the government. She had no intention of dodging the war work she was legally obliged to do. She would work anywhere she could find an approved position. But it was more than flesh could bear to put up with Caro's cold shoulder for however many more years this war would last, and anywhere else would do, frankly. She'd bus it all the way to Timbuktu tomorrow if there was a vacancy for a hard-working girl.

But could she persuade Mrs Topping, the Land Girls' coordinator for this remote part of Cornwall, to let her move district?

Lucky, lucky Alice, she kept thinking. She was escaping

to Bude on the north coast, miles away from sleepy Porthcurno. Especially when her gaze was drawn to an advertisement that read: *Help Needed at Roskilly Dairy in Bude. Shop and farm work. Good rates paid. Training will be given.* That sounded just the ticket. Then her heart sank, recalling how old the newspaper was and how notoriously hard it was for Land Girls to arrange a transfer. It was probably a waste of time even trying . . .

'I'm ready for bed.' Caroline threw her magazine aside, yawned extravagantly, and turned over in bed, saying in a cold voice, 'Put out the light, Pickles. It's late.'

Penny said nothing but folded the newspaper to the dairy farm advertisement and tucked it carefully under her bed.

Pickles.

That nickname, which she'd thought terribly funny when Caro first gave it to her two years ago, now struck her as simply mean. She liked pickles, yes. And cheese too, truth be told. She liked food of all varieties. But that didn't mean she had to put up with being called *Pickles* for the rest of her life.

Penny snapped out the light and lay down, imagining what it would be like to start afresh in a new place. She need never tell anyone about that horrid nickname. She could be plain Penny again. She could be *herself*.

The next morning, Penny rather cheekily asked for the day off and to her surprise her request was granted. Joe seemed distracted when she asked him, and it soon became clear why. As she hurried back up to her attic bedroom to change into civvies, she overheard Violet and

Joe in the kitchen, arguing about Alice leaving the farm. Violet didn't sound very happy, though it was hard to be sure how Joe felt, as he answered everything in the same mumbling monotone.

Leaning over the banister, Penny nearly jumped out of her skin when a strict voice said behind her, 'Eavesdroppers hear no good of themselves, missy.'

Blushing, she turned to find Alice's grandmother glaring at her.

'Sorry,' Penny said swiftly, 'I was just curious . . . I heard about Alice leaving, you see.' She bit her lip. 'We all going to miss her.'

Sheila's glare softened, and she tutted under her breath. 'That's for bloomin' certain. I told the silly girl not to go. But she won't listen to me. Got her heart set on this Bude nonsense.' She made a harumphing noise under her breath. 'Printing press, indeed! It's reading too many books, that's what this is. It's addled her brains.'

Relieved that her rude eavesdropping had been forgotten, Penny agreed. 'I don't know how she can do it. Leave home, I mean. It was bad enough joining the Land Girls' Army. But at least I was sent here with the other two, straight from the Land Girls' training course. I didn't have to come on my own.'

'Our Alice has always been a rum 'un. Takes after her dad, I suppose.' Sheila stopped and shook her head, abruptly changing the subject. 'Well, I can't stand here chatting to you. I've got jam to make.' And she bustled on down the stairs.

Up in her room, Penny changed quickly into civvies, pulled on her walking boots and grabbed her bag. Then she dashed back down the stairs, for she knew the bus was due in Porthcurno shortly.

It was a warm and sunny September day and she enjoyed the brisk walk down into the village. But she admitted to some trepidation as she rehearsed her request to the local Land Girls' coordinator, who was based in Penzance. In the end though, Mrs Topping heard her rambling explanation without any sign of annoyance, nodded briefly and took the newspaper cutting to study it.

'Ah yes, the dairy in Bude. They've had trouble recruiting staff and it's a vital local outlet for fresh food supplies, so it comes under approved war work.' She took a quick note of the details. 'I'll be in touch with them and let you know as soon as a transfer can be arranged.'

Penny stared at her in amazement. 'You mean . . . I can go? Just like that?'

'The longer the war goes on, the more this kind of thing happens.' The coordinator shrugged, sitting down behind her desk in the small office. 'We try to encourage Land Girls to stay with the same farming outfit throughout the war. But it's not always practical. And if you're as unhappy as you say you are—'

'I am,' Penny exclaimed, nodding fervently.

'Then the best thing all round is for you to move to a different farm. Bad feelings can infect everyone in a working unit. Best sort it out as soon as possible.' Mrs Topping paused, studying her. 'Though the work in Bude will be very different to what you're used to at Postbridge Farm.'

'What do you mean? More livestock than arable?'

'That, yes, but I don't believe they're looking for a Land

24

Girl, per se. The Roskillys also run a farm shop in the town itself. You may be required to work there, not on the land.'

'I don't mind. In fact, shop work sounds rather fun, and it would make a nice change.' Penny smiled shyly. 'I miss being around people, if you see what I mean.'

'Very common with Land Girls, especially on these more remote farms,' Mrs Topping nodded, picking up the telephone. 'Well, leave it with me. I'll see what I can do.'

After being promised that she would hear back from Mrs Topping within the week, Penny wandered about Penzance in the sunshine, quite shocked at how quickly things were moving. Now, at last, she began to have niggling fears that she might have made a mistake. What if her co-workers at the dairy farm turned out to be even worse than Caroline and Selina? But that was a risk she'd have to take.

She spent a very pleasant hour in a smart Penzance teashop, lingering over a pot of tea and a tasty slice of fruit cake, and finished her library book before returning it. The librarian asked if she would be taking another book out, and Penny felt wildly liberated as she shook her head, saying, 'No, thank you. I'll be moving away soon.'

Back at the farm that evening, she managed to grab a word with Alice before dinner. 'I've spoken to the local coordinator,' she whispered, 'and she's getting back to me.'

Alice narrowed her eyes. 'Give you the green light, did she?'

Penny nodded. 'Apparently, it happens all the time. Land Girls getting restless or falling out with people and moving to different farms. She's writing to the dairy farmer in

Bude, but I doubt they'll say no. They've been having trouble getting staff.'

'I wonder why.' Alice frowned. 'Maybe it ain't such a nice place to work.'

Penny flushed, though she herself had wondered about that too. 'I couldn't say. But I'm willing to give it a try. Besides, she said the work may be in the farm shop, not on the land. Which would suit me fine, especially with us going into autumn. I've spent enough days knee-deep in mud and getting drenched to the bone, thank you very much.' She hurried into the kitchen, following the gorgeous smell of supper cooking. 'A dry, comfortable shift in a farm shop would do me nicely.'

'Hang on a tick.' Alice touched her arm. 'If you get word before Saturday,' she said in her ear, 'you can travel with me. I've told my family and they're not happy, but what can I do about that? It's war work. There's no dodgin' it.'

'I'd like that, thank you.'

'What are you two girls whispering about?' Violet demanded, standing in the middle of the kitchen with her hands on her hips. 'Dinner's ready,' she told them. 'Wash your hands and sit down before it gets cold.'

Penny grinned at Alice, and they both hurried to obey, though they had to wait their turn while the three evacuee kids who lived at the farm finished washing their own hands. They were noisy little blighters but she had to admit the farm had been livelier since they'd moved in last summer, just before Violet and Joe had married. Eustace and little Timothy were still school age, but Janice had finished her education and was helping out around the farm now.

By the time they sat down, Penny's tummy was rumbling,

thanks to the rich aroma of the large meat pie Violet had just brought out of the oven. Her pies were always more gravy than meat, due to increasingly stingy rationing at the butcher's shop, but the creamy mashed potatoes and home-grown boiled veg usually made up for it. For Penny, that had always been the best thing about living on a farm – all the fresh food.

Towards the end of the meal, as the busy scraping of knives and forks began to be drowned out by the hum of cheerful conversation, Alice pushed back her chair, stood up and tapped her tea mug with a spoon.

'Could I have everybody's attention, please?' she demanded nervously, looking much younger than her eighteen years.

They all looked up in surprise from their dinner plates. Even the three evacuee children stopped chatting and giggling among themselves for a moment, turning to stare from their end of the table.

Silence fell.

'Oh, here we go,' Violet muttered, shaking her head in disapproval.

'Hush, love,' Joe warned her.

'Let the girl say her piece,' Sheila told her daughter, and Violet's lips compressed, though she said nothing more. 'Come along, Alice love . . . let's hear it.'

A slight flush in her cheeks, her air defensive, Alice told them, 'I'm leaving the farm. In fact, I'm leaving this part of Cornwall. I've been drafted for war work on the north coast, up near Devon. I'll be leaving Monday.' When nobody spoke, her voice tailed off. 'That's it, I suppose. That's what I needed to tell you.'

Caroline was staring up at her, her thin brows arched. 'Goodness. What kind of war work?'

'Printing,' Alice told her awkwardly.

Selina stifled a snort '*Printing*? I've never heard that be considered war work,' she remarked, but gave a shrug, returning to her dinner. 'Well, safe travels. Good luck with it.'

'Yes,' Caroline agreed, throwing the younger girl a bland smile. 'Good luck.' She hesitated though, glancing at Violet and Joe. 'I take it you don't approve, Mrs Postbridge?'

'That's none of your business,' Joe grumbled.

'Sorry, I'm sure,' Caroline said tartly, and also returned to her dinner. But she was careful to say nothing more.

Penny knew that neither of the Land Girls would dare disrespect the farmer. He was the one holding the purse strings, after all, since the money for their wages went direct to Joe, who then distributed them after deducting a weekly amount to cover food and accommodation. Caroline might have an acid tongue but she knew better than to bite the hand that fed her.

'I'm sure we all wish you very well with your new work, Alice,' Sheila said primly.

'Thanks, Gran.' Alice sat down again, not catching anyone's eye.

It seemed the announcement was at an end. But Penny had other ideas. As Joe and Violet picked up their knives and forks again, she forced herself to her feet.

Everyone stared at her instead. With heat in her cheeks, Penny burst out, 'I've applied for a new position too,' and saw Caroline's eyes widen, fixing on her face in disbelief. 'I'm sorry to be leaving you, Joe, and you too, Violet. I only hope you can find a replacement Land Girl soon.'

'You're leaving too?' Violet looked horrified. 'But why? Are you not happy here, love?'

Penny glanced at Caroline and then away, not wanting to cause a scene by revealing how she'd fallen out with her fellow workers. 'Of course not. I just felt like a change, that's all. So I'll be travelling up to Bude with Alice on Monday. That's where my new job is, you see. And I'm sorry for the short notice.' She paused, horribly intimidated by the silence around the dinner table. 'Look, I'm not good at making speeches. The thing is, I've had a cracking time here in Porthcurno and I'll miss you all. But I . . . I've made my mind up, so there it is.'

And she sat down heavily, feeling wobbly and unable to eat another mouthful, which was very unlike her.

'Well, I never!' Alice's grandmother exclaimed.

'You sly thing.' Selina clapped a hand over her mouth, staring at Penny. 'You're serious? You're not pulling our legs? You're really leaving the farm?'

'Good riddance is what I say,' Caroline muttered, but subsided into silence on meeting Violet's thunderous stare.

Joe rubbed his forehead with a dirty fist, looking troubled. 'That's a turn-up, and no mistake. Are you sure it's allowed? I mean, I don't want to stop you, Penny, if your heart's set on a move, but—'

'We *need* you here,' Violet said more forcefully. 'You can't go.'

'Now, Vi . . .' Joe began, frowning.

'Mrs Topping says I can go,' Penny interrupted hurriedly, shaken by the difficult reception of her news but holding

Violet's stern gaze as best she could. 'She says I'm allowed to transfer, so long as it's approved war work. And it is.'

Joe nodded. 'Of course you can move placements. If the coordinator says it's allowed, then that's an end to the matter.' He sighed, glancing at his wife. 'I'd best start looking for a new Land Girl straightaway. It'll be harvest time soon.'

'Maybe I could help out with the harvest,' Violet told him.

Sheila chuckled, and after a moment's baffled silence, Joe joined in with his deep, rich, rumbling laughter.

'Thank you kindly, but I don't think that would be a good idea, Vi,' he told her.

'Whyever not?' Violet looked offended.

Awkwardly, Joe patted his wife's hand. 'You're a talented woman and I'm proud you're my wife. But you're no farmhand, that's for certain.'

'Well, of all the ungrateful . . .' Violet got to her feet and began collecting the dirty plates for washing, her movements brisk and no-nonsense. She was a tall, imposing woman with fair hair set in soft rolls above a high forehead, and she had a sharp tongue when she wanted. Tonight though, she gave Penny a strained smile as she scooped up her plate. 'I won't deny, it's going to cost me and Joe a few headaches trying to replace you. But good luck with your new job, love. Let us know how you get on once you're settled, all right?' she added, looking more resigned than annoyed. 'Or Joe will be fretting about you forever after.'

'Yes, Violet. Thank you.'

Violet sighed and moved on, heading for the sink with the dirty dishes.

'See?' Across the table, Alice gave her a conspiratorial nod. 'That weren't so bad. And now it's all agreed.'

Penny smiled back at her friend, though inside she was still nervous. It was such a big change to make. 'Here's to our new life,' she said, and bravely raised her mug of lukewarm tea, looking up and down the table. 'To Bude.'

'To Bude,' the others echoed, slurping at their mugs.

'And all who sail in her,' little Timothy chirped up, and everybody laughed.

CHAPTER THREE

Bude, North Cornwall, September 1943

'Ugh, this sign is so mucky.' Rolling up her sleeves, Florence rubbed grime from the painted wooden sign so vigorously, the stepladder beneath her feet rattled and her bucket of warm foamy water, set on the top step beside her feet, slopped over. 'I should never have left my spring cleaning so late, but it's been such a difficult year.'

'You can't blame yourself, Flo. What with losing Percy and all . . . Oh, do be careful!' Her elderly neighbour, Doreen, watching from below, gave a shriek as Florence lurched sideways, straining to reach the furthest edges of the sign. 'You might fall.'

'It can't be helped. I need to clean the whole thing, not just the middle,' Florence groaned, glancing down as warm water seeped through her shoes, dampening her stockings. 'Though I seem to be cleaning myself more than this dratted sign.'

Hurrying to finish, she wiped another clean swathe

across the cheerful yellow and green sign that her husband had designed. It was good to see the name of his beloved boarding house no longer obscured by months of dirt. *Her* boarding house now, she mentally corrected herself. Percy had been gone over a year now, killed on a flying mission to God knows where, as nobody had ever given her details.

Now the first anniversary of his death had passed, it was high time she accepted that she was alone and moved on with her life. She was thirty-five years old, for goodness' sake, and knew that her husband would not have wanted her endlessly pining for him. But it was so hard.

She'd loved Percy dearly. He'd been such a happy-go-lucky fellow, always smiling and telling jokes, lighting up the place with his cheery presence. The boarding house felt so cold and empty without him, especially in the long evenings when she was sitting alone by the wireless, listening to war reports and darning linen until her fingers cramped. She missed him so much, it was like a hole in her heart that she had to rub every now and then, hoping to remove the ache. But it never went away.

Her only consolation was Billy, their son, a sweet, chubby-cheeked three-year-old who was her pride and joy. The little darling slept like an angel but made up for it during the day, tottering about the place and creating havoc.

She didn't know what she would have done without Billy to distract her in those first few months after losing his father. Or without her wonderful friend Charlotte, who lived three doors down and at this very moment was looking after Billy while Florence worked. Charlotte had a four-year-old of her own, a pretty cherub named Emily, who doted on Billy and insisted on him playing at her house as often as possible.

Of course, Florence reciprocated, having Emily over for tea or to play with Billy, but never as frequently as the other way around, for her work at the boarding house was so taxing. Thankfully, Charlotte didn't seem to mind an extra child in the house, especially as Florence always made sure she wasn't out of pocket when it came to providing lunch or tea.

'Lovely ladies,' a smooth American voice, deep and mellow, hailed them from behind, startling her. 'I'm looking for Mrs Florence Pritchard. Would you happen to know where I can find her?'

'Oh!' Doreen exclaimed, sounding flustered.

Florence turned in surprise, dripping washcloth in hand, to find a stranger smiling up at her. He was wearing an American army jacket in dark olive green with a matching belt, four bright buttons catching the sunlight, pale taupe trousers with a pinkish hue, and shiny brown shoes. His sleek dark hair was cut short, with a beret worn at a jaunty angle. He was in his mid-thirties, she guessed, not much older than herself.

The soldier's dark eyes sparkled up at her with good-natured amusement and she was instantly aware of her legs on show. Ridiculously, as though she were some inexperienced girl, her cheeks heated and she bit her lip.

Maybe this style for shorter skirts wasn't such a good thing after all, she thought. It might save on fabric, but if it exposed one to such impudent stares . . .

'I'm Mrs Pritchard,' she admitted, coming down the stepladder rather too hurriedly. As it shook, Doreen cried out and made a feeble grab for it, but not before the American had dived forward, holding the stepladder steady as Florence descended more carefully.

'There you go, ma'am,' he said with a wink.

'Thank you,' she said primly.

'My pleasure.'

Dropping the washcloth into her bucket, she glanced up at the half-cleaned sign with an inward sigh. Maybe later she'd have a chance to finish the job.

'How may I help you?' she asked, drying her hands on her apron.

He touched his cap respectfully. 'Ma'am, I'm Staff Sergeant Miles Miller and I've been directed to you by the town clerk. He led me to understand you run an association of boarding house owners in this town.'

'Oh, hardly.' She felt again the weight of sadness under which she'd woken that morning, and shook her head, trying to smile and failing. 'My late husband Percy chaired the Bude association for a time, but we haven't had any meetings since before the war. Too many members signed up or were drafted.' Covertly, tucking her fair curls back behind her flimsy headscarf, she studied the soldier, thoroughly intrigued. 'I don't understand though, Staff Sergeant Miller. You're US army? What are you doing in Bude?'

'That's what I'd like to discuss with you, ma'am.' He glanced at Doreen, and then indicated the door to the boarding house. 'Maybe inside? Privately?'

'Well, I'm rather busy . . .' she began uncertainly, and he grinned.

'You need this sign cleaned up, is that it?' When she

nodded, he took the bucket and washcloth from her. 'Allow me, ma'am.'

Confidently, the American officer headed up the stepladder one-handed. Soon, the sign was shining in the morning sunshine, once again clearly reading *OCEAN VIEW BOARDING HOUSE: Prop. Mr P. Pritchard.* The soldier came down the ladder at the same pace he'd gone up, still holding the bucket. She reached for it automatically but he shook his head.

'Show me where to tip away this dirty water and I'd be glad to do it for you, ma'am.'

Florence exchanged astonished glances with Doreen. 'Thank you,' she told him, pointing out the grating further along the street.

'I'd best call on Angela at Number Ten,' Doreen murmured, edging away. 'See if that nasty cough of hers is any better.' And she disappeared down the sunlit street, no doubt eager to share this exciting gossip as soon as possible.

When he'd finished, Florence took the empty bucket and showed him into the boarding house. 'This way.' The officer insisted on bringing the stepladder, neatly folded under one arm, and replacing it in the utility space under the stairs. 'Can I offer you some tea, Staff Sergeant Miller?'

'No, thank you, ma'am. And Sergeant is just fine.'

Leading him into the airy sitting room used for residents, she sat in the armchair beside the hearth and folded her hands into her lap, waiting.

Sergeant Miller studied the room with an intelligent gaze, his large frame dominating the space, and then took a seat opposite her.

'It's like this, you see,' he began, crossing one leg over

the other, 'we're looking to commandeer the whole town. Boarding houses in the first instance, and then private homes with any spare rooms. It's a major undertaking, so the town clerk suggested we approach the boarding house association and coordinate with you guys first.' He stopped, his mouth quirking. 'Pardon me, I meant the ladies and gentlemen of the association.'

She blinked, struggling to take in what he was saying. 'Forgive me but I'm not clear on what you're asking. You want to commandeer *the whole town*?' Her mind was reeling. 'For what, exactly?'

'To house the Second Battalion US Rangers, ma'am.' He looked embarrassed. 'I probably should have started with that, huh?' When she said nothing, still staring, he added confidentially, 'The thing is, I'm new to this role. Liaison officer. I'm still learning the ropes, as it were. You may have to cut me some slack.'

'Cut you some . . . I'm sorry, I still don't understand.' She sat up straight, hands clasped tight in her lap. 'Why on earth are the US Rangers—'

'Second Battalion Rangers,' he corrected her.

'Thank you, yes, the Second Battalion Rangers, coming to Bude, of all places?' She hesitated, feeling faint at the thought of such a massive undertaking. 'And when are they due to arrive?' She was praying he would not say imminently, for she had just closed for a week of cleaning and stock-taking at the end of the summer season, and everything was at sixes and sevens.

But to her relief he said, 'Not yet,' and then qualified that with a less certain: 'Sometime in the next one to two months. Most probably.' He paused. 'Unless orders change.'

'You don't know, in other words.'

'Officially, ma'am, it should be before Christmas. But between you and me,' he added uncomfortably, 'it could be any day now. Or never.'

'Good grief.'

'I'm one of the advance party, here to smooth the way for if or when the battalion does arrive. There are two of us.' He glanced about the sunny front room. 'We're in need of accommodation. Preferably somewhere close to where we'll be billeting the troops, so we can talk to all the landlords and private homeowners ahead of installation. Make sure there are no hard feelings, and iron out any issues before they can become a problem.' His friendly gaze came back to her face and he smiled. 'You wouldn't happen to have a couple of rooms available here, would you, ma'am? We'd only need half-board. Breakfast and dinner, and we'll lunch out.'

It was on the tip of her tongue to say no, and the place was closed to guests, but instead she heard herself say pleasantly, 'Of course, Sergeant. If you can give me a few hours to sort out two rooms, I'd be happy to have you here.' And then could have bitten her tongue out, for what on earth was she thinking, agreeing to provide accommodation when the whole house was stripped and bare, ready for a thorough cleaning and for any repairs to take place?

She had a new long-term guest due on Monday too, a Miss Alice Fisher, and had intended to repaint the back bedroom before her arrival. This would now force her to do everything in a tearing hurry, which she disliked, as that was when mistakes were made.

But she could hardly take it back now. His smile had

deepened, his eyes crinkling. And his accent, a deep drawl, was really quite charming.

'Thank you kindly, ma'am, that's mighty good of you.' He stood and gave her a nod. 'I'll show myself out. We've somewhere to stay tonight, but we'll be back tomorrow afternoon.' They shook hands. 'Hopefully, we can get all this sorted out in double quick time. I've just come from Scotland. It only took a few days there, but it was a much smaller place and the troops will mostly be under canvas up there, it looks like.'

'The battalion's going to Scotland first? And then here?' She was amazed.

'Oh, we move about pretty quick,' he assured her, grinning.

They were still holding hands, she realised with a start, his warm grip enveloping hers, and she released him, stepping back.

'Well, I'll see you tomorrow,' she stammered.

He touched his cap again, a sign of respect, and then said in a lower voice, 'No need, I'm sure, to ask you to keep this to yourself for now, ma'am? It's still hush-hush, as you British like to put it.'

'Of course.'

When he'd gone, Florence stood in a daze for several minutes, and then gave a cry before dashing to the linen closet to count how many bedsheets, pillowcases and blankets were still good enough to use for guests. She had a thousand jobs to do if her boarding house was to welcome a dozen or so American troops this winter.

* * *

When it was time to collect her son from Charlotte's house, Florence pulled on a cardigan and began to walk uphill into town. The row of boarding houses where she lived on Down's View felt very rural, out among the marshy, green downs near the sea, but was in fact only a brisk ten-minute walk from the town centre.

It was a sunny evening and still mild as the season moved into autumn, though a stiff breeze gusting off the Atlantic caught her skirt and made it flutter.

She adored living here in Bude, waking up every morning to salty air and the wide-open skies above the ocean outside her window. But despite having her son to care for, she did feel lonely at times, without Percy to keep her company, her beloved soulmate and helpmeet.

Her family lived in the rural city of Exeter in neighbouring Devon, where she'd grown up as an only child until the age of twelve, when her sister Imogen had been born. It was also where she'd first met her husband, Percy.

They had bumped into each other at the Exeter Christmas market, quite literally, for she had been carrying a stack of presents and he had been walking with his head down, studying a newspaper, and collided with her. Much apologetic laughter had ensued. She'd been captivated at once by his droll humour, but impressed by his wisdom too, for Percy had been much older than her, almost thirty to her still naïve twenty-four. His apology had been to carry her shopping home for her, a walk of some twenty minutes, so she'd offered him tea on arrival. Percy, whose mother had died when he was young, had been staying with relatives over the Christmas period, but spent those few heady days escorting her about the town instead.

Before he'd returned to Cornwall, where he worked in his father's boarding house, Percy had invited Florence to come to stay in Bude that summer. Within a few weeks of her visit, they'd become engaged. And when his father died the following year, leaving Percy the boarding house, it had seemed quite natural for them to marry and run the place together.

For seven glorious years, they had been deliriously happy, living and working together as man and wife. Her only regret was that they'd only been able to have one child, although Billy was enough of a handful at times, so goodness knows how she would have managed alone with more than one.

After Percy's death, her parents had written to ask if she wished to sell the boarding house and move back in with them in Exeter. But there was no going back to her childhood home. She was a grown woman now, with her own way of doing things. Much as she loved her parents, she could never live with them again. Not without going barmy. Especially with Billy in tow.

Charlotte's home was a pretty cottage at the crest of the hill, its chimney smoking cosily. She knocked and the door was thrown open by her friend, an animated expression on her face. Charlotte was in her late twenties and petite, with dark curly hair she wore in a short bob, not even brushing her shoulders. She always gave Florence the impression of someone in a hurry, though in the nicest possible way.

'I'm sorry I'm late,' Florence began guiltily, but her friend shook her head.

'Oh, don't worry about that.' Charlotte beckoned her

inside. 'Quick, come and see what your Billy's been up to. It's so sweet.'

Inside the cottage, she found her little son nursing a ragdoll while four-year-old Emily stirred an imaginary stew of autumn leaves in a pot beside the hearth.

'They're playing at keeping house,' Charlotte whispered in her ear, unable to contain her giggles as Billy swung the ragdoll violently back and forth, its floppy head dangling. 'Oh, not too hard, Billy,' she gasped between laughs. 'Poor baby needs gentle handling.'

Noticing the remains of a meal on the table, Florence bit her lip. 'You've fed him too? That's so kind. What do I owe you?'

'Never mind that. How about you take Emily tomorrow afternoon instead? Say from two until five o'clock?' Charlotte pulled a face. 'I'm always in such a rush these days, I'd like some special time just for me,' she whispered, checking to be sure her daughter wasn't listening. 'If you can manage that?'

'Of course, I'd love to have Emily over for tea.'

Florence stayed for a quick cuppa, both women laughing over their children's antics, and then Charlotte said it was time for Emily's bath.

'Come on, Billy,' Florence told her son, finding his shoes and bundling him into his coat and hat. 'It's long past your bedtime.'

Tramping home with Billy, the little boy tugged free of her hand and toddled ahead of her, seemingly untired by his long afternoon of play.

Florence glanced north towards the clustered army barrack huts on the hilltop at Cleave Camp. The camp lay a few miles from Bude but was always lit up by the setting sun as it dipped towards the horizon each evening. As she watched, a small plane came into land at the airstrip there, tilting its wings to catch the gleams of sunset before straightening up.

It was a reassuring sight, for although they had not suffered too badly from bombing up here, she knew the rest of Cornwall had been battered in recent months, and she suspected a strong army presence with an airfield nearby might be deterring the bombers. Though sooner or later they might decide to flatten Cleave Camp anyway, or one of the new military installations here in Bude.

There was really no knowing where bombs might fall next.

'The enemy's getting desperate,' one of her friends had told her, learning of a recent bombing raid on Penzance. But a man in the pub had suggested the constant bombardment was being done to soften up the Cornish, ready for an invasion force. Such a horrible thought.

Reaching the boarding house, Billy ran inside, chortling as he stripped off his hat and coat, cheerfully shouting, 'No bed, no bed, no bed.'

Chuckling under her breath, Florence pursued her son inside, gave him a quick flannel wash and coaxed him into his pyjamas. 'Better lie down, young man, or there'll be no story time,' she told him, patting the narrow cot at the end of her bed where he slept. 'You want to know what happened to the prince after he came home from talking sense into the giants, don't you?'

Billy clambered into bed at once, nodding eagerly. The story was one she had spun out of her own imagination, involving a prince whose kingdom had been under threat from bad-tempered giants. 'More Prince Billy!' he urged her, for this fictional prince just happened to share his name, and he settled down under the covers ready for the next instalment. 'Tell story, Mummy.'

Gently, in a soft voice that dropped ever lower as the boy's eyelids began to droop, Florence continued with her tale of a Cornish prince in an enchanted castle, and how he'd discovered on returning home from the peace talks that his madcap mother had taken up bicycling in his absence. Now Prince Billy needed to learn how to ride a bicycle too, so he could keep a careful eye on his mother whenever she rode out to explore their kingdom . . .

Once his breathing had relaxed into sleep, she tiptoed from the room and headed slowly downstairs. Before locking up the house for the evening, she stepped outside to wander the small front garden and simply daydream for a few precious moments, as she often did when the boarding house was closed to guests and life was less frenetic.

After bending to sniff her fragrant pots of rosemary and thyme, Florence sat on the rustic wooden bench and gazed across the rolling downs, thinking of all the times she and Percy had walked there together at dusk, hand in hand, admiring the view over the silvery bay.

'Oh, Percy,' she murmured, as though he were sitting there beside her. 'I miss you so awfully. This damn war . . .'

The only reply she got was the whisper of the sea as it came running over the flat sands and the steady darkening of the sky towards sunset.

CHAPTER FOUR

Bude, North Cornwall, October 1943

As the train pulled into the station at Bude, Alice was instantly reminded of another train journey she had undertaken a few years before and was struck by the similarities. Then, she had been fleeing the London Blitz with her aunt Violet and her older sister Lily, barely any possessions to her name and no idea what might await her in Cornwall. Once again, her battered suitcase only contained a few changes of clothing, plus a winter coat and sturdy shoes, and as for knowing what lay ahead, she had even less idea this time around. At least on that occasion, they'd been collected from the station by Great-Uncle Stanley. But their stay at his farm had not been of long duration, Stanley having laid hands on Lily, so Violet had packed their bags and dragged them both out of there, while their Great-Aunt Margaret had stood about shrieking and blaming Lily.

Alice had been too young to understand what was

happening at the time. Looking back though, she shuddered and hoped fervently that nothing so unpleasant would ever befall her.

As they tumbled out onto the platform, steam surrounding them and shrouding the small station in white, Penny nudged her and pointed up at a flock of large grey birds passing overhead. 'Geese,' she whispered excitedly.

Penny's letter of authority had only arrived on Friday, giving Penny the weekend to pack and say her final goodbyes. The Land Girl had seemed surprisingly tearful to be leaving her companions on the farm, considering that she'd argued with both Caroline and Selina. But they had been together a long time and Alice supposed their bonds of friendship must have remained strong, even after such a horrid falling-out.

She had felt a pang herself on leaving her family, who had all insisted on waving them off at the bus stop in Porthcurno, tears flowing and white hankies fluttering in the air, as though she and Penny were off to war and not simply heading north up the Cornish coast. Gran had pressed paste sandwiches and a bag of apples on them, and her elderly beau from the village shop, Arnold Newton, had even contributed two bottles of ginger beer, wishing them well for the journey with an unexpectedly kindly wink.

But she had never made any close 'bosom' friends, either in Porthcurno or while working at the school in Penzance, so it was with an open mind and an eager heart that she had sat staring out of the train window as they chuffed their way north from Penzance to Bude.

She was eighteen. Her life was just beginning, and who knew what interesting new people she might meet in Bude?

Now she stared upwards at the ghostly birds flapping seawards against a pale blue sky, and felt a shiver of apprehension, as though someone had walked across her grave. But she smiled at Penny and gripped the handle of her suitcase, determined not to be silly and superstitious. 'It's quite a walk up into town,' she told her friend, 'so we'd better get going. Ready?'

Penny looked flustered but nodded. 'Ready as I'll ever be, I suppose. Though Lord knows what I'll do if this Mrs Pritchard turns me away. What's the address of her boarding house?'

'Downs View Road. Other side of town, I think.' Alice had found an old map of North Cornwall among Joe's books and spotted the location of the 'downs' at Bude, which ran close to the cliffs.

Hurrying out of the station, they followed the crowd of passengers heading on foot into Bude. The road ran along the river for a stretch and the view out to sea was quite lovely. Tall reeds and grasses grew thick at each side of the sparkling waters, and birds drifted in flocks midstream, their pale reflections quivering. They soon passed a wayside inn doing brisk business, an ancient cart still drawn by a carthorse pulled up outside as the drayman delivered barrels of beer down a ramp, like something out of Victorian times.

Up ahead, a narrow bridge spanned the river, and just before that point, the road into town peeled off to the right, growing rapidly steeper.

'This is a hill and a half,' Penny managed to say, puffing as they climbed. 'It's worse than the track to the top pastures at Postbridge Farm. I only hope I won't have to trot up and down this street every day. Though I suppose it would keep me fit,' she added dubiously.

Alice, who was thin and wiry, found the hill less of a struggle. Besides, the shops they passed easily distracted her from the steep climb, their front windows packed with interesting wares. She particularly noticed that none of the shop windows had been boarded up, as they so often were in Penzance, and guessed that Bude must not have suffered regular bombing raids as they had done on the south coast of Cornwall. But the hill steepened towards the end, so that even she was breathing heavily by the time they had nearly reached the brow, where the road forked.

'Where now?' Penny asked, her cheeks flushed.

Pausing outside the large, whitewashed façade of the telephone exchange, Alice asked a passer-by for help.

'Downs View Road?' The woman pointed further up the hill. 'Take a right turn at the picture house and follow the road to Poughill,' she said, and then laughed. 'Though that won't be very helpful, as it's not signposted. They took down all the signposts in case of invasion. Better just keep walking until you're nearly at the church, and then turn left towards the sea.'

Alice and Penny both thanked her but glanced at each other in apprehension.

'Quite a trek, this boarding house,' Penny muttered.

As they reached the peak of the hill though, pausing outside Bude's cinema, they were rewarded with such a beautiful view, the land falling away across soft green downs towards the sea, that Alice felt it had been worth the long walk.

'Goodness, what a glorious view . . . I can see why

Bude is such a popular resort.' Alice and Penny followed the road towards the church as directed. 'Here we are.' On their left, they could see a row of tall Victorian houses stretching almost all the way to the sea, their elegant fronts facing the Downs. The sun came out from behind a cloud as they carried their bags wearily along the road, finally coming to Ocean View Boarding House. 'This is the one.'

It was a double-fronted, three-storey building, painted a delicate salmon pink with white window frames and a dusky red front door. The first-floor rooms at the front each had a narrow balcony, with foliage from potted plants peeping through the railings.

When Alice knocked, the front door swung open to reveal a smiling blonde in dungarees, a paintbrush in her hand and a smear of white paint on her cheek, who did not look even remotely like the Gorgon landlady of her imagination. For a start, she was far younger than Alice had expected, being maybe in her mid-thirties. And she had kind, understanding eyes that reminded her of Hazel, who was about the same age and one of the nicest people in the world.

'You must be Miss Fisher,' the woman said, and peered past her at Penny, who was biting her lip with nerves for having turned up without a reservation. 'And you've brought a friend. Hello, it's lovely to meet you both. I'm Mrs Pritchard. Though I'm afraid you've arrived a little earlier than expected.' She held up the paintbrush. 'I was just touching up the paintwork in your room. I hope you don't mind the smell of fresh paint.'

'Not me,' Alice lied valiantly, her nose already wrinkling.

'This here is Penelope Brown. She's 'oping to get a room too. D'you have any spare?'

Mrs Pritchard's face fell. 'Well, the problem is, although they're standing empty at the moment, all my guest rooms apart from yours are already spoken for.'

Penny threw Alice an anguished glance. 'Oh blow, I was worried that might be the case.' She looked glumly up and down the road, asking, 'Do you think one of the other boarding houses might have space for me?'

'Most are in the same position as me, I'm afraid. In fact, the whole town's about to be invaded.'

'*Invaded*?' Alice wondered what on earth she could mean.

'Oh, not by the Germans. Don't look so worried!' Mrs Pritchard bit her lip, laughing. 'Look, never mind. I'll just have to make one of my two-beds into a three-bed,' she told them. 'I'm sure it won't be a problem. Please come in, both of you.'

The boarding house was clean and tidy inside, if a little old-fashioned. Framed watercolours of Cornish scenery and sepia photographs of elderly relatives on the seafront hung in the long hallway, and there was a smell of lavender and beeswax polish in the air. The landlady showed them briefly around the downstairs, which consisted of a front parlour with views over the Downs, and a cosy dining room at the rear.

After explaining a few house rules, such as not inviting men back to their rooms – at which Alice and Penny grinned at each other in embarrassment – they were taken upstairs and shown into the small back bedroom that Mrs Pritchard had been painting. Sure enough, there was a strong smell of fresh paint. But the sash window had been pushed up to air the room and Alice was sure it would be gone in a day or so.

The room was sparsely furnished with a narrow bed, dressing table and chest of drawers, a cupboard set into the wall, and an old armchair with a sagging seat near a neatly swept hearth. Alice peered out of the window, her heart lightening. She felt sure she could be happy here, and although the view was not of the ocean as advertised, but of a backyard and gate, she preferred to be looking at other people's back gardens and houses than the blinding white skies above the Atlantic.

Mrs Pritchard, who seemed a cheerful woman, showed them the room next door, which was to be Penny's bedroom. The mattress was bare and the whitewashed walls were drab and also in need of fresh paint, but Penny seemed perfectly happy. She had been sharing with Caroline and Selina since being drafted into the Women's Land Army to Postbridge Farm, so presumably a room of her own was the height of luxury, as indeed it had been for Alice once Lily went away to work, leaving her the large double attic room all to herself.

'Now, let's sort out names. You're Miss Fisher,' Mrs Pritchard said, smiling at Alice.

'Yes,' Penny answered for her, 'and I'm Penny.' She threw an accusing look at Alice. '*Not* Penelope.'

'Understood,' the landlady said, placing her paintbrush and tin of paint on the landing, ready for removal. 'My name's Florence. You can call me Flo when we're alone together if you like, but I'd prefer Mrs Pritchard or Mrs P when we're in in company. You see,' the landlady added shyly, 'I have two gentlemen lodging here too.'

Penny stared. 'Gentlemen?'

'Soldiers,' Mrs Pritchard elaborated. 'I expect you'll meet them soon enough.'

Alice was surprised though she said nothing. *Soldiers? Staying in a boarding house?* It seemed rather irregular.

'Now,' Mrs Prichard hurried on, 'I'll drum up some fresh linen for your bed, Penny. Don't forget, supper is at six, and if you're ever going out for the evening meal, try to let me know in advance. I hope,' she added, 'that you'll both be very comfortable here. And if you girls need anything, just let me know. If ever you can't find me downstairs, my room's that one,' she said, pointing along the landing to a door marked *Private*. 'Though my three-year-old son shares with me, so if you can avoid knocking after dinnertime that would be appreciated.' She winked. 'Billy's a good sleeper, but it's best not to risk disturbing him.'

With that, she bustled away, leaving the two girls to unpack their bags.

'Goodness, she was far nicer than I imagined,' Penny said, looking a little awestruck. 'And the house is very clean and tidy. Always a good sign, my mother would say.' She tested the mattress with a few tentative bounces and her eyes widened. 'This bed's wonderfully soft too, no lumps.' But Alice could tell that she was worried.

'What's the matter?'

'Oh, I'm only thinking of my war work placement.' Penny's smile faltered. 'Thing is, it's all very well having that letter in my pocket, giving me permission to work at the dairy. But maybe I won't get along with the farmer. Maybe I'll be out on my ear within a week. And then what would I do?'

'I wouldn't worry about it, love,' Alice said, trying to be reassuring. 'You get along with most people. It's more likely me who'll get the shove. I always manage to put someone's back up,' she admitted, adding with a grimace, 'most times without even knowing how I did it.'

And she headed back into her own room to unpack.

At six o'clock sharp, a dinner gong sounded downstairs.

The dining room held only three tables and a sideboard. But each table had four seats, which gave her the rough capacity of the boarding house. It looked like it would be a cosy enough room after dark, hung with red curtains with thick black lining to shut out the light once evening fell, and a large hearth with a mantelpiece and oval mirror. A clock stood on the mantel alongside pretty china and brass ornaments of the kind Gran liked to collect. At that hour the heavy curtains were wide open. Since the room itself faced north though, it was chilly, and the fire had not been lit. The grate, she noticed, was empty, as was the coal scuttle that stood alongside. Too early in the year, Alice guessed, for such luxuries.

One of the tables had been laid for four people, and as she came into the room, two men who had been seated there abruptly stood, smiling at her in welcome.

Alice couldn't believe her eyes. 'You . . . You're *American* soldiers,' she blurted out, staring from one to the other in disbelief. She recognised their distinctive dark olive jackets and khaki shirt-ties from American movies and Pathé newsreels she'd seen at the picture house. 'But what on earth are you doing in Cornwall?'

'It's a mighty long tale, Miss,' the taller one said, grinning as he pulled out the chair next to him. 'Care to take a seat while we tell it? I'm Staff Sergeant Miles Miller and this is Corporal Ken Jones.'

'I'm Alice Fisher,' she said, and shook their hands, still bemused.

She was sitting down just as Penny came hurrying along the hallway, plaiting her hair and humming a merry tune. Her friend stopped dead in the doorway, staring wide-mouthed at the two soldiers, who instantly pushed back their chairs and stood to attention again, their faces respectful.

'This must be our other fellow guest,' the dark-haired sergeant said, with a significant glance at his companion. 'Mrs Prichard told us to expect company tonight.'

'She certainly did.' The corporal stepped smartly to usher Penny into her seat, who sank into it with a stunned expression, gawping up at him with eyes like saucers.

'Yes,' Alice whispered to her, leaning across, 'they're not British soldiers. Try not to stare.' She said more loudly, 'This is my friend Penny Brown.'

'Nice to meet you both, Miss Brown, Miss Fisher.' The sergeant smiled at them both in turn. 'We're here as liaison officers for the Rangers.'

Alice was impressed. 'You're *US Rangers*?'

'You've heard of us?'

'Of course. You're very famous . . . as soldiers go.'

'Why, thank you. You might as well know, it's likely the townsfolk will have quite a few of us on their hands soon, so we're here to make sure there's enough accommodation in Bude to go around, and to begin making arrangements for . . .' The sergeant fell silent as Mrs Prichard swung

54

through the door from the kitchen carrying a large soup tureen. 'Ah, supper. I'm starving.'

'I could eat a horse,' Corporal Jones agreed, tucking a napkin into his collar with a wink. He was blond and cheerful, with a strong jaw and muscular build.

The landlady set the soup tureen on the table before fetching four soup bowls and spoons from the sideboard. 'It's leek and potato,' she explained hurriedly. 'Not terribly exciting but needs must.'

'We don't have leek and potato soup in the States,' Sergeant Miller reassured her. 'So it's pretty exotic to us. Thank you, Mrs P.'

The dark-haired sergeant liked the landlady, Alice decided, watching his gaze follow her around the table as she served them. And Mrs Pritchard liked him too, she suspected, because the woman barely made eye contact with him at all, though she had beamed at the other soldier without hesitation when he thanked her.

The soup was good, and the bread rolls were soft and fresh from the oven. 'Even better than my gran's rolls,' she admitted, a little surprised.

Mrs Pritchard smiled at Alice in her friendly fashion, placed glasses and a jug of water on the table, and left them to eat.

'I'm going to like it here,' Penny whispered to her under cover of spoons scraping bowls as the two men devoured their soup with every sign of enthusiastic hunger.

Alice concentrated on her own soup, though her head was whirling with thoughts. 'Me too,' she murmured back.

* * *

Once dusk had fallen and the blackout curtains had been drawn across, the two soldiers went upstairs after an hour of playing cards in the front room, and even Penny yawned and stumbled up to bed, saying wearily, 'Goodness, I'm too tired to stand . . . See you in the morning, Alice.'

As soon as the sound of people moving about upstairs had stopped, Alice got up and turned off the wireless. As she did so, she heard an odd little click from outside the window, as though somebody had opened or closed the front gate. But who on earth would be out there at this late hour? Mrs Pritchard had gone up to bed ages since and she was the only one still up.

A funny sound outside in the night . . . This was precisely the sort of thing she would be trained to investigate, wasn't it?

Silently, she removed her coat from the hall stand where she'd hung it earlier, wrapped herself in it, and stepped out into the quiet evening air.

It was dark and there were no lights showing anywhere, everyone respecting the lights-out curfew. The small front garden appeared to be empty.

She stepped to the gate. Ahead, the Downs stretched invisibly in the darkness, and to her right she could hear the ocean breaking gently on rocks. Uphill to the left stood the town, smothered in black, all windows curtained against any chance of bombers.

She must have been mistaken about hearing the front gate click . . .

Then she caught the faint click of heels and spotted a shadowy, stooped figure hurrying away down the road as though fearful of being out after lights-out. An elderly lady, judging by the old-fashioned coat and glint of silvered hair sticking out from under her hat.

Alice hesitated, one hand on the gate latch. Should she sneak after the woman and see where else she was going? It would be good practice at the top-secret trade she had come here to learn. But their visitor was probably just one of Mrs Pritchard's elderly neighbours, come to ask something, but retreating on seeing the place in darkness.

Besides, there was no moon tonight. In this darkness, she might lose her way back to the boarding house, which would hardly be a good start.

'I need a torch,' she said under her breath, wishing she'd thought to bring one from the farm.

Someone above her cleared their throat, and she jerked instinctively back into the dark shrubbery beside the front door, staring upwards.

It was Sergeant Miller, the US Ranger, standing on a balcony outside a front upstairs window. Had he heard her come out of the house? As Alice watched, he casually lit a cigarette and tossed the match over the balcony, the acrid scent of burning tobacco thickening the night air.

Alice took a few tentative steps towards the front door, trying not to be seen or to rustle the spiky bush at her back. That was what a spy would do, wasn't it?

But before she could make her escape, the American said clearly, 'Goodnight, Miss Fisher,' stepped back into his room and closed the balcony door.

She groaned, covering her face. *Oh yes, very stealthy, my girl,* she told herself derisively. *You'll go far.*

CHAPTER FIVE

Following the complicated instructions given to her by the landlady, Penny made her way into Bude before climbing uphill again on the far side of town, seagulls crying overhead. The shops she passed, mostly still closed at that early hour, included a family butcher and two greengrocers, an antique shop, and a large haberdashery stocked with rolls of tempting, colourful fabric and ribbons. It struck her as a busy and cheerful little town, no doubt due to its many visitors during the summer season, though the streets and houses were quiet now the good weather was beginning to wane. None of the shops had been boarded up to protect against bombing, which relieved her mind. She had feared that moving to a town would be more dangerous than living in the countryside, but perhaps this northern resort had not suffered as much damage during the war as more popular Cornish towns further south.

Penny paused outside the fabric shop, peering at the jolly window display with interest. But she didn't linger there. She could not be sure how much further it would be to the farm and she did not dare be late on her first day.

It was a grey, overcast morning but there was no rain. It seemed like a long walk through rows of elegant townhouses and more spacious residences with gardens further out of the town centre. The track up to the farmhouse itself was muddy but she was used to that, navigating the puddles and mud ruts skilfully.

Beyond the farmhouse, several fields stretched lush and green, dotted with black-and-white heifers. It was obviously a large herd, and she could see why they needed extra help now that so many young men had gone off to war. As she approached the farmhouse, a dog burst out barking and leaping about her. But again, she was used to dogs and didn't flinch.

'Down, boy,' she told him in a firm voice, and the animal hurriedly sank onto his haunches, wagging his tail fiercely and mock-growling at her.

A boy emerged in the doorway to the farm, peering at her. 'What do you want?' he demanded in a surly manner.

'Is the farmer at home?' Penny asked, horribly nervous. His unwelcoming manner was not helping. 'Or Mrs Roskilly?'

'Dad's in the cowshed,' the boy called back, though 'boy' wasn't quite the right description for him. He was tall and lanky, with ginger hair falling in his eyes, and looked at least sixteen. Maybe seventeen. Certainly, he was not much older than Alice, who was only eighteen. Though Alice was mature for her age, Penny considered, so that it often felt as though there wasn't much of an age difference between them. 'Mum's at the shop in town.'

Penny blinked, belatedly realising that the letter had instructed her to make herself known at the shop in town, not at the farmhouse itself. 'Oh right,' she said lamely. 'I'm sorry to have disturbed you.' But as she turned away, she realised she didn't know exactly where the shop was located. 'Erm, is the shop far? I don't know the way.'

Looking bored, the boy rattled off a series of directions that left her dizzy, and then slammed back into the house, whistling for the dog as he did so.

'Oh dear,' Penny muttered, and headed back to the muddy puddles towards the town.

This time, she got the letter out of her pocket and reread it, paying careful attention to the address of the shop. That was where Farmer Roskilly sold his produce, as well as select produce from other farmers in the area. She'd expected to be working on the land at least some of the time. But there was every chance she would end up serving customers in the farm shop.

At least the hours would be more civilised, she thought with a grin. But she'd never done anything like that before in her life, so it was with a genuine sense of trepidation that she wiped her shoes before entering the farm shop, pulled off her woollen beret and twisted it between both hands.

A stout woman with flushed cheeks and grey-streaked hair under a knotted chiffon headscarf turned towards her from behind the counter, asking cheerfully as she wiped her hands on her apron, 'What can I do for you, my love?'

Trembling, Penny began in a quavering voice, 'I'm Penny Brown, I'm here about the job.' She indicated her breeches and green jumper, and the beret. 'I'm a Land Girl.'

'Oh, you're the Land Girl they've sent us, are you?' The friendly smile disappeared and the woman looked her up and down as though she were a maggot in an apple. 'You're not what I expected. How old are you?'

'Twenty-two.'

'You look older. Do you have any experience?'

'I've been working on a farm in Porthcurno for the past couple of years. Mostly arable land, though there is a small herd of cows, so I've done a little herding, milking and churning. I'm not afraid of livestock or hard work.'

Her look was dry. 'I meant experience serving in a shop.'

Penny felt intimidated by her terse manner and fierce stare. 'No, sorry. But I'm willing to learn.' When the woman exhaled noisily, she plucked up courage to ask, 'Are you Mrs Roskilly?'

'That's me,' the woman agreed. 'I don't doubt you're a good worker on the land. But we don't need farmhands. We've got two stout girls already up at the farm, Sadie and Rosie. What we need most is someone to help in the shop, and sometimes bring the churns down and any fresh eggs or veg from the farm of a morning. You'll need to be at the farm for six o'clock sharp some days, to bring down the produce to be sold that day, and to wait on customers in the shop from seven until half past four closing. But you'll stay behind until gone five most days, sometimes later, to wipe down the counters, mop the floors, and clean the shop windows.' She paused, adding reluctantly, 'We're closed Sundays, so you may please yourself that day. And I'll allow you one afternoon off per week. Wednesdays would suit.'

'Yes, Mrs Roskilly,' she said.

'Though you can't work in the shop dressed like that.' The farmer's wife balled her hands into fists and stuck them on her ample hips, glaring at Penny as though she had come to work deliberately dressed in the wrong style. 'Have you nothing else to wear?'

'I've a skirt and blouse.'

'That will do, for starters. You're staying at the Land Girls' place over in Holsworthy, I take it?'

'No,' Penny admitted. 'Because I asked to change area, I'm having to find my own accommodation. They don't have room for me at the Holsworthy hostel. I'm at a boarding house on Downs View Road instead.'

'Very nice,' Mrs Philip said, and raised her eyebrows. 'Sounds like you've fallen on your feet there, my girl.' She saw a customer come into the shop and her entire demeanour changed, the sour look on her face changing to a ready smile. 'Mrs Thrupp, how lovely to see you. Are you well? What can I get for you this morning? I've got some lovely fresh-made butter, just brought down from the farm.' She gave the elderly lady a wink. 'How's your ration book looking this week?'

Penny shrank aside as the farmer's wife served the customer, who stopped to cast her an astonished look, no doubt wondering what on earth a Land Girl was doing in a farm shop in the town centre.

As soon as the woman had left, Mrs Roskilly turned to her with a sharp nod. 'Get changed into something more suitable and come straight back. And don't expect any pay for this morning, not turning up an hour late and looking like that.' She leant over the counter, glancing down at Penny's feet, and shook her head in horror. 'And clean those shoes before you come back. You look like you've fallen into a pigsty.'

By the time Penny had hurried all the way back to Downs View, cleaned her shoes and changed into her skirt and blouse before trudging to the shop again, it was almost lunchtime. Half a day's wages gone already, she thought miserably. But she was determined to make this new placement work, for the alternative was returning to Joe's farm with her tail between her legs. How the other Land Girls would laugh if she did that! No, she must swallow her resentment and focus on pleasing her new employers, even if Mrs Roskilly was shaping up to be a real dragon. Besides, she comforted herself, she wasn't on her own in Bude and could always laugh about it at the end of the day with Alice.

The farmer, whose name was Graham, was at the shop, unloading milk churns from his van. He looked her up and down in much the same way his wife had, except the way he studied her figure made her uncomfortable.

'Ah now, Jean said you was a big girl,' he remarked with apparent satisfaction in a thick Cornish accent, and nodded. 'She were right.'

A big girl?

Heat bloomed in Penny's cheeks as she realised what he meant, but she didn't dare say a word. It would be too awful to cause a row on her first day, especially after turning up late and in the wrong gear.

The farmer lifted a large milk churn out of the back of his van and gestured for her to take it. 'That needs to go to the back of the shop. There's an alleyway just there. See it?'

Penny bent to the churn, but could barely lift it off the ground, it was so heavy. She strained until she was red in the face, half carrying, half dragging it to the mouth of the alleyway before having to stop, panting for breath.

A burst of laughter greeted this huge effort, and she looked back to see the farmer, his wife and son, and two young women in Land Girl breeches – presumably Sadie and Rosie – mocking her with sniggers and jokey comments from the door of the shop.

Indignation burst inside her and she straightened, snapping out, 'I'm doing my best. What's so bloody funny?'

The laughter stopped.

The Land Girls glanced at each other and jumped into the van without a word. The farmer's wife gave an outraged gasp and turned to her husband, saying, 'Did you hear that bad language? We've been asking and asking for weeks, and this is what they send us. Rough as slurry, she is.' She shook her head vehemently. 'She can't work in the shop. Not with that tongue on her.'

Penny bit her lip, blushing fierily. Why hadn't she just kept her stupid mouth shut?

Standing in the shop doorway, the lanky boy grinned and folded his arms as though this dressing-down of the new girl was hugely entertaining.

'Now,' the farmer said with a laugh, 'don't take on. She'll do, right enough.' He jerked his head towards his son, his smile disappearing. 'Well, don't just stand there, you lazy lummox. Help the girl get the churn down the back alley. Then show her where to stow her coat.' His eyes narrowed on the boy's face. 'And no funny business, do you hear?'

'Yes, Dad.'

Secretly thankful that she didn't have to manhandle the milk churn all the way down the narrow alleyway to the back of the shop, Penny stood aside and let him do the honours. Inside the back room of the shop, he grudgingly showed her the coat pegs and nodded to the outside convenience before leading her behind the counter. There she found the farmer's wife serving a gentleman, her manner once again polite and smiling. But once the customer had left the shop, Mrs Roskilly turned to her and examined her outfit with eagle eyes.

'That's better, I suppose.' She rummaged in a drawer for a hair net and clips, handing them over with a sharp warning not to dawdle while putting them on. 'I'll show you how to deal with the ration books first, because that's the most complicated part of the business. Then the weighing scales and the till. You won't be taught how to use the meat cutter or the cheese wire for at least a week or two, until we can be sure you won't do yourself a mischief. They're dangerous items, see?'

'Yes, Mrs Roskilly.'

She was glad to see that the boy had vanished, though she later caught a glimpse of him kicking a stone down the road, whistling and with his hands in his pockets. Her own mother, seeing that kind of behaviour, would have called him a juvenile delinquent. But Mrs Roskilly seemed oblivious to her son, only once calling out to him to stop fooling about in the road, and that was just before he was nearly hit by an army truck trundling past. Indeed, she went to the door of the shop and waved her fist at the truck driver, who ignored her completely.

'Idiot driver!' she called after him. 'You could have hit my boy!'

Perhaps, Penny thought to herself as she cleaned the weighing scales according to her new employer's exacting instructions, her boy ought not to have been standing in the road then.

But again she said nothing.

It was a long afternoon and surprisingly tiring, especially the times when there were no customers, which wasn't uncommon. Penny, who was accustomed to hard labour and an endless list of chores to be done around the farm, found it rather exhausting just to stand about in an idle manner, sweeping the same stretch of floor again and again, or rearranging items on the shelves as she waited for someone she could serve at the till. Though, in fact, Mrs Roskilly never permitted her to press any key on the till – a machine that she regarded with as much dread as awe – or to serve behind the counter. The most she was ever allowed to do was to weigh vegetables or measure out sugar or flour to the exact specifications permitted in the ration book, or sometimes to run and fetch canned goods from the shelves at the back of the shop.

'Thank you, my dear,' Mrs Roskilly would say each time she performed one of these tasks, smiling as benignly as though Penny was her own offspring. But as soon as the shop was empty again, she would glare at her. 'Get on with your work, then. That floor isn't going to sweep itself.'

'Yes, Mrs Roskilly.'

The shop door stood open most of the time, presumably to entice passers-by onto the premises. But since it was

October, a sharp wind kept the place uncomfortably cold, which was good for preserving the dairy produce, meats and vegetables, but not so wonderful for Penny's feet and legs. She was used to wearing warm trousers that kept out the cold even on winter days and the pristine white apron Mrs Roskilly had given her was no substitute. Her woollen stockings were old, worn through in places, and the skirt only reached to her knees. Her blouse fastened at the wrist with an old-fashioned button, but the material was thin. By the time the shop closed at four-thirty, she was chilled to the bone and shivering.

Mrs Roskilly, overseeing the cleaning work at the end of Penny's shift, spotted this and said, 'You'd best wear a cardigan tomorrow, foolish girl, or you'll be in bed with pneumonia by the end of the week.'

Penny, whose only cardigan was showing holes at the elbows and would never meet Mrs Roskilly's high standards, did not dare comment, but merely nodded. Perhaps, she thought nervously, Alice would have a cardigan she could borrow. Though she couldn't remember seeing one among her belongings.

The late afternoon was grey and grim on her way home, and the sight of the sea merely made her wish for her cosy bed. But when Penny dragged herself back to the boarding house, she found loud music playing and poked her head around the half-open door to the front room to find the two American soldiers gathered about a gramophone, discussing which recording to play next. When they saw her, they yanked the needle off the record, apologising for having disturbed her.

'No, please don't stop,' Penny said shyly, coming into the room. 'I liked that music. What was it?'

'It's "Chattanooga Choo Choo", recorded by Glenn Miller and his orchestra. Miles brought it over with him specially.'

'Glenn *Miller*?' Penny stared at the sergeant, whose surname was also Miller.

Miles laughed. 'No relation, sorry. I wish . . . But no, it's a common enough name in the States.'

'You've never heard it before?' the fair-haired corporal asked, clearly surprised. 'It was top of the US billboard for weeks when it came out. All the rage among the troops.'

Penny rolled her eyes. 'I've been living on a farm in the middle of nowhere since war broke out.'

'Ah, I get it.' He showed her the record with its handsome gold writing. 'Looks nice though, doesn't it? We didn't think we'd be able to listen to it here. But as it turns out, Mrs P's late husband had a gramophone player, and she brought it down from the attic for us.' He gave her a wink. 'Do you dance, at least?'

'I . . . I don't think so,' she stammered, and both men laughed.

'Well, it's never too late to learn,' Corporal Jones said reassuringly, and nodded to the sergeant to put the needle back on the recording. 'Let's have that again, shall we, Miles? From the beginning.' He held out a hand to her. 'Would you care to dance, Miss Penny?'

She blushed. 'Yes, thank you.'

The music blasted out again, louder than Joe had ever listened to the wireless back at Postbridge Farm, and Penny found herself dancing with the American, whose steps were smooth and experienced, but who thankfully didn't seem to mind whirling about the room with someone who could barely keep up.

Just as she was getting dizzy, the other Ranger tapped Corporal Jones on the shoulder, saying, 'Hey, Ken, mind if I cut in?' and they swapped places with a grin, the corporal lighting a cigarette while the sergeant danced with Penny. Miles had kind eyes and moved a little slower than his friend, which made the complicated dance steps easier to follow. The record was played several times over, until Penny stumbled over a foot stool and sank down in exhaustion, laughing fit to burst.

'My poor feet,' she exclaimed, but although her toes and heels were indeed throbbing after that long day in the shop, she didn't mind. 'I told you I couldn't dance.' Her heart was thumping fast and she was breathless. 'Oh, but that was the best fun I've had in simply ages.' She'd barely ever danced in her life and now had *two* dance partners all to herself! Caroline and Selina would have turned green with envy to see her . . . 'Thank you, Corporal Jones. Thank you, Sergeant Miller.'

'Thank you for the dance, Miss Penny. You'll soon get the hang of it. But call me Miles, won't you?' Miles lit her a cigarette and she took it, inhaling cautiously, though she had never smoked in her life. When she choked and spluttered, handing it back to him with a grimace, he laughed and she found herself grinning too. 'That's a first too, I'm guessing?'

'You must think me awfully dull.'

'Not a bit of it,' Miles said, throwing himself into the chair next to hers, a glass in his hand. 'The colour's back in your cheeks, at least. You looked dead beat when you came in.' He offered her the glass with a smile. 'And this should do the rest.'

'Is that gin?' she asked suspiciously.

'Moonshine.'

'What on earth's *that*?'

'Bathtub gin . . . home-made liquor. Don't tell me you've never had a drink before?' The soldier's brows arched, and she hurriedly shook her head, not wanting to seem green.

'No, I've drunk alcohol before. I'm not terribly keen on gin, that's all.' He was still holding the glass out though, so Penny took it with a wild laugh. 'Still, beggars can't be choosers.' The fiery liquid burnt her throat and heated her belly, but she took another swig. 'Goodness me!'

'The girl's got gumption,' Corporal Jones said, laughing.

'Hey, go easy on that stuff,' Miles drawled, though she noticed he'd poured himself some too. 'Here's to our boys,' he added, raising his glass in a toast. 'Americans, British, Allied forces . . .'

'To our boys,' Penny and Corporal Jones both murmured, downing more 'moonshine'.

Soon, Penny had to close her eyes. The room was spinning. She had intended to go straight upstairs on coming in, to change her stockings and have a quick wash before supper at six. But none of that seemed to matter anymore. She kicked off her shoes and drew her stockinged feet up onto the seat of her chair, giggling at the thought of what awful Mrs Roskilly would say if she could see her meek shopgirl now.

She couldn't remember feeling this happy in months. Maybe even years. Maybe she had *never* felt this happy before.

'I feel . . . happy,' she whispered into the silence, and then bit her lip in chagrin, not daring to look up at them. 'Gosh, how is that possible? I must be such a wicked person. How can anyone be *happy* when this dreadful war is still going on?'

'Sometimes letting yourself be happy is the only way to handle war,' Corporal Jones said in a low voice, and she looked up to see his face swimming, the room somehow misty. 'Because you never know when your number's up, right? Might as well dance and drink and—' He broke off, glancing up as Miles made some protest. 'And enjoy life while you can,' he finished.

'Yes,' Penny whispered, understanding that point of view, and knocked back the last of her bathtub gin in response, choking as it hit the back of her throat. 'Though this stuff is still horrid!' she added with a shudder.

CHAPTER SIX

Pinning out her washing in a stiff breeze, Florence caught the distant throb of engines and turned with a sinking heart to study the grey expanse of sky between her and the Atlantic Ocean. Fresh from the mangle, the still-damp tablecloth flapped and fluttered into her face as she paused, one peg already in place, the other hovering in mid-air . . .

Approaching planes, to be sure. And more than a few. But were they friend or foe?

They'd been lucky in Bude, as daily newspaper headlines attested. Hardly any munitions had been dropped on this idyllic northern stretch of coast, while Cornish villages and towns further south and west had suffered frequent bombings during this dreadful war.

Nothing as bad as they'd had it in London, of course, where street after street had been erased, with thousands killed and whole families displaced.

But one bomb would be enough to level her humble boarding house, Florence thought with an inner shudder of trepidation, or any of her neighbours' homes. And the enemy was rumoured to be favouring incendiaries these days, sneaky little devices that wreaked havoc through fire instead, dropped willy-nilly on roofs and hard-to-access places where they could burn undetected until the whole place was ablaze.

'Mummy! Mummy!' Billy came running into the yard, his face ablaze with excitement. 'Door! Lady!'

'There's a lady at the door for me?' she roughly translated, still staring into the sky. A few silvery specks had appeared in the distance, sunlight glinting off bodywork. Hurriedly thrusting the peg home across the corner of the tablecloth, she stuck out her hand. 'Come here, Billy, there's a love.'

'Playin',' Billy insisted.

The noise of the planes grew louder. Breath tangled in her throat, her chest tight. They were turning inland. Towards Bude?

'Hang on, we might need to run for the cellar,' she said urgently, reaching for him. But, at that moment, she saw the lead plane more clearly and recognised the markings. Her body sagged in relief. It was one of theirs. 'Oh, for goodness' sake!' Somehow, she found a lopsided smile for her son, who was still gazing up at her, his face perplexed. 'A lady at the door, you said? I'll be right there, dearest. Yes, you go and play.'

Abandoning her washing basket in the yard, Florence hurried through the house to the front door, drying her hands on her apron and quickly checking in the mirror that her hairnet was straight before pulling the door open.

'Hello,' she said, blinking in surprise. It was only Sally, their postie, a cheerful, bouncy woman in her fifties who always seemed to have time for a lengthy chat, even when Florence didn't. 'Sorry to have kept you waiting, Sally. You should have left it in the hall. Another parcel, is it?' She groaned inwardly at the familiar handwriting on the brown paper.

'That's right.' Sally handed it over with a smile and a wink. 'Exeter postmark. Looks like it's from your mum again.' She seemed to make it her business to know who each letter or parcel was from, which Florence found a little disconcerting. 'That's the second one this month.'

'She means well.' Florence took the small parcel with a grimace. 'Ever since I told her we'd been struggling a little, my mother's been sending me hand-me-downs from her neighbour's boys for Billy.'

'Ah, bless her, my old ma was just the same.' Sally settled her postman's cap more firmly on her silvering hair as the breeze threatened to snatch it off, and then launched into a lengthy anecdote about her late mother's thriftiness.

Florence was far too polite to show her boredom. But thankfully, just as she was losing the will to live, the garden gate banged, and she looked past Sally to see the broad figure of Staff Sergeant Miles Miller coming down the path.

'Oh dear,' Florence said with a quick, apologetic smile, 'I'm so sorry to interrupt you, Sally, but I'll have to go. This is one of my guests and I need to have a quick word with him. See you tomorrow, perhaps?'

'Righty-oh.' Unperturbed, Sally shouldered her bag and continued on her rounds, though with a curious sideways glance at Miles, who was a real eye-catcher, Florence had to admit.

'I'm sorry to have scared your visitor away,' Sergeant

Miller said politely as he followed her back inside the boarding house.

'My visitor?' Florence didn't understand at first. 'Oh, you mean Sally? She's the postie . . . our postwoman, that is. She was delivering this parcel, that's all.'

'Allow me.' He took the parcel from her as she struggled to close the front door with it under her arm. 'Where shall I put it?'

'Just there, thank you.' Florence felt awkward but smiled as he placed it carefully on the hall table for her.

'You wanted a word with me?'

She stared, then remembered the silly excuse she'd made to escape another of Sally's interminable anecdotes. 'Oh, erm, yes . . .' She racked her brain for something to say.

'Or was that just a way to bring your conversation with the postwoman to a quick end?' he suggested astutely, one eyebrow arched.

'Oh dear.' Florence bit her lip, blushing. 'Guilty as charged!'

'Not guilty at all. You were simply too busy to chat, but too polite to point that out.'

'Are you a mind-reader?' she asked, laughing.

'No, but I have five sisters.'

'Five.' She stared. 'Goodness, that must have been hard work for your mother.'

'On the contrary, she's always said her five girls were far less trouble than her three boys.' He was smiling now too.

She sighed, nodding. 'I have to say, my Billy is quite a handful. I only have the one, so can't compare him to a girl. But he certainly has me on the go from dawn until dusk.' Belatedly, she recalled that her little boy had been left on his own while she was talking on the doorstep to the postwoman, and she threw an anxious glance down the hall towards her own living quarters. 'In fact, I really ought to check on him. Lord only knows what he'll be up to.'

'In that case,' he said, removing his smart uniform cap and folding it, 'I'll let you go about your duties while I take myself off to my room.'

She watched as he began to ascend the stairs, his back very straight, and then dashed back through to find Billy.

To her relief, her son was seated cross-legged on the floor of the kitchen, playing with a wooden train and making puffing noises as he rolled the painted engine back and forth across the floor.

'Good boy,' she told him, and he rewarded her with a winning smile, showing pearly front teeth.

Florence felt happy, watching him play. 'Where is that train off to?' she asked, kneeling beside him. Some days, his childish world of make-believe was so much more appealing than the real one she had to live in as a grown-up. 'Somewhere exciting, I hope.'

'Prince Billy,' he told her, meaning the fairy-tale character she had created for his bedtime stories. 'Go beach!'

'The train is taking Prince Billy to the seaside?'

He nodded vigorously. 'Long . . . long, long.'

'It's a long way?'

'*Long*,' Billy agreed approvingly and rolled the engine around himself in a wide circle. 'Woo-woo!' He mimicked a train's whistle. 'Tunnel,' he added, mispronouncing the word slightly, and rolled the train under his other hand to hide it. 'Dark . . .' His voice had dropped to a whisper.

'But Prince Billy isn't scared of the dark, is he? He's too brave for that.'

'No.' Billy pushed his chest out proudly, but rolled the train back out into the light all the same. 'Train! Woo-woo!'

Florence ruffled his hair. 'One day we'll take the train like we used to with Daddy, and go through lots of tunnels and whizz out into the light again.' She sighed, for train tickets were so expensive and most civilian travel was restricted these days to prioritise war-connected journeys. 'Maybe once the war's over.'

She tried not to consider what would happen if England and her allies lost the war. It was simply too horrid to contemplate.

While Billy was still occupied with his train, she slipped into the backyard to finish pegging out the washing. Once she'd completed that task, one eye on the unsettled skies in case of rain sweeping in off the Atlantic, she dragged the heavy, old-fashioned mangle back into the outbuilding and returned to the kitchen. Her chores included preparations for that evening's dinner, peeling the vegetables and leaving them to one side, covered with a damp cloth.

Finally, she mopped out the kitchen, made a quick lunch for Billy and, while he was munching, sat down at last to open the parcel from her mother.

A letter accompanied the neatly folded hand-me-down clothes.

Dear Flo,

I hope this letter finds you and Billy well. I'm sending you more clothes as I know how fast children grow. I'm sure you'll find a use for them, and if not, you must know other ladies with sons who would benefit from a few extra pairs of short trousers.

Some family news. I'm afraid your sister has been behaving in a difficult fashion again, and your father and I are at our wits' end. I won't be so indiscreet as to put anything down in a letter. But we've both decided she needs time away from Exeter. As you'll recall, the state of her nerves earned her a medical exemption from war work. But your father and I both believe some form of steady work and responsibility could only benefit her, and might indeed be the very thing she needs to put her back on the straight and narrow.

So we gave her an ultimatum. To live with you in Bude and help out around the boarding house, or leave home, apply for war work in one of those factories up north, and fend for herself for once. Needless to say, she prefers to come to you.

In your last letter, you mentioned how hard it was to look after Billy and keep the place running, especially now you may be having soldiers billeted on you. I'm sure this extra help will be welcome, and although I know you and Imogen haven't seen eye to eye in the past, I'm hoping you girls can use this time to get past your differences and learn to be good sisters to each other.

I'm sorry if you feel inconvenienced. But this is about family and blood is thicker than water. Besides, your little sister needs a proper example set for her, and we know you're the best person to do that.

*I can't be sure when Imogen will travel down to
you, but it should be soon. We'll try to let you know
in advance of the date.*
God bless,
Your loving mother, Hyacinth

Florence groaned, reading through this letter twice with
a heavy sensation in the pit of her stomach. Imogen to
come and live with her in Bude? At twenty-three now, her
sister was her junior by twelve years, the two of them as
unlike each other as chalk and cheese. It would be a
complete disaster. For starters, Imogen hated the thought
of hard work, and would almost certainly cause trouble in
Bude, having a careless tongue and a flirtatious manner
that put most women's backs up. Especially the married
ones . . .

No, her sister couldn't possibly come to stay. For starters,
she had no spare rooms. But even as she got up to fetch
pen and paper to reply to her parents, her eye fell on the
date at the top of the letter. *Two weeks ago?* There'd been
talk of postal disruptions but that was ridiculous.

Sitting down again heavily, she muttered, 'For Pete's
sake,' and saw Billy's gaze swivel from his lunch to her
face.

'Wass matter, Mummy?'

Florence straightened, summoning a smile for his
favourite new phrase, one she often used to him when he
was unhappy. 'Nothing, darling,' she told him firmly. 'Have
you finished that bread and cheese?'

Billy shook his head, chewing reluctantly and lingering
over the crust, which she always insisted that he eat.

'Your Aunty Imogen is coming to stay with us,' she told him, resigning herself to that fact, since the time for dissuading her parents had already long passed. 'There are no rooms spare so we'll have to share.'

'Aunty Migen,' he said, grinning.

'I've told you about her before. She was at your christening.' Like the bad fairy, Florence thought, and then chided herself for being unfair. Imogen wasn't deliberately disruptive. She was a fragile person, that was all. 'But you won't remember that.' Florence began to tidy the table again. 'Time for your nap now.'

Billy growled and swung his legs in violent disapproval of this idea, which proved just how much he needed forty winks.

Setting his plate in the sink, Florence glanced out of the window and moaned. 'Rain!' she exclaimed, and dashed out to rescue her clothes off the line before they got a second impromptu dunking . . .

After Billy's nap, Florence got him ready for an outing, dragging on a woollen hat and fastening the toggles on his winter coat, her favourite acquisition from among her mum's hand-me-downs. She had noticed that her monthly delivery of two large sacks of potatoes from Farmer Roskilly had not yet arrived, and they had none left. One of the perks of running a boarding house was her ability to buy in bulk, though even that was rationed now. But since the delivery van had not called yet, she would have to fetch a pound or two of potatoes from the shop for tonight's dinner. So a quick trip into town was called for.

'Mittens?' she asked, casting about for the cosy blue

mittens his paternal great-grandmother had kindly knitted and sent in late September, just in time for the weather to turn less hospitable. Edith lived further down the northern coast, near the small port of St Ives, with her second husband. But she rarely visited, for she had a serious arthritic hip that limited her ability to travel. Since she'd lost Percy, Florence had not felt able to make the trip on her own with Billy, though she hoped to do so early next spring, before the boarding house became too busy with guests. Edith was a lovely old lady and they often corresponded by post; it would be nice to see her again, and to let Billy get properly acquainted with his great-grandmother.

'Ah, here they are.' She crouched down beside her son. 'Hands up, there's a good boy.'

Though it would break her heart to remember every step of that journey, how Percy had proudly carried his baby son onto the train and shown him the passing countryside through clouds of steam . . .

'No cry, Mummy,' Billy said gently, touching her cheek with his mittened hand.

With a shock, Florence realised he was right. A solitary tear was rolling down her cheek . . .

'Oh.' Hurriedly, she wiped it away, pinning a bright smile to her face instead. 'Silly Mummy. Must be this cold weather, making my eyes water. Now, are we ready?'

Billy nodded vehemently.

'Good,' Florence said, pulling on her own coat and hat, and taking his hand. 'Then let's go.'

But on the doorstep, she found the two sacks of potatoes that she'd been expecting, and blew out her cheeks, shaking her head.

'Oh, bother. Why didn't the farmer's van call at the back of the house?' she muttered to herself. 'Now I'll have to drag these two sacks through to the kitchen myself.'

Footsteps on the stairs made her turn. It was Sergeant Miles Miller again, this time on his way out. He touched his cap. 'Mrs Pritchard.' He glanced at the bulging sacks of potatoes and back at her face, guessing her predicament. 'Can I carry those for you, ma'am?'

That slow drawling accent again . . . it was so charming. She felt an instinctive prickle of annoyance, which was hugely unfair to him, of course. The sergeant couldn't help having such a lovely speaking voice and a smile that could warm the hardest heart. But she had grown used to a certain level of independence as a widow, doing even the heaviest and most physically exacting jobs herself. It had opened her eyes to what a woman could do on her own. Still, there was no point in refusing someone's help purely on principle. And she had no desire to strain her back lifting those heavy sacks . . .

'Thank you,' she said warily, 'that would be very kind of you.'

'Kitchen?'

Nodding, she watched, speechless with disbelief, as the American hoisted one of the large sacks over his shoulder as though it weighed next to nothing. Goodness, the muscles that must lie under that smart uniform, she thought . . . and then blushed at the way her mind was wandering.

Hurriedly, she sat Billy on the bench in the front garden to wait while she directed the sergeant where to place the potatoes. As he brought the second sack through, the kitchen door gave its usual creak, and he glanced up at the top hinge, frowning.

'That door needs a spot of grease,' Sergeant Miller commented, dropping the sack where she had indicated and turning his attention to the hinge instead. 'Happy to fix the squeak if you've a can of oil to hand.'

Florence drew a sharp breath, ruffled by the soldier's blithe assumption that she was happy for him to make himself useful about the place. Carrying sacks of potatoes that she would have struggled to handle was one thing. But performing odd jobs about the house too? Unaware of her scrutiny, he swung the door back and forth experimentally, his head cocked, listening to the creaky hinge.

What next, she wondered hotly? Advice on how to run a guest house or raise her son in the absence of a father figure? No doubt he thought a woman on her own could never be as competent as a man at household maintenance, and that she would welcome his interference with open arms . . . Well, she would soon put him straight there.

'No need for that,' she told him. 'I can do it myself.'

His gaze returned to her face, eyes narrowing as though he could, once again, read her thoughts. 'My apologies, ma'am,' he said in his slow drawl. 'I didn't intend to push myself in where I'm not wanted.'

She blushed at that, feeling horribly ungrateful. 'No, it's fine . . . Thank you, but you're a guest and I can manage jobs like that on my own.'

'Of course,' Sergeant Miller said simply.

He opened the creaking door for her and they went back down the hall together. Outside, she called Billy to her, and the American officer smiled down at her son with easy good humour. It was hard to resist that smile, she thought, her annoyance falling away. It suited his lean face better than the stern expression she'd often seen him adopt in company with his fellow soldier.

'Going into town?' he enquired.

She no longer had potatoes to buy, but they were still in need of fresh greens. She indicated the covered shopping basket over her arm. 'A few errands to run, yes.'

'Might I beg a favour, ma'am?'

Florence looked up at him warily. Sergeant Miller hadn't struck her as the type to take advantage, but perhaps there was a less palatable reason for his offers of help about the house . . .

'What . . . what kind of favour?' she asked, clutching Billy's hand so tightly that he glanced up at her with accusing eyes.

'I need a guide to the town,' Miles explained, though she was discomforted to realise he'd noticed her moment of distrust, his hesitation unmistakable. 'We anticipate the troops' arrival soon, and we're still looking for more places to commandeer for the whole winter, especially a venue large enough to accommodate all the officers. It would be good to get a genuine townsperson's view of the place. Shortcuts, for instance, or the low-down on local characters.'

Relieved that his 'favour' meant nothing untoward, her lips quirked at his curious Americanisms, and saw his brows tug together. 'I'm sorry,' she explained, 'it's just the way you talk . . . It's so different.'

His face relaxed. 'Unlike the quaint way the Cornish talk, you mean?'

'Quaint?' Her eyes widened, and then she smiled, seeing that he was teasing her. 'Oh . . . well, if you need a guide, I'd be happy to point out the larger venues that might be able to accommodate your officers. Though I need to hurry or I won't get all my chores done, and then your evening meal will be late on the table.'

'We can't have that,' he agreed solemnly, and glanced at her large wicker shopping basket. 'May I carry that for you, ma'am?'

'It's not heavy, thank you,' she said primly, and nodded to Doreen with a smile, who was chatting over the garden wall to one of their other elderly neighbours. 'Good afternoon.'

Both old ladies turned as one to stare after them, faces alive with curiosity under their knotted headscarves. No doubt tongues would soon be wagging all over town that she'd been seen out walking with a handsome American officer, Florence thought with an inward sigh. If only her gossipy neighbours knew how much his offers to 'help' left her bristling, they might be less inclined to jump to the wrong conclusion.

They crossed the road together as they approached the town, Billy beginning to skip between them, keen to visit the shops. 'Ahead of you is the Bude picture house,' she told Sergeant Miller, nodding towards the large, ornate building. 'Will the troops make use of *that*, do you think?'

'I'd say that's a certainty, ma'am,' he said with a twinkle in his eye. 'Our boys need their entertainment. They love music and the movies, that's for sure.'

She could readily believe that. He and his fellow officer had developed a habit of playing the gramophone loudly in the evenings after dinner, listening to jazz and big-band music while they smoked and drank in the small front room. Not that she really minded that, since it didn't seem to disturb Billy too much. Indeed, she had brought Percy's old gramophone down from the attic herself when Corporal Jones had politely asked if she had one in the house. Sometimes, though, listening to the faint strains of music, she would twirl about her bedroom in her stockinged feet, remembering how she and Percy had danced when they were courting.

How long ago those happy days seemed now. Like another world . . .

Sergeant Miller glanced down at her abstracted expression, frowning. 'Has *our* music been disturbing you, ma'am? I know we've gotten lively of late and I apologise. Sometimes the young ladies come down to join us for a dance and a little conversation. Nothing you wouldn't approve of, I'm sure. Just letting off steam after a long day. But we can call a halt if you prefer.'

Embarrassed to be thought such a killjoy, she stammered, 'Goodness, no. You and the corporal are guests. You must do as you like.'

He hesitated, then his generous mouth broke in a smile. 'In that case, I'd be mighty pleased if you'd join us for a dance yourself one evening, ma'am.'

'*Me?*' Her voice was a squeak. She shook her head, utterly thrown by the mental image of dancing with this man, whose constant, well-meaning interference was driving her up the wall . . . Why on earth was he even suggesting it? She wasn't some pretty young thing like Penny and Alice. Or was this him taking pity on a lonely widow? Her cheeks flared with heat. 'That's very kind, but I couldn't possibly. I . . . I have Billy to look after.'

The sergeant inclined his head, accepting that excuse without comment. But she thought she detected disappointment in his face. Or was that merely her imagination?

CHAPTER SEVEN

Alice circled the block three times, each time staring at her intended destination, a small printers' workshop down an alleyway off Belle Vue Road, with quick intensity before moving on, in case anyone should spot her taking an interest.

Finally, she plucked up courage to march up to the front entrance, where a sign swung behind the dingy glass door panel, saying CLOSED.

Despite this, she knocked and took a step back, studying the place at closer quarters. The workshop was a low, single-storey building set slightly off the road, roughly fifty feet down an alley, dominated by higher buildings on either side with shopfronts and accommodation above.

There was no answer, so she rapped on the glass again, this time more loudly, and from inside, a muffled voice barked out, 'Door's open.'

Clutching her mysterious summons, Alice pushed the door and went inside.

The workshop was dusty, laid to floorboards, and the air

was thick with cigarette smoke. The small front office held a desk and several work stations, all littered with machinery, sundry items like scissors and glue pots and guillotines, plus rolls of white paper and printed sheets. Some sheets had been knocked to the floor and trodden on, perhaps months ago, the print faded and bearing dirty scuff marks. A further door at the back led into a second, even dustier-looking space containing what appeared to be a printing press.

There was a thin, wizened man bending over an old typewriter at a desk near the back, a screwdriver in one hand and a metal canister of oil in the other. He didn't look up but continued fiddling with the typewriter, even though a bell above the door had jangled loudly at her entrance. A cigarette dangled from his lips as though permanently stuck there, and every now and then he took a drag on it. His black overalls were smeared with oil and greasy fingerprints as though he were a car mechanic, not a printer. But she supposed the work involved in maintaining a printing workshop to be not dissimilar to that of a garage mechanic.

Alice coughed, the smoky atmosphere tickling her throat. 'Hello, I'm Alice Fisher. I was told to report here today for, erm, war work.' She held up the letter, but the man continued fiddling with the typewriter, head down. 'Is this the right place?'

The man looked up at last, studying her with narrowed blue eyes, crinkled and creased, his weather-beaten face a mass of deep-set wrinkles. 'No, you won't do,' he said after a brief head-to-toe examination that took in her beret, best skirt and blouse, woollen stockings and black shoes. 'Best go back where you came from, Miss.'

'I'm sorry?'

'You should apply for a factory job if you want war work. Or take up nursing. That's best for the likes of you.' The printer returned to the typewriter, delicately squirting oil into the roller mechanism. 'Close the door on your way out, there's a good girl.'

Alice had never been so excruciatingly embarrassed in all her born days. Her first impulse was to do exactly what he said and crawl back to the boarding house in defeat. Then she recalled all the times Aunty Violet had been told no, and how she'd never taken that as an answer, even finding them work and a roof over their heads when her great-aunt and uncle threw them out soon after their arrival in Cornwall. Aunty Vi would have stood firm and insisted on being given a fair crack.

'You don't understand,' she said, though she was quaking inwardly. 'This letter . . .

'I'm not interested in your letter.' He pointed to the door again without lifting his head. 'Off with you now. I'm a busy man.'

Alice took a deep breath and said, as firmly as she could, 'No.'

He looked up at this, eyebrows shooting. 'Beg pardon?'

'I said, no. I've been told to come here. Belle Vue Printers. I'm expected.' She took a few unsteady steps towards his cluttered desk and laid the letter down on top of his typewriter. The thin sheet immediately began to bloom with faint oil patches. 'It says *right there* to report to this address,' she added, tapping the letter. 'Miss Alice Fisher. That's me.'

'Is it now?' The man didn't so much as glance at the sheet, looking directly at her with a fixed stare.

'I'm not asking for no special favours,' she went on. 'Someone seems to think I should be here, so here I am. I don't mind if all you want me to do is sweep the floor. It does need sweeping, after all, if you don't mind me saying so.' At this, his eyebrows rose even higher and he glanced around the workshop in mild surprise, as though this was the first time he'd even noticed the mess. 'But you're not sending me away, Mister. Not on my first day. Just so we're clear.'

'I see.' His thin, greasy roll-up fell out of his mouth onto the floor. He pressed a booted foot on it, still holding her gaze. 'Miss Alice Fisher, eh?'

She swallowed. 'That's right.'

'And that accent?' He put down the oil canister. 'East End?'

'Near enough. Dagenham.'

'Stick with *near enough*.' His eyes narrowed on her face. 'When someone's questioning you, stay silent if you can. And if you can't, never volunteer more than you need. Got that?'

She nodded, her heart thudding, and leant forward to retrieve her precious letter. 'Does that mean I can stay?'

'It means we'll see.'

Alice almost smiled, taking that as a yes, but decided not to push her luck. Not with this man.

He wiped an oily hand on his overalls and stuck it out to her. 'Pleased to meet you, Miss Alice Fisher. I'm Sidney. You won't need no more than that,' he added sternly as they shook hands. 'And don't ever call me Sid. Is that clear?'

'Yes, sir.'

His dark, bushy brows drew together. 'Not sir. Sidney. That's what everyone calls me.'

'Yes, Sidney,' she said promptly.

He produced a printed sheet from a desk drawer and held it out, along with a fountain pen. 'Read this and sign at the end.'

'What is it?'

'Official Secrets Act.'

Her eyes widened, but she nodded, read the printed document through carefully and then signed her name at the bottom. She had no intention of doing or saying anything that might damage England's chances of winning the war, so she was happy to sign an agreement not to do so.

'All right, you'd better go through.' Putting her signed sheet back into the drawer, Sidney nodded her towards the dusty office with its silent printing press. 'Out the back door and down into the shelter.'

She blinked, not understanding. 'Are we expecting an air raid?'

'Stop asking questions.'

Biting her lip to prevent a sharp response, Alice nodded, pushed the letter into her coat pocket, and followed his instructions.

Out the back of the print workshop, she found a curved tin structure, rather like an Anderson shelter but larger. Ducking through the salt-speckled door, she saw a set of steps ahead in the gloom with light showing below. Cautiously, she went down the steps and found herself in a narrow underground room with a desk and chair set beside a blackboard on an easel, and two short rows of chairs facing them. Like a classroom, she thought, her gaze instantly drawn to an odd series of chalked words on a blackboard.

The place was empty, but as she stood there, uncertain, she heard conversation and footsteps behind her, and three men and a young woman came down the steps. They all fell silent on seeing her, and the young woman, a pretty girl with lively eyes and short chestnut hair, set hands on hips and looked her up and down. She looked to be about nineteen or twenty, at a guess.

'Well,' she said, with an affected toss of her head, 'look what the cat dragged in. This the new recruit? I give her two weeks, tops. Then she'll be back to Mummy and Daddy, tail between her legs.'

The young men laughed, though uncomfortably.

The tallest among them put out a hand to Alice, who shook it, her smile perfunctory. 'Hello,' he told her, 'don't mind Sophy. If anyone's a cat, it's her. My name's Jasper. Stout chap with the beard is Barnabas, and that there is Spotty Patrick.' He raised his brows when she said nothing. 'And you are?'

Alice hesitated, looking at each of them in turn, uncertain how to introduce herself. *Never volunteer more than you need.* But she hadn't been told not to give anyone her name, had she? And these appeared to be her fellow trainees, so it was probably safe.

'Alice,' she said simply, omitting her last name this time. Exactly as they had done. Then she glanced at Sophy, not unpleasantly but putting her straight. 'And I can't go running to Mummy and Daddy because they're both dead.'

This wasn't entirely true, as her father was on a secret mission for the British government behind enemy lines. But Ernest Fisher had been officially 'presumed dead' and that was all she intended to say on the subject.

A short silence followed this pronouncement.

Sophy flushed and turned away to find a seat, while Barnabas and Jasper dug their hands in their pockets, looking awkward.

Only Patrick smiled in easy sympathy, coming to shake her hand. He wasn't *that* spotty, Alice thought, studying his face. But maybe he had been once and the nickname had stuck. 'We're both in the same boat, by the sound of it,' he told her. 'I lost my mother as a baby, and my father too this past year. It's not easy being an orphan.' But his eyes were less friendly than his words.

Before she could reply, more footsteps heralded the arrival of Sidney, who came limping down the steps and across the mud floor, a folder tucked under his arm, another roll-up stuck to his lip. Seeing him without a work desk in the way, she realised belatedly that he had a false leg, just like her uncle Joe, only he didn't bother with a stick.

'No more bickering,' Sidney said shortly, as though he'd caught every word of their conversation, which was surely impossible. 'Take a seat, ladies and gentlemen. I hope you've all had a chance to meet Alice. She'll be out with Barnabas this week and Sophy next week. Is that understood?'

There was muttered assent as they all drew out chairs and sat down. Alice took a seat alone on the second row behind Sophy, who glanced back at her sharply.

'This week, we'll be going over some basics, since Alice

has just joined us. Starting with surveillance.' Sidney rubbed off the odd words chalked on the board and began to sketch out a map. Watching eagerly, Alice quickly realised it was a map of a town centre, with buildings marked with letters of the alphabet and labelled as shops, residentials or public use, and roads designated with numbers. He put down the chalk and asked, 'Now, if you had to watch point B from both front and rear without being noticed, which positions might you take up and how many people would that involve?' He nodded to Patrick, who had his hand up. 'Well?'

Alice listened as Patrick described how he would tackle the surveillance and was surprised when Sidney contradicted one part of his plan, explaining how exposed he would be leaving his 'man' in front of F, which was a residential building, with no useful doorways to duck into or window shopping available for cover.

'Alice,' Sidney said, turning his intent gaze in her direction, 'where would you put your second agent in this instance?'

'The library,' she said without hesitation.

Sophy threw an irritated glance over her shoulder. 'It's too far away to be an effective surveillance point.'

'But it's got better cover. You could lurk inside for ages without arousing suspicion, pretending to be looking at books,' Alice pointed out, hoping she hadn't got it wrong, 'and watch through the doorway or window.'

To her relief, Sidney nodded. 'Good work.' His gaze went to Barnabas. 'Later, I'd like you to take Alice round the town and show her some of our assembly points.' He looked back at Alice. 'Those are prearranged places where we know to gather after an operation or in the event of an emergency.'

'So we don't come back here?' Alice asked, puzzled.

'Never.' Sidney drew on his roll-up and let the thin smoke drift slowly out of one corner of his mouth. 'This is HQ. And in an emergency situation, you should always assume HQ has been compromised. Barnabas will talk you through the rest. He's our most experienced trainee.' He paused. 'Once you're ready, you can partner with Sophy. She's been learning how to tail someone in a pair situation, but only in a male-female dynamic. Two girls together will make a useful contrast.'

He turned again to the map, beginning to discuss potential escape routes if spotted and pursued during a surveillance operation.

Sophy's back had straightened and her chin was jutting out, and Alice knew she was annoyed. It was possible she was uncomfortable with the idea of partnering with a newcomer. Or perhaps she resented Alice having made a better suggestion about where to conceal yourself while watching a target. Though that would be silly, given it was Alice's first day of training and she'd probably make a fool of herself with an embarrassing suggestion soon enough. Sophy had nothing to worry about.

Still, the niggling worry that she'd somehow trodden on the other girl's toes wouldn't go away.

As soon as there was a break for tea and a smoke, she went straight up to Sophy and said, not bothering to mess about, 'We seem to have got off on the wrong foot. Have I done something to offend you?'

Sophy stared at her, astonished. 'Of course not. Whatever

makes you say that?' and then marched off outside, not waiting for an answer. 'I'm dying for a cigarette. You coming, Pat?'

Patrick gave Alice a wry shrug and followed the other girl up the steps.

Not the friendly response she'd been hoping for, but Alice tried not to let it bother her. She and her sister Lily had come in for some nasty taunts at the start of the war because of their half-German father and she was used to shrugging off hostility. But it would be awkward if Sophy kept up her unfriendly behaviour for weeks or even months on this training course.

'You've put her nose out of joint,' Jasper murmured, coming up behind her.

Alice glanced back at him. 'Have I? How?'

'By being a girl.'

She didn't understand that and wrinkled her nose.

'Before you came along, it was just Sophy and three boys,' he elaborated, following her up the steps. 'Now she's got a rival.'

'But I'm *not* her rival,' Alice said, surprised and a little alarmed by this idea. 'I don't even know what you mean by that.'

Jasper raised his brows. 'You're an unusual girl, aren't you?' But he laughed. 'Put simply, most personnel selected for this course are male and have some previous combat training. You know . . . Firearms, hand-to-hand, special operations. Not casting aspersions on the fairer sex, you understand, but there aren't many women in that position. So it was a big thing when Sophy was selected.' He winked, grinning. 'But she's no longer so special, if there are two of you.'

They had come out into the fresh, salty sea air. Sophy was standing across the small backyard with Barnabas and Patrick, all three rolling cigarettes, deep in conversation. Alice studied the dark-haired girl with interest.

'How was she selected?' she asked.

'I think she was training for the Wrens and someone gave her a tap on the shoulder.' Jasper glanced at her. 'And you?'

'I . . . I was working in a school in Penzance. As a teaching assistant.' She hesitated, feeling herself to be on boggy ground. 'I got a letter telling me to report here.'

'You weren't already in combat training?'

'No.'

'Had you done any previous training? Maybe in Signals?'

'No.'

'Then how on earth . . .' Her fellow trainee's gaze narrowed on her face. 'Alice, do you have a contact within the service? Or in the government?' His voice had dropped to a whisper. A cold shiver ran through her as Jasper looked her up and down, his face speculative. 'A family connection, perhaps . . . Who's your father?'

The shock of that last question left her breathless.

'N-Nobody special,' she stammered, not meeting his eyes, and hurried towards Sidney as he came up from the shelter with a tray of tin mugs and a teapot. 'Oh, a cuppa. Bloomin' marvellous. My mouth's dry as ashes.'

She had to be more careful what she said, Alice realised, forcing a smile to her lips as she took the tray from Sidney. Or she could be putting her dad in serious danger. Not to mention herself.

CHAPTER EIGHT

Thankfully, working in the Bude dairy shop had improved since Penny's awful first day on the job. She had invested in another pair of woollen stockings, despite the extravagance, and now wore two pairs to work. This kept her legs from getting too chilly while standing about for long periods in the cold. She wore a vest under her blouse and a cardigan borrowed from Alice on top, and now that she had adjusted to the draughts and windy gusts that blew in through the permanently opening and closing shop door, she no longer felt the cold so much.

No, her problems these days were more to do with her employers and their extended family, none of whom were particularly pleasant people. But it was steady work, and some of the customers were nice enough, especially the old gentlemen, who always had a smile for her and a word of encouragement.

Today though, old gentlemen seemed to be thin on the ground, and several times she came under Mrs Roskilly's eagle eye and was reprimanded for making a mistake, either giving the wrong change again or being too slow to return to the counter when called.

'Penny,' her employer called sharply from the back of the shop, 'what on earth is this? If you've no customers, you'd better come here and explain yourself.'

The shop was unfortunately empty.

Penny lifted the counter and hurried through the narrow aisles, her heart sinking at the angry note in Mrs Roskilly's voice. She found her employer at the back, stooped over the lowest shelf of canned goods. 'Yes, Mrs Roskilly?'

'This is bully beef,' Mrs Roskilly said, holding up a can of corned beef. 'We don't put canned meat next to canned vegetables, do we?'

'No, Mrs Roskilly.'

'And yet you've shelved an entire box of bully beef in the wrong place.' The woman straightened, her lips pursed, bright scarlet lipstick seeping into the deep creases beside her mouth. 'It will all have to be moved.'

Penny had a strong suspicion that one of Mrs Roskilly's sons had unpacked that particular box of goods. But there was no use saying so. Mrs Roskilly idolised her sons and would not hear a word against them. Whereas she was only too happy to berate Penny for every tiny mistake or misdemeanour.

'I'll move them to the correct shelf straightaway. I'm very sorry.'

'I should hope so. Don't let it happen again.'

'No, Mrs Roskilly.'

As soon as she'd gone, Penny dropped to her knees on the hard stone floor and began removing the corned beef from the shelf of canned vegetables.

As she did so, a pair of dirty, scuffed boots stopped beside her.

'Is that bully beef?' a cheerful Cornish voice asked, and she glanced up in surprise at a young man in loose trousers and a thick, close-knitted jumper. 'I could do with a can, while you're down there.'

She selected a can and held it up to him, smiling shyly. 'There you go.'

He had a silky thatch of thick fair hair that flopped carelessly over his forehead, a round, grinning face with a healthy flush, and ears that stood out like jug handles.

'It's for my ma,' he explained, although she had not asked. 'She's sick of fish. And I can't blame her.'

'Can't you?' Penny was entranced by his fresh good looks and that creamy Cornish accent, so much richer than her own dull Home Counties accent.

'I'm a fisherman, see.' He grinned down at her. 'Like my pa before me, and his before that. The family business, you could say.'

'I see.'

'The *Mary Jane*, that's our boat.' He nodded over his shoulder. 'She's in dry dock right now, with Pa working on her. Just a few repairs. But we'll be going out again before the winter storms set in.'

He was certainly a talker, Penny thought, mesmerised by the deep, rolling lilt of his voice. She was usually the one who wouldn't shut up. Famous for it, in fact. But already he had shifted into talking about the weather, and how the fish were too canny to be caught these days, and how the war was going on, while she knelt there, unmoving, unspeaking, her wide eyes fixed on his face.

'Penny, are you ever going to finish restacking that shelf?' Mrs Roskilly demanded with obvious restraint, appearing from behind the aisle divider.

'Sorry,' Penny breathed. Fumbling all the corned beef cans into her arms, she threw him a harried smile before dashing away to reshelve them in the correct place.

The shop owner had given the young man a forbidding look too. 'Can I help you, John Pascoe?'

'That you can, Mrs Roskilly,' he said irreverently, tossing her the can of corned beef. 'I'll have this, thank you, and an ounce of baccy for my pa. To be put on the slate, Ma says. She'll call in with the ration books first thing tomorrow.'

'Hmm,' was all Mrs Roskilly said, but didn't refuse him tick, as she sometimes did when customers came in and asked for items to be put 'on the slate' or 'on tick', which Penny had discovered meant to be paid for later, either when the ration book was produced or, for some off-ration goods, when they had enough money.

In a trance, Penny watched the young man until he had taken his goods and left the shop with a casual, 'Cheerio,' and a wave in her direction. Then realised belatedly that she had shelved all the cans of corned beef upside-down.

'Drat,' she muttered, and hurriedly set to work adjusting the row before Mrs Roskilly could spot her mistake and give her what for. But her heart was thudding and she couldn't seem to concentrate on her work.

So that was his name, she thought, biting her lip.

John Pascoe.

'I've never met a fisherman before,' she mentioned to

Mrs Roskilly later, while being shown how to use the wire cheese cutter. 'I imagine it must be very hard work. All those days at sea.'

'Weeks at sea, sometimes,' Mrs Roskilly corrected her, and shook her head. 'He's a young rascal, that John Pascoe. Like his father before him.'

'You know his father too?' Penny looked at her wonderingly.

'When I was a lass, yes, and we were at school together. My mother warned me about him and she was right to do so. I was better off with Mr Roskilly.' The woman's brows tugged together in sudden alarm. 'Here, watch what you're doing with that cheese wire, girl! You nearly sliced your finger off.'

'Oops.' Penny sucked her fingertip, which was bleeding slightly.

'Best go and clean yourself up in the back,' Mrs Roskilly told her, frowning darkly. 'Can't have you bleeding over the goods.'

'No, Mrs Roskilly.'

'And no more mooning over that young John Pascoe. I'll not have any funny business in this shop. Is that clear?'

Lunchtime came, and Mrs Roskilly provided her with one of her own home-baked Cornish pasties on sale in the shop – a simple twist of pastry with meat and potato tucked inside – and reminded her not to be late back.

'Forty-five minutes is more than enough for your lunch break,' her boss told her, handing over the still-warm Cornish pasty wrapped in a sheet of old newspaper. 'Make sure you get back here in good time. I've an appointment with the doctor for my chilblains this afternoon, and I can't leave the shop unattended.'

Clutching her lunch, Penny fairly flew down the road, people scattering out of the way in surprise as she clattered across the bridge into the other side of town. No time today for admiring the ducks and swans on the river, or stopping to buy her weekly bag of aniseed balls or jelly beans with her ration book. No, for she was intent on spotting the *Mary Jane* among the boats in dry dock along the harbourside.

She slowed to a more sedate pace on reaching the harbour walkway, for the tide was almost fully in that lunchtime and flecks of sea foam, whipped up by the sea breeze, had left the stones slippery and precarious.

Grey-bearded fishermen in thick jumpers, smoking pipes and chatting as they worked, sat along the harbour, mending what looked like lobster or crab pots, darning nets or hammering nails into long planks. One or two looked up at her curiously as she passed, but there were others sitting or standing along the harbour wall to eat their lunch, so she merely smiled and fetched out her pasty.

As she walked, she unwrapped the newspaper and nibbled at one corner, her stomach rumbling as she belatedly realised how hungry she was. 'Mmm,' she said to herself, biting more deeply into the thin, crumbling pastry to reach the meaty filling.

Sadly, the meat was chewy and tasteless, and there were only a few chunks of potato smeared with gravy. It would keep her going until suppertime, Penny told herself, trying not to pull a face. 'Worse where there's none,' her mother would have said, urging her to eat up, regardless of the taste.

Abruptly, she stopped dead and hurriedly swallowed the last few bites of the pasty. Propped up on wooden stilts, a dirty-hulled vessel lay just ahead on the harbourside. MARY JANE was the name painted in large black letters on the planks facing her. A seagull sat perched on the boat's hull, but flew away with a haunting screech as a man's head popped out from under the boat. His wild grey hair was covered with a woollen hat and he had a grizzled beard, kept surprisingly trim given his dishevelled look. 'John?' he was calling out, glancing up and down the harbourside. Could this be Mr Pascoe Senior, she wondered? 'John? Where are you, boy?'

Blushing, embarrassed in case she was caught looking for the very boat he'd mentioned, Penny looked hurriedly about for the young man she'd met in the dairy. To her relief, there was no sign of him.

But the old fisherman had seen her looking. 'Ahoy there, Miss,' he said in a thick Cornish accent, beckoning her over, and she froze, staring at him wide-eyed, still clutching the greasy newspaper her pasty had been wrapped in. 'Ha' seen a young man in your travels, about this high?' he asked, gesturing with his hand. 'Wi' fair hair and a gormless look about him? I sent him to fetch me a pinch or two of baccy an hour ago, and I'm beginning to think he may ha' taken a tumble off them cliffs there,' he added, nodding towards the high, craggy cliffs that rose around the harbour. 'He'd best ha' a good excuse for skipping out, that's all I can say.'

Penny shook her head. 'I've not seen him, sorry.' She blushed even deeper, realising that wasn't entirely true. 'Not since he bought the baccy . . . I mean, the tobacco.

In the dairy shop, that is. That's where I saw him.' She was babbling, she realised.

'Oh aye? You saw my grandson in the shop, did you?' He rubbed his beard thoughtfully. 'That's no Cornish accent. Evacuee, are you?'

Her brows rose. 'I'm not a schoolgirl,' she said, a little offended. 'I work in the dairy. And I ought to be getting back there. Excuse me.'

'Eh, watch out, there!' He was pointing behind her, alarm in his face.

Too late.

She'd already stumbled backwards over a coiled length of rope and gone sprawling. 'Ow,' she muttered, wincing and hobbling as she staggered back to her feet.

It felt like she'd grazed her knee through the woollen stockings. Her left ankle hurt like billy-oh too. Could it be twisted? Now she would be late back to work, having to limp all the way. And Mrs Roskilly had been so insistent that she should return on time.

She'd be lucky not to lose her position over this.

Turning with a muffled cry of pain, awkwardly favouring her good ankle, she came face to face with John Pascoe, who had been walking along the harbour with his hands in his pockets, whistling. The young man slowed his steps, staring. He looked surprised to see her again, as well he might. Worse, she thought with a burst of flushed humiliation, he must have seen her fall over the rope coil in that ungainly fashion.

'Hello again,' John said. 'I see you've met my grandpa.'

'Yes.' She gave him a pained smile, wishing the ground would swallow her up and be done with it. 'I have to go, I'm afraid. I'm running awfully late.'

'You'll not be running anywhere, by the looks of it. Hurt yourself?'

'My . . . my ankle.'

'Well, only one thing for it,' he said simply, and scooped her up in his arms. She lay against his chest in silent amazement, her face scarlet, heart thumping. 'Back to the dairy shop, is it?'

'Thank you,' she gulped.

Mrs Roskilly's face was a picture when John entered the dairy, setting her back on her feet with a nod, only a little breathless, as though she had weighed nothing on the long climb up from the harbour. Which was clearly not the case, she thought, burning with embarrassment as she explained to her speechless employer what had happened.

Once he'd turned and disappeared, Mrs Roskilly glared round at her. 'I knew you were trouble, girl!' She gave a hiss of frustration, seeing Penny lean against the counter, her ankle still throbbing and twice its usual size. 'And you can't work in that state. Or walk, by the look of you. I'll have to get my husband to run you back to Downs View Road. Bang goes my doctor's appointment.'

'I'm so sorry,' Penny burst out, biting her lip with remorse. 'Please don't cancel your appointment because of me. There's no need for me to leave early. I . . . I'll sit on a stool behind the counter to man the till. How's that?'

'Hmm,' was all Mrs Roskilly said to this, her lips pursed, but didn't refuse the offer, disappearing into the back to fetch a stool for her.

Penny sagged, rubbing her sore ankle. Goodness, what a hero John was, she thought. Mentally, she relived every step of that uphill journey, held safely in his arms while passers-by stared at them in amused surprise. She'd never really been interested in the opposite sex before, but he was the boy for her, no doubt about it.

Though she knew instinctively what Selina and Caroline would say if they were here. That John Pascoe with his carefree smile and tall, handsome figure was far too good for someone like 'Penny Pickles' and she should stop kidding herself.

And perhaps they would be right.

CHAPTER NINE

Florence was so exhausted, she could have lain down on the floor of the back parlour and slept right there, without any problem. After an intensive morning cleaning and repainting the attic rooms ready for new guests, she had been run off her feet all afternoon without any chance of a sit-down. Charlotte's little girl Emily had come around to play with Billy for a few hours while Charlotte went to the library and caught up with her laundry. The two children had needed careful supervision to prevent squabbling and accidents. They'd played happily together at first, but then aeroplanes had flown low overhead on their way to Cleave Camp above Bude, frightening Emily with the deep hum of their engines, and it had taken almost half an hour to calm the girl down.

Billy had stared at his friend in surprise, for he loved the sound of planes, but his clumsy hug had made no difference to her wails of 'Bad men! Bad men!'

Going out into the yard, Florence told Emily, 'They're not the bad men's planes. They're our planes, and we should be jolly glad to see them. In fact, Billy's daddy flew planes . . .'

Her heart squeezed in pain at the memory and she stuttered into silence, not wanting to remind Billy of his father's loss, though he'd been so small at the time, he couldn't remember his father now. Which was awfully sad, but perhaps for the best.

Smiling down at the little girl, Florence dried her tears with a handkerchief. 'Next time,' she added, 'maybe we could give them a friendly wave as they fly overhead. Would you like that?'

But Emily shrank away, seemingly convinced that the planes were enemy fighters, there to rain fire on the town.

Sighing, Florence took them back indoors and removed their coats and hats. After they'd played with their toys for a while, she sat one child on each knee beside the low fire burning in the grate and told them a long, richly detailed story about Prince Billy and his cousin Princess Emily who made friends with a family of ogres living near their castle, after realising that ogres were not scary after all but were in fact very good at juggling and telling jokes.

Afterwards, both children clamoured to hear more stories. But Florence, conscious of the time, asked them to put their scattered toys back into the toy box instead – for all the good that ever did, but it was a good way to keep them safely occupied – and she hurried away to sweep and dust.

This weekly chore complete, she checked on the children again and was amused to find them both asleep on the sofa, warm and with flushed cheeks.

Quietly, she tiptoed out and spent the next half hour in

the kitchen, making a fish pie for her guests' supper, every now and then peeking into the back parlour to reassure herself that both her charges were still dozing.

By the time Charlotte finally arrived to collect her daughter, just as the daylight was beginning to fail, Emily was sitting up and playing with her ragdoll, while Billy ran up and down the hall, shouting a few thankfully incoherent words from a song he'd overheard the American officers singing a few days before. It was not a suitable song for a child, in her opinion, but her son seemed to take delight in her exasperated protests.

'I'm so sorry,' she told Charlotte as her friend bundled Emily into her coat and hat, ready for the short walk home. 'I've asked him not to keep singing that awful song. Something he picked up from the Americans who are staying here.'

Her friend looked at her curiously. 'I've heard there are going to be hundreds of American troops here soon, not just the two you have. One of my neighbours knows the town clerk's wife, and *she* says they're going to be stationed in the town for some time. Months, maybe. Is that true?'

'I don't know about hundreds,' she admitted, truthfully enough, 'but I believe the United States have already sent troops over to England, yes. And some of them may be stationed in and around Bude. Though I don't know how many.'

'Goodness me. But why here?'

'Something to do with the coast hereabouts, as I understand it. They want to train on the beaches.' That was something Sergeant Miller had let slip the other day in idle conversation. 'But you didn't hear that from me, all right?'

'Oh, mum's the word,' her friend agreed, but she was looking concerned. 'Though I don't know how we'll cope if the town is overrun with Americans.'

'If it helps us win the war, I don't think we have a right to complain,' Florence pointed out.

Her friend, whose husband was away on active service, had to agree with that. With a smile, she bid Florence goodnight, heading off into a beautiful orange dusk as the sun set over the ocean to the west.

Hit by a sudden wave of exhaustion, Florence caught her son, who was still running about, clapping his hands and shouting the words to that unfortunate song, and said firmly, 'Time for some peace and quiet, Billy. Do you want another nap or would you prefer to play quietly with your toys?'

'Toys,' he told her, his face sullen.

'That's a good boy.' She set her son down on the rug in front of his wooden train, hurriedly went about closing the blackout curtains, and then sank into an armchair beside him. The back parlour was gloomy but warm. The fire, behind its fireguard, ticked over softly into smouldering embers.

Wearily, Florence allowed her eyelids to close.

Ten minutes' rest, she promised herself, and then she would have to bustle back into the kitchen to put the pie into the oven for supper.

The next thing she knew, Sergeant Miller was stooping over her, saying gently, 'Mrs Pritchard? Time to wake up, ma'am.'

She sat up with a start, eyes wide, a swift apology on her lips. 'I'm so sorry. I fell asleep. My goodness, is that the time?' She stared in horror at the mantelpiece clock. It was gone six o'clock.

Ordinarily, she served dinner at six. Her poor guests must have been sitting waiting in the dining room for a meal that never came.

'I'll bring your dinner through straightaway,' she stammered, turning towards the kitchen, only to realise with a shock that she had forgotten to put the pie in the oven.

'What is it, ma'am?' Sergeant Miller, who had been obediently heading back towards the dining room, stopped. His eyes were concerned. 'Is something wrong? Can I help you?'

Horribly embarrassed, she explained about the pie. 'It won't be ready for ages.' Close to tears, she bit her lip. 'I'll have to make something else. Though I'm not sure what we have. Bread and cheese, perhaps. I'm so sorry.'

To her astonishment, the American did not even seem angry. He merely smiled and nodded. 'Don't you worry, ma'am. Leave everything to me.'

Before she could enquire what he meant, the officer had left the room.

Hurriedly, Florence took her son through to the kitchen and made him a helping of bread and cheese, with a glass of milk and a rosy apple cut into slices for his pudding. While he was eating, she put the pie in the oven. Once cooked, it could be left on the cold shelf in the pantry to be eaten tomorrow, if still good. Though what the sergeant had planned for tonight, she could not imagine.

Much to her relief, Billy tucked into his simple meal without complaint and had soon cleared his plate and was yawning, ready for a quick wash before bed.

Once her son was clean and sleeping in his cot at the end of her bed, Florence quietly washed her own face, tidied her hair and changed her dress, which had become badly creased during her nap.

She didn't know why on earth she was worrying about her appearance, given that she was a widow and had nobody to impress. But perhaps her pride had been stung lately, spotting her reflection in the mirror and seeing how tired and drawn she looked, no longer pretty and fresh-faced – not like her two young guests, Alice and Penny.

She had heard the Americans talking to the girls some evenings while they were playing music and dancing. She probably ought to put her foot down. Some landladies along the road had already been muttering about loud music and irregular goings-on after dark.

But why shouldn't they dance?

There was a war on, for goodness' sake. Hitler could invade at any moment, and none of them could be sure they would survive this. Especially those two brave young men, who had signed up to fight for freedom and decency.

Downstairs, Penny and Alice were already seated in the dining room alongside Corporal Jones, chatting as they waited for their evening meal. Florence peeked out of the kitchen door at them, utterly at a loss for what to feed them, except more bread and cheese. Which was hardly the daily hot meal they were paying for. But she had not shopped properly for days now, due to the sheer weight of chores and the fatigue of running around after little Billy, and the pantry was bare.

'I'm so sorry,' Florence said, horribly embarrassed, fastening on her apron as she came through the kitchen door, 'but supper will be a little delayed. You see, I . . . I fell asleep and—'

But as she began to explain her predicament, they all heard booted feet coming along the hallway, and suddenly Sergeant Miles Miller was there, holding a large package in his arms.

It smelt delicious.

'Whatever is that?' Florence cried, her astonished gaze flashing to his face. 'It smells like . . . *fish and chips*?'

'Food identified correctly, ma'am,' Miles said with a wink, and set the fish and chips on the table, still tightly wrapped in oily newspaper. 'Fish and chips for all of us. With plenty of salt and vinegar. Help yourselves.'

'Oh, you wonderful man,' she choked, and then recalled herself. Goodness, whatever was the matter with her? Dropping her guard like that . . . Though it was awfully kind of the sergeant to have rescued them from bread and cheese for supper. And to think she had been so horrid to him over wanting to oil that squeaky hinge in the kitchen . . .

Blinking away tears of gratitude, she said in a stilted voice, back on her dignity, 'I'd better fetch plates and cutlery,' and turned back to the kitchen.

'Don't bother with that,' Alice told her, dragging on her arm. 'We can eat 'em out the wrappin's . . . Sit down and tuck in, Mrs P.' And indeed the other officer had already begun unwrapping the fish, a broad grin on his face. 'See?

There's plenty to go around. And fingers is all we need for fish and chips. Not knives and forks.'

'Mmm, what a feast!' Penny exclaimed, tearing off a scrap of newspaper to make herself a makeshift plate, onto which she dragged a heap of glistening, well-salted chips and a portion of golden-fried fish, batter curling crisply at the edges.

'You know what, Sarge? You're a proper gent, you are,' Alice told Miles in her East End accent, offering him a fat chip.

'Am I now? I'm guessing that's a compliment,' Miles smiled, popping the chip in his mouth as he drew up a seat to the small dining table. There really wasn't enough room for all of them, yet somehow they squeezed in.

Florence found herself smiling, her spirits lifting, and not simply because she didn't need to dash off and rustle up some supper for everyone as she had expected. Perhaps it wasn't so bad to have someone to help out occasionally. Though she didn't want to feel beholden to Sergeant Miller. It wouldn't be right.

'Sergeant, you must let me know what I owe you,' she whispered to him as they all helped themselves to fish and chips. It was hard not to think of him as 'Miles' in the privacy of her own head, but was she careful to stick to his proper title out loud. 'These are off-ration.'

'No need,' he insisted, shaking his head when she protested. 'This is my treat.' He gave her an odd look. 'Besides, you may not be so grateful when you hear my news.'

'What do you mean? What news?'

'Only that the Yankees are coming to town.'

She stared at him, baffled. 'I'm sorry? The *Yankees*?'

'The Americans, ma'am,' he explained. 'They're due to arrive in Bude next week. The Second Battalion Rangers.'

'So soon?' She ate in silence for a while, worried that the house was barely ready to receive more guests. 'Will there be government help for people who take billeted soldiers?' she asked at last. 'The cost of all the food, the upkeep of the rooms . . .'

'No need for you to worry, ma'am. We're setting up a big chow house down the road, beachside. It should cater for most of the men.'

'*Chow house*?'

He grinned at her puzzled expression. 'That's what we call a canteen. Somewhere the men can eat. Mealtimes may be irregular, you see. What with all the early morning training, mostly down on the beach.'

Florence was relieved. 'Thank you for setting my mind at rest.'

'My pleasure,' he said, and his gaze held hers a fraction longer than was entirely polite.

Florence removed a few bones from the fish before popping it in her mouth, wishing the sergeant wasn't quite so handsome. And did he have to sit so close? Their knees were touching. But it would be rude to shift her chair away.

'Early morning training on the beach?' Sharp-eared Alice had overheard them. 'That sounds exciting,' she said, addressing both Americans. 'Doing what, exactly? Or is it all hush-hush?'

Florence regarded her young guest with amusement, trying not to smile. Alice was only eighteen, yet she had an unusually direct way of talking. Most girls her age had to be coaxed into conversation when men were in the room. Alice showed no such nervousness around the opposite sex. Yet she wasn't flirtatious either, as Florence's younger sister Imogen had been at the same age. She was simply honest and straightforward. It was rather refreshing.

'I'm sorry, Miss.' Miles hesitated, glancing at the corporal. 'You're right . . . We're not at liberty to say. I hope you understand.'

'Of course.' Alice continued to eat, nodding. 'Quite right.'

Penny had finished her meal already and was wiping her hands on a napkin. 'That was marvellous,' she said enthusiastically, 'thank you, Miles.' She beamed at Alice. 'I say, this is awfully exciting, isn't it? Compared to life on the farm, I mean.'

'I suppose so,' Alice agreed, focused on her chips.

When the meal was finished, Florence rose to clear the table and fetch a pot of tea for everyone.

'Let me help you with that,' Sergeant Miller said, getting to his feet.

'Oh no, you stay there,' Florence told him in a hurry, not quite comfortable with the idea of being alone with this great hulking American in her tiny kitchen. 'Let me fetch out a big pot of tea for everyone. It's the least I can do after such a lovely treat.'

But Miles ignored her, scrunching up the greasy newspaper scraps and nodding to his corporal. 'Ken, give me a hand, would you?'

Together, both men carried the soiled newspaper into the kitchen for disposal. Afterwards, they wiped the table and then washed their hands with soap in a business-like manner at the sink, the air soon redolent of coal tar, while

Florence filled the teapot and carried out cups and saucers on a tray.

She couldn't help wondering if Sergeant Miller had understood the reason for her hesitation and deliberately asked his fellow officer to accompany him, so she wouldn't feel awkward being alone with him.

Well, she would soon be in a house full of American soldiers, Florence reminded herself. And she was a widow and a mother, hardly an inexperienced young woman like Alice and Penny. It was foolish to be making such a fuss over nothing.

Yes, she'd banged knees with Sergeant Miller tonight, and experienced an odd flutter in her heart. So what? The Americans wouldn't be posted in Bude forever, and once they'd moved on, she would be alone once more, and thank goodness for that. A little momentary silliness over a man in uniform hardly seemed worth worrying her head over.

Sitting down next to Miles again, she thanked him when he insisted on pouring the tea for everyone, and didn't worry when their knees brushed again. Where was the harm? The truth was, he was good company, and she couldn't help noticing that her constant fretting over jobs to be done seemed to fade into the background whenever he was in the room. There was something so relaxing about that smile and slow drawl of his . . .

They were sitting about merrily, sipping cups of tea and chatting, when a familiar wail split the air above.

'Oh no,' Florence gasped, jumping up so hard the cups rattled in their saucers. 'The air-raid siren.' She was thrown by the horrid, fearful sound; they hardly ever had the siren go off after dark in Bude. 'The nearest shelter is next door's cellar at the back of the house. You can go through the kitchen.'

As they scrambled for the back door, she bit her lip, trying not to panic. 'Blasted Germans. I'll have to wake Billy and carry him out to the shelter.'

'I'll give you a hand,' Sergeant Miller said, and this time she did not protest.

CHAPTER TEN

Alice sat beside Penny on a rickety, worm-eaten bench with no back, hands resting on her knees, wishing she'd had time to fetch her latest novel to read after the siren went off. The cellar under next door's boarding house – the entire row overlooking the Downs seemed to consist mostly of hotels and boarding houses – was spacious enough, but damp and draughty, with grey mould patches infecting one wall. And there was nothing to do but sit and wait until the air raid was over.

'Cold,' young Billy moaned, seated on his mother's lap. Florence adjusted the blanket she'd wrapped him in, apologising yet again for having woken the boy.

''Ere, look at this, Billy,' Alice said, taking an old flyer from her pocket – one she had picked up from the floor of the printing workshop – and, with a few practised twists, folding it into the shape of a swan. This she handed to the boy, who took it hesitantly and stared down at the paper bird in bewilderment. 'It's a swan,' she explained. 'It's a Japanese art called origami.'

'Goodness,' Florence said, her thinly sketched eyebrows rising high. 'Japanese? Wherever did you learn that, Alice?'

'From a library book.'

'I wish I had more time for reading these days.' Florence nudged her son. 'Say thank you to Miss Fisher, Billy.'

'Fanks,' the boy muttered, holding the paper swan limply.

The two American officers had been helping older residents and guests down the cellar steps, but now that nobody else appeared to be coming, they came over to sit beside Florence and Alice. She studied both men with interest, trying not to make her observation too obvious, as she had been taught in her 'surveillance' classes, pretending to look past the Americans at somebody else while secretly making a note of their features, clothes and demeanour. It was useful practice and helped pass the time.

'Let's have a sing-song, shall we?' someone shouted above the chatter, and voices dropped, people glancing at each other in uncertainty.

Beside her, Penny groaned and rolled her eyes. 'Just as I was nodding off too,' she whispered to Alice.

'How about a sea shanty?' the rambling old gent suggested, and launched into song without waiting for a reply, his voice thin and rusty. Slowly, others joined in, until roughly half those in the shelter were singing.

Alice knew neither the tune nor the words. There hadn't been much call for sea shanties in Dagenham. But she soon picked up the chorus and joined in, glad of an excuse to glance around at people without seeming rude. Her instructors had insisted that trainees should take every opportunity to study those around them, not merely as a way of practising their surveillance skills, but in case they spotted anything genuinely untoward or out of the ordinary.

Needless to say, she saw nothing untoward in the cellar.

As the words to the song died away and people smiled around at each other, the gloomy space decidedly lighter, Penny leant towards her and said urgently, 'Alice, what was that song your gran was forever singing in the kitchen at Joe's farm?'

'Song?' Alice echoed blankly.

'You know the one . . .' Penny nudged her and began to hum a tune.

'Do you mean "Knees Up Mother Brown"?'

'That's the one. Go on, sing it.'

Alice's eyes widened. '*Me*? I'm no bloomin' good at singing.'

'Don't worry,' Penny said cheerfully. 'I'll sing along with you, once you've got started.'

'How about *you* start off and I join in later?' Alice felt cornered.

Her grandmother and Aunty Violet were the performers of the family. They didn't care what people thought so long as they were having a good time. She had known Gran to jump on a chair wearing a pan on her head, with its lid and a wooden spoon in hand, and play along with the spoon to whatever song she was singing, dancing up and down on the chair while everyone around the dinner table clapped and cheered.

But she wasn't anything like Gran and the thought of people staring at her while she attempted to sing had her transfixed in horror.

'Because I don't know the words as well as you, silly,' Penny pointed out.

Their hushed altercation had drawn the attention of the two American officers. Corporal Jones grinned at them, saying, 'What are you two young ladies whispering about?'

Alice said nothing, but Penny practically seized this opportunity to embarrass her, saying loudly, 'Alice knows a song we could sing. An East End song, I think. It's jolly good fun.'

Everyone immediately began petitioning Alice to stand up and sing her song.

'I'll never forgive you for this,' she whispered to Penny, who was laughing now and digging her in the ribs to make her stand up.

'Come along, girl, let's hear your ditty,' the rambling old man urged her, showing a gap in his front teeth as he nodded and smiled at her encouragingly. 'No more of this shillyshallying about.'

'Oh, for goodness' sake,' Alice muttered under her breath, but got to her feet, clammy palms on her skirt. 'Erm, it goes a bit like this . . .' And she began to sing, in a wavering voice, the opening words to 'Knees Up Mother Brown', or the closest to them she could remember.

As Penny joined in, and their voices grew stronger, several other people began to sing along with them, and after the first few lines, nearly everybody was singing. They ended the song with gusto and laughter, some of the older ladies even getting to their feet and rustling their skirts about, performing a shuffling dance on the spot, much to everyone's amusement.

Applause followed this, and Alice sank back onto the bench with relief, breathing rapidly, her cheeks scarlet.

'There,' Penny exclaimed, clapping her hands and giggling, 'I told you people would love that song.'

'They did, didn't they?' Alice tried to smile, but to her embarrassment, her mouth crumpled. She was choking, her throat contracting painfully. Then her vision blurred with tears, something wet trickling down her cheek and into the corner of her mouth. What on earth was wrong with her? 'Oh . . . Oh dear.'

Penny was staring at her, eyes wide. 'Alice? You're crying.'

'N-No, I'm not.'

'Hey, you can talk to me, you know, and it won't go any further.' Penny leant towards her, lowering her voice to a whisper. 'Whatever's the matter?'

'I . . . I don't know,' Alice mumbled, hurriedly drying damp cheeks with the backs of her hands, utterly baffled.

'I think I do.' Putting an arm about her shoulders, Penny gave her a tight squeeze. 'Gosh, what a rubbish friend I am. No wonder you didn't want to sing that song. You're *homesick*, aren't you?'

Alice didn't know how to reply to that. Was she homesick? But even as she considered the question, a tidal wave of emotion flooded her chest and more tears rolled down her cheeks. Maybe she was and hadn't even realised until now. The thought startled her.

'Poor love . . . Here, take this.' Withdrawing a handkerchief from her sleeve, Penny handed it over. 'I'm sorry I made you cry. But you'll see your gran and your Aunty Violet soon enough, I'm sure.' She gave Alice a shy peck on the cheek. 'You could write and ask them to visit you one weekend when they're free. What do you think?'

'Yes,' Alice gulped. 'I . . . I'd like that.'

But inside, she was confused by her own behaviour. She

had burst into tears and in public too. The girl who never cried, according to her family.

Sometimes, Alice thought, she honestly didn't know what was going on inside her own head. She always tried to be logical and to look at things as unemotionally as possible. But it seemed she couldn't avoid being human. And she did miss being at the farm with Gran and her aunt and the three evacuee children, and Joe too of course, or visiting Lily and her new husband Tristan in their cosy cottage in St Ives. Lily had written recently to say she was expecting a baby, but Alice had missed all the excitement that must have caused at home. Not that she was interested in babies, or not yet, as her gran would say. But it would have been nice to see Lily again and make a few sisterly jokes about how big she'd be growing soon.

When the all-clear finally sounded an hour later, they stumbled out into a gloomy evening that smelt fresh and clean, no smouldering overtones left behind by the dropping of incendiary devices.

Florence, walking behind them with Billy asleep on her hip, said quietly, 'I expect the airfield at Camp Cleave called to say a wave of bombers had been spotted along the coast, only they turned in a different direction and passed Bude by.' She gave the girls a reassuring smile. 'They often pass us by.'

At the back door, Florence nodded the girls to go straight inside. 'It's not locked. Who's going to break in during an air raid?' she told them as Penny groped her way inside. 'Best wait until we're all inside though before turning the lights on. Safety first, let's not forget the blackout.'

* * *

126

Upstairs on the landing, Penny yawned extravagantly behind her hand, her eyelids drooping, and said goodnight to Alice. 'I'm going to wash and turn in for the night. See you at breakfast. Unless you've got another early start tomorrow.'

Creaking a floorboard underfoot, Alice shrugged. 'It's possible. Sometimes I need to be out by six. I'll have to check my rota.'

'Goodness, they do work you hard at that printers' shop.'

Once her friend had gone to fetch her towel and washbag, Alice slipped into her own bedroom and sat on the bed, staring at nothing. Why on earth had she cried tonight? And over an old song, for goodness' sake? Lily would have laughed herself silly to see it. Or would she?

She and her older sister Lily had often squabbled as kids, especially during that dark year, back in Dagenham, when their father had been listed as 'missing in action, presumed dead' and their mother, Betsy Fisher, had been killed by a bomb strike. Everything had been falling apart in their lives, most of their schoolfriends had already been evacuated, and nobody had known when and where the next bomb would fall, the Germans flattening every street for miles, leaving nothing but rubble behind . . .

But then Aunty Violet had decided to take them down to quiet, rural Cornwall with her and their lives had changed forever.

It had been frightening at first. Yet somehow Aunty Violet had held their small family unit together. And once Gran had followed them down to Cornwall, the world had seemed to brighten, despite bombs still falling and bad news from the front line, where the constant war was reported to be swinging Mr Hitler's way.

To escape the horrors of that time, Alice had locked herself into the books and stories she loved, while Lily mocked her for being a bookworm. But as Lily had grown older, she'd grown more caring. Working as a trainee nurse, looking after wounded soldiers at the convalescent home in St Ives, had softened her heart and left her with practical skills too. Now she was a midwife, tending pregnant women and newborn babies, and with her own baby on the way.

But had Alice changed too? She'd certainly never expected to cry in public like she'd done in the shelter. And what had set her off? Only a song from the old days and a few hazy memories from her childhood. A mental image of her gran dancing on the kitchen table with a saucepan on her head . . .

A noise made her stiffen. Something small and hard had struck her bedroom window, the crack muffled by the thick folds of her blackout curtain.

'What on earth . . . ?'

Jumping up, Alice snapped off the bedside lamp and stood listening, tense and alert. A moment later, the crack came again, and this time she was able to interpret it.

Someone was throwing stones up at her window.

Kneeling on the lumpy mattress, Alice lifted one corner of the blackout curtain and peered down into the gloomy backyard. It was still dark but she could see a shadowy figure there, arm raised as though about to throw another stone. Presumably seeing her looking down, the arm was lowered and the figure stepped back, beckoning her instead to come down and join them.

It looked to be spotty Patrick, one of the other trainees at the printers' workshop.

She pushed up the sash window, careful not to make any noise that could alert others in the household to their unusual conversation taking place.

'Patrick?' She was astonished. 'What in gawd's name are you doing here at this time of night?'

'Come down,' Patrick whispered hoarsely. 'Night-time training.'

Dimly, she recalled the instructors warning them that some training sessions might take place at night, and to keep boots and warm clothes at the ready, just in case.

'Meet me at the front,' she told him, also in a whisper.

'No, you have to climb out the window,' he insisted, and again beckoned her to come down. 'It's part of the training. Use the drainpipe to climb onto that low roof.'

She looked where he was pointing and her brows rose steeply. 'Shin down the drainpipe? In a skirt? Are you crazy?'

There was a short silence. 'We never get this problem with the boys,' he said at last, scratching his head. 'Don't you have any trousers?'

Alice did own a pair of trousers, as it happened. Auntie Vi had found an old second-hand pair for her at a church sale back when Uncle Joe had asked her to help out around the farm. They weren't exactly flattering and she had last worn them to muck out the chicken coop. But it was dark outside and it wasn't as though they were being judged on their elegant clothing.

'Hang on a tick.'

Alice let the curtain drop, snapped on the light again,

rummaged in her bottom drawer for the trousers, and pulled them on. After that, all that was needed was for her to pull on a woolly black beret, a pair of gloves and her work boots.

Hurrying back to the window, she pushed it open as far as it would go and slipped one leg over the sill. Peering down from her first-floor window made her feel slightly nauseous. A faint sliver of moon hung behind ragged clouds, but there wasn't enough light to be shinning down a drainpipe at this height.

Taking a deep breath, she swung her second leg over the sill. The drainpipe was within reach. But only just. Shuffling slowly across, Alice wriggled one foot after the other onto its metal supports. Wrapping both arms around its cold circumference, she got onto the drainpipe and clung there like a monkey, not daring to move in case the whole structure broke off the wall and clattered to the yard below, taking her with it.

'Lower your right leg slightly,' Patrick whispered up hoarsely, 'and shift your grip downwards at the same time. Another few inches. Can you feel the next bracket? Put your foot on it . . . That's it. Now the other foot.'

Soon he had talked her down within reach of the flat roof above the back porch. From there, she lowered herself gingerly by her arms, dropping the last few feet into the yard. She rolled on landing as she'd been taught in class, copying how parachutists were supposed to land to avoid serious injury.

Unfortunately, it wasn't soft ground she was landing on but hard stone, and there were several large plant pots in the way of her enthusiastic 'roll'.

'Ow,' she exclaimed, rubbing the back of her head.

'Hush, can't you?' Frowning, he held out a hand to help her up. 'Come on,' he whispered impatiently, 'let's get going. After all this delay, I bet we'll be the last to reach the rendezvous point.' Shaking his head, Patrick walked away without waiting for her. 'I knew this would happen. As soon as I drew the short straw, I knew it wasn't my lucky day.'

Alice ran after him in the darkness. 'You drew *straws* to decide who should fetch me?' She felt her temper rise. 'Why? Coz I'm a bleedin' girl?'

'Because you're a liability,' he snapped back.

'Ta, I'll bear that in mind,' she said sharply, and strode ahead, glad of her long legs as she soon left him behind.

She'd thought Patrick was all right when she first met him, sympathising with him over the 'spotty' nickname. Now she realised he could be cruel as well. But she'd known from the start this wouldn't be a walk in the park. Most of the other recruits had been selected from the military and possessed skills she'd never had a chance to learn. A few were much older too, in their mid-twenties. But someone had put her forward for this opportunity, maybe her own father, and she was determined not to let him down . . .

CHAPTER ELEVEN

To Penny's astonishment, the young fisherman was waiting outside the dairy when she finished work a few days later. She felt the oddest fluttering in her tummy on seeing him and put it down stoutly to having missed her lunch that day, as Mrs Roskilly had made her work through her lunch break to make up for her late arrival that morning.

John Pascoe had been leaning against the wall, fiddling with the buttons on his jacket, but straightened up as she drew level with him. 'Hello,' he said cheerfully. 'Finished work? I wondered if you fancied going to the pictures?'

'With you?' Penny asked, more in shock than bad manners.

Boys never asked her out on dates. She was lucky to get a second glance from most of them, let alone an invitation to watch a film, presumably at their expense.

'Unless you've some objection?' He grinned at her expression. 'What is it? Never heard a fisherman use a long word before? I know you're from up country, but we do read here in Cornwall. My ma likes to see me with a book in my hand when I'm onshore. She says we only get one brain and need to use it as much as possible.'

'Quite right too.' Penny didn't know why she was so nervous. He was a perfectly ordinary young man, if you ignored the fact that he was strikingly attractive with all that fair hair and quick movements like a dancer. 'What's on at the pictures this week?'

'I guess we'll find out once we get there.' He held out his arm. 'Care to walk up there with me? While you're thinking about it.'

Impressed by his confidence, Penny linked her arm with his, and together they began to walk up the steep hill towards the picture house at the very top of Belle Vue, which was on her way home anyway.

She had never been much of a talker, but luckily John had plenty to say for himself. Listening to him rattling away, she soon lost her initial nerves and chatted with him quite easily, as though they'd been friends forever.

When they reached the cinema, people were already queueing to get in. There was a film poster outside, and she went to study it anxiously, not wanting to waste her time on a film that would bore her.

'Oh, how marvellous!' she exclaimed, recognising the actor and actress on the colourful film poster. 'It's Judy Garland and Gene Kelly in *For Me and My Gal*.'

'You like the sound of that?'

'Rather!' Penny's cheeks grew warm. 'Judy Garland's voice is just wonderful. And Gene Kelly . . . Well, he's smashing.'

'*Smashing*, eh? I can see I've got a serious rival in Gene Kelly.' John's grin widened at her surprised expression. 'You want to go in with me?'

She hesitated, torn. 'It'll mean missing my supper. Mrs Pritchard serves a hot meal at six. If I'm late, I may not get any.'

'My mother always keeps a plate of something warm on the range for me. You can share mine, if you like.'

'Go home with you, you mean?' She was secretly scandalised. Go home with him on a first date? She didn't know much, but she knew that wasn't the usual way of things. But she was curious to meet his mother and see where he lived. Besides, she hated missing her supper. 'That's very kind of you,' she agreed shyly. 'I don't mind if I do. Though I'm not sure how much money I have on me for a ticket,' she admitted, trying to recall how much it cost to get in.

'I'll pay for both of us,' John said smoothly, jingling change in his pocket. 'It's a good trade, fishing. And there's always plenty to eat too.'

Penny turned away, smiling, for she wasn't sure what to make of that statement. Was he seriously advertising himself as a good provider? She barely knew him . . .

As they reached the head of the queue, a deep rumbling made everybody turn and stare at the road. Up the steep, winding main street, the gloomy light of the setting sun glinting off windscreens, came a cavalcade of army vehicles driving almost nose to tail. A portly man in overalls, crossing the road with his nose in a newspaper, leapt out of the way in surprise as the lead vehicle beeped its horn.

'What on earth?' Penny murmured.

'They don't look like our army vehicles,' John said, studying the steady procession of cars, vans and covered trucks as it passed. 'Nor the uniforms neither. And where are they headed? There's nowhere to go but back out of Bude.' He was frowning. 'Wonder if they've lost their way.'

But Penny knew instantly who they were.

'You're right, they're not ours,' she whispered, clinging to his arm. 'Those are the US Rangers.'

The army vehicles had disappeared from view, presumably on their way along the road to Poughill, a small hamlet on the north side of Bude.

'*Rangers?*' John turned to stare at her. 'My pa said he'd heard down the pub there were to be American troops stationed here this winter. But how d'you know about them?'

Shyly, she explained about the two American officers staying in her boarding house and how they had been talking for days now about the arrival of the Second Battalion Rangers.

'They'll be *hundreds* of US soldiers in Bude soon, Sergeant Miller says. Most of them to be billeted on the townsfolk.'

'People will have to give up their spare rooms?' He looked astonished.

'That's what he said. But the Americans are going to help us win the war,' she pointed out, remembering what Sergeant Miller and Florence had been discussing over fish and chips the other night. 'So we should help them out in return, don't you think?'

'Can't argue with that.' John turned to pay for their tickets, a thoughtful look on his face.

They were ushered inside the cinema, where the lights were already out, a young girl with a torch showing them to their seats. In the darkness, he added under his breath,

'Besides, what do I know? I won't have to go to war.' There was an edge to his voice that surprised her. 'Fishermen are like farmers. Exempt from being called up.' John waited patiently until she'd taken her seat, and then sat down beside her. 'You don't mind, I take it?'

'I think it's rather romantic, having American soldiers around the town. It will certainly liven things up.' Penny dwelt on the evenings when she and sometimes even Alice had danced with the officers downstairs, listening to music with a fast beat that she'd never heard before but which was awfully exciting. But she was careful not to mention that. 'Besides, I doubt they're going to stay long. They seem to be moving from place to place while they're over here in England.'

John leant towards her. 'Sorry, you misunderstood.' He was very close, she realised, his breath warm on her cheek. 'I meant, you don't mind that I'm not a soldier, that I'll never be called up to serve our country? Because some girls do mind.'

'Of course I don't mind. We need fish,' Penny said simply.

He laughed, straightening. 'That we do.'

With a flourish, the big screen at the front of the picture house flickered with light, and they both faced front, staring up with interest as the first pictures appeared and music began to play.

'Oh, I love Gene Kelly,' Penny whispered, clasping her hands in her lap.

By the time the film and the news reels had ended, and they'd followed the shuffling crowd outside, the air was chill and it was dark over Bude. In the distance the incoming tide whispered gently up the foreshore, clouds fine and wispy as they hung over the faint silvery glimmer of the sea. Still locked in the unreal world of the film, Penny hummed under her breath and swayed as though dancing, looking wistfully down towards the sea.

John, mistaking her movements for a shiver, reminded her in practical tones to put her coat back on. He was no Gene Kelly, that was for sure. But he was at least interested in her, and maybe he was even a little better-looking than Gene Kelly. She bet he would look fine in a striped suit and tap shoes . . .

'It's chilly tonight,' he added. 'Winter's setting in. Can you feel it?'

'Unfortunately, yes.'

Penny slipped her arms into the coat before buttoning it against the cold evening air, still looking down towards the sea. A car drove past them slowly, no headlights on, taking the tight corner at walking pace, the hour being past curfew for lights. She thought of the recent air raid, studying the dark skies above in trepidation. But there was no sign of any enemy aircraft tonight, thank goodness.

'This way.'

John led her downhill through shadowy alleys and across the narrow bridge towards the harbour, Penny gripping his sleeve all the way in case she lost her footing in the dark. At last, he stopped before a row of low-built cottages, their chimneys smoking gently, and pushed through a sturdy front door with Penny a step behind him.

Penny found herself in a cosy sitting room with a fire burning low in the hearth. Beyond them, a woman was already standing in the doorway through to what looked to be the kitchen, hands on her hips, glaring at them both.

'Evenin', Ma,' John said easily, shutting the front door.

'Who's this, then?' his mother demanded, looking Penny up and down. She was a small woman with skin like tanned leather and tiny dark eyes that gleamed in the firelight. She wore a patterned dress in a muddy shade of brown and grey, with a pinny tied about her narrow waist, and clogs on her feet. 'You never said you was bringing anybody home. And certainly not a girl.'

'This is Penny, Ma. I took her to the pictures and the film finished late, so she missed her supper. I said she could share mine.'

'Hmm,' the woman said, pursing her lips in disapproval.

After kissing his mother on the cheek, John strolled past her into the kitchen, again beckoning Penny to follow. The kitchen was smaller and warmer than the sitting room, an ancient range dominating the room, a table and chairs, and a set of battered old pans hanging from a rack near the window.

The old fisherman she'd met on the quay sat at the table, hunched over a tin of tobacco. He glanced up at their arrival, greeting them both with a knowing grunt. The other man, who looked like the same man except thirty years younger, stood up to shake her hand, bearded and with curious blue eyes.

'How do?' Mr Pascoe asked, as cheery as his son. 'John's told us all about you. Working in the dairy, are you? I knew her as a girl, Mrs Roskilly.' He chortled. 'A right handful, that one.'

'Yes, she said she'd known you at school,' Penny agreed

without thinking, and saw his wife's eyes narrow, so decided not to elaborate. To her relief, John's father made no further comment either.

John said, 'I'm going to share my supper with Penny. She's not eaten yet.'

'Well, you're welcome here.' John's father pulled out a chair for her, flashing a look at his wife. 'If you fetch out the pie, love, I'll see to cutlery for them. And maybe you could make a fresh brew?'

Silently, Mrs Pascoe bent to retrieve a large pie dish from the depths of the oven, plus a plate of veg from the stove top that had been covered with a tea towel. Two-thirds of the pie had been eaten, but the remainder was unlike anything she'd ever seen before, with two shiny fish-heads peeking out of the pastry.

'I say, that smells delicious,' Penny exclaimed with genuine enthusiasm, her tummy rumbling. 'But what are those fish-heads about?'

'Those are pilchards, looking up at the stars. My ma's cooking is legendary and Stargazy Pie is her speciality,' John told her with a wink. 'An old Cornish recipe.'

His father handed over clean cutlery. 'Best tuck in quick, lass,' he instructed her kindly. 'Or John will take the lot. Except the greens, of course. We always had to force greens down his throat, ever since he were a young lad.'

John took this in good sort, grinning, while the old man fell to laughing soundlessly, packing his pipe with tobacco as he watched them finish off the pie and vegetables.

'Any war stories at the pictures?' John's father asked. 'What were they saying on the newsreels?'

'Same old nonsense, how we're doing well and thrashing

the enemy, when anyone with eyes can see that we're not.' John paused in his eating, looking up at them all. 'Here's some Bude news though . . . The Americans have arrived. You said you'd heard rumours about them coming, Pa. Well, they're here.'

'Oh aye?' His father glanced at the old man, who grunted under his breath again. 'You saw troops in the town?'

While he finished off his supper, John described what they'd seen in the queue for the picture house, and his family listened intently.

Penny listened too, not sure when she'd last enjoyed herself so much. It was almost like being back at the farm, with everyone chatting around the dinner table, and she had to admit the Pascoes had put her at ease after a shy start . . .

John insisted on walking her back through town to Downs View Road. The stars were out, the clouds had drifted gently away, and it was a lovely evening. As they walked, a slight sea breeze ruffling Penny's skirt and hair, John pointed out the constellations. 'That up there is Orion,' he said, showing her where to look. 'See the three stars, slanted in a row? That's his belt. And that over there is his club.'

'Amazing,' Penny breathed, craning her neck to look up at the stars, winking bright against the black velvet of the sky.

'We use the Pole Star sometimes, out on the sea, to navigate by. Though nowadays we have all the up-to-date instruments too. Not that we need them,' he chuckled. 'Granddad could sail us home blindfold, as anyone in Bude could tell you. He knows these waters like the back of his hand.'

'But aren't you ever scared?'

John lowered his hand from where he'd been pointing at the Pole Star, and stared at her, perplexed. 'Scared? Of what?'

'I don't know ... Big storms, I suppose, or German submarines.'

John pulled a face. 'Submarines, maybe.' He took off his cap, scratched his head, and then put his cap back on. 'At the dead of night, you can get to wondering what's underneath the boat. It's not the easiest place to be when it's pitch-black, I can tell you. But when it's broad daylight and the fish are nipping, I'm at my happiest out there on the ocean.'

'Is it the freedom you like? Life on the ocean wave and all that?'

'That, yes, but also . . .' John hesitated, and she could tell he was trying to get the words right. She liked that about him. He was an honest soul, not just saying things to impress her. 'It's a blessed big place, the open sea. And there you are, on a little boat, just two or three men trying to make a living from the fish and not drown, and it certainly makes you think.'

'Think what?'

'How insignificant we are. Little specks on a huge ocean. It makes you not take life too seriously. That's what my dad says, anyway.'

'And what do you say?'

John tapped the side of his nose, grinning down at her through the gloom. 'I'll tell you what's in my noggin one day, I promise. But not tonight.' They had reached the boarding house. John politely held the gate open for her. 'Thank you for coming out with me.'

'Thank you for inviting me.'

'I hope my ma didn't put you off too much.'

Penny laughed. 'I've met worse.'

'I don't believe that. But I'm glad to hear you say it. So,' he added softly, glancing up at the boarding house, which lay in darkness, 'would you care to walk out with me again one evening? Or at a weekend, if you're not working?'

Her cheeks warming, Penny nodded. 'I don't see why not.'

'I'll say goodnight then.' John took her by surprise, bending to kiss her on the lips. It was only a fleeting contact and then he was gone, disappearing back into the dark. But she felt the shock of it on her lips afterwards, a warmth and tingling from where their lips had touched.

Fumbling for her house key, Penny jumped at a voice behind her.

'Blimey, who was that, then?' It was Alice, appearing mysteriously out of the shrubbery at the front of the house. 'You're a dark horse, Penny Brown, and no mistake. I had no idea you were courting.'

'Good grief, Alice! You nearly gave me a heart attack. What on earth were you doing, hiding in that bush?' Penny demanded, blushing fierily as she realised her friend must have overheard everything they had been saying. Not to mention witnessing that kiss!

'Sorry about that.' Alice looked suitably chastened. 'I was getting in a few lungfuls of sea air when I heard you two comin' down the road and didn't know who it was.'

She hesitated. 'I was curious, so I ducked behind the bush and kept quiet. I . . . I couldn't exactly come out once I'd caught on that it was only you, could I? That bloke would have thought me barmy, hiding in a bush.'

'I can't imagine why,' Penny muttered, fitting her key to the lock. 'Curious to see who it was? Why on earth would you be curious?'

'Oh, I dunno . . . You get some funny sorts in Cornwall, don't you?'

'Hmm.' Penny couldn't help thinking that Alice was one of those 'funny sorts' but didn't want to upset her by saying so. But that reminded her . . . 'By the way, did you hear an odd noise the other night, after the air raid?'

'Eh?'

'I swear I could hear a man talking in our backyard. And then it sounded like someone was shinning up – or maybe down – the drainpipe.'

'Blimey.' Alice's eyes had widened. 'Did . . . Did you see who it was?'

'Goodness, no. I was too scared to lift the blackout curtains,' Penny admitted, 'and then it all went quiet again, so there wasn't any point.'

'Sorry, didn't hear a thing. Maybe you, erm, imagined it.'

A little annoyed, Penny threw her friend a glance but again decided not to say anything. It had probably just been one of Mrs Pritchard's neighbours, messing about in the back lane. She hadn't imagined hearing voices though . . .

Alice followed her inside the house, which lay dark and silent. No doubt the landlady had long since gone to bed, and thank goodness there hadn't been a repeat air raid tonight.

'By the way, did you know the US Rangers arrived this evening?' Alice asked in a whisper as they tiptoed up the stairs.

Penny nodded vehemently. 'I was outside the picture house. It was such an impressive sight. So many jeeps and trucks!'

'That's just the tip of the iceberg, Sergeant Miller says. He and Corporal Jones went out to meet them and I happened to be coming along the street. The rest will be arriving over the next couple of days.'

'However are we supposed to accommodate so many troops in this small town?' Penny shook her head, yawning as she opened her bedroom door. 'It's going to be a circus. Gosh, I'm tired.'

'Me too,' Alice agreed, but hesitated, glancing back as she opened her own bedroom door. 'What's his name, by the way?'

Momentarily confused, Penny stared round at her. 'Who?'

'Rudolph Valentino, who do you think? The boy you was kissin' outside just now, of course.'

'*Hush!*' But Penny had to suppress a smile at the Valentino reference. Hardly, she thought, given how fleeting that kiss had been. Though she imagined he wouldn't take much encouraging to go further. 'He's John Pascoe. A fisherman. Rather dishy, don't you think?'

'It was dark, and I was looking at him through a bush. But . . .' There was a long pause. 'I suppose he might have been dishy, yes.'

'Alice Fisher, you are incorrigible.'

'Thank you,' Alice said with an enigmatic smile, and disappeared into her room.

In her own bedroom, Penny shrugged out of her coat, pulled off her hat, and stood staring at herself in the wall mirror. She was still a little breathless. Her cheeks were flushed, her eyes wide and glittering, lips parted. She half expected to see a mark where he'd kissed her, but her lips looked perfectly normal, apart from being chapped after the recent spell of cold weather.

Her first ever kiss!

Too late, she recalled Mrs Roskilly's dire warnings about girls who failed to keep a proper distance from boys. Should she have slapped his face for kissing her, rather than standing there astonished and enjoying the moment?

Would he now take further liberties with her because she hadn't shrieked and boxed his ears?

The thought of John taking further liberties with her made Penny bite her lip and stare at herself, bolt-eyed, in the mirror. Far from being shocked by the idea, she was excited. That probably made her a bad person, at least as far as Mrs Roskilly was concerned.

Penny stuck her chin in the air, staring back at her reflection rebelliously. She was sick of being known as 'shy' and well behaved. She was determined to squeeze every possible ounce of enjoyment out of life, and if that meant being spotted in the street kissing a boy she hardly knew, then so be it.

It was nobody's business but her own what she chose to do with her life.

CHAPTER TWELVE

Once the American Rangers had begun to arrive in Bude, life changed rapidly for Florence. For a start, she had attended a public meeting of householders and been allotted eight more servicemen, much to her shock, which meant some would have to bunk three to a room. She'd been promised extra mattresses and bedding too, thank goodness. No extra help around the place though, which was worrying when she had young Billy to care for on top of all her other duties.

But at least those householders giving up their spare rooms, attic spaces or damp basements – voluntarily or not – to accommodate American troops had been assured that most meals would be taken down at the 'chow house' currently being set up on the beach at Crooklets, a stone's throw from her own boarding house. That ought to take some of the pressure off the ordinary people of Bude.

But there had been a suggestion that a few meals might still need to be taken on the premises, and with a house bursting at the seams with large, hungry soldiers, she could only hope that would not be a frequent occurrence.

But it was clear that life would not be the same again until the US troops had moved on again. From eight o'clock in the morning, the men of the Second Battalion Rangers had been knocking at her door, singly or in twos and threes, kitbags thrown over their broad shoulders, smart in their grey-green uniforms with olive shirts and matching neckties.

Though flustered by the sheer number of new arrivals, Florence had politely taken the men up to their rooms, pointing out the bathroom and WC convenience, one upstairs – a real luxury, and one that Percy had insisted on installing, saying it would increase the cachet of their premises – and the other out in the backyard, rougher but still well maintained. Then she had shown them the front sitting room where they could gather for socials and listen to the wireless or gramophone. She pointed out the rules to them, which she had handwritten neatly and set in a frame at the base of the stairs. Not that she cared much for rules. But with so many men in her overflowing boarding house, she thought warily, keeping order might become important.

To her relief, Sergeant Miller had requested to stay on with her, even though Corporal Jones was moving to an officers' placement further into town. 'I'd like to keep an eye on things at this end of the town,' he told her, watching the new arrivals stamping up and down the stairs. 'Assuming you don't mind.'

'Not at all,' Florence replied, readily agreeing to the

arrangement, for she was not altogether comfortable at coping with the troops alone. 'In fact, I'm pleased. So many new faces . . . It's good to know one of you by name, at least.'

His mouth quirked in a smile. 'I'm sure you'll learn their names soon enough. You're a very sociable lady.'

What did he mean by that, she wondered?

She hoped the sergeant didn't think she was a flirt. But she had to admit to a strong attraction to him, which was increasingly difficult to suppress. His smile was rare, yes, but so inviting . . .

By early afternoon, the US soldiers had all been shown their rooms and were assembled in the sitting room for a briefing by Sergeant Miller. Florence had just put Billy down for his after-lunch nap and was sweeping the hall free of dried mud that had inadvertently come in on their boots. Dreamily, she was listening to the men's muffled voices through the wall when someone rang the front doorbell again.

Surprised, for all her rooms were now occupied and she had ticked off all the names against the list Miles had given her, Florence set aside her broom. She checked her reflection, wiped her hands on her apron, and answered the door with a polite smile.

'Hello, Flo,' her younger sister said sweetly, standing on the doorstep with a suitcase in each hand, wearing a tightly fitted cream jacket over a navy blue, knee-length dress. When Florence said nothing, her heart thudding and her tummy plummeting, her sister added, rather less sweetly, 'Well? Aren't you going to invite me in? It's a horridly long journey on the train from Exeter and my feet are aching.'

Guiltily aware that she wasn't being particularly welcoming, Florence stood aside and let her sister in. Ever since her mother had written to warn her that Imogen might be travelling down to stay with her, she'd been hoping that day would never come, as Imogen was notorious for her last-minute changes of plan. But that had been a false hope, hadn't it?

'Sorry, I'd forgotten you were coming,' she fibbed to conceal her confusion and disappointment. 'Let me take your luggage.'

Imogen did not protest but handed over her suitcases, already stripping off her thin leather gloves and staring about the place with an assessing eye as though she had just bought it. She was about Florence's own height and build, yet somehow always looked far more delicate, tottering past on high heels that matched her perfectly seamed black stockings. Her eyebrows had been drawn finely with a pencil, high above thick-lashed hazel eyes, powdered complexion as pale as a china doll's, her mouth a brightly painted scarlet bow, drawing the eye.

'Nothing's changed since my last visit, I see,' her sister commented with a sigh, and then glanced quickly back at her. 'But I suppose you've not had much time to redecorate.' She paused. 'I was sorry to hear about Percy. Truly.'

Florence sucked in a painful breath. 'Thank you.'

'I wish I could have made it down for the funeral. And I ought to have written afterwards. But you know how it's been . . . This awful war.' She made a dismissive gesture with her gloves. 'I was so busy with war work, around that whole time, I barely had a minute to myself. I was helping old Major Tomlinson organise the Home Guard. They'd be lost without someone to deal with all the paperwork.'

'Of course,' Florence nodded, determined not to show scorn at such a flimsy excuse. Besides, her parents had already apologised for Imogen's absence at the funeral, claiming she was too unwell to leave Exeter. Since Imogen was infamous for her frequent bouts of illness and accompanying fits of melancholy, Florence had not questioned it. But now it struck her that Imogen had simply feared the idea of attending a funeral, facing up to all the uncomfortable realities of death, given how easily she could become depressed. 'I hope they'll cope without you.'

'Oh, I trained up a replacement Girl Friday before leaving,' Imogen said airily, heading down the hall. 'Besides, I felt like a different view in the morning, you know?'

She stopped beside the public sitting room, and before Florence could warn her not to go in there, had pushed through the partially open door. Imogen stopped dead on the threshold, staring in at all the American troops, her hand drifting instinctively to plump up her pretty hair. The gathered troops were all in uniform, some lounging on the seats, some standing, a few smoking, all fresh-faced young men.

Florence, right behind her, caught a glimpse of Sergeant Miller's astonished expression and felt her heart sink in dismay.

'Oh goodness,' Imogen said faintly, taking in the scene, 'talk about a different view . . . Are you gentlemen all here for me?' Her lips quivered in a smile. 'How very sweet of you.'

The soldiers laughed. All except for Sergeant Miller.

'Imogen,' Florence hissed, pulling her hurriedly out of the sitting room, 'you can't go in there. It's guests only.' She met her sister's indignant stare. 'Let's go into the kitchen and have a cup of tea, shall we? You must be dying of thirst after your long journey. And I'd like to hear about everything you've been doing these past few years.'

Her sister began to protest but Florence paid no attention.

'So sorry,' Florence mouthed, directing the remark to Sergeant Miller, and pulled the door firmly shut.

Then she fled after her sister, only stopping to pick up the two suitcases.

She found Imogen already seated at the kitchen table, her coat draped over the seat back, hands raised to unpin her stylish blue hat, an accusing look on her face.

'There was no need to be so rude to me in front of all those men.'

Florence put down the cases and drew a deep breath, trying not to lose her temper. 'I didn't mean to be rude, but that was a private meeting. Official military business.'

'Who are they, anyway?' Imogen was now looking absentmindedly at the closed door, a secret smile dancing about her lips, as though reliving that moment when the soldiers laughed. 'Goodness, all those men. So many of them . . .'

'They're not men. They're US Rangers.'

'They looked like men to me.' Smoothing an automatic hand along her velvety blue hat, Imogen watched her put the kettle on. 'Wait . . . *US Rangers*? Ah, I understand now. The unusual uniforms. That officer's odd accent. They're

151

Americans.' Her smile grew. 'That one's quite a specimen, isn't he? Very handsome.'

Anger mixed with fear flared through Florence's mind. 'Don't.'

'Don't what?'

'You know very well what I'm talking about, Imogen. Leave him alone. Leave them all alone. They're here for specialist training. And all hush-hush too. If the Germans knew . . .'

'They probably already know,' Imogen said with a shrug. 'The enemy have spies everywhere.'

'Not all the way out here.'

'Well, that's where you're wrong. Because I have it on excellent authority that there are Nazi spies and sympathisers all over this country. They're honeycombed into every town and village, hiding in plain sight.'

'Oh, don't be ridiculous. What *excellent authority*?' Florence set out the cups and saucers for tea. 'Did your old Major Tomlinson tell you that?'

'Don't be silly, Flo. Anyway, it's common knowledge back in Exeter.' Imogen crossed her legs, showing off those elegant seamed black stockings, almost certainly silk, which Florence couldn't possibly afford as a widowed mother, scrimping and saving for every penny, not in a month of Sundays. 'That's why we have to be so careful what we say in public. You know, *loose lips sink ships*? Because you never know who's standing next to you in the queue at the butcher's.'

'Even here in Cornwall?'

'Everywhere, Flo.'

'Hmm.'

Making the tea without pushing that topic any further, Florence had to admit that she'd seen similar warnings on recent government pamphlets. The sort that Alice was printing all day and most evenings at that print workshop in town. Indeed, there were so many pamphlets and public information posters these days, it was hard to keep up with current advice. The poor girl certainly worked long enough hours . . .

She set out a few ginger snaps on a plate, the last of a batch of biscuits she'd made the previous week, and poured tea for her sister while Imogen hunted through her handbag.

'Mother wrote you a letter.' Imogen held it out. 'The latest news and all that. Father's health. You know what a fuss he makes over every little sniffle.'

'Thank you.' Flo took it, tucking it into her apron pocket to read later, away from Imogen's curious eyes. 'Biscuit?'

'No, thank you.' Her sister was eyeing the home-made biscuits with disdain.

'Oh, well.' Florence bit into a ginger snap and grimaced. Perhaps they had grown a little stale, despite being kept in a tin. But she ate it anyway.

'So, where's little Billy? Has he grown much? I haven't seen him since the christening.'

'He's quite a bit bigger now,' Florence said drily. 'And having his nap. I'll get him up later and you can see him then.' She hesitated, her mind whirling as she considered the enormity of the changes ahead. Her younger sister here, living in the same house, and for goodness knows how long . . . 'So, what are your plans while in Bude? I mean, do you have any idea how long you'll be staying here?'

A cloud passed over Imogen's face. 'You should know, I didn't exactly come of my own accord,' she said stiffly.

'I'm aware.'

'Which means I don't know when I'll be allowed back home.'

'Mother and Father only have your own welfare in mind, I'm sure. I was told you'd had some problems? And that time away from Exeter might help.'

Imogen's eyes dimmed, a faint suggestion of tears gleaming there as she looked down at her teacup. 'There was a gentleman,' she said softly. 'At least, I thought he was a gentleman . . .'

'I see.'

'I doubt it. You and Percy were so happy.' Her sister flashed her an unhappy look. 'I haven't been so lucky. They see . . . this,' she added, indicating her figure and prettily arranged hair, 'and they only want one thing. Except I'm always fooled and think it's love.' Her voice choked, and she fell silent for a moment. 'But I'm determined never to make the same mistake again. I'm done with men.'

Flo, while sympathetic, had heard this speech before. Several times. 'Planning to take holy orders, are you?'

Imogen gave her a long, accusing stare. 'I should have known you would be mean to me,' she said eventually. 'My own sister!'

'I'm sorry.' Florence was genuinely contrite. 'It does sound like you've had a difficult time and need a change of scenery.' She bit into another limp ginger snap without thinking. 'Thing is, Immi, I'd forgotten you were coming and I've given up all my rooms to the Rangers. So you'll have to share with me, I suppose.' She ignored Imogen's horrified exclamation and pushed on. 'And I'm rushed off my feet here and have almost no help. If you're going to stay, you can't be a guest. You'll need to work.'

'Work?' Imogen looked up at her, wide-eyed.

'When Mother wrote to say you'd be coming to stay with me, she told me you'd agreed to help out here.' Florence felt she needed to put her foot down firmly from the start. 'I hope you're not going back on that arrangement.'

With obvious difficulty, her sister replied, 'I wouldn't dream of it. It's just that I've been struggling with my moods, and I'd appreciate a few days' grace from work to recover. Just long enough for me to settle in and maybe find out more about the town. I've barely set foot here before. It would be nice to take a look around before being plunged into hard labour.'

Florence had to suppress an unladylike snort. 'Hard labour? It's mostly just housework.'

'Mother never made me do housework.'

'I'm not Mother.'

'Oh, I know *that*.' Imogen raised her gaze to Florence's face, a calm dignity in her expression. 'But I shall pull my weight from first thing tomorrow morning, if that's what you want.' Delicately, she took a sip of tea and then studied the teacup with apparent interest before replacing it gently in the saucer. 'I can start work today, in fact. Before I've even unpacked. Just give me a job and I'll do it.'

Florence took a deep breath. She would sound like a monster if she accepted that offer and made Imogen start work straight after arriving. Even tomorrow would seem like unnecessary haste now, after what she'd said. Well, not *what* her sister had said, but the way she'd said it. Her tone, her careful emphasis . . .

'Of course not,' she heard herself say, 'there's no need to be ridiculous. You're right. You should take a few days to find your feet. Bude is a lovely little town. And there are plenty of excellent walks right from the doorstep, especially towards the beach and along the coast.' Her teeth came together with a snap as she saw the gleam in Imogen's eyes and realised she had tumbled right into her trap. But she would have lost face by admitting it. Better to try for a magnanimous air. 'Let me take those cases upstairs for you. You can unpack and have a nice lie-down before supper.' Anything to get rid of her for a few hours, she thought grimly.

'A lie-down? Gosh, what a horrid thought. Only old ladies have lie-downs at this time of day, and I'm barely twenty-three.' Imogen nibbled at a ginger snap and then replaced it on the plate with a shudder, despite the little bite she'd taken out of it. 'No, I'll go out and take some air. Have a look at the town. That was a good suggestion of yours, Flo.' A smile lurked on her lips as she rummaged in her bag again and withdrew a compact mirror to check her reflection before applying fresh lipstick. 'Maybe one of those nice Rangers could escort me into town, since I'm a stranger here.'

'They're strangers here too.'

'Marvellous.' Imogen's eyes twinkled. 'We could discover the place together, then. How wonderfully romantic. I do love men in uniform.'

Giving up, Florence took the cup and saucers to the sink to wash them. Her little sister would never change her ways, so there was no point wishing for it. 'You must do as you wish,' she said wearily as she finished and reached for a tea towel, turning to find the kitchen empty.

Her sister had already gone.

Later, heading up to the bathroom to give it a good cleaning, she encountered a wild-eyed Alice on the stairs, her long blonde hair tousled and in disarray, her cardigan wrongly buttoned up. 'Day off?' she assumed cheerfully, for she hardly ever saw the girl these days. 'About time too. They seem to be working you like a slave at that printers.'

Alice stared at her. 'No, I . . . I slept in. I didn't mean to.' Her cheeks were still flushed with sleep. 'My bloomin' alarm clock must have stopped. What's the time, Mrs P?'

'Past three o'clock.'

'Gawd blimey!' Alice dashed past her and down the stairs, one untied shoelace dangerously trailing, moaning, 'I'm for the high jump now, and no mistake.'

'Oh dear.' Florence watched the girl grab her coat off the hall stand and thump through the front door, which slammed shut behind her.

Too many late nights and early mornings, she thought sympathetically, and shook her head as she continued up the stairs, armed with her cleaning bucket. They really shouldn't be working these young people so hard.

'Excuse me, ma'am.' One of the fresh-faced US Rangers had come hurrying out of his room, still settling his cap on short-cropped, white-blond hair. He saluted her briefly and then hurtled down the stairs at much the same speed as Alice, swiftly followed by another young soldier, barely indistinguishable from the first, who also saluted her with a grin before running after his friend, calling, 'Hey, wait for me, Trasker!'

'Such lovely boys,' she murmured, smiling. Then opened the bathroom door to find a horrid mess of shaving cream in the sink, the tap still running, a dirty towel trodden on the floor, and the window wide open, letting in a sharp draught. 'Oh . . . blast.'

CHAPTER THIRTEEN

Alice was still winding her scarf about her neck as she ran, laces flapping, along Downs View Road and towards town. Never had the distance to work seemed so long. Her heart was pounding, her head spinning. She simply couldn't believe how late she had slept. Not even late morning but midafternoon! Though she'd been working so many late nights recently, being taught how to conduct surveillance on a house in the early hours or follow someone unseen after dark, it was a wonder she wasn't still asleep . . .

She recalled hearing snatches of noise, the thud of boots on the stairs, men's voices echoing through the house, and yet she hadn't stirred, listening to these sounds in a thickly dozing trance, nestled deep under the blanket, eyes firmly closed, her body too heavy to move of its own accord.

Panic seized her as she bit her lip and tried to imagine the possible punishments for turning up halfway through the afternoon. Alice turned cold and began to shiver at the thought of being dressed-down good and proper in front of all the other trainees.

Oh, the shame of it!

She stumbled as she dashed down Belle Vue and breathlessly flung herself down the narrow alleyway. The bell over the door to the printers' workshop jangled violently as she burst through it, a desperate apology ready on her lips, only to find the place deserted.

Gasping, she ran through to the back room, but that too was empty, though the printing press was still hot to the touch, which suggested work had only recently ceased. Among their other duties, the trainees were expected to take turns printing government literature, to keep up their cover. Huge stacks of new pamphlets lay in boxes beside the machine, a few poorly printed ones scattered about the floor as discards. To anyone else, it might have looked like the place had been ransacked . . . But it was just untidy.

'About time too, Miss Fisher.'

She turned, flushing at the heavy irony in that voice, to face the new instructor, Mr Rawlings, who'd come down from London a few days ago to oversee their training while Sidney was away.

'I'm sorry, Mr Rawlings, sir,' she stammered, 'I know how late I am . . . But you see, my alarm clock stopped and I didn't wake up until just now.'

His brows rose. 'Sleeping Beauty, are you?'

Alice bit her lip at this taunt, glaring at the man with barely concealed dislike. It hadn't been her fault she'd overslept. It was all these long hours that were to blame.

Mr Rawlings was a large man in early middle age who always wore a smart suit jacket and tie, with well-polished shoes and cufflinks in his shirt sleeves. He had a slight limp when he walked, and the rumour went that he'd been wounded early in the war and had to retire from active service, but now worked for the Secret Service and sometimes, it was suggested, Mr Winston Churchill himself.

'I say, he's very stylish,' Sophy had murmured on Rawlings' first day with the team, gazing at him admiringly. A 'posh nob' was what Alice had called him later, and Rawlings had spoken like one too, all la-di-dah with his cut-glass BBC accent, confirming her suspicions.

She hadn't been as impressed by his expensive suit as the other girl. But then, she'd seen plenty of posh gents at Porthcurno. Yes, and met them too, sometimes in the company of George Cotterill, who ran Eastern House. Types like Rawlings were always in and out of the listening station at Porthcurno, men working for the government, often on top-secret business, wearing smart suits and hats, and speaking like they had bloomin' marbles in their mouths . . . They weren't nothing special.

All the same, this particular posh gent had the power to dismiss her from training.

'It was a mistake, that's all. And I'll make it up to you. I'll give up my afternoon off and I'll take a double shift on the printing.' Alice crossed her fingers behind her back. Her heart was thumping painfully, and not just from the mad pace at which she'd crossed Bude. 'Honest, Mr Rawlings, please give me another chance. It will never, *ever* happen again, I promise.' She crossed herself fervently. 'Cross my heart and swear to die.'

Rawlings came closer, looking her up and down. 'Have you looked in a mirror this morning, Miss Fisher?'

'Erm, no.'

'Then I suggest you do, and soon,' he said gently. 'And then rectify what you see. In particular, your clothing.' His gaze dropped to her woolly cardigan, which she only now realised, on glancing down at herself in horror, was hopelessly misbuttoned. One of her shoelaces was also undone and her skirt appeared to be on the wrong way round. 'Can't have agents of the government wandering the streets of this country looking like scarecrows, can we? Not even trainee ones. Unless, that is, they have been ordered to stuff straw in their shirts and stand in a field to overhear what the crows are saying.'

Her blush deepened at his tone. 'Yes, sir.' Then blinked. 'I mean, no, sir.'

'Three bags full, sir?'

'I'm ever so sorry,' she burst out. 'That bloomin' clock . . . But it's all them early shifts we've been pulling. And the all-nighters too. We went traipsing all over the town until gawd knows what hour the other night, climbing up and down drainpipes like a regular tea leaf, and when I finally got to bed last night—'

'Tea leaf?' he interrupted, frowning.

'Thief,' she explained, feeling foolish. 'Sorry, sir. It's rhyming slang.'

'You're a Cockney?'

Alice shook her head, but stuck her chin out. 'Dagenham,' she told him proudly. 'East of London, yes, but not within the sound of Bow Bells,' she added, outlining the usual definition of a Cockney in case he didn't know it.

But it seemed Mr Rawlings did know, for he was already nodding. 'Of course.' He looked her up and down again,

nodding. 'Alice Fisher. *Fisher.* Yes, I seem to recall . . .'
Then he clammed up, looking away, and she wondered
what he'd been about to say. He thrust his hands into his
trouser pockets. 'Late nights and stopped alarm clocks are
no excuse for missing roll call.'

'No, sir.' She waited miserably to be dismissed.

'But as this is a first offence . . .' He paused, regarding
her steadily. 'It is a first offence, isn't it? Since I don't have
Sidney's order book to hand.'

'First offence, yes,' she agreed eagerly, thankful that she
wasn't to be sent home. 'I ain't never been late before, I
swear.'

'All right, then let this be a lesson to you to keep your
equipment in good order, Miss Fisher. Which means your
alarm clock, in this instance.' He raised his brows at her
meaningfully. 'Yes?'

'Yes, sir.'

'People have died before now through sleeping in and
missing a vital rendezvous.'

'During training?'

Rawlings bit back a laugh. 'Maybe not during training,
no.' He rocked back on his heels, studying her. 'Sidney said
you were a live wire, and I'm glad to see he wasn't wrong.
I wonder . . .' He jiggled loose change in his pocket, his
face preoccupied. 'I may have a job for you in a few weeks.'

'A special mission?' she asked excitedly.

He seemed amused by her eagerness. 'I suppose you
could call it that, yes. Nothing too dangerous, of course.
You're still a trainee. But you might enjoy the challenge.'
He studied her. 'If you think you're ready.'

'I'm more than ready, sir. I'm so ready, I can't even . . .'

Alice's heart was nearly bursting. Then she realised she didn't have a clue what kind of special mission he was suggesting and it might be a good idea to check first. 'Ready for what though, exactly?'

'For an adventure,' he told her, with a solemn wink.

They were interrupted by the other trainees returning from town. Jasper strolled in, chatting to Sophy, who seemed bored, barely listening to him. Barnabas was arguing with a new recruit over which of them could hold their breath for longer, while Patrick was walking while scribbling something in a notebook with such deep concentration, he almost collided with Alice.

'Hey, watch out there, lad,' Rawlings exclaimed, and Patrick staggered backwards, dropping his notebook.

'Sorry, Alice. Didn't see you there.'

'No harm done, I'm sure.' Alice stooped to retrieve his notebook, which was lying open, face up. She glanced at his odd handwriting before closing the book and handing it back to him with a grin. 'Blimey, your scrawl's worse than mine.'

Patrick reddened but gave her a muttered word of thanks before hurrying after the others for debriefing, followed by Rawlings.

It was only after Patrick had gone that Alice, trailing after the group, realised with a shock that he didn't have bad handwriting. The few lines she'd glimpsed in his notebook had been written *in code*.

When she finally got back to the boarding house that evening, after hours of reading manuals on surveillance techniques and making notes, Alice felt almost too tired to eat. Her tummy was rumbling madly though, for she'd skipped breakfast and lunch by sleeping so long. And her ears were buzzing. It was as if she could hear voices rumbling in the distance.

Wearily, she unwrapped her scarf, shrugged out of her coat and hat, and hung all three on the coat rack in the hall before trailing down to the dining room, her feet like lead.

On opening the door, she discovered the buzzing wasn't her imagination. The room was full of soldiers, all apparently talking at once, and in deep American accents. They were American Rangers, maybe a dozen of them, still in their uniforms but clearly off duty, chatting together over cups of coffee, the air thick with smoke from their cigarettes.

Alice stared at them, baffled. 'What on earth?'

To her relief, she spotted Penny across the room and raised a hand to catch her attention. Her friend, who'd been chatting to one of the men, got up and rushed over.

'I say, isn't this amazing?' Penny gushed. 'I've never seen so many soldiers in one room in all my life.'

'Yes, but I'm confused. Where've they all come from?' With a start, Alice realised she was swaying on her feet and leant against the wall to support herself. Goodness, she must be hungrier than she'd thought. But with all these strange hours and long shifts, she was losing track of mealtimes, which was very unlike her.

'Up north, I heard. Somewhere in Scotland?' Thankfully, Penny seemed too distracted by the soldiers to have noticed Alice swaying about like a drunk. 'They moved in this afternoon while I was working at the dairy.

Florence says they were awfully noisy. Banging up and down stairs. And they left a terrible mess in the bathroom, apparently. But Imogen says we'll have to accept a little disruption, on account of how much the Americans are helping with the war.' Her face was flushed with excitement. 'Anyway, it's true. I mean, they were even talking about US troops on the newsreel at the picture house. Everyone's saying how we're bound to win the war now that America has sent so many troops.' She grabbed Alice's arm, hissing dramatically into her ear, 'And don't they look smashing?'

Alice did vaguely recall Sophy telling her that the Americans were moving into billets today while she was struggling to study the surveillance manuals. But somehow it hadn't penetrated her brain properly.

'So we have Rangers in the house. Well, it was only a matter of time.' Alice bit her lip against another wave of hunger, her tummy rumbling loudly. 'Is there anything to eat? Or have they guzzled everything in the kitchen?'

'Oh no,' Penny said, grinning, 'they haven't eaten here. They had their supper down the road at the chow house because Florence can't be expected to feed all these people. This is just coffee. And I think some of them are drinking moonshine too,' she added in a whisper.

Alice had been offered moonshine by Corporal Jones one evening – what her gran would call 'bathtub gin' – but had declined. She liked to keep her wits about herself, and besides, that stuff always made her face bright red.

'Well, that's something, at least. Where is Florence? I hope there'll be a hot meal for tea tonight. Because I'm bloomin' starving. I swear my stomach thinks my throat's been cut.' She paused, frowning. 'Hang on, who's Imogen?'

Penny gasped. 'I'd forgotten, you haven't met Imogen yet. She only arrived today too. Come on, let's find her.'

'But who is she, for gawd's sake?' Alice had to shout to be heard over a loud burst of laughter from the men, who were making fun of one of the soldiers.

'She's Florence's sister,' Penny exclaimed, laughing merrily. 'You'll love her. Oh wait, I think she's in the middle of that big group of soldiers, so you'll have to meet her later. Now, come on, let's get you fed.' And she dragged an astonished Alice through several tightly packed tables of American soldiers and into the kitchen. Several of the men glanced up at them with appreciative smiles but both Penny and Alice ignored them, though as soon as the kitchen door had closed behind them, cutting out the noise and drifting cigarette smoke, Penny dropped Alice's hand and burst out in giggles. 'I'm so glad I came with you to Bude, Alice. I'm having the time of my life.'

Florence was at the sink in her apron, washing up cups. 'Oh good, you're back, Alice,' she said, turning her head, a harassed look on her face. Her little son Billy was still awake, which was unusual at this time of the evening, sitting on the floor with his favourite wooden train. He looked heavy-eyed but was quiet enough, his thumb tucked in his mouth. And, for once, Florence didn't remonstrate with him for sucking it when she glanced around at the boy in a distracted way. 'I've been keeping your dinner warm on the range.' She paused. 'I'm sorry about all the noise. But I did warn you that the place might be swarming with new, erm, guests soon.'

'I don't mind,' Alice said, and drew out a chair. 'There's nowhere free in the dining room for me to eat my meal. Would it be all right for me to take it in here instead? Just for tonight?'

'Of course.' Florence brought her cutlery, water, and a napkin while Penny slipped back out into the throng, clearly finding the peace and quiet of the kitchen too boring. Then she took a covered plate off the stove top and placed it in front of Alice. 'It's your favourite tonight. Bangers and mash.'

'Oh, Mrs Pritchard,' Alice murmured, 'I could kiss you.'

Florence laughed, and put the kettle back onto the hot plate to boil. 'You may change your mind when you taste those sausages. There's more meat in the gravy, if you ask me.'

'I'm so hungry tonight, I could probably eat this napkin and be happy.' Alice shovelled a heap of gravy-streaked mashed potato onto her fork before devouring it in one mouthful, unladylike behaviour that would have earned her a scold from her gran if she'd been there. 'Mmm,' she said indistinctly. 'Fanks, diss tastes so cood.'

Florence, with another quick glance at Billy, sat down beside her at the kitchen table. 'I'm truly sorry about the disruption,' she told Alice earnestly. 'The problem was, Miles . . . I mean, *Sergeant Miller* took his meal in the dining room with Penny earlier, and when the soldiers began to return from their first training sessions, they naturally gravitated towards him.' She got up to check the blackout blind was secure before turning to make the tea. 'Tomorrow, I'll make it clear they need to use the sitting room for socialising instead. They're all lovely boys, but we can't allow them to stop you eating your meals out there. You're my guest too.'

Alice cut up her two sausages into tiny circular slices to make the food last longer, rolling them about in the thin gravy before popping them in her mouth.

It was hard not to remember those big slap-up meals Gran had prepared on Sundays for the whole family before the war. Her mum Betsy and Aunty Violet had always helped out with the veg while her dad carved the meat, but Gran had been in charge of cooking the Sunday roast and preparing the gravy, so rich and succulent, with shreds of meat bobbing about in it . . .

'You all right, love?' Florence had put a hand on her arm.

'What?' Alice realised she had stopped eating and was staring into space, her tired head swirling with memories of happier times. 'Oh, yes . . . Sorry.' She tucked in again. 'Penny said your sister's come to stay,' she added indistinctly, even though Aunty Violet had told her often enough not to talk with her mouth full.

'Imogen, yes.' Florence poured them both a steaming cuppa and pushed Alice's towards her with a sigh. 'She's sharing with me and Billy at the moment. Though it's a bit of a squeeze, to be honest.' She hesitated. 'If many more soldiers are billeted here, I may have to ask you to share with Penny for a few months. But I'll do my best to avoid that.'

Alice nodded, frowning. 'Ta, Mrs P.'

She didn't mind sharing with Penny, if push came to shove. It would only be awkward if one of the other trainees came around again, throwing pebbles up at her window in the night. Penny might think she had a boyfriend, and that would be embarrassing.

Besides, what if this special job with Mr Rawlings involved her being away overnight? She'd have to come up with a bloomin' good story to explain *that*.

CHAPTER FOURTEEN

Life changed irrevocably after the Americans came to Bude. US soldiers were constantly walking the streets, training on the beaches and cliffs, going on marches up and down the rugged coastline, queueing to make international calls outside the telephone exchange, and best of all, soldiers popping into the dairy shop every day for tobacco or something quick and easy to eat.

'What's a Hershey bar?' Mrs Roskilly demanded as another disgruntled-looking young soldier left the dairy shop. 'That's the fourth time this week I've been asked for a Hershey bar. Some kind of American chocolate bar, the young man said. As if we stock things like that in Cornwall. Haven't they ever heard of rationing?'

'I don't think the war has affected them as badly over in the States,' Penny told her boss shyly. 'At least, that's what I've heard from the troops billeted where I'm living. They do have rationing of a sort, though, and something called "thrift stamps" but it's been nothing like our ration books here. Anyway, they're setting up a special shop soon for the troops to get the sort of items they like from home.' Or so Corporal Jones had told her the other evening, excited by the news. The new shop was going to be run by the Rangers themselves, situated just down the hill from the telephone exchange. 'So they won't be bothering you for Hershey bars much longer.'

'There are troops billeted in your boarding house?' Mrs Roskilly laughed, rolling her eyes. 'Dearie me. You'll never look twice at John Pascoe now, will you? Not when there's all these young American boys everywhere.' She shook her head in mock disapproval, though Penny could tell the farmer's wife was fishing for gossip to pass on to her friends. 'I've heard they play music until all hours too. And smoke and drink like nobody's business.'

Her husband, who'd been busy rolling barrels down the side alley, had come into the shop, wiping his hands on his trousers. 'Nothing wrong with a smoke or a drink now and then. Can't blame a man for that. And they'll be off fighting soon enough. Might as well have fun while they're here in Bude.' He winked at Penny in a disconcerting way. 'Happen there'll be one or two lads with their eye on you, young miss. Maybe more than an eye, eh? Best watch out you don't get a reputation.'

'Best watch I don't give you a clip round the ear, Graham,' his wife told him severely. 'Have you finished unloading them barrels?'

Sheepishly admitting that he hadn't, Mr Roskilly hurried back outside to finish unloading the farm van.

Penny bent her head to the cheese counter again, which she had been assiduously cleaning.

'He's not wrong though,' Mrs Roskilly said, arms folded,

watching Penny work. Her lips were pursed, eyes narrowed. 'I won't have girls working in my shop who think they can swan off with any young man they like. I'll not have talk.' She paused. 'Is that clear?'

'Perfectly, Mrs Roskilly,' Penny said, her head still bent, pretending she had found a particularly stubborn piece of grime in an obscure corner of the cheese shelf, though in fact the whole counter was so spotlessly clean, she could have eaten her dinner off it.

'There's a look about you lately . . .' Mrs Roskilly tutted, studying her. 'Well, you're old enough to make your own decisions. Just watch yourself, that's all I'm saying.'

To Penny's relief, the bell over the door jangled and three young soldiers strolled in, laughing and chatting together in their interesting American drawls. Penny looked across at them, but warily, one eye on her employer, only to see Mrs Roskilly produce a warmly inviting smile, pat her hairnet, and hurry to the counter to serve them herself.

'Yes, my dears, what can I do you for?'

Suppressing a chuckle, Penny nipped into the back to wash her hands at the sink and check her reflection at the same time. It was true, she did have a glow about her face these days, and it was hard not to speculate, as Mrs Roskilly had done, that it was down to all these good-looking young men on every street corner. She had never taken so much interest in her own appearance either, getting up early to do her hair and make-up and even once or twice to run an iron over her work blouse and skirt.

And she did like the idea of walking out with one of the American soldiers, it couldn't be denied. What a lark that would be!

But at the back of her mind, she was guiltily aware that she had not been down to the harbour to see if John was still ashore, or if he had gone out on the boat with his father and grandfather yet. He hadn't been in the shop recently, and nor had they, which suggested the three men had gone out fishing and might be gone a long time. She couldn't be sure he wasn't still in Bude though.

She and John Pascoe had enjoyed a lovely night at the picture house, with a tasty dinner at his parents' cottage afterwards. But that didn't mean she was promised to him in any way, nor he to her. So why did she feel guilty about chatting or dancing until the early hours with the American Rangers billeted in her boarding house? She and John weren't walking out, just testing each other out. She was still a free agent. So why shouldn't she flirt with a few handsome strangers in uniform?

Because you'll get a bad reputation, my girl, Penny thought sternly, echoing Mrs Roskilly's words of warning.

During her lunch break, she grabbed one of Mrs Roskilly's pasties as usual and hurried down to the harbour to see if John's boat, the *Mary Jane*, was still in dry dock or had gone out. She couldn't see the vessel anywhere and, after asking a few of the fishermen mending their nets on the quayside, discovered that the *Mary Jane* had indeed been taken out in search of a good catch, and might not be back in port for some days.

She thanked the men she'd approached and wandered on, feeling a bit lost. The tide was a long way out, though just on the turn, and a few people were walking their dogs along the sand. This end of the northern coast was not as heavily mined or defended as the beaches were further south, so it was possible for Penny to stretch her legs on the sands and get a few bracing lungfuls of fresh air, watching the tide come in.

Having finished the Cornish pasty, she walked on slowly in the shadow of the rugged cliffs. She was mindful of the time, as Mrs Roskilly had started docking her an hour's pay whenever she was late back, but although her twisted ankle had recovered well, the odd niggle made her wary of hurrying too much and setting it off again.

There were small red flags set into the sands at intervals ahead, as though marking out a special area. But since the only people nearby were men in uniform talking earnestly in a group, their heads bent over what looked like a map, she continued walking. It was a pleasant day and her mood soon lifted. The weather was breezy but not as cold as it had been lately, for the sun was out and striking the churning shallows with golden light. Above the roar of the incoming tide, she heard an odd noise in the distance but couldn't make out what it was.

Rounding the rocks that stuck out of the wet sands, Penny was astonished to see dozens of men in dark green clothing scaling the cliffs at Crooklets Beach, just ahead of her.

It had to be the US Rangers, she realised, peering at the climbers through sun glare from behind a raised hand. She'd heard talk of them training on the beach, but never seen it with her own eyes, and certainly hadn't envisaged them climbing up the sheer, jagged rocks of the cliff face itself. It all seemed very organised, however.

The soldiers had thrown down lengths of knotted rope,

and some were climbing up while others climbed down, a man in uniform yelling down at them through a loud-hailer from the cliffs. Up above, men with packs on their backs were quick-marching in groups up the steep green stretch, singing a song to keep them in time, the tune carrying all the way to the beach below. Others were crawling across the sand on their bellies under rolls of barbed wire, clutching rifles and with tin helmets strapped on firmly, while what sounded like firecrackers were exploded over their heads, thrown by men sitting in the open back of a military van.

It was such an amazing sight that Penny stopped dead to stare, mouth open, and only belatedly realised that her shoes were sinking into the wet sand and likely to be ruined.

'Drat!' Cursing under her breath, she dragged her feet out of the oozing sands and began to hurry on around the base of the cliffs.

'Hey, you there! Out the way!'

Penny stared up in surprise, her steps slowing. The man with the loudhailer up on the cliffs appeared to be waving violently in her direction and yelling into his contraption like mad. She frowned. Was he yelling at *her*?

But there was no time to consider that question. For, at that moment, two large men in uniform came out of nowhere, grabbed her by the upper arms and began to manhandle her off the beach between them.

Protesting, Penny demanded that they let her go, but the men paid no attention to her cries. 'What on earth are you doing? How dare you?'

The soldiers were so strong and fast, they lifted her feet clean off the sand, so she was almost flying. By the time they got her off the beach and onto the foreshore where tents had been set up on the muddy ground, the area crowded with army jeeps and other vehicles, she was furious and indignant.

'Who . . . Who are you?' she demanded breathlessly as they set her down again on dry land. 'And what do you think you're doing?'

'Second Battalion US Rangers at your service, ma'am,' one of the men said, releasing her with a brisk nod. 'Apologies if we upset you. But it was vital to move you out of the field of engagement.'

'The *what* of *who*?' Penny straightened her rumpled clothing, glaring at the man.

'We're running war games here, ma'am,' the other soldier told her, his tone disapproving. 'What Jones here is failing to mention, is that you were in the way. You wouldn't want to get hurt, would you? We certainly wouldn't want any civilians being harmed during our time in Bude.'

'Well, you could have said something to warn us off,' she snapped, thoroughly discombobulated. 'Put up a barricade or posted a few sentries.'

'Didn't you see the red flags on the beach?'

'Oh.' Penny flushed, belatedly recalling the line of red flags that she had indeed spotted and ignored. 'Well, yes, but I didn't know what they were for. You need a written sign. Something to make it clear it's a danger zone. *Stay off the beach*, for instance, with a skull and crossbones underneath.'

Jones grinned. 'We're working on it, ma'am. Early days yet. I'm sure we'll get all that sorted out soon enough. Again, you have our apologies.'

'Hmm,' was all Penny could say to that.

The two men moved away, and Penny straightened her hat, feeling quite put out. But then she recognised a few of the soldiers among those leaning against a nearby jeep, and hurried over to them, her heart lifting.

She had spoken to Dean and Alan several times at the boarding house. Their rooms were on the same landing as hers, only two rooms along, which meant they shared a bathroom. If her mother knew about that, she would put her foot down and insist on Penny moving to an all-ladies boarding house, if such an old-fashioned establishment were still to be found in Bude. But luckily her mother had no idea of her circumstances.

Besides, having to share a bathroom with young men was just one of the hazards of war, wasn't it? Though once she had spotted Alan coming out with only a towel wrapped about his waist, and had hurriedly shut her bedroom door again, blushing fiercely.

'Hello,' she said now, feeling a little embarrassed, for they must have witnessed her being dragged off the beach by those two burly soldiers. 'I nearly got myself blown up. Did you see?'

'We could hardly miss it,' Dean said, chuckling.

To her annoyance, even Alan was laughing too. 'I'm afraid so, Miss Penny. I gotta say, your face was a picture.' He paused, looking at her more closely, concern in his soft brown eyes that reminded her of a spaniel. 'Hey, I hope you weren't hurt?'

'Don't worry about me, I'll live,' Penny said lightly, forcing a smile to her lips. She didn't want them to think she was the kind of girl who would get upset over something so trivial. Besides, it had been her own fault, paying no attention to that row of red warning flags further down the beach. 'So, what are you boys doing? Not very much, by the look of it.'

'We're *observing*,' Dean told her, clearly offended by the suggestion that they were lazing about. 'We've been tasked with observing the proceedings and making a full report on what we see. Because we'll be doing it ourselves tomorrow.' He glanced up at the thickening clouds overhead. 'I just hope this weather holds. I've heard it rains a lot in Cornwall and I hate playing war games in the rain.' The way he pronounced 'Cornwall', as though it were two separate words, made her bite back a smile.

'That's because he doesn't like getting his smart hairdo wet,' Alan said, and received a mock punch to the arm from his friend.

'You'll pay for that,' Dean said, but with an answering grin.

'I'd better leave you to your "observing", then.' Penny was aware of a senior-looking Ranger with slicked-back grey hair and a frown on his face headed their way. 'Before I get you two into trouble for chatting to the locals. See you back at the boarding house!' She hurried away, quickly threading a path through the parked vehicles and billowing tents on the foreshore, tripping over several sets of guy ropes and almost colliding with a man carrying a chin-high stack of metal containers. 'Oops, sorry.'

As she stumbled on, past the hastily converted 'chow house' where the Rangers ate their meals and through a small crowd of locals who'd gathered on the marshy downs to watch the shenanigans, she felt herself grabbed for a second time, and was amazed to find John Pascoe staring down at her.

'Goodness!' she exclaimed, reeling back. 'I thought you were at sea. The *Mary Jane* has gone out. What are you still doing in Bude?'

John released her, and she realised with a shock that his left arm was in a sling. 'Banged myself falling down the harbour steps,' he admitted gruffly, 'didn't I?'

'Oh no, how awful. Is it broken?'

'Not as bad as all that. Doc says it's just a sprain and some bruising. But he told my pa I mustn't go out on the water. Not for a few weeks at least.' John sounded grumpy. 'He and Granddad have gone out on the *Mary Jane* on their own instead. I only hope they'll be safe without me.'

'I thought they were both experienced fishermen?'

'Experienced, aye. But getting on a bit. It's hard labour, working a fishing boat all hours of the day and night.' He pulled a face. 'Pa was furious with me for hurting meself.'

'That's hardly fair. It's not your fault you fell down the steps.'

'Well, Pa had just warned me they were slippery, and I weren't rightly looking where I was going. So maybe it was my fault,' John chuckled. 'A boat was coming into the harbour just then, and the skipper yelled out my name, so I raised my hand and shouted back. Next thing I know, I'm on my back at the bottom of the steps, and my arm . . . You can see for yourself,' he told her, lifting away some of the sling to reveal a forearm bruised black-and-blue and gouged by a nasty gash. When she gasped, he said hurriedly, 'It's not half as bad as it looks. But I'm landlocked for now.'

'Poor John. Still, at least it wasn't your head.'

'Oh, it wouldn't have been so bad if I'd hit my head. Where there's no sense, there's no feeling,' he added with a wink, 'or so my ma's always telling us.' He looked past her at the American soldiers still dashing about on the beach, throwing explosives that cracked and banged every few minutes. 'I saw you getting in trouble with the Yanks just now. What was all that about?'

Embarrassed, Penny explained about the red flags and the soldiers dragging her off the beach. 'But I wasn't to know, was I?' He was laughing, so she laughed too. 'They're going to set up a warning sign soon, the Americans told me. So it won't happen to anyone else. Cold comfort for me, though.'

'And the two men you were talking to just now?

'What?' Penny was taken aback, and abruptly recalled what Mrs Roskilly had said about her reputation. 'H-Have you been spying on me, John?' She was stammering, her face hot, for she disliked the idea of her behaviour being monitored. Her overprotective mother had done that when she was younger, always checking who she was talking to and why, and it had driven her crazy. That was one reason she'd fled her home to become a Land Girl far away in Cornwall. 'Because you've no right.'

John looked sheepish. 'No need to spy. I've got eyes, haven't I?' He gestured back down the beach to where the Americans were clustered by the jeeps, watching the others training on the beach. 'I've nothing much to do at home, so I came down here to see what these Americans are up to. And what's the first thing I see? Only Miss Penny Brown being dragged off the beach like a German spy and interrogated by two damn Yanks. Though it was a funny old interrogation,' he added suspiciously, 'for I saw the three of you laughing away together, chummy as anything.'

'Their names are Dean and Alan, if you must know, and they're staying at the same boarding house as me on Downs View Road. And I'm not a German spy, thank you,' she insisted, very much on her dignity, though she hoped that had only been a joke. 'I was out for a walk on the beach and managed to find myself in the wrong place, that's all.'

John said nothing for a moment, looking her up and down. 'Wrong footwear for walking on the beach, I'd say,' he commented at last. 'You need boots.'

'Yes, they're a bit soggy. And so are my stockings, which is a nuisance. I'll have to rinse them out and hang them up to dry when I get home.' She looked down at her feet in remorse. 'It was skirting all those big rocks that did it. I'd forgotten how wet the sand gets between rock pools. Even when the sun's out, like today.'

To her relief, he seemed to have let it go that she'd been so friendly with the American boys. They chatted about the changeable weather for a few minutes, then John asked, looking puzzled, 'By the way, shouldn't you be working?'

'Oh, damn and blast,' she muttered, realising she'd completely forgotten the time. 'Sorry, I have to dash.' Penny turned away, already heading away from him. 'I'll be as late as stink. Mrs Roskilly will have a fit.'

'Can I see you later?' John called after her, laughing.

'Come to the shop at five,' she shouted over her shoulder, beginning to run along the cliff-path, her feet squelching in wet, sandy shoes. 'Unless I've been given my marching orders by then!'

They had parted company amicably enough, despite an initial awkwardness over her hobnobbing with the Americans. But her head was whirling. She needed to decide if she was going to take John Pascoe seriously. Because if they were *courting*, instead of just friends, she would have to give the Rangers a wide berth in future, in case they got the wrong idea. Which could prove awfully difficult, given they were all packed into Ocean View Boarding House together like sardines in a tin . . .

CHAPTER FIFTEEN

The morning sunshine had long since retreated and the afternoon grown chilly by the time Florence hurried out to unpeg her washing from the line in the backyard, having noted slowly gathering clouds from the west.

Setting aside the full basket of clean linen for ironing later, Florence bustled through to mop the hall floor before any soldiers returned from their training exercises for a wash and a smoke, which they often did before heading down to the beachside 'chow house' for their evening meal. They had been asked by Miles to remove their boots at the door and not traipse mud through the house, but being mostly very young men, they inevitably forgot or perhaps couldn't be bothered at the end of a long weary day, leaving dirty boot prints and even unsightly clumps of mud on the hall tiles and up the stairs.

To cope with this issue, Florence had taken to sweeping the hall and stairs every morning after the men had gone out for the day, and mopping the tiled floor every second afternoon before they came back.

She had almost finished mopping the hall when she heard raised voices outside the boarding house and frowned. They were women's voices, and one of them she recognised as belonging to her sister. Putting aside her mop and bucket, she trod carefully over the wet tiles to the door, opened it a crack and peered outside.

Sure enough, Imogen was leaning over the garden gate, talking in a strained, high-pitched tone to her neighbour, Doreen. The older woman looked quite shocked and kept shaking her head, insisting vehemently that Imogen did not know what she was talking about and that she ought to mind her manners.

Florence's heart sank. She didn't want to interfere between the two women but knew she must. These were her neighbours, this was her town, and if Imogen was behaving badly, it could only reflect on her own reputation.

She went outside, shivering in the sharp salt wind off the sea and drawing her cardigan closer. 'Is anything the matter?' she asked with a smile, trying to be diplomatic. 'Imogen, I'm sure if you have something to say to Doreen, you should invite her in for a nice cup of tea and we can all talk together, like civilised people.' *Not yell at her over the garden wall like a fishwife*, she continued in her head, but was too polite to say so out loud.

'It's all right, I've got this under control,' Imogen told her, a flash of irritation in her pretty eyes as she turned to her sister. 'No need to push your beak in where it's not wanted, Flo.'

Florence took a deep breath and struggled against a wave of bitter resentment. Why, oh why, did she have to give house room to her nasty little sister? Why couldn't she simply send her away and be done with it?

Her jaw set hard as she processed the unpalatable reasons. Because her mother and father had asked her to take Imogen for a few months. Her parents were good, caring people but, reading between the lines of her mother's awkwardly phrased letter, they needed a little time away from Imogen. A respite from her difficult behaviour, perhaps, or simply time to be alone together as a couple without Imogen's almost *dramatic* presence in the house.

She understood why Imogen had been 'sent' to her. But she still wished that she didn't have to cope with her. Didn't she have enough on her plate with Billy? Thankfully, her son was playing at his friend Emily's house this afternoon, which was one less thing for her to worry about.

'Doreen, I'm so sorry if there's been a misunderstanding between you and my sister.' She nudged past Imogen to open the garden gate in smiling invitation. 'Let's not stand about in this cold wind. Won't you come inside for a nice cup of tea? I'm sure I have some sponge cake too.' She knew that Doreen was very partial to sponge cake.

But her older neighbour wasn't to be mollified with promises of tea and cake. She shook her head, her silvery-white hair blowing in the wind, and walked on towards town with a muttered, 'No, thank you.'

Mortified, Florence watched her until she was out of sight before turning to Imogen in despair. 'Whatever made you pick an argument with Doreen? She's one of my closest neighbours, for goodness' sake. And eighty years old, if she's a day. Are you out of your mind?'

Far from being embarrassed, Imogen merely gave her a cool, unreadable look and headed back inside. 'She was being nosy.'

'Old ladies are always nosy, you know that,' Florence said impatiently, following her into the house. 'Oh, watch out for the wet floor!' But it was too late. Her sister had already trod straight through the mopped area in her high-heeled shoes, leaving a series of odd marks behind on the gleaming wet tiles, like the prints of a wading bird on a riverbank. 'For Pete's sake, Imogen! Look what you've done now . . .'

But her sister had simply carried on walking and was out of sight.

Florence stood a moment in fuming silence, staring at those marks on the tiles. Her heart felt like it would burst. It was silly, perhaps, to get so upset over such a trivial thing. But just then it seemed to encapsulate everything about her sister that was careless, selfish and dismissive of other people's efforts. Grabbing up the mop, Florence sloshed it back and forth over the spoilt area, not caring if she was leaving the tiles too wet to dry properly before the girls came back for their supper. She felt like crying, but she knew she was more angry than unhappy. Why did Imogen have to be so spiteful? And why couldn't her sister have chosen somewhere else to live, rather than with her? It simply wasn't *fair*.

Afterwards, she sighed and fetched a clean cloth from the cupboard under the stairs, got down gingerly on hands and knees, and dried up the glistening pools of water left behind by the over-wet mop.

Just as she was reaching for the last 'puddle' on a distant

tile, the front door opened and she looked up in dismay to find Sergeant Miller standing there.

'I'm sorry,' he said in his deep, rich voice, surveying the clean bright hallway floor. 'Should I take my boots off before coming in?'

'Are they dirty?' she asked, hurriedly dabbing at the last wet tile.

Bending slightly, he checked the soles of both boots with a conscientious expression, and then shook his head. 'Clean as a whistle. I've been into town for a meeting today, not down at the training zone. Besides,' he added with a smile, 'I wiped my boots on the doormat before opening the door, just to be sure.'

'Then I can't see any reason for you to remove them.'

Goodness, how pompous that had sounded. Florence wished she could be more natural with him, as she had been when they'd first met. Though she knew why she was sometimes uncomfortable when they were alone together. After her initial uncertainty about him, a few smiles and playful remarks between them had been a bit of fun, making her feel young again. But she could not allow this – whatever it was – to become more serious, especially while Billy was still so young and impressionable; he would not understand his widowed mother taking an interest in another man.

Leaning forward, she made to get up off her knees, and found him beside her in a trice, holding out a large, masculine hand as a support.

'Let me help you up, ma'am.'

'Thank you.'

Florence struggled to her feet with his aid, not terribly

gracefully, and caught sight of her reflection in the incriminating hall mirror. Her hair was dishevelled after she'd stood in the wind to unpeg the washing, and her bold red lipstick, applied first thing that morning, had long since faded to an indistinct pinkish colour which did nothing to offset the pallor in her cheeks.

Her appearance shouldn't matter. She was in her own home, and with a man she had come to consider a friend. Nothing more. Yet it did matter, and enough to make her want to run scurrying for a hairbrush and to retouch her lipstick.

Why?

As she came to her feet, her hand still clasped in his, Florence realised with a shock how close they were to touching *elsewhere*. Chest to chest. Maybe even hip to hip. Taking a hurried step back to correct her position, she came up against the wall, and her eyes flew wide, her breath expelled in a soundless 'oh'.

'Careful there.' He released her, but slowly, his gaze holding hers.

'I should get on,' she stammered, looking anywhere but at him, her pale cheeks suddenly hot in some schoolgirlish way. 'So much to do . . .'

But he didn't move, still looking at her in that curiously intent way, their faces mere inches apart.

Abruptly, with a flash of insight that left her dazed, Florence understood why the sight of her unkempt reflection had left her embarrassed, and why she increasingly felt so awkward around this man . . .

The door to the kitchen banged as they stared at each other, and Imogen came wandering out of the adjacent dining room, heels clacking on the tiled floor. 'Flo, where do you keep the sugar?' she demanded, her voice dying away as she encountered the two of them in the hallway, though thankfully no longer so close, for at the sound of her approach, Sergeant Miller had taken two well-spaced steps backwards and clasped his hands behind his back, standing ramrod straight, as though enacting some military ceremony.

'Hello again,' Imogen added, looking him up and down with interest, for although she must have seen Miles about the place quite frequently since her arrival, Florence had been careful not to introduce him to her sister. 'Sorry if I'm interrupting.'

'Interrupting?' Florence echoed sharply. 'Goodness me, what on earth could you be interrupting?' She stooped to gather her cleaning things. 'Sergeant Miller and I have been discussing the, erm, protocol for boots in the house.'

'Is that so?' Imogen's gaze flicked between the two of them with prickling interest. 'The boots protocol . . . Well, well.'

Miles looked uneasy, as well he might. But he didn't contradict Florence. 'It's not right that Mrs Pritchard should waste her time cleaning up after our men like this. Not when there's such a simple preventative measure, such as removing boots before entering the property. That's not the Rangers' way.' He drew himself up even straighter, nodding to Florence. 'I'll make that clear to the men tonight – you have my word, ma'am.'

'Thank you.'

Imogen had not been thrown off the scent though. Eyeing Miles, she played with her hair, which she always wore loose without a hairnet, a natural curl to the glossy dark waves nestling on her shoulder. 'I say,' she murmured, 'you wouldn't happen to be any good at loosening stuck windows, would you?'

'Imogen, no,' Florence said, eyes widening.

Her sister had been complaining ever since she arrived that the old sash window in their shared bedroom wouldn't open more than a few inches. It was an issue that Florence had been aware of for years and hadn't bothered to rectify, for Billy also shared that room and she didn't like the idea of her impulsive son being able to throw the window open on a whim. Now her sister was demanding that one of their guests take a look at the mechanism, which was quite outrageous . . .

But she wasn't simply scandalised by the impudence of Imogen's request. She was also mortified at the thought of Miles entering her bedroom and being in her private space. He would hardly miss the framed photograph of her and Percy on their wedding day or beaming together over Billy at his christening, or her perfume bottles and pots of cream among all those odds and ends she kept on her dressing table, and no doubt a pair or two of stockings or other undergarments draped over the mirror or the iron-frame bedstead. And now that Imogen was sharing with her, there would be her dresses, skirts and blouses strewn around the room in disarray, for Imogen was not a tidy houseguest.

Miles began, 'I don't have much time . . .' But seeing Imogen's downcast look, he added politely, 'I could have a quick look now, if you like. Whereabouts is this window?'

'Upstairs,' Imogen said, utterly shameless, and led him

up to their bedroom, throwing a look back at her sister that could only be interpreted as triumphant.

Florence stood to watch them go, wringing her hands in anxiety. Perhaps she was being overprotective towards her son, who was still too young to be able to open such a heavy window, and it was true that the room was becoming awfully stuffy now three of them were sharing it. A little more fresh air would be welcome in the mornings, even if the weather was growing colder with every day that passed.

But she knew that Imogen had asked Miles to look at that window for other reasons than needing fresh air.

On the face of it, her request must have appeared innocent enough. An upstairs window was stuck. Miles was a strong man, a soldier, in his prime. To him, it would be the work of a few minutes to loosen the paint-locked frame with a hard shove, or gauge whether the problem required a chisel and hammer as well.

But to Florence, it had been a deliberate provocation. A show of feminine strength by her little sister. A demonstration that she was still young and pretty and could wind a man around her little finger if she wished. That on the strength of a few words and a smile she could get that handsome man up into her bedroom – their bedroom – and there wasn't anything Florence could do about it. Or not without seeming petty-minded and jealous.

Which was ridiculous. Florence wasn't even remotely jealous. Jealous of what, anyway? That an American officer Florence had come to like would be spending a few minutes alone with her sister in the intimate space of a bedroom?

She wasn't Imogen's mother or nursemaid. Her sister was a grown woman and must do as she pleased. And she herself was a widow, with a child to consider.

But the ache in her heart was real, as was the desire to call after Miles and order him to come back downstairs. Even now, she could hear their muffled voices and the lilt of Imogen's laughter, and her jaw clenched hard as she listened.

How dare her sister do this? How dare she? Because Florence *was* jealous. She was as jealous as hell, in fact. Her throat had clogged up with tears and she could scarcely breathe for fear of bursting with fury and distress. It was pointless to deny it. Somehow, and she had no real idea how or when it had occurred, she had become *infatuated* with Sergeant Miles Miller, and worst of all, her sister knew it.

CHAPTER SIXTEEN

It was coming up to Christmas when Alice finally received a reply to her letter home. She'd written to Aunt Violet several weeks before, giving her as much news as she was allowed, given the secrecy of her war work, and eagerly asking for news of home in return. She'd also asked whether it would be possible for them to visit her and Penny in Bude. It was really herself who was longing to see her family, but Penny missed being at the farm too and would have been unhappy to think she was not included.

Indeed, she felt a little guilty about Penny. Her friend had partly come to Bude to keep her company, and yet they'd hardly seen each other since arriving, except for a few evenings spent with the Rangers, dancing and listening to music.

Since Penny had recently confided that she was walking out with a young fisherman, Alice had included this interesting nugget of information in her last letter to her aunt too, knowing it would shock the Land Girls at Joe's farm. Mealtime conversations between the Land Girls had been interspersed with giggling comments about boys and who fancied whom, much to Joe's discomfort. Caroline and Selina had also joked about Penny, saying she was 'too tubby' and 'shy' to find a boyfriend. Alice imagined their noses must have been put out of joint to discover that 'Pickles', as they'd meanly nicknamed her, once free of a dreary life in the sticks, had found herself a nice young man.

Florence handed her the letter from home as she came in from work, on a cold December evening, saying, 'Something for you at last today, Alice. I hope it's good news.'

Thanking her, Alice had dashed upstairs to change out of her work clothes before supper. Then she sat on the bed and opened the letter. Sure enough, it was from Aunt Violet.

Dearest Alice,

We were all so excited to receive your last letter, which I read out at supper so the Land Girls could hear too, hope you don't mind. The girls hooted when they heard about Penny's young man. Though I suspect Caroline was a little jealous. She and her latest beau seemed to have fallen out recently. So thank you for writing again and I'm sorry it's taken so long for me to reply. Life has been hectic here on the farm.

A new Land Girl arrived late October to take Penny's place. Her name is Joan and she's lovely, if a little quiet, and comes from North London. But she's had her work cut out with us, poor lamb. You see, back in November, Joe cracked a bone in his foot, messing about with the tractor, and the doctor insisted he had to rest it for a few weeks, which was a bit of a disaster. As you'll remember, Joe finds it hard enough to get up to the top fields in winter with his false leg, let alone down again. So having the other foot bandaged up and out of action made it impossible for him, poor soul.

Thankfully, Caroline and Selina pulled their weight as usual, with Joan helping out as best she knew how, so Joe barely had to lift a finger the whole time. His foot's better now, bless him, and only gives him the odd twinge. And we're all extremely thankful for that, as Joe with a sore foot was awful grumpy. He weren't cut out to sit around in an armchair reading the newspapers, that's for sure.

Once he was out of bandages, we gave the girls a slap-up dinner as a thank you for all their hard work, and we even had some of Mum's home-made wine and a knees-up around the table. You know how your gran loves to entertain, and once she'd had a few glasses of the elderflower wine, she rolled out all the old songs from our Dagenham days, while her beau, Arnold Newton, played the spoons. It was such a sight! We all wished you'd been there. And after the Land Girls had gone up to bed, we drank a toast to absent friends, meaning you, your sister Lily, and You Know Who as well.

Lily wrote to us last month too. She says her pregnancy is going nicely, even though she's still working. I've written to tell her she should stop work *now and rest until the baby comes. But you know how stubborn your sister is. She wrote back to say there's a war on, as if I hadn't noticed, and nobody can take time off. I don't see how her resting is going to make any difference to Mr Hitler. But there's no arguing with Lily. I only pray everything will be well. She's not due until late next spring though, so I suppose I'm probably making a fuss about nothing as usual.*

Now for our big news. Arnold Newton from the village shop has only gone and asked your gran to marry him. You could have knocked me down with a feather when Mum came waltzing in to tell me. She was pink with delight, I swear, and as giddy as a schoolgirl. Joe said she looked twenty years younger. I didn't know what to say, but luckily Joe said congratulations from the both of us. But I do worry about her marrying again at her time of life. I'm not saying she's an old lady. But she's no spring chicken either, and as I said to Joe afterwards, when Mum couldn't hear me, I worry about her beau too. Your gran's a bit of a handful and old Arnie's not getting any younger. I only hope it won't be the death of him, tying the knot again at his age.

Anyway, so there's to be another wedding in the family. Mum says you and Lily must be there to see her wed, come hell or high water. So it's going to be a grand old affair at Porthcurno Church, probably sometime in early spring. As soon as your gran knows the date, she'll write and let you know. Oh, and she says you're to make sure Penny comes too.

It wouldn't be right if she wasn't at the wedding. Our Land Girls are part of the family now and we'd all love to see her again. Do write and let us know how she's getting on in Bude. Caroline is forever asking if we've had any news of her. I think she's missing Penny something rotten, though she won't admit it.

Anyway, I must dash. Joe and I are taking Mum into Penzance so she can shop for wedding clothes. Not for her, but for Arnie. Whatever next? Apparently, he's got one suit and only worn it twice, once for his wedding and once for his wife's funeral, and he can't fit into it no more. Mum's decided to splash out on some posh material and run him up a new suit on the sewing machine. As if she knows the first thing about men's tailoring, Lord love us. I only hope it doesn't end in disaster and he's walking down the aisle with his hems up around his ankles and his jacket lopsided.

Well, cheerio, love. I can't promise to visit you for Christmas, what with petrol rationing and the difficulty of getting a train ticket without good cause. But I'll try to send a parcel to cheer you up nearer the time. I hope they're not working you too hard in that printing shop.

Missing you, with much love, your Aunty Violet and Uncle Joe xxx

Alice read the letter carefully twice, and then pulled her feet up onto the bed, tucked her head onto her folded arms, and had a little cry.

She wasn't truly unhappy here in Bude, just a little *homesick*, as Penny had termed it. And she'd hoped for a Christmas visit from her aunt, at least. But clearly that was impossible. She was enjoying the war work placement, despite a few clashes and misunderstandings with others on the training course – Sophy in particular, who seemed to delight in making life awkward for her.

Alice really couldn't understand why Sophy was so bloomin' mean and toffee-nosed at times. As the only other girl on the course, by rights they ought to be *friends*.

So yes, the training was difficult and challenging, but it was also everything she'd ever hoped to do. And she wouldn't give it up for the world. Only sometimes she did miss having a large, noisy, loving family about her . . .

At last, she blew her nose, dried her eyes, and read the letter a third time. Her gaze lingered over the telling phrases, 'we drank a toast to absent friends' and 'to You Know Who'.

She did know who.

Her father, Ernest Fisher, who was supposed to be dead. A spy for the British government, working undercover behind enemy lines somewhere, and the bravest man she knew.

Carefully, Alice folded her aunt's letter and put it away in the old cake tin where she kept her most precious items. She was wondering where her father was right now, if he was safe, and whether he had indeed been the one to recommend her for this training course in Bude. But who else could have done it? No, her dad had been behind this placement, for sure.

* * *

Only the next day, her good mood evaporated when she was paired with Sophy for a hand-to-hand fighting session. No doubt the instructors had decided that girl against boy would be too one-sided and might lead to injury. Alice, on the other hand, felt sure she would be more likely to face a male opponent in the field, and that replicating that challenging situation at least once would be better than facing someone her own build every time they trained.

Clearly, Sophy felt the same, for the other girl threw her a poisonous glance from under long lashes and made a loud protest. 'Can't I fight one of the others? Spotty Patrick, perhaps, or Jasper?'

But Sidney, who was overseeing that morning's session, ignored the interruption and continued to outline the exercise. 'You need to avoid inflicting serious harm on each other,' he continued steadily, 'but if the odd punch or kick from your opponent lands, let that be a lesson to defend yourself better.' They were down in the underground shelter where one of the assistants had dragged out a few thin mats to cushion any falls, though Alice doubted they would be much use. 'First, take up position like this. Like a boxing match. Except there are no rules in this fight. The only goal is to win, by whatever means necessary.'

He gestured to Treve, a small, wizened old Cornishman who sometimes instructed them in firearms handling and combat, and the old man left his stool and shuffled over. The two men opposed each other with fists up, and slowly began to circle each other.

'Be aware,' Sidney went on, 'your opponent may have a concealed weapon. A knife or even a pistol. So always be on the lookout for any tendency to protect one side, as that will likely be where the weapon is concealed. Equally, it could show you where your opponent is weak or already wounded. So you should then target that side, and watch he doesn't reach for a weapon in any moments of confusion, hoping to take you unawares.' He nodded to Treve, who threw a punch, which Sidney deflected. But as he took a step back, Treve almost effortlessly hooked a foot about his ankle and brought Sidney crashing to the ground.

Treve gave him a hand up, grinning.

Dusting himself down, Sidney looked around at them all, watching in awe on the sidelines. 'What are you waiting for?' He shook his head impatiently. 'Come on, this is a life-or-death struggle against the enemy. You don't need permission to defend your country. Get into position and let's see those fists.' He nodded to Jasper, who had already turned to his partner, Barnabas, fists up. 'That's the ticket, boy. Keep those hands nice and high, defending your face. Thumbs on the outside.' He demonstrated, tucking his thumb safely over his curled middle fingers. 'We don't want any broken thumbs, thank you.'

Alice dragged one of the mats into a clear space and waited, both fists defending her face, thumbs on the outside. Her dad had shown her and Lily how to fist-fight when they were small children, and though it had only been for fun, Alice had never forgotten.

Reluctantly, Sophy followed, though disdained the protection of a mat. The two girls circled each other, slightly crouched as Sidney had shown them.

'Now, try to land a punch,' Sidney shouted, and there was a flurry of movement and noise, as everyone lunged at once, parrying blows or landing them amid general laughter. Except for Sophy, who still seemed to be distracted.

'Ow!' Sophy reeled back, clutching her nose, eyes wide with shock. 'I . . . I wasn't ready.'

Alice kept her fists up, just in case the other girl came back at her with a vengeful blow. But Sophy merely squealed and ran for the steps out of the shelter, a trickle of blood escaping below her clamped hand.

Surprised, Alice watched her go, and then looked to Sidney and Treve, who were both chuckling. 'Sorry,' she said, feeling some contrition was demanded, as the other trainees were glaring at her with accusation. 'She said she wasn't ready. I didn't realise.'

'That's her hard cheese, then,' Treve growled in a thick Cornish accent. 'Besides, that's no way to fight. Enemy don't wait for you to be *ready*.'

'True enough,' Sidney agreed, nodding. 'Nicely done, Alice.' He hesitated though, glancing around at Mr Rawlings, who'd come in a few minutes earlier to watch the training. The two men exchanged a look, then he added, 'Best go and check how she is, though. We don't want to look like brutes.'

Feeling guilty, Alice went up the steps after her wounded opponent. The yard was empty, but she found Sophy in the printing workshop, slumped on a low stool with a bloodied handkerchief pressed to her nose, still making little whimpering noises.

'Get lost,' Sophy told her indistinctly, glancing round at her.

Alice chewed on her lip. 'I don't think I should. Sidney told me to come and check you were all right.'

'Well, you've checked. Now you can get knotted.'

'Try tilting your head back,' she suggested, remembering how Gran had always dealt with nosebleeds. It was obvious Sophy had been crying, which made her feel awful. Apart from the odd squabble with her sister growing up, she'd never hit anyone before. She'd certainly never caused a loss of blood before and felt a little shocked by how easy it had been. 'I'm sorry you got hurt. I didn't mean to hit you so hard.' She hesitated, then added helpfully, 'Would you like me to put a key down your back?' That technique was infallible with nosebleeds, according to her gran.

'Go to hell.'

Alice was sorry the other girl had received such a hard bop on the nose but she couldn't help feeling aggrieved at how badly she was taking it.

'Hang on, this ain't my fault,' Alice told her, a little hotly. 'You weren't protecting your face properly. That's why you got a smack in the hooter.'

'Because I wasn't ready.'

'You never said so.'

'I clearly wasn't ready. Any fool could have seen that. Even an East End idiot like you.' Sophy lowered the bloodied handkerchief, glaring at her. 'You're a bully. You did it deliberately.'

'No.' Alice shook her head, upset now. Not least by the insults. 'Honest, I would never do that.'

'Liar.'

'I'm not lying.' Alice felt her temper rise and couldn't seem to calm herself down. East End idiot? A bully and a liar? Her cheeks flushed. 'Stop it.'

'Make me.'

'What . . . What do you mean?

When Alice stared at her in hurt and confusion, Sophy gave a brittle laugh. 'You really are stupid, aren't you? Make me stop, then. Right here and now. No mats and no instructors. Just you and me.' She tossed the bloodied hanky to the ground and launched herself towards Alice, not with her fists up like before, but with hands like claws, each fingernail painted bright scarlet. 'Last girl standing wins.'

Backing away in surprise, Alice tripped over a box of government flyers and barely got a chance to straighten up before Sophy's nails had scratched her cheek. With a cry of pain, she swung wildly without even looking, one fist and then the other, making contact again, and Sophy staggered back with a cry.

'Good God, stop this at once! Alice, what on earth are you doing?'

Rawlings was standing in the doorway to the print workshop, staring at them both, an astonished expression on his face.

Sophy turned her bloodstained face towards him, suddenly weeping. 'She hit me again, sir,' she sniffed. 'No warning, nothing. She's horrible.'

''Ere, th-that's not true,' Alice stammered. 'Sophy was the one who attacked me.' She put a hand to the stinging scratch on her cheek and realised with a shock that she was bleeding.

'So, you didn't hit her again?' Rawlings demanded.

'Well . . .' Alice frowned, wanting to be truthful. 'Yes, I did. But I couldn't help it. I was bloomin' defending meself, weren't I?'

It was the truth. But she could tell from Rawlings' face that he didn't believe her. Sophy, meanwhile, was sobbing her heart out as though she'd just witnessed a basket of kittens being drowned. Alice felt like crying too, but simply folded her arms and waited for the inevitable. She knew which one of them looked guilty and it weren't Sophy.

She'd made a right mess of things, hadn't she? Now she'd probably let her dad down by getting thrown off the training course, and there weren't nothing she could do about it.

CHAPTER SEVENTEEN

Penny lowered herself gingerly from the ladder and into John's waiting arms. She gave a little squeak of alarm as the boat skittered beneath the new weight, adjusted itself and steadied, its old timbers creaking and protesting. 'Oh Lord, I feel seasick already. Does it always move up and down like this?'

John burst out laughing. 'Mostly, aye. But you get used to it. Only, do try to remember, a boat is a *she*. Not an *it*.' He put a hand lovingly on the wooden deck rail, worn smooth with age. 'You don't want to hurt her feelings, do you? Poor ol' *Mary Jane*.'

'However can you hurt a boat's feelings?' Penny demanded, and then added hurriedly, seeing his frown, 'Oh, I forgot. You're all terribly superstitious, aren't you? I suppose it's risking your life on the open sea that does it. Sorry, I didn't mean to ruin your luck, honest.'

'Ah, it'll take more than a slip of the tongue to ruin our luck,' John's grandfather told her cheerfully. The old man, standing above them on the quayside, waved his hand as he set off back to their cottage. 'I'll see you boys dreckly. Tatty-bye for now.'

John caught her surprised look and whispered in her ear, 'Grandpa doesn't unload the fish these days. Got a bad back. That's why I'm here, see? To help Pa get the fish out and off to market.'

'*Dreckly?*' she whispered, puzzled.

He laughed. 'It means . . . *straightaway*, but in a little while too. A Cornish word. You've never heard it?'

'Once or twice,' she admitted shyly. 'Only I never knew before exactly what it meant. Thank you.'

His father was busy further along the deck, bending to load a crate with fresh-caught fish, their plump, shining bodies hauled out from a deep pit with wooden sides set on the open deck. Once full, he handed this heavy crate to John, who placed it effortlessly on his shoulder, climbed the iron rungs of the ladder and hoisted it up to a man waiting above them on the quayside.

As he scaled the ladder, the small boat swayed, so that Penny was obliged to plant her feet firmly to avoid staggering about.

'There you go, Frank,' John said, adding, 'There's a few more herring to come yet.'

Frank grunted, taking the crate. 'Nice day for it.'

'Can't complain.'

The man, who was wearing a rubber apron and a woolly hat against the cold, carried the fish crate along the quay and slung it into the back of an elderly van painted with the words, *Frank's Fish Stall*, in elegant cursive alongside a depiction of a shiny fat herring. Then he came back for the next load, which John had already fetched to hand up to him.

As this process went on, Penny went to peer down into the pit of fish. There, dozens of large, wet, silvery-grey herring lay piled on top of one another, round blank eyes staring up at her, their scales shining in the cold December sunshine. Despite taking a practical view of fishery and farming, she still shuddered at the sight of so much death. On the other hand, people were *desperate* for protein. The longer the war went on and the tighter rationing restrictions grew, the less meat and fish were available to eat. Being able to put fresh food on the table to keep people's strength and spirits up was so important, she couldn't afford to be squeamish about how that food was provided.

'Was it a good catch, would you say?' she asked John, who was helping his father shovel more fish into a fresh crate.

'Not too bad. Though it could have been larger.' He glanced at his father, who seemed tired, with hunched shoulders and dark shadows under his eyes. 'How was the trip, Pa? We didn't expect to see you for a few more days. Did the fish dry up?'

'No, the herring were plentiful and eager for the net.' John's father straightened and scratched his head, looking glum. 'We were turned back, that's what happened. Us and a few others too. By the coast guard.'

'What?' John looked thunderstruck.

'German submarines been sighted in the area, they said. So they told us to turn back to harbour before the job were half done,' he said in a low voice, glancing over his shoulder as though to check he was not being overheard. But the man in the rubber apron was busy securing the crates in his van, and the other fishermen along the quayside were equally occupied, swabbing down their decks or discharging their own haul of fish. 'We didn't want to mess with no German subs, so your grandpa and I came back, like we was told.' He shrugged. 'Maybe we'll head out again early spring. So long as there ain't no storms a-brewing.'

'My arm's good as new now. I'll come out with you next time. Grandpa can stay home for a rest.' John gave a whistle under his breath, glancing out to sea. 'But German submarines? That's not good.'

'No, it ain't. But don't you go spreading that about the town, boy. We was told special to keep it mum.' His father laid a finger across his lips. 'Under our hats, so to speak. No sense worriting people for no good cause.'

'I won't say a word,' John agreed.

The fisherman looked at her and Penny hurriedly shook her head. 'Me neither,' she assured him. 'But how frightening for you both. I think you're awfully brave, Mr Pascoe, to be going out on the sea when we're at war.'

'Brave?' John's dad gave a chuckle, slapping his son on the back. 'I like this new girl of yours, John. She's got a sense of humour, eh? But come along, best stop gabbing and get the rest of this fish unloaded. I'm ready for my bath, I tell you now.'

The two men fell back to work, shovelling the bright silvery bodies of fish into crates. Penny, feeling a bit out of place, watched them for a few minutes and then wandered to the side of the boat, careful not to get tangled in their piled-up nettings or coils of rope. She stared down into the greeny-blue water of the harbour. There was a little oil floating in spirals on the surface of the water as the tide ebbed and flowed around them, the boat swaying to the same rhythm. The timbers creaked gently and the smell of salt was everywhere.

She wondered what it would feel like to be out on the open sea in the *Mary Jane*, the wind in her hair and the rolling swell of the ocean below them. Maybe one day she might be offered a chance to find out . . .

Despite this amusing thought, she was feeling a bit off-balance. Not because of the dancing boat, or the thought of those German submarines, cutting invisibly through the black deep off the Cornish coast. Everyone knew the Germans to be out there somewhere, far beneath the surface, hunting for boats to sink or maybe waiting to support a landing invasion force. That was an old fear and one that no longer kept her awake at night. No, this odd feeling in her tummy was something different.

Your new girl, John.

What on earth had he meant by that? *New girl*? That suggested there had been a *previous* girl. Who could he be talking about?

John appeared by her side. 'How's about I give you a quick tour of the boat while Pa finishes up that last crate of fish? He don't need me no more.' He took her hand. 'You've never been on a fishing boat before, have you?'

She shook her head, smiling. 'I'd like that, thank you. Show me your *Mary Jane*.'

It wasn't a large craft, and she imagined it must be quite a squeeze when there were three men aboard. There was a little wheelhouse, where the fishermen could keep dry and warm while steering the ship on a cold stormy night. And there was a hatch with wooden steps leading down into the sleeping quarters.

John helped her down these creaking steps, laughing every time she squealed and gripped the rails when the boat moved unexpectedly. 'A boat's like a horse, Penny. You can't expect her to stay still the whole time. Just go with it and ride her. It becomes second nature after a while.'

From above, they heard footsteps crossing the deck, no doubt John's dad climbing the ladder to hand over another crate of fish to the man on the quay. The boat dipped and ducked again at this small exchange of weight, and she gave a little cry, staggering sideways.

Thankfully, John was right beside her and caught her before she could bang her head on the wall cupboard. 'Careful there,' he said softly and pulled her towards him.

She did not resist though felt shy with his arm about her waist, aware that they were completely alone. Hurriedly, she examined the cabin, avoiding his interested gaze. There were two double bunks, set into the wall. Room for four men if needed, though only two were made up with blankets and a bolster pillow. There was barely any room to stand between them.

He saw her eyeing the bunks dubiously, for they were short and narrow and looked decidedly uncomfortable. 'It can be a bit of a squeeze down here,' he admitted. 'And one time Pa fell out of the top bunk in a storm and broke his collarbone. But it ain't a bad life.'

'Rather you than me.' She hadn't enjoyed being taken unawares by the boat moving while still in harbour. 'Especially when this boat – I mean, the *Mary Jane* – keeps going up and down.'

'She goes up and down a mite more when we're at sea,' he said, laughing.

'Ugh.' The small fishing boat had steadied – his father must have stopped climbing up and down the ladder onto the quay – but Penny was still horrified by the thought of being tossed about in a violent storm. 'You're amazing for doing this job, John. And we certainly need the fish as a nation, with Germany blowing up all our supply ships. But I couldn't do it.'

'Well, that's not surprising.' John gave her a wink. 'You're a girl, for starters.'

'I'm glad you've noticed.'

'Aye, but you weren't bred to it neither,' he pointed out kindly. 'You're not from fishing folk.'

'True. My father's an accountant,' she admitted, a little awkwardly for she had never talked to him about her family before. Her home life all seemed so far away and almost unreal, that old life she had lived before the war. 'A bit dull compared to a life at sea.'

'I don't mind dull.' To her surprise, his hands framed her face and slowly, his gaze locked on hers, he bent his head and kissed her.

It was very different from when he'd kissed her before, the evening after they'd been to the pictures together. That kiss had been quick and friendly, and although it had left her surprised and pleased, it had not made her dizzy. This kiss did.

She clung onto his shoulders and closed her eyes, and thought a hundred things all at once, none of them making much sense. But oh goodness, he was a good kisser. Not that she had any experience whatsoever at kissing. He was her first boyfriend, if she could call him that yet. But she felt sure, having heard the other girls at the farm talk about bad kissers, that she would know if he was no good. As the kiss went on, heat crept into her cheeks and she became a little breathless.

At last, he released her and she stared mistily into his eyes, unable to say a word.

'Ah, you're a wonder, Penny,' he told her.

'Am I?' Her hands were still on his shoulders. She let him go, awkward now the kiss was over. 'Why am I a wonder?'

'You just are.' John was studying her, a troubled expression in his eyes. Perhaps she wasn't a good kisser. He'd probably kissed dozens of girls and had a fair idea of how it should be done. While she was a complete novice.

A thumping on the roof of the cabin jerked her out of her reverie. His dad shouted through the timbers, 'I know what's going on down there, you two lovebirds.' His laughter rang out. 'Come up here, John, and lend a hand. I'm ready to go ashore.'

Mortified, Penny hurried back to the steps without a word and climbed out with John close behind her. She was too embarrassed to look his father in the eye. *Lovebirds*, indeed.

'Well, I should be going too,' she said, hot-cheeked. 'Thank you very much for the tour of the *Mary Jane*,' she added, and turned to shake John's hand, as formally as though they had been perfect strangers.

But John pulled her close instead, planting a kiss on her cheek. 'Wait, and I'll walk you home when we're done securing the boat.' It was a Saturday afternoon and she was not working that day. 'Or into town, if you like.'

Flustered, she agreed and climbed carefully up the iron

ladder onto the sunny quayside to wait for him. There were two small children playing jacks a short distance away, and she wandered along to watch them, lost in her own thoughts. Should she get so serious with John when she was still so young and inexperienced? A kiss or two didn't matter much. But there'd been something more in his eyes back there . . . And what had he meant by calling her a 'wonder'?

The sun was warm on her face but the wind off the sea that lifted her hair was chilly, reminding her that Christmas was only a few days away. She expected it would be a small group at the boarding house sitting down to Christmas lunch together. Probably just her, Alice, Florence and her sister Imogen, and little Billy.

She didn't mind a quiet Christmas celebration. But the last few Christmases, spent at Postbridge Farm with the other Land Girls, had been noisy, fun affairs with impromptu songs and dancing around the table. Her landlady was a perfectly nice woman, but she doubted that Florence went in for singing and dancing, even at Christmas. And there was an odd tension between her and her sister Imogen, who had appeared out of nowhere and now seemed to be living with them permanently. Penny wasn't sure she liked Imogen much. But she didn't really know the woman, so was giving her the benefit of the doubt.

Hearing voices at her back, she turned to see John and his father on the quayside, checking the ropes were secure on the *Mary Jane*.

To her surprise, a young woman approached John and gave him a peck on the cheek. Far from rebuffing her, John grinned and fell into an easy conversation with her.

Penny stared, wide-eyed and astonished.

The girl had curly red hair, cut dramatically short, with a green beret pressed down on her curls and a pretty matching cardigan. She was petite too, her head barely reaching John's chin. The folds of her dark skirt flapped about her knees in the sea breeze and she wore ankle boots that showed off shapely calves.

Penny started towards them, feeling a little indignant. Then her steps faltered and she stopped. What right did she have to demand this girl's name and her business? John and she didn't have an understanding, as such. They only saw each other occasionally, and even though they had kissed – twice now – nothing had been said formally about them being boyfriend and girlfriend.

Blood pounding in her ears, she dimly recalled John's father saying something about *this new girl of yours*. Her eyes narrowed on the girl's face as John, his father and the newcomer turned and began to stroll towards her.

Was this his *previous* girlfriend?

'Hello,' the redhead said on coming face to face with her. 'I'm Daphne. You must be Penny. The one who used to be a Land Girl. John's mother told me all about you.' The girl stuck out a hand and they shook hands. 'I can see why you'd make a good Land Girl,' she added, looking Penny up and down. 'Big, strapping, and strong enough to drag a bull around by his nose ring, I daresay.' And she laughed merrily, as though this were a great joke.

Astonished, Penny did not know how to respond to this unexpected mockery. Always a little sensitive about her weight, she realised the other girl must be trying to make her feel unattractive, though she had no idea why if Daphne

215

and John were no longer a couple. But she'd been brought up to be polite, no matter the provocation, so she kept smiling and said, 'Hello,' in return, but couldn't resist adding lightly, '*Daphne*, did you say?' and wrinkled her nose as though puzzled. 'Funny, that . . . John's never mentioned you to me. But it's nice to meet you.'

Daphne glared at her, no longer laughing.

'Oh, I clean forgot . . .' Penny glanced at John, who was looking uncomfortable and unsure how to react. 'There's an urgent chore I need to run in town. I'd better hurry. Thanks for showing me around the *Mary Jane*. See you another time, perhaps?'

Without waiting for a response, she strode away along the quay towards town, head held high.

Behind her, she heard John calling her name but she didn't stop or turn around. Not least because she had tears in her eyes, a little shaken up after her uncharacteristic cattiness towards the other girl. She didn't feel guilty though, only angry. She hadn't started that spat, and the 'big, strapping' remark still rankled.

John hadn't stepped in to defend her, she recalled. In fact, he hadn't said a single blasted word throughout that awkward encounter.

Constantly replaying the scene in her head and wishing she had not said what she'd said or had been more measured in her response, Penny began to wonder why John had remained silent. Had he been too embarrassed to get involved or had he secretly been siding with the other girl? Either way, she had not felt supported by him in that moment.

An angry sense of hurt continued to simmer inside her

as Penny tried to decide what best to do. Before today, she had considered herself attracted to John but still undecided about him. They came from very different backgrounds, after all, and his mother hadn't been exactly friendly towards her, which suggested there might be trouble if the relationship turned serious later on.

But the truth was, John seemed to be the one who was undecided, maybe because he had other options he hadn't mentioned. Like Daphne . . .

That possibility cut deep in a way that took her by surprise. Perhaps she'd grown more attached to John than she'd realised, and a clean break was the only thing that could save her from looking like a fool.

CHAPTER EIGHTEEN

Sitting in the small back room reserved for staff, Florence cuddled her son on her lap. Billy was squirming and giggling as she tickled him, which he loved. After playing together in the backyard, she had brought him inside out of the cold. He ought to have gone upstairs for a nap, but today she had wanted to spend a little extra time with him, as that was often when she felt happiest, just sitting with her son and enjoying being his mother. So she had drawn him onto her knee and told him another story about Prince Billy. This one had involved a golden ball and a land overrun by fire-breathing dragons which the young prince was destined to defeat.

Billy had listened to this story with shining eyes, but then asked, 'Tell story about Spitfires!' He'd made the noise of a plane engine roaring through the sky. 'Rrrr . . . Spitfires!'

At first, she'd felt inadequate to the task, not knowing much about fighter planes and worrying that it was a bit bloodthirsty for such a small child. But she'd done her best, craftily incorporating Spitfires into the fairy story she had already told him, so that the young prince grew up to be a fighter pilot and took on the dragons in his glorious flying machine.

Billy had seemed much excited by this twist in the tale, and after she'd finished the story, had demanded to be tickled. Grinning, she turned her fingers into spidery claws, ran them up his sides, and tickled her son while he squirmed on her knee, both of them laughing . . .

Their chuckles and giggles were interrupted by Imogen barging into the room. 'There you are at last!' Imogen was flushed and agitated. 'I've been hunting for you high and low.'

Florence stopped tickling Billy, alarmed. 'Whatever for?'

'That Sergeant Miller you're so friendly with . . . He came back early from the beach and was asking for you, maybe twenty minutes ago? He'd looked in the kitchen and dining room, but you weren't there, and he had some work to do, so asked me to pass on the message. Only I was busy at first, writing my journal, and then I couldn't find you either . . .' Her sister was breathless, an irritable note in her voice. 'I swear I checked in here ten minutes ago and the room was empty.'

'Yes, Billy and I were outside in the backyard, planting up bulbs in one of the flower beds. Well, I was planting bulbs and Billy was digging a hole.'

'To 'Stralia!' Billy embellished triumphantly. He'd been using an old wooden spoon to make holes in the soil, since her trowel was too heavy for him. When she'd told him about the sunny continent on the other side of the world, whose brave soldiers were their long-term allies in the fight against Germany, he had not unnaturally tried to dig a tunnel there . . .

'*Australia*?' Imogen raised her brows, glancing at him. 'You'd have to dig a pretty big hole to reach the other side of the world.'

'Big hole,' Billy repeated, nodding earnestly.

'Billy, why don't you play with your toys before nap time?' Reluctantly, Florence set her son on his feet and watched as he tottered away to the open toy chest, making a beeline for his train as usual. 'The sergeant wants to . . . to speak to me, did you say?' she asked her sister, getting to her feet. 'I wonder why.'

Suddenly nervous, she smoothed her hair with an automatic hand, recalling how windy it had been in the garden earlier. Had she checked her reflection on coming back inside? Probably not, which meant her hair must look a fright. Or at least in need of a good combing . . .

'He didn't say. Though I got the impression it was urgent.'

'Goodness me. Well, thank you for letting me know.' Florence removed her tatty but comfortable shawl and shook out the creases in her skirt, trying to conceal how flustered she felt. 'In that case, I'd better go and find him. Are you free to watch Billy for me? I'll only be a few minutes.'

Imogen sighed. 'I suppose so.' But she was already smiling as she knelt beside her nephew and began asking about his train. Her sister had a surprising affinity for children, Florence thought, considering her more autocratic behaviour with adults. But perhaps that was because they didn't mind her abrupt manners quite so much.

When Florence went hesitantly up the stairs and

knocked on Miles's bedroom door, there was no answer. Hurriedly, she slipped into her own room to tidy her appearance before going back downstairs in search of him, eventually finding the sergeant seated on the bench in the front garden, where he was studying a book in failing sunlight. He seemed to fit a natural setting better than the boarding house rooms, somehow at one with the elements. Which made sense, since from the way he'd talked about Texas once or twice, it sounded as though he'd led quite an active, outdoor life before the war. The sea winds kept snatching at the pages of his book but he didn't seem to mind, head bent, still reading intently . . .

'Sergeant?' she said awkwardly, and his head jerked around at her voice. Seeing her there, he closed the book and jumped to his feet. Her nerves jangled as she closed the front door and took a few steps towards him, her whole body on edge. 'You . . . You wanted to speak to me?' she asked, not quite able to meet his gaze.

'I hope so, ma'am. I'm sorry to be dragging you away from your work,' Miles said with his usual politeness, 'but I need to ask you a question.'

'A question? That sounds serious.' Her heart sank, though she didn't really know why. Perhaps she had hoped it would be a personal matter rather than something relating to the boarding house. But she was just being foolish, allowing her silly thoughts about him to become more than mere daydreams. 'Well, I'm here now. So you'd better ask it.'

Miles tucked his book under one arm and drew off his cap, folding it between his hands. He was wearing full uniform, as usual, and looked devastatingly handsome and

221

brave. Which were definitely *not* thoughts she ought to be having about one of her own guests, she told herself sternly. Talk about unprofessional!

'Feel free to say no, ma'am,' he began awkwardly, 'and perhaps I shouldn't even be asking, but there's a dance in town tomorrow night.' He paused and she could only stare at him, her eyes widening, as she wondered what on earth was coming next. Surely he wasn't going to ask her to . . . ? 'I know this is short notice, but would you like to accompany me there?'

But yes, he was going to ask that.

Oh Lord.

Florence couldn't breathe properly, her chest felt so tight. Of all the questions he might have asked, a date had not been something she'd considered. She blinked, opening her mouth to say, *No, thank you, that's out of the question.* But then closed it again on the radical thought, *why not?*

'Tomorrow night?' she echoed in a faint voice, thinking rapidly. 'Christmas Eve?'

'That's right. It's a Christmas dance for the officers. There'll be entertainment laid on, with dancing too, and you'd be coming as my special guest.' Miles waited, watching her earnestly. 'If you were to say yes, that is.'

She was blushing, she realised. Her eyes met his and a thrill ran through her. She should say no, of course. She was a widow and a mother, for goodness' sake. And he was a soldier, bound for the front line. They both knew the odds were against him coming back alive. And if by some miracle he did survive the onslaught, it was unlikely he would travel all the way back to this quiet corner of Cornwall after the war. He was an American, not an

Englishman, and he would quite rightly be returning to his own shores once it was all over.

So, this was a moment in time, not the start of something serious between them. Not a forever thing, like her love for Percy. She could seize it or let it go. But if she chose the latter, would she spend the rest of her life eaten up with regret and wondering, *what if?*

Dizzily, from a great distance, she heard herself say, 'Yes, thank you, Sergeant Miller. I would very much like to go to the dance with you.'

A light came into his face, which she recognised as happiness, for she was experiencing the same burst of happiness inside herself.

No, happiness was too ordinary a word. It was joy she was feeling, a joy that would not be denied. Not even because she was a widow and a mother, and a woman who ought to know better. Just for this one special moment in time, she refused to conform to traditions or to know better. She wanted joy in her life even if it could only be for the briefest of times.

'That's dandy,' he said with obvious relief, replacing his cap on his head. 'I'll pick you up at seven tomorrow, then,' he added, and, moving past her, held open the front door. 'I'd better let you get back to your work.'

She dared not meet his eyes or pass too close, for fear the hot spark within her would blaze into a full-blown fire and begin raging out of control. Instead, murmuring something indistinct, Florence followed him inside and watched silently as he walked upstairs, the book still under his arm. All the same, even without words, something had shifted between them . . .

He was actually whistling, she realised, his shoulders back, his gait relaxed.

Why? Because she'd said yes and now they were going on a date together? It hardly seemed possible that such a small thing could change a person *physically*. Yet she felt a similar shift inside herself too. A slow relaxation of muscles and sinews that had been tensed for years . . . She had said yes to Sergeant Miller and she didn't regret it. And goodness, it had been so long since she'd thrown off her apron and workaday clothes and dressed up for *a dance*.

It was like something out of that old fairy tale, the one about Cinderella and Prince Charming . . .

She knew again that deep moment of inner joy and wondered if Miles was feeling something akin to that too. Or was that expecting too much? Perhaps it was enough to feel happy and content in the moment, to be looking forward to a few pleasant hours at the Christmas dance, and to let all other considerations go . . .

Some people might disapprove – she knew that. But she steadfastly refused to feel bad about saying yes. The world was in ruins, she reminded herself, and this single moment of happiness had presented itself like a miracle. Besides, her mind was already busy with vexed questions, such as who would look after Billy while she was out, what she would wear to the dance, and whether her best dancing shoes would still fit?

Finding Imogen looking restless and bored in the snug, she said quickly, 'Thank you for looking after him,' and allowed her sister to hurry away without mentioning the dance to her. She needed to check it was all right with

Billy first before admitting to her sister that she had accepted a date. Because if her son was unhappy about it, she couldn't possibly be happy either and would have to tell Sergeant Miller it was all off.

Crouching down beside Billy, who looked up at her in surprise, she asked, her fingers crossed on both hands, 'Will you mind terribly, darling, if Mummy goes out tomorrow evening? I'm sure Aunty Imogen will sit with you. Or maybe Charlotte.' She gave her son a tentative smile. 'It would be after your bedtime and only for a few hours, I promise. In fact, I daresay you won't even notice I'm not here.'

Billy frowned as he considered this unusual request. Then he held up his hands and she drew him swiftly into her arms. 'Aunty Migen,' he said firmly, unable to say Imogen correctly.

Relief flooded her at this easy acceptance. 'You like Aunty Imogen, don't you?' The boy liked her sister's sparky nature and her way of chuckling and playing wild games with him. Florence began to allow herself to feel more excited . . . She *would* be going to the ball, it seemed. 'I'll ask if she's free to look after you.'

Satisfied with this, he returned to his toys. 'Choo choo!' Billy chanted, running his toy train along the edge of the rug. 'Choo choo!'

The following evening, Miles came to collect her just after six o'clock as arranged. The sergeant gave a low whistle as she came along the hall in her best frock and heels, a jacket around her shoulders to ward off the cold, with a shawl on top.

'Shall we go?' he murmured, and she blushed, taking the arm he held out to her.

The town was shrouded in darkness, for it was gone curfew and any lights that might have shown in the houses had been blacked out to avoid providing a target for enemy bombers. They walked along the road together, her hand resting on his arm, with Florence hoping to goodness that she wouldn't trip over anything in the dark – though she knew Miles would catch her in a heartbeat if she did. It was a warm, comfortable thought, accompanied by a sense of security she hadn't felt in a long, long time.

'Was that your friend Charlotte I saw earlier,' he asked politely, 'collecting Billy?'

'Yes, she's a gem.' Florence bit her lip. 'I did ask my sister if she could look after him, but, well, she's going to the dance herself.' In fact, Imogen had only left the house ten minutes earlier, also on the arm of a charming young officer. She didn't know where Imogen had met him and would have liked to ask Miles what kind of man he was, but she hadn't caught the officer's name, so her curiosity would have to wait. 'I'll be picking Billy up in the morning, since I wasn't sure how late the dance would run and it wouldn't be fair to ask Charlotte to wait up for hours.'

Because of this, she was determined to keep a clear head and not drink too much, however tempting it might be to let her hair down for once, in case it led to her sleeping in. Besides, she wouldn't want to give rise to any local gossip by getting tipsy in public.

Bad enough that she was attending this dance with one of her own lodgers – that was enough to set tongues wagging in a rural backwater like Bude – but to stagger home the worse for the drink, in full sight of any neighbours who just 'happened' to be watching, would mark her out as a Fallen Woman. It was a frustrating fact in this day and age, but while Imogen would be given some leeway as a single woman, widowhood was still considered sacrosanct by some of the older ladies on Downs View Road.

Especially perhaps Doreen, for the old lady was already in a bad mood with them following that uncomfortable argument the other day.

But she had decided to put all that old-fashioned nonsense aside and simply follow her instincts. Percy wouldn't have expected her to spend the rest of her life in mourning. He had been a good man and a gentle, loving husband. If he were here to see her walking out with an American officer, he would probably have told her, 'Have a wonderful time, Flo. Kick up your heels, my darling, and enjoy your life.'

'What's your poison, by the way?' Miles asked, interrupting her thoughts.

'I'm sorry?'

'What do you like to drink?' He smiled at her sideways, his face a glimmer in the evening gloom. 'You never join us in the evenings, so I haven't had a chance to find out.'

Most evenings, much to the annoyance of some citizens, the soldiers' billets came alive, filling Bude with music and laughter. 'Making a damn ruckus,' the butcher had muttered under his breath the other day when another customer in the queue had complained about noisy gramophones late at night. 'But we've got to be grateful to them, I suppose.'

'The Americans won't be here long, dear,' his wife had

soothed him, arranging a new window display of cuts of meat, though the produce all looked rather meagre compared to its pre-war glory. 'Gone by spring, they say.'

Spring? It was already Christmas, Florence had thought, her heart aching for all the fresh-faced young soldiers she passed in the street when out shopping or visiting Charlotte. Billy always saluted them, shouting, 'Ten'tion!' and the young men would salute back at him, grinning. One day, the town would wake up as usual and they would all be gone, she'd realised, suddenly listless and unhappy. Gone where, though?

'Oh, a glass of wine will be fine,' she told Miles. 'Or whatever's on offer. I know rationing is so tight these days. Though perhaps you brought your own supplies over from the States?'

'Something like that.'

'You seem incredibly well organised, I have to say.' She hesitated. 'By the way, have you heard yet how long the Rangers will be staying in Bude?'

He said nothing for a moment, and then said in cautious tones, 'Let's not talk about the Rangers or the war tonight. Do you mind?'

'I'm sorry.'

'No need to apologise, ma'am,' he told her firmly. 'The thing is, it's a dance. And a Christmas dance at that. A time for us to forget all that nonsense and simply have fun.'

'Of course, quite right.'

'The troops have their own celebrations in a few days,' he told her, 'in case you think only officers get to dance in this unit.' She couldn't see him smiling, but she could hear the humour in his deep, rich voice. 'But the officers have to oversee their celebrations, so we can't host both on the same night.'

'And who oversees the officers?' she couldn't help asking, a little mischievously.

He gave a chuckle. 'I guess we'll have to keep ourselves in check,' he admitted, and glanced her way. 'I only hope that won't be too difficult.'

Another joke.

Dutifully, she laughed. But she felt a frisson of excitement at the way his gaze moved over her, and her breathing quickened. She had dragged out her highest pair of heels from a box under the bed, which she had often worn before falling pregnant with Billy, and these were forcing her to walk slow and steady, back straight, toes pointed. And the unaccustomed feel of the only silk stockings she owned, and which she had carefully resurrected from her bottom drawer, against her skin was a constant reminder of her femininity. She had not felt *feminine* in such a long time. Not like this, at any rate, all her senses fully alive and prickling, nerves alert to his proximity, her hip occasionally brushing his as they walked.

'You can't keep calling me ma'am,' she pointed out. 'Not when we're going to a dance together.'

'You prefer Mrs Pritchard?'

'I prefer Florence.'

'Florence it is, then.' Reaching the outskirts of town, he slowed and helped her to cross the street, for it would have been easy to turn an ankle in heels in the darkness.

They went down Belle Vue until they reached the Grenville Hotel. That was where the officers were being housed. From outside, it seemed to be in darkness, for the blackout was being rigorously observed. But as soon as they passed through this shielded doorway, they found themselves in the hotel lobby, where officers with ladies on their arms were chatting to each other and enjoying drinks before the main event of the evening, which was to be the dancing. Through the double doors into the dance room, Florence could see the band setting up, ready to play, some of the men already tuning their instruments. She recognised a musician friend, a grey-haired woman sitting with her violin tucked under her chin, and gave her a merry wave.

'Hello, Flo,' an excited voice said in her ear, and she turned, startled, to see her sister Imogen standing behind her, a vision of loveliness in a deep blue dress that nipped in at her waist and flared over her hips, cinched with a broad scarlet belt that matched her lipstick. 'Isn't this divine? All these officers . . .' Her eyes were dancing with excitement.

'Yes, they're wonderful,' Florence replied, and then threw a glance towards Miles. 'You're an officer. Aren't you eligible to live here with the others?'

'I was invited, yes, but I declined. Someone needs to be on the ground, to keep an eye on what's going on down among the men.' He hesitated, and then added, 'Besides, I'm happy where I am at Ocean View. You run a comfortable house, if you don't mind me saying so.'

She blushed.

Behind her, Imogen turned impatiently to the young man who was escorting her. 'When will the dancing begin, do you think? I'm longing to dance. It's been ages . . . My feet are tapping already.'

A young man came past with a tray of drinks, and Miles deftly provided them all with a glass of bubbly. It was unlikely to be French Champagne, Florence thought, sipping it thoughtfully, as that was impossible to get hold of these days. But it was fizzy and pleasantly cold.

'Enjoy that glass while it lasts,' Miles murmured, watching her. 'It'll be light beer after this. Soldiers' rations.'

People were already being ushered into the hall, so they followed the crowd, glasses in hand. One of the senior officers stood on a raised platform at one end of the long room to address them all. 'Tonight, we celebrate Christmas Eve. And I want to thank the good people of Bude for having taken us into their homes and their hearts this Christmas.' There was a roar of approval from the listening men. 'Let us drink a toast to the good men of the Second Ranger Battalion and to our commander in chief, Colonel James Earl Rudder who will lead us to victory . . . just as soon as we're given the nod.' More cheering and applause. 'We've been training long and hard, and we're ready, more than ready, and I know we'll do our country proud in this fight.' He raised his glass high. 'America the Brave!'

'America the Brave!' The toast was repeated in a triumphant shout around the room, and then everyone drank.

Nodding to the band leader, the officer said, 'Now, let's have music and dancing. I expect to see every Ranger on the floor tonight, showing these beautiful ladies from Bude exactly how well we Americans do *everything*, including dance.'

To a burst of laughter, the band began to play a jaunty tune. Groups of couples began to congregate on the dance floor, young men in uniform, young women in party frocks, the room soon a swirl of bright colour and movement.

Miles drained his glass, and then looked into Florence's eyes. 'Shall we?'

'I'd be delighted.' She took his hand, smiling, but almost gasped when he whirled her onto the dance floor, an arm snug about her waist as though they would be waltzing, his gaze locked with hers. 'Oh goodness.'

As the music changed tempo, faster and more snappy, Miles spun her around like a top before catching her again, dancing with her in the jaunty new American style.

Florence was breathless and exhilarated, following his lead as he showed her all the new dance moves that he and the other young officers seemed to know off by heart. She had feared dancing in high heels again after so long wearing flats, but in fact she was so swept away by the insistent beat of the music, she quite forgot she was wearing heels at all. Out of the corner of her eye, she spotted her sister dancing fast and furiously with one man, only to be claimed by another officer, who spun her away, both men laughing uproariously. Imogen didn't seem to mind swapping partners, clearly enjoying herself. Florence felt a little concern, watching her sister, but had to admit that it was lovely to see Imogen in such high spirits. She only hoped there would not be a price to pay for her exuberance.

Miles noticed her gaze and said reassuringly in her ear, 'There's no harm in it. They're both solid young officers and won't take advantage of her. But I can go over there and make sure of it, if you like.'

Florence immediately felt guilty. 'That's very kind of

you, Miles, but no thank you. I'm not Imogen's jailer. Besides, she's a grown woman. She knows her own mind.'

'That she surely does,' he agreed wryly.

The dancing went on for what felt like forever. Florence could not remember when she had last enjoyed herself so much. But eventually she became tired, and stumbled once or twice. Miles, an arm about her waist, said with a grin, 'Time for a breather, perhaps? There's a quiet place I know.'

Her head still whirling, she went with him into the corridor, and it was only once they were alone together in a darkened side room that she realised she ought to have refused.

'Hey, don't look so scared,' he said, checking the blackout curtain before switching on a table lamp. It was a small library with armchairs and a pool table. He came back to her. 'You just looked like you needed some time out.' His long finger brushed her cheek. 'You're flushed.'

She said nothing, staring up at him.

'We'll go back in a minute,' he added, 'and I'll fetch you another drink. How about it?'

Florence nodded silently.

'Maybe I'm out of order,' he said, taking both her hands, 'but I can't help noticing how you're always looking out for other people . . . Alice and Penny, your sister Imogen, those young Rangers you chat to every day on their way in and out of the house. You don't just make their beds and tidy their rooms. You ask questions and you listen to their answers, and you take all their troubles on yourself. You *care*.' He shook his head when she protested. 'I've seen it with my own eyes, Florence, especially with those two young women. You're like a second mother to them. And

I'm not saying you shouldn't do it, because I've seen how you love to *connect* with people. But sometimes you need to let them make their own mistakes.' He paused. 'Like Imogen, for example.'

'You think I'm interfering with her life?' she whispered.

'I think you need someone to look after you for a change. Someone who'll be the strong one, so you don't need to,' he said, adding softly, 'Someone to be your rock.'

Their eyes met, then Miles bent his head and kissed her. The kiss itself only lasted a few seconds. But, as soon as their lips touched, Florence knew it was ridiculous to keep pushing away her feelings. She had thought this a passing infatuation but she needed to stop pretending. She had fallen deeply in love with her American Ranger. And he was going to leave for the front soon and break her heart forever.

CHAPTER NINETEEN

To her relief and astonishment, Alice was not thrown off the training course for having punched Sophy in the nose. After the ruckus had died down, she was openly berated and made to apologise to Sophy, who was still weeping and glaring at her balefully. But nothing worse. It had been deeply unfair but Alice didn't bother complaining.

However, a few days after that, Rawlings caught Alice's arm at the end of a training session, holding her back from leaving. 'I'd like a word with you. Away from here. Come on, get your coat.'

He took her to a quiet side-street café, ushering her to a small corner table where he removed his stylish fedora, smoothed back his hair, and ordered them both a round of tea and cakes.

'You're a handful, Alice,' he said, 'and no mistake. But I think you could make a useful operative in time and with proper handling.' He saw the excitement in her eyes and shook his head, smiling. 'However, you're not there yet, and maybe you never will be. So don't get your hopes up. I need you to stop messing about with these petty squabbles and focus on your training.'

Their tea arrived on a tray and they waited in silence until the waitress had laid out the teapot and cups and saucers and bustled away again.

Then Alice leant forward. 'Sophy started that bloomin' squabble, not me,' she whispered crossly.

'*Focus.*' He glanced at the teapot. 'You can be Mother.'

'Hmm.' Alice poured them both a cup of tea through the strainer, added a dash of milk, took a long refreshing slurp, ignoring his raised eyebrows, and then tried again without the cross tone. 'All right. I shouldn't 'a done it. I lost me 'ead. How's that?'

'Much better,' he said approvingly. 'But in future, you're going to *keep* your head. Whatever the provocation. Is that clear?'

Alice eyed the plate of cakes that had appeared on the table while he was speaking. 'Yes, sir.' It took all her willpower not to grab one of the dainty pink sponge cakes and stuff it into her mouth, she was so famished, having skipped lunch that day in order to take some books back to the library and check a few new ones out. She couldn't drop off to sleep without at least one novel on the go, kept at her bedside.

Spotting her hungry stare, Rawlings laughed. 'Go ahead, take one. Take two, in fact. They're for you, not me.'

While she crammed in sponge cake and swigged tea thirstily, her instructor took a good half hour to remind her why she'd wanted to work for the British Secret Service in the first place and how hard she would need to train if that dream was to become a reality. He tore a strip off her for having punched Sophy and made her feel downright rotten. But then he cheered her up again by reminding her that he still had her in mind for a 'special mission' and that she was not going to be thrown off the course as she'd feared.

'Not this time, anyway,' he concluded, with a warning stare. 'But one more incident like that—'

'I'm goin' to keep me nose clean from now on,' Alice insisted, wiping her mouth with a napkin as she'd seen him do earlier. 'Honest, guv.'

Sure enough, shortly before they were given a few days' leave for Christmas, Rawlings took Alice, Patrick and Sophy into the frosty yard, where they stood nervously stamping their feet and swinging their arms to keep warm, wondering what it was all about.

'I hope you enjoy your time off,' Rawlings told the three of them, 'but soon after you come back, you'll be going on a special mission. This mission forms an important part of your training. It will be a challenge and a test, and you'll need all your wits about you.' He paused. 'In particular, you'll need to work as a team, not merely as individuals.'

Alice glanced at the other two, and wished she had not been put in a group with them, given that she'd punched Sophy in the nose not so long ago. But she half suspected this grouping might be part of her punishment.

Rawlings continued smoothly, 'I've put the initial details in this envelope.' He handed them each a small envelope. 'Take this home and study it over the Christmas break, and I want you back here on top form.' He paused. 'Alice, would you stay behind for a moment? I need a quick word.'

When the others had gone, Alice clasped her hands behind her back and stood waiting, unsure what was coming next. Not more tea and cake though, judging by his stern expression.

Rawlings studied her. 'I expect you think I've been unfair, putting you in a group with Sophy.'

'I don't think she likes me very much,' she said candidly. 'Not surprising, given I smacked her in the nose. I still say it was *her* fault, but I daresay she's none too keen on me. Which is fine, as I ain't keen on her neither.'

His lips twitched. 'In my opinion, you were both to blame for what happened.' He saw her raised eyebrows and shook his head. 'I told you, there'll always be times when you need to stay calm and resist turning a disagreement into an all-out brawl. Self-control is incredibly important in this line of work, Alice. You need to understand that and master it, or you might as well go home now. Am I making myself clear?'

'Yes, sir,' she said, resigning herself to another long-winded lecture on discipline and biting her lip so she wouldn't say anything cheeky.

His mouth quirked in a smile. 'Your face is an open book, Alice. You need to work on that too. You'd be no good in a poker game. If there's one skill you desperately need to learn, it's how to conceal what you're thinking.'

Alice tried not to grin.

'Talkin' of open books,' she said, a memory flashing through her head, 'I saw one of the boys' notebooks by accident a while back. It was written in code.'

'Patrick's notebook, by any chance?'

She hadn't named names, not wanting to get any of her fellow trainees in trouble. But it seemed pointless to deny it now. 'That's right,' she agreed in surprise. 'I . . . I didn't know if it was important. Perhaps I shouldn't have said nuffin.'

'No, I'm glad we have that kind of trust. There should be trust between an agent and their handler.'

She blushed, stupidly pleased by the way he'd referred to her as an 'agent' when she was still basically a raw recruit to the service.

'Don't worry about it. Patrick's on a mission of his own. Watching someone for me.'

'Oh,' she said, curious now.

'Need-to-know basis only,' he added, seeing her expression. 'Sorry.'

'Right you are, guv.'

'On a different note, before you go, I have something for you,' he said softly, and handed her a small plain postcard. 'Don't mention it or show it to anyone else though. Not even your family. I'm perfectly serious about that.'

Alice studied the postcard with a frown, turning it over. There was no name and address, no picture on the front of the postcard, and no stamp either. But there was a message on the back.

It read simply, *I'm proud of you. Merry Christmas. x*

She recognised the handwriting at once. It was from her father, Ernest Fisher. *I'm proud of you.* Alice turned the card over in her hand, and then stared at him wonderingly, tears in her eyes. 'Where did you . . . I mean, how on earth . .' Her voice shook.

Rawlings merely smiled, tapped his nose and walked away.

Christmas at Ocean View Boarding House was quiet and peaceful. Florence uncomplainingly cooked the dinner all morning while Penny kept Billy busy and out of the kitchen, and Imogen laid the table. Alice sat on the sofa and flicked through a women's magazine. Meanwhile, Imogen constructed an amazing table centrepiece that would have left even Alice's exacting gran sighing with delight, dressed with glossy ivy leaves, plump red berries, and a few delicate sprigs of mistletoe, all draped over a log.

Imogen brought a surprising liveliness to the gathering, for it had turned out that she loved to sing, and so entertained them all with popular songs, accompanied by Miles humming the tune and tapping the floor, while Florence was preparing the meal. She had a good voice too, singing several Vera Lynn tunes so beautifully it turned Penny's eyes misty, and had even Alice recalling the family she'd left in Porthcurno, for Gran had always loved listening to Vera Lynn on the wireless. Up at the farm, they would be enjoying their Christmas meal without Alice this year, a thought that made her feel homesick again.

It was her first Christmas away from home and she felt it keenly. But at least she had Penny there, one familiar figure from her past, and the two of them joined in with the Vera Lynn choruses, swaying and giggling as they sung together.

Then it was time to sit down to eat, and that was fun too, everyone laughing and sharing stories of how Christmas had been before the war.

Alice had Penny opposite her, Billy on her left side and Imogen on her right. At one end of the table sat Florence, who had whisked off her gravy-stained apron to reveal a pretty, knee-length black dress with a white lace collar, while at the other end Miles was standing to carve the bird. Although the soldiers and officers were all having their own Christmas lunch elsewhere, the sergeant had chosen to eat with them instead. Alice guessed it must have something to do with his liking for Florence, which he was no longer trying to conceal, or not among this small gathering, at any rate. Florence too seemed to be smiling at him more than usual, and in a shy way that reminded her of Aunty Violet and Uncle Joe, back when they were first courting . . .

Imogen, who had also dressed up for Christmas lunch, was scooping sprouts out of the serving dish. 'Before the war, I found Christmas boring,' she remarked, 'always the same old traditions. Now, Christmas feels bright and cheerful, a complete contrast to everything else in this drab old world.'

'Yes,' Penny agreed enthusiastically, dropping a thick blob of chestnut puree onto her plate, 'and I'm looking forward to this glorious feast. Thank you so much, Florence, for cooking it for us.' Penny helped herself to some of the turkey that Miles had been carving silently. 'But how on earth did you get hold of a turkey? A real turkey!'

'I found that wonderful bird lying on my kitchen table yesterday morning, plucked and ready for the oven.' Florence blushed, glancing up at Miles, whose face was impassive. 'I think you'll find the gentleman with the large carving knife in his hand may have pulled some strings for us. Though how he managed it, I still don't know. But I'm eternally grateful. We didn't get turkey last year or the year before. In fact, we had rabbit stew last year. Tasty but chewy. You're not keen on rabbit, Billy, are you?'

But Billy was too busy wrinkling his nose as he chewed on a sprout and then spat it out again. 'Wassat? S'gusting!' he exclaimed.

They all laughed.

Eagerly, Alice tucked into her meal, not caring where the turkey had come from but happy that she had some and it tasted good, especially with thick gravy, something they hadn't enjoyed for a long time. She thought fleetingly again of Gran and Violet and dear Joe, and wished she was back at the farm and could see the evacuees chasing each other around excitedly on Christmas morning. But mostly she was thinking of the special mission and what it might entail.

Last night, she'd opened the envelope that Rawlings had given them and sat reading its contents. Their mission was to locate and follow a certain member of the US Rangers. It sounded awfully exciting. She only hoped the American they would be tailing knew all about their mission and had given permission to be followed.

After lunch, they played Charades together, which was good fun. Alice had often played it at the farm and was good at guessing the names of books and films. They all sang a little more and listened to the wireless too, but when it grew dark, Alice crept away to her room to read a book. It had been a lovely day, but she did miss her family . . .

On Boxing Day afternoon, Florence called up the stairs

to her with a hint of laughter in her voice. 'Alice? You'd better come downstairs.'

It was long past lunch, and Alice had been reading lazily in her room again, enjoying the quiet and solitude of the Christmas holidays. She certainly didn't want to bestir herself for no good reason.

Rather grumpily, she closed her book and went downstairs, only to find herself staring, mouth open, at a grinning Aunt Violet, her sister Lily – looking very pregnant in a large white smock dress – her wonderful gran in a purple knitted hat, Uncle Joe leaning on his stick, and even white-haired old Mr Newton, all of them on the doorstep, beaming at her.

'Merry Christmas, love!' Gran cried in her husky voice, opening her arms wide, and Alice ran into them, sobbing.

They wandered down towards the sea together, going slow for Mr Newton's sake, who leant on her gran's arm the whole way, precariously waving his stick while admiring the view. Just behind them, Alice walked between her uncle and aunt, so glad of their company, she felt like hugging them both again, with Lily to her right. It felt like old times, and yet, there was a slight shock in her heart, seeing her loved ones here in Bude and so unexpectedly.

'How on earth did you manage it?' Alice asked, her voice high-pitched with excitement. 'I thought you couldn't come to see me.'

'I saved up my petrol ration,' Joe told her with a wink. 'It meant fewer trips into Penzance for a good long while but your aunt was determined. You know what she's like when she gets a notion into her head. Stubborner than a mule.'

'Excuse me, Mr Postbridge?' Aunty Violet demanded, arching thin brows at him. In a smart blue dress, she looked healthy and happy, and prettier than Alice had ever seen her. 'What was that you said?'

'Nothing, Mrs Postbridge,' Joe replied placidly. 'Just clearing my throat.'

'So I should think. Mule, indeed.' But Aunty Violet wasn't really cross, giving a little chuckle. She cast Alice a shrewd glance that took her in from head to toe. 'You look thinner than before. Aren't they feeding you properly back there?' She jerked her head back towards the boarding house. 'That the landlady? Mrs Pritchard, was it? Young for a widow. I expected a much older woman.'

Briefly, Alice explained Florence's circumstances, as best she understood them, and touched briefly on the other people in the boarding house, describing as many of the American Rangers as she knew by name. They had called up the stairs for Penny before leaving the house, sure she would want to see the old gang from Postbridge Farm. But there had been no reply and Alice suspected that Penny had gone out for an afternoon stroll as she often did in her spare time, loving the fresh salty air. But it was not a problem, for they could all catch up later.

'Poor lady,' Joe remarked, his brow quirking. 'It can't have been easy for her. Does she have children?'

Joe had been wounded early in the war, losing a leg and having a false one fitted, which was why he now walked with a stick. Soon after, he had lost his beloved mum to a bomb. That bomb had been a horrible mistake, or so folk had speculated; the Germans had been looking for nearby Eastern House, the government listening station, when they'd dropped bombs on the isolated farm instead.

That had been before Joe and Violet got hitched. A nasty rumour had spread about tiny Porthcurno that Violet was to blame for the bombing, being sister-in-law to Alice's German-born dad and possibly an enemy informant, and although Joe had never believed such a dreadful lie, things had become difficult for a while between them. Thankfully, Joe had eventually seen that smear for what it was, and he and Violet had returned to courting in earnest.

'A little boy called Billy,' Alice told them. 'He's three years old and a bit of a rascal.'

'They're all rascals at that age,' Gran called back to them.

'Goodness, Gran,' Lily exclaimed, incredulous, for the older couple were walking several feet ahead, 'you must have ears in the back of your head.' And she and Alice exchanged a laughing look, while Violet and Joe both chuckled under their breath.

'Eyes too, remember,' their gran replied with a mock snap in her voice, 'so watch it, you cheeky lot.'

Alice wasn't fazed. She knew her gran loved them all dearly. Just as she loved the three evacuee children they'd taken on at the farm.

'Talking of rascals,' she said to her aunt and uncle, 'where are Eustace and little Timothy?'

'Lord bless you,' Violet said, laughing. 'How much room do you suppose Joe has in his old van? We left the boys at the farm with their sister Janice to look after them. She's old enough now, and a sensible girl she's turned out to be too, after that wobble she had last year. Besides,' she added practically, 'we'll be driving back after we've sat down for a spot of tea with you, Alice love, for the farm can't be left to run itself.'

'But it'll be dark by then,' Alice gasped.

'Joe can cope. He knows these roads like the back of his hand.'

Uncle Joe nodded. 'Had a friend in Bude before the war. Often drove up here then for a day out.' He sighed. 'He's away fighting somewhere, last I heard.'

Alice glanced at her sister. 'No Tristan? Or wasn't there room in the van for him either?'

She had got to know her sister's husband, Tristan Minear, quite well while she was working in Penzance, where he'd been living on his father's farm with his sister, Demelza. Both the Minears were blessed with huge smiles and a mop of bright, reddish curls that made them instantly recognisable about town. They'd lost their mum at a young age and been brought up on the farm by their dad, an irascible old curmudgeon whom Alice had avoided whenever possible. Farmer Minear had been horrid to Lily, especially after Tristan had returned home from the war badly burnt.

Luckily, on starting work as a midwife in St Ives, Lily had been given a tiny cottage of her own, so when she and Tristan married later that year, they'd had a home to move into. Now she was carrying a baby of her own, and it was clear from her sister's sweet, shining countenance that she was ecstatic about it.

'Tris couldn't be spared from his work with the Fire Service,' Lily admitted, a flash of sorrow in her eyes that was quickly replaced by a smile. 'But he sends his love.

246

And we both hope you'll come to the christening in St Ives, once this one's born.' And she rubbed her rounded bump with affection.

'Don't mention the christening!' Aunty Violet and Gran both cried in unison, and Gran crossed herself, shaking her head in consternation.

'Whyever not?' Alice asked, perplexed.

'It's bad luck,' Violet explained in a low voice, 'given she's not even had the baby yet. In case it jinxes you.'

'These young people,' Gran was complaining to her beau, Mr Newton, their silvery heads bent together. 'They know *nothing* about life.'

'Aye, they're all wet behind the ears,' Mr Newton grumbled in his deep, gravelly voice.

Lily merely smiled and shook her head, unbothered by superstitious fears.

'Anyway,' Violet continued, hugging Alice close, 'I've some amazing news of my own to tell you,' she murmured in her ear.

'*We've* amazing news of *our own* to tell you,' Joe corrected her, shooting his wife a secret smile. 'It takes two, you know.'

'Joseph Postbridge!' Violet exclaimed, scandalised, but then spoilt the effect by giggling. 'We'll have less of that talk, thank you.'

Joe grinned.

'What do you mean? What news, Aunty Vi?' Alice asked, even more mystified and worried in case it was going to mean yet more upheaval.

'There's to be yet another addition to the family,' her aunt told her softly.

'You've not taken on *more* evacuees?'

'For goodness' sake!' her sister chortled. 'Alice Fisher, for an eighteen-year-old, you can be a chump at times.'

'I'll be nineteen soon,' Alice muttered, but nobody was listening.

'Your aunt's expecting a baby,' Joe explained, 'and I couldn't be prouder.'

Alice's heart leapt.

'Early days though,' Violet added hurriedly. 'So it's not common knowledge. But I wanted you to know, love.'

He and Violet exchanged a speaking look that made Alice's toes curl with embarrassment. But she loved seeing it too, for she had missed the love and joyful chaos of life on Joe's farm. And she was ecstatic for them.

'That's marvellous news,' Alice cried, and hugged them both, one after the other. Then she hugged Lily too, for good measure, even though her large tummy got in the way. 'It seems everyone's having babies these days.'

'That's the war for you,' Mr Newton rumbled.

'Now, don't you think about joining 'em, Alice,' Gran warned her, wagging a finger. 'You're scarce out of school.' But she gave Alice, Lily and Violet an indulgent smile. 'Ah, but look at you, all my lovely girls together again. Does my old heart good to see it.' She winked at Alice. 'And you'll come and be my bridesmaid, won't you, love? Once Arnie and I have settled on a date?'

'You want me for a *bridesmaid*?' Alice gulped, her eyes brimming with happy tears. 'Oh, Gran . . . Of course I will.'

'Blimey, that's a relief.' Gran blew out her cheeks. 'Otherwise, I'd ha' lugged your bridesmaid's dress all the way here for nuffin.'

'You did *what*?'

'I brought your frock with me, so we could check how it fits. Can't leave that kind of thing to chance, love. Don't worry, us girls will leave Joe and Arnie downstairs having a cuppa, and nip up to your room for a fitting,' she said, adding with a grin, 'and a bloomin' good chinwag about the wedding, How's that?'

'I'd love that, Gran,' Alice said, so happy inside she could almost have burst with it.

Down on the beach, they could hear the US Rangers training, even though it was Boxing Day. Someone was barking orders in a hoarse military voice, and the sound of firecrackers kept going off, presumably to mimic gunfire. Men in camouflage were just visible scaling the rugged cliff face towards a pillbox-style lookout station they'd built into the rock so the troops could stage assaults on it from the beach below.

'Eh, that looks interesting.' Old Mr Newton began heading that way, dragging Gran along with him. 'Better than all this talk of weddings and babies.'

Laughing, they gave up chatting and followed Mr Newton towards the barrier the Americans had erected across the entrance to the beach, to watch the US Rangers being put through their paces. Beyond the barbed wire and the echo of firecrackers, the vast Atlantic shimmered and rippled in the breeze, a silvery blue with soft, rolling waves.

'Blow me, look at them climb that cliff with just a bit o' rope!' Joe exclaimed, staring. 'Did you ever see anything like it, Arnie?'

'Never in my life,' the old chap admitted, equally impressed.

But much to the men's disappointment, Gran soon insisted they return to the boarding house, explaining to Alice on the way how she and Vi had made the wedding cake between them, with a little help from Arnie in getting an extra packet of dried fruit on the quiet, since their ration books wouldn't stretch to that amount. The cake was maturing in a tin until it was ready to ice, Gran told her, kept moist with the odd spoonful of brandy. 'Though how we'll manage to cover it in royal icing,' she muttered as they reached Ocean View, 'I've no bloomin' idea. That many eggs and that much icing sugar?'

'We'll cope, Mum,' Violet told her calmly. 'Won't we, Joe?'

'Aye, with a little help from our neighbours. We'll have a whip-round in Porthcurno, see who's got any sugar going begging. As for the eggs . . . Well, a few days of extra seed might encourage our best layers to make more of an effort,' Joe chuckled.

'Come on, love,' Gran said, bustling in through the door. 'Which one is your room? I can't wait to see you in this dress. Ran it up myself on the Singer the other week. It'll look smashin' – just wait and see.'

Upstairs, Alice found herself surrounded by the female members of the family – her gran, Aunty Violet and Lily – all crammed into her tiny bedroom, helping her try on the dress she'd be wearing at the wedding. She had gasped on first seeing it – a bright yellow ankle-length frock with a dreadful lace collar and old-fashioned flounces at the hem – and then caught Lily's stern eye and hurriedly turned her gasp into a cry of admiration instead.

'Goodness, it's so . . . yellow.' Alice, though never much

interested in fashion, had cringed inwardly at the thought of being seen in public in such a flouncy dress. 'Though I, erm, love it. Such a cheerful colour.' She fingered the lace frill dubiously. 'Do we really need this?'

'It matches the lace on my wedding dress,' Gran insisted, pulling the frock down over her head. Once it was on, flounces and all, she stepped back to admire the effect. 'Oh now, don't she look a picture, Vi?'

Lily smothered a laugh.

Aunty Violet bit her lip and turned away, rummaging for a hanky, which she used to dab her apparently watering eyes. 'Yes, Mum . . . A picture indeed.' And made a snorting noise, ignoring Alice's pained expression. 'Beautiful.'

'Though it needs taking up a few inches,' Gran said thoughtfully, eyeing the flouncy hem. 'I knew you were tall but I've made it too long now. You'll look like a bloomin' Victorian in that . . . Hand me my bag, would you, Lily? There's pins in there. Now, don't you worry, love,' she told Alice firmly, 'we'll soon fix you up.'

'Thanks, Gran,' Alice said faintly, though in truth she wasn't *too* unhappy, even though the dress was a raging monstrosity and would make her look like a buttercup at the wedding. She had her family around her again and she hadn't laughed so much in weeks. 'Congratulations on the baby, Aunty Vi,' she said. 'And thank you all for coming to visit me. You, Gran, Lily . . . and Joe and Mr Newton too.' She beamed, her eyes growing a little misty. 'This has been the best Christmas present ever.'

CHAPTER TWENTY

On a bright morning soon after the Christmas break, Penny was just on her way out of the boarding house, hoping to take a walk in the sunshine during her day off, when she stopped dead, her heart leaping. John Pascoe was walking down the road towards her, a rucksack on his back and his hands in his pockets, head up, whistling a tune. He looked as though he didn't have a care in the world . . .

The mere sight of him made her glow with happiness, which was ridiculous. The last time she'd seen John, he'd been chatting to a pretty girl on the quayside, Daphne, who'd then made a sly comment to Penny, mocking her weight. Affronted, she'd stalked away from the pair of them without looking back.

Since then, she'd regretted her behaviour and wished she had stayed to talk to John about it. But she'd felt so hurt and frankly *embarrassed* by what the girl had said, she hadn't been able even to look him in the face.

John had come into the dairy shop two days later, stoutly asking to speak to her, but Penny had shaken her head, hurrying into the back room to busy herself with mopping the floor there. The whole episode had still felt too raw for her to talk about it without the danger of bursting into tears, and she didn't want him to see her crying. She knew they hadn't formalised their courting and he was free to see other girls, just as she'd spent some evenings dancing and drinking with the Americans, though it had all been perfectly innocent. But deep down inside, she'd been afraid that he preferred Daphne and wished to tell her that . . .

But he'd been much in her thoughts lately. Alice had terrified her the other day, showing her a government brochure on what to do in the event of an invasion: hiding under the kitchen table, barricading the house with furniture, or arming yourself with garden tools. Seeing John, so strong and confident, strolling towards her now as though he owned the place, pushed those fears of invasion away. It seemed impossible that the Germans could ever gain a foothold in Cornwall, however many submarines and armed men in jackboots and metal helmets they sent, when there were men like John Pascoe here to defend the coast.

She'd written something similar about John in a letter she'd sent to her parents just before Christmas. Though she knew her overprotective father would go spare if he thought she was dating anyone, so she'd cautiously described him as a 'nice local boy I've met'.

She could have gone back inside the boarding house and refused to speak to John. But that would have been cowardly. Instead, she stood her ground until he was at the garden gate, and then said coolly, 'Hello, John,' knitting her fingers together in the warm gloves she was wearing. 'What are you doing here?'

'I would have thought that was obvious. I've come to see you.' John's gaze held hers, and a little thrill ran through her. 'If you want to see me, that is.'

She couldn't help asking, 'Who was she? That girl on the quay, I mean. You seemed on very good terms.'

Goodness, Penny thought, blushing fiercely, she sounded jealous, and she hadn't meant to. She had intended to dismiss him in a disinterested way.

'Just a friend from my school days. If you'd stuck around, I would have introduced you. But you ran off like your house was on fire.' He frowned, digging his hands deeper into his pockets. 'I can't help it if Daphne came up to me and started asking how I was. What was I supposed to do? Chuck her in the harbour?'

'So she means nothing to you?'

'She's a nice enough girl, and we went to school together. But that's all there is to it.' John paused. 'I'm keen on *you* though.' He looked down at his feet, a red tinge to his cheeks. 'Spent all Christmas thinking about you. I even asked my grandpa's advice after you refused to look at me in the shop. He told me to come and speak to you again when you weren't working. He said, sometimes it takes a few goes to catch a fish.'

Penny wanted to laugh but didn't. 'I'm not a fish.'

'I never said you was. It's just another of Grandpa's old sayings.' He took a deep breath. 'So, how about it? Would you like to forget what happened? Or is it over forever? Because if it's over forever, I'll have to eat and drink all the sandwiches and beer in this rucksack, and then I'll probably fall asleep drunk, and my ma won't be too happy with me.'

Penny glanced at the rucksack on his back. 'You packed a picnic?'

'I thought that, if you were free, we could take a walk along the cliffs heading north,' and he jerked his head towards the cliffs to the right side of the bay. They were high and rugged but there was soft grass along the top and a fine view over the sea. Penny had walked there once or twice herself. 'You can see all the way up to Cleave Camp once you get clear of Bude. There's a sheltered spot where we could stop and have our picnic, and then walk back. It's a fine day,' he ended persuasively, 'and if we steer clear of where the Americans are training, we shouldn't run into trouble.'

'I am free and I wouldn't say no to a picnic on the cliffs,' Penny admitted, her heart beating fast. She did like John, and she was sorry that she'd made him uncomfortable after that episode on the harbour. 'I'm dressed for a walk anyway, so shall we go?'

Since the base of the cliff-path was blocked by a wall of barbed wire and sentry posts, they followed the path designated for civilian use that led between the few scattered houses at the end of Downs View Road, emerging eventually on the lush green expanse of Maer Cliff. The sea shone cold and bright in the distance and a chill wind stirred the short grasses underfoot. They walked side by side along the meandering uphill path, sometimes passed by squads of Rangers on a march, for the American soldiers often went on day-long marches along the north coast, returning to the boarding house exhausted and footsore, sometimes long after dark. The tide was out and ridges of black rocks in the beachy coves below were exposed, like the ribs of a gigantic dinosaur half-buried in sand.

They walked close to the crumbling edge of the cliff at times, but most of it was marked *No Admittance*, for the Americans were using much of that stretch of coastline for their training manoeuvres.

'I wish I could have seen these cliffs before the war,' Penny remarked as they began the long trudge up a particularly steep slope. 'Florence says she often walked here with her husband Percy, but it's all barbed wire now, and there are soldiers everywhere . . . I wish I could have seen it when it was unspoilt.'

'Aye, it was a lovely place to be on a summer's day before the war. My family often took a walk up here on a Sunday afternoon after lunch, and you'd see other families doing the same. Walking the dog or young couples hand in hand. But the view is the same.' He pointed along the steepening coastline, which stretched upwards and away in the hazy distance, the sea almost white where it met the horizon. 'See up there, a few miles on?' She followed his arm and vaguely saw a collection of what might be huts on the highest point visible. 'That's Cleave Camp. They've an airfield. Several friends have been posted there for training. Sometimes I wish . . .' He broke off, frowning.

'That you could be up there with them? That you'd signed up to do your bit?'

John nodded abruptly. 'I feel idle, sitting at home when there's a war on.'

'But there's a reason your occupation is reserved,' Penny pointed out calmly. 'It's all very well for women to work with the Fire Service or ambulance driving or to do factory work in place of the men who've gone to war, but there were some jobs where you need a man's strength or years of skilled experience and know-how, like you and your dad, used to being on the winter sea in the pitch-black and cold. Goodness, I wouldn't know what to do if a storm blew in or the nets got caught up.' On impulse, Penny reached out and took his hand. 'You've done the right thing. You're needed here, John. And don't ever think otherwise.'

He glanced down at their hands, joined at hip level, and smiled. His gaze met hers. 'You're a kindly soul, Miss Penny, and I'm sorry I didn't come after you down at the harbour. I made a mistake. I know that now and I hope you can forgive me.'

Guilt soared through her. 'No, it was my fault. I shouldn't have stormed off like that without even waiting to hear who that girl was or why you were talking to her. I behaved very badly. You've no need to apologise.'

'Well, I'm sorry anyway.' He squeezed her hand and then released it. 'Another five minutes and there's a good spot for a picnic, with somewhere sheltered to sit. I've beer and sandwiches and a few squares of chocolate apiece.'

'What's in the sandwiches?'

'Fish paste, I think.' Seeing her expression, he threw back his head, laughing. 'We like fish in our family. If you spend much time with me, you'll have to learn to like fish too.'

Penny's heart thumped and she held her breath, which was tricky, as they were still walking uphill. She came to a halt, looking at him shyly. 'Am I going to be spending much time with you?'

'Would you like to?' John asked seriously, standing in front of her as though to shield her from the sea breeze. Her hair was blowing into her face, and he lifted his hand, tidying the wayward strands with a sudden smile. 'Please say yes.'

That smile was impossible to resist. As were the promptings of her heart. There was just something about John that made her feel . . . safe.

'Yes,' she whispered.

The promised sheltered spot was a stony outcrop where they were able to sit with their backs to the sun-warmed stone, a rug spread on the damp ground, while they ate their sandwiches and chocolate, and drank their bottles of beer. The sun glistened and sparkled on the ocean for as far as the eye could see, and while they enjoyed their beer, John told her amusing and sometimes hair-raising anecdotes of his time at sea.

Penny wasn't sure she entirely believed all his stories, some of which were a little far-fetched, especially when he spoke spookily of 'monsters' in the deep knocking on the bottom of the trawler. But she laughed anyway, and drew her knees up and her coat close to keep warm, and in return found herself telling him stories of her days as a Land Girl. Such as when she'd slipped in thick mud and had to walk a mile back to the farm, caked with mud from head to foot. Or when the tractor had accidentally rolled downhill on its own while they all ran after it, shrieking . . . But when she spoke of Selina and Caroline, her voice faltered, and he quickly guessed that things had gone wrong between the three girls.

'That can happen when people work closely together,' he said reassuringly. 'I'm sure it wasn't your fault.'

'I hope not. Anyway, that's why I chose to leave the farm and come to Bude with Alice. To see a bit more of the world and meet interesting people.'

John eyed her thoughtfully. 'Am I interesting?'

'Goodness, what a question!' She finished her beer and got to her feet, avoiding his gaze. 'We'd better head back. This wind is getting cold.'

He knelt to pack the remnants of their picnic in his rucksack, then strapped it to his back again. 'It was a serious question,' he said at last, swinging to face her.

'Of course you're interesting.'

'Why don't I believe you?' John cupped her cheek and his gaze sought hers, not allowing her to hide. 'What are we doing here? Playing games? Because I could do that with any girl.' His voice had dropped to a husky whisper. 'I don't want to play games with you, Penny.'

'I . . . I don't know what you mean.'

But she did know and was scared. He was asking her to make a choice. And she wasn't sure she was ready to do that.

'I may not live on Downs View Road,' he told her carefully, 'but I hear things. Such as the wild parties they hold there. Dancing and drinking until all hours.' She blushed and he nodded. 'The American troops . . . They're *interesting*, aren't they? From the other side of that big wide ocean.' He nodded to the shining Atlantic at her back, where they could hear the approaching drone of an aeroplane engine. 'And I'm just a Bude boy.'

She didn't know what to say.

The sound of gunfire made them both spin in alarm, their conversation pushed to one side as they ducked instinctively behind the rocky outcrop, staring along the cliff.

'What on earth?' John straightened, staring from behind a raised hand. 'Oh, I see. It's only target practice. Look.' He pointed to a line of big guns further along the cliff, being manned by soldiers, though by their uniforms they seemed to be their own home-grown British troops, not Americans. 'They must have come down from Cleave Camp.'

The soldiers were shooting at a large, off-white balloon-style target being dragged by the aeroplane they'd heard.

They watched for a moment, John seeming fascinated, then he noticed her pale cheeks and breathless silence.

'Are you all right?' He was frowning.

'I just get so scared, that's all.' Penny shivered, dragging her coat tight and wishing the wind was not so chill. 'It's being on the Cornish coast that does it. The south coast of England is mined and defended for miles, but they haven't bothered so much with Cornwall.' She ran a hand over her eyes. 'When I was at Porthcurno, I felt much safer. There were lookouts everywhere you looked and the beach was heavily mined.'

Hurriedly, Penny stopped herself before she betrayed any government secrets, since the tiny village of Porthcurno housed a vital top-secret listening station that she wasn't supposed to know about. Though most villagers did, of course.

'Alice brought back more information the other day about what to do if we get invaded,' she continued more carefully. 'But what *can* we do? I mean, the Rangers are here right now, and that makes me feel much safer. But they won't be here forever. And then it'll be down to us. And maybe a handful of soldiers from Cleave Camp. We're so far from anywhere, it would take ages to get help from the army. And you know the locals will all be rounded up and shot within hours of a German invasion. What chance would any of us have?' She was sobbing, she realised with shock, and stuttered to a halt. 'Oh dear.'

'Hey, come here.' His arms enfolded her. 'You can always rely on me to protect you. Me and my pa. Yes, and Grandpa too. Besides, we've a good volunteer unit in the town, mostly veterans, retrained and ready.' He chuckled. 'They might be getting on a bit but those old boys can still shoot straight and handle a bayonet. We don't need the Americans. Them Jerries set so much as a toe on our Cornish shores, we'll give 'em what for. You'll see.'

Penny nodded, and hoped he was right. Which felt about right, given how the war kept lurching on from bad to worse. All they had left was hope, wasn't it?

CHAPTER TWENTY-ONE

It was late evening by the time Florence finally put aside her knitting and got up out of her tatty but comfortable armchair, meaning to carry Billy back up to bed. The soldiers, partying noisily in the front room, had disturbed him, which was unusual, so she'd brought the boy downstairs to sit with her by the fireside, wrapped in a blanket while he played drowsily with a box of wooden building blocks. Eventually, of course, he'd tumbled to sleep on the rug, and she had left him to sleep for a while, just to be sure, while she clacked her needles softly, knitting him a blue scarf.

Once the fire had burnt down to slumbering embers, she scooped her son lovingly into her arms and was struggling with the latch when someone knocked at the door.

'Oh yes, please come in,' she said thankfully, taking a step back.

As she'd suspected, it was Miles.

Ever since the night of the Christmas Eve dance when

they'd kissed, Miles had been coming to visit her in the 'snug', as she called this private sitting room at the back of the house. Not that he ever made advances towards her when they were alone together, always the perfect gentleman. A little too perfect, she sometimes felt, wishing he would kiss her again. But although they were never physically intimate, they had talked for hours, quietly and in depth, while his soldiers caroused next door.

They had spoken of the war and of life in general, but also more specifically of family ties and love. Shyly, Florence had told him more about her dear Percy. She'd admitted that, although she missed her husband terribly, she could now imagine moving on with her life, while she was careful not to be too specific about what that might entail. She hadn't wanted Miles to think she was angling for a marriage proposal.

'It would be for Billy's sake as much as my own,' she had added shyly, for having a widow as his only parent could not be ideal for an intrepid young child like Billy. Though she didn't say as much to Miles, as Billy grew into boyhood, she suspected he would soon long for a father who could teach him to fish or how to kick a football. Not that a mother couldn't do such things, but she felt strongly that a boy needed a father figure about the place too, as a role model and to lead by example. And she had no particular attachment to widowhood. Indeed, though she kept silent about this too, she often yearned for a man's touch again and for strong arms about her, keeping her safe and warm at night.

Was it wrong to wish for such things in this age of women's liberation, she wondered? The war had demonstrated beyond doubt that women could be just as strong and capable as men. Wrong or not, however, Florence did sometimes wish that some of her heavier responsibilities – not to mention her fears – could be lifted from her shoulders.

Miles, in his turn, had gradually confided his own private thoughts and history to her. How he had grown up in a rural area, though the weather in Texas was very different from the mild climate of Cornwall. And how he feared for his father's health back home in America and wished he could be there, taking on daily tasks that his father could barely perform, being infirm. He had a mother too, who sounded rather delicate. It was clear that he doted on 'Momma' as well as 'Pops', and as their eldest son had been doted on in turn. Despite these factors, he didn't regret coming to fight the Nazis, saying it was every man's duty, 'to defeat fascism once and for all'.

Now, Miles glanced at the child in her arms and offered to carry him upstairs. When she protested, he smiled. 'The boy weighs less than a feather to me,' he whispered, and she reluctantly handed Billy over.

Florence followed him up the gloomy staircase to the room on the first floor that she shared with both Billy and now Imogen. The landing lay in darkness. She imagined that Alice and Penny must be in their respective bedrooms, probably asleep by now, or else downstairs with the Rangers, listening to music, which they often did in the long evenings.

'In here,' she whispered, and opened her bedroom door with a slight creaking sound, only to stop dead in shock.

The bedside lamp was already on, and there, on the bed

she shared with her sister, Imogen was kissing one of the US soldiers billeted on them. Thankfully they were both fully clothed, but indignation held her motionless for several seconds before she exclaimed, 'Imogen! What on earth do you think you you're doing?'

Imogen sat up with a start, looking flushed and dishevelled. The US soldier with her was Private Carson, and that was probably what shocked Florence the most, for he was such a nice young man, always polite and smiling.

'Flo, for goodness' sake! Can't I get a moment's privacy in this house?' Imogen demanded, tidying her mussed-up hair. She did not seem to think she had done anything wrong, and indeed her eyes flashed fire at both Florence and Miles, standing behind her with Billy in his arms. 'I'm sorry if I've shocked you both. But I'm not a nun, you know. And there isn't a law against it,' she added drily.

Miles glanced at Florence questioningly, and she pointed him towards the cot where Billy slept, though he was getting rather too large for it these days and would soon need a small bed of his own. Miles laid the boy down to sleep, tucking the blanket around him with tender care, and then straightened, instantly back to being a military man, his hands clasped behind his back as he faced the young man.

Private Carson had leapt off the bed at the sight of his superior officer, pulling down his uniform jacket and running a hand over his short hair, his face as flushed as Imogen's. 'I know how it looks, Sergeant, but I swear, nothing happened.'

'You're dismissed for the night, Private. I'll speak to you

first thing tomorrow morning, when I shall expect a full explanation of what happened here tonight. First, however, you will apologise to Mrs Pritchard. This is her bedroom and you should never have set foot across the threshold. Nor will you again.'

'No, Sergeant.' The young man turned to Florence, saying apologetically, 'I'm so sorry, Mrs Pritchard. It'll never happen again. You have my word.'

'Dismissed, Private,' Miles barked.

Private Carson practically ran from the room, saluting Miles hastily at the door.

Florence touched Miles's sleeve and said softly, though she was boiling with temper inside, 'We mustn't wake Billy.' She hesitated, avoiding looking at her sister, though she knew a showdown between them was inevitable. Something needed to be done about Imogen's behaviour, and straightaway. 'You'd better let me deal with this now.' By *this*, she meant Imogen, of course.

Thankfully, Miles seemed to understand. He searched her face, and then nodded. 'Whatever you think best, ma'am,' he said and, with a quick glance at Imogen, took himself off to bed, closing the door behind him.

Taking a deep and almost painful breath into her lungs, Florence turned back to her sister, and said with careful restraint, 'I think you'd better leave. Tomorrow morning. I can walk with you to the train station if you like, to help carry your bags. But you must leave.'

Imogen stared at her blankly, her eyes stretched wide. 'You must be joking,' she said at last, and ducked to look in the dressing table mirror, checking her reflection. Seeming reassured by what she saw, she turned to face

Florence, folding her arms across her chest. 'It was just a kiss and a cuddle, that's all. I don't know what all the fuss is about.' Her attitude was cool and dismissive.

Florence realised that her hands had clenched into fists and made a conscious effort to relax them. She did not want to fight with her younger sister. Not least because her young son was sleeping only a few feet away.

'I'm not even remotely joking,' she told her in a low voice, standing straight-backed, her chin up. 'I've had enough of you, Imogen. I want you out of here. I'm sorry, but there's no point pretending anymore. You're a disruptive influence on Billy and this household. And that's my final word on the matter.'

She turned away, meaning to go back downstairs to lock up and check the house was secure before returning to bed herself.

But Imogen, crossing the room in a flash, dragged her back by the arm. 'You can't be serious. It was nothing. You're making a mountain out of a molehill. Don't be so ridiculous, Flo. Goodness gracious, anyone would think I'd had sex with the man!'

Florence, outraged by this dreadful comment, especially with her son in the room, could not help herself. Her hand swept up and she slapped her sister about the face. Instantly, she regretted it and bit her lip. She'd let her temper get the better of her. But there was no taking it back.

The two women stared at each other, Florence tense and silent, Imogen with a red, spreading stain on her cheek and her chest heaving.

'Well,' Imogen gasped, 'at last we see your true colours.

Florence the bully. Florence the harridan. Florence the frustrated widow!'

Florence sucked in a sharp breath and hurriedly left the bedroom before she could be tempted to say something she might regret, closing the door behind her. But she was shaking and her knees felt weak as she groped her way down the dark stairs, desperate not to meet any of the young men in the front room, who were still playing music and talking in their deep voices, telling jokes and anecdotes, and occasionally bursting into riotous laughter.

Florence stopped outside the door to the front sitting room and listened for a moment. She heard a deep rumbling voice, and then the music was turned down. Now it was quieter, she caught the lighter tones of girls' voices, and recognised at least one of them. Penny was in there, enjoying the soldiers' company. Perhaps Alice was in there too.

Ridiculously, she felt a stab of envy at the freedom of these young girls. A freedom she had never known, or not on the same scale. Since war had broken out, nobody seemed to care what anyone did anymore, however outrageous or shocking. Maybe her sister was right to mock her for prudery and righteous indignation. Maybe she was indeed a 'frustrated widow' and ought to stop living in the past and start seeing life as these younger people did . . . Like mayflies, living it up while they could. Living hard and fast and not regretting anything. Because tomorrow might be too late.

Though she was not *old*, was she? She was only thirty-five.

She had told her sister to leave. First thing in the

morning. Now she regretted that impulse, feeling cruel and uncharitable. Her sister was young and found it hard to control her impulses. Imogen ought never to have taken that man to their bedroom where Billy slept, it was true . . . But that didn't mean she deserved to be thrown out on the streets.

And she'd promised their parents she would look after Imogen, that she would shelter and house her younger sister and try to keep her out of the sort of embarrassing scrapes she was so good at tumbling into.

She had failed miserably; that was obvious. Imogen was incorrigible and out of control. Or maybe she was just making the most of her life at a precarious time, and Florence and their parents were both stick-in-the-muds who couldn't see beyond their own noses.

Florence gave a loud sob, clasping a quick hand to her mouth to stifle the sound. What on earth should she do now? She couldn't go back up there and share the bed with her sister. Not after that appalling slap, which she ought never to have dealt her.

Why had she done it? She would have to apologise, though Imogen never apologised. But two wrongs didn't make a right.

The door to the sitting room began to open and she hurried on along the darkened passageway, fearful of being caught listening at keyholes, but was stopped by the murmur of her name.

Florence turned, her heart thudding. It was Miles.

She felt thrown off-balance, seeing him loom so large in the gloom of the hallway. 'I . . . I thought you'd gone to bed,' she stammered.

'I was telling the guys to turn the music down and start winding the party up,' he explained in a low voice. 'It's not right for them to be keeping you up so late. Besides, they've a full day of training scheduled for tomorrow. Things are getting intense. If they're too tired, mistakes could be made. And mistakes cost lives.'

'Yes, of course. Thank you.' She didn't know what else to say.

Florence stared at him, remembering how they had witnessed Imogen and Private Carson kissing on the bed, and realised that she'd been secretly wishing it could have been her and Miles. A warm flush crept across her cheeks and she could not seem to look away from him. By the look in his face, she guessed he must be thinking much the same thing. It was the look of a lover, not a soldier.

'Florence,' he said intensely, their eyes locked, but at that moment the door to the guests' sitting room opened and young men poured out, mock-whispering and supporting each other up the stairs to bed. Others, who had come visiting from other billets, called out, 'Goodnight,' and stumbled out of the front door, leaving it wide open, with several local girls giggling in high heels.

Penny appeared too, deep in conversation with one of the young soldiers, and they both went upstairs together, though to Florence's relief it didn't strike her as a romantic relationship. It sounded more as though they were discussing politics. Deep down, Penny still seemed as shy as she had been on first arriving at Downs View Road. But the American soldiers were so friendly and easy to talk to, compared to their own more reserved menfolk, she could perfectly understand why Penny spent so long chatting to those young men every night . . .

None of them appeared to have noticed the couple standing silently in the shadows at the other end of the passageway.

A blast of cold, wintry air came swirling about the hall and Florence hugged herself, shivering. Miles strode down to the entrance and closed the front door firmly after the last of the visitors, securing it with bolt and key before looking back at her searchingly.

But the spell was broken and she could only shake her head, slipping away into the shadows. It was madness, and they both knew it.

She had loved a man once with all her heart and soul, but lost him prematurely to the war. She could not bear to love another man only to lose him the same way.

The next morning, Florence woke early, having spent a disturbed and deeply uncomfortable night in her armchair at the cold hearthside, a blanket over her knees. She had barely slept at all, mulling over her dreadful row with her sister, and when she had finally dropped off to sleep, her dreams had been troubled.

By the clock on the mantelpiece, it was nearly six-thirty in the morning. Still dark outside but not too early to begin her working day.

There was always something useful to do in a large boarding house, as she'd discovered before they had even opened their doors to guests, and long before Herr Hitler had been anything other than another foreign name in the newspapers. How that odd little man had changed all their lives for the worse, to be sure, she thought, pushing off the blanket and standing up. But she had grown to know her neighbours better since losing Percy and having to rely heavily on their support and friendship. Not that she was happy to be at war with Germany, and certainly not for so many years, but at least this shared adversity had brought the community closer together.

She stretched and yawned, shaking off her drowsiness, then heard a creak from the stairs followed by a low knock at the door shortly afterwards. Florence turned, hurriedly raking fingers through her messy hair, wondering who on earth it could be at this hour.

'Yes?'

But the door opened to reveal Imogen.

Her sister looked not to have spent an easy night either. There were dark shadows under her eyes and a wan, drained look to her usually vibrant countenance.

'May I come in?' Imogen whispered.

'Of course.' Florence stood stiffly, waiting. Her sister had never asked permission to enter the snug before. But then, Florence had never felt the need to spend a night there either.

Imogen closed the door and crept inside, wearing her belted dressing gown, a sumptuous scarlet flannel she had owned since before the war, and with her feet in slippers. She turned a pale face to Florence's, a tear sliding down her cheek.

'I'm sorry,' Imogen began, her voice breaking on the unaccustomed words, her look pathetic. 'You were right. I should have known better. On your bed, and when Billy sleeps there too . . . It was outrageous of me and you have every right to throw me out on the streets. But please, I beg of you to give me a second chance.' Her voice throbbed with emotion. 'Not because I'm your sister, but because you know I have nowhere else to go.'

Florence took a deep breath, steeling herself against the pleading look in her sister's face. She had seen this performance many times before after one of Imogen's 'episodes', this tear-stained apology, and knew that giving in would rapidly convert that look to one of triumphant pleasure. It still had the power to touch her heart though.

'You're not homeless,' she pointed out calmly. 'You can go home to Mother and Father.'

'They threw me out!'

'That's not true, Imogen. They suggested you should go away for a while, that's all. To give them a little respite from precisely this sort of behaviour.'

'They'll never take me back,' Imogen insisted.

Florence hesitated, considering that possibility. 'If I write to them, explaining that I no longer have space for you here, you can take my letter with you.'

'It won't make any difference.' Her sister sounded desperate. Another tear slipped down her cheek. 'Please, Flo . . . I'll do anything.' She wrung her hands. 'I . . . I haven't been helping around the place as I promised, but I'll change. Give me a job to do, I'll do it, no complaining.'

'The outside lavatory needs a thorough clean,' Florence said deliberately, just to see how she would react.

To her surprise, Imogen nodded enthusiastically, as though she'd suggested trying on the crown jewels. 'Oh yes, I can do that. Nothing easier, in fact. I'm a whizz with a mop and bucket once I get going. If you tell me where the soda crystals are kept, I'll get dressed and see to that straightaway.' Her smile was tremulous. 'I'll have your outside convenience sparkling in no time.'

Stunned, Florence stared at her.

'Does . . . does this mean I can stay?' Imogen added meekly, peering at her through tear-drenched eyelashes.

'Let's see how well you do the job first.' Florence still wasn't convinced. 'Besides, I know you, Imogen. If you've got that unfortunate young man in your sights, nothing I say will prevent you from snaring him. And I won't have these soldiers' hearts toyed with, do you hear me?' Her voice rose, despite her attempt at self-control. 'These brave young men will be off to the front soon, and you and I both know what that means. Private Carson may never come back. It's downright wicked to raise his hopes of a relationship with you and then dash them, right before he goes off to fight.'

'Who says I'm going to dash them?' Imogen demanded, momentarily losing her pleading look.

'Ah, there's the real Immi,' Florence said with satisfaction.

'No,' her sister insisted, shaking her head. 'All right, it's not a forever love. But he doesn't want that, anyway. He told me himself, he has a girl back in the States.'

'And you still kissed him?' Florence was scandalised.

'Nick was lonely and unhappy. The other men laugh at him for never trying to get a girl,' Imogen shrugged. 'Our little kiss last night will put paid to that. I was being kind, that's all. Not leading him on.'

'Oh, Immi . . .'

Her sister ran up and hugged her. 'Please say I can stay? You know I can't go home, and I've been declared unfit for war work because of my nerves, so I'll be homeless and penniless if you make me leave.' Her eyes shone with tears again. 'I swear, I'll pull my weight with chores and I'll never even glance twice at the Rangers again. You'll hardly notice I'm here.'

Florence gave a hollow laugh at this unlikely thought, but nodded, sure she was making a mistake but unable to say no to her incorrigible little sister. 'Very well, you can stay,' she agreed with a sigh. 'Just try to steady on a bit and think harder before plunging into things . . .'

'The way you do, you mean?'

Surprised, Florence hesitated before saying slowly, 'I suppose so, yes. Just please don't make me regret this.'

'I won't,' Imogen promised, and hugged her tighter.

Florence did not draw back, but her thoughts were in a whirl. *The way you do, you mean?* Was that really how she came across to her sister? As someone very cautious and unlikely to take risks?

Despite common sense telling her it was nonsense, it still hurt to be perceived that way. In her sister's eyes at least, she must appear dull and uninteresting.

If only she and Immi could have been closer as children . . . But being so much older, Florence had sometimes felt more like a mother to her than an older sibling. The distance between them was not entirely down to the age gap, however, and she knew it. She had been standoffish and uncommunicative sometimes when perhaps she ought to have been more open and sympathetic towards Imogen's escapades. Yes, they were chalk and cheese, and she often struggled to understand her nervy, impulsive sister. But they were bound by blood and family ties, and that had to mean something, didn't it?

Drawing in a shaky breath, Florence closed her eyes and relaxed into the hug, allowing her sister's unexpected warmth to envelop her.

Well, she would do better in future, she told herself firmly. She would work hard to make *friends* with her sister, however unlikely the prospect of success.

The thought made her smile.

'You know,' Imogen said wistfully, drawing back to study her, 'you could try being more like me. You're too serious about everything. Quite like an old lady at times.' Her smile was mischievous. 'Maybe stop fretting so much and live a little?'

'Do you remember what I just said,' Florence asked, 'about not making me *regret* letting you stay?'

'Oh, Flo . . .' With a carefree laugh, Imogen skipped to the door, flinging it open with one of her dramatic gestures. Her mood had skyrocketed back to happy again, it seemed. Triumphant, even. 'You can't fool me. I know you don't mean it.'

'Outside lavatory,' Florence told her sternly.

'On my way!'

CHAPTER TWENTY-TWO

There had been some commotion late at night. But there was always some commotion in the evenings at the boarding house, so Alice had not paid much attention, merely rolling over and pulling her covers over her head. Now she could hear voices again, as she quietly washed and dressed in the milky gloom before dawn, ignoring her need for more sleep. Someone else burning the candle at both ends, she guessed.

She had to be in town by seven o'clock, and didn't like hurrying, so had woken early to prepare in good time, despite being tired.

Today was the big day. The day of their special mission for Rawlings.

She felt uneasy, for she didn't know exactly what to expect, not only from the mission itself but from the other two trainees on her team. Patrick wasn't a bad bloke, even if he did think her lack of military training made her a liability, but Sophy had never hidden the fact that she didn't like Alice, even before getting a bop on the nose.

Now, of course, she must absolutely *hate* Alice, which might be a problem if they needed to rely on each other in the field.

Alice grinned, lacing up her shoes. 'In the field' was an expression she had begun to use quite often, despite not having heard it much before coming to Bude. It was what Barnabas called 'spy talk'.

Dragging on her winter coat and gloves, she made her way downstairs as quietly as possible, avoiding the creaking stair near the bottom. She had to unlock and unbolt the front door, letting herself out. From the sound of voices in the back room, Mrs P was up and about, so it would be acceptable to leave the front door unlocked.

Outside, the cold dark greeted her, though the sky was glimmering with light across the sea. She could see fishing boats bobbing out on the tide and wondered if Penny's new fellow was out there. John Pascoe. The *Mary Jane* was the name of his boat, Penny had told her.

Alice wasn't sure how serious it was between Penny and the young fisherman. They seemed to fall out surprisingly often, and Penny still spent most evenings with the Rangers. But then, she'd noticed Aunty Vi and Uncle Joe often having little spats, and she knew how much they loved each other. And Penny never flirted with the Americans, only danced and chatted.

Alice supposed it must be awkward, having strong feelings for someone else, and perhaps a few fiery words simply couldn't be helped. Maybe one day she would find out. But she was in no hurry to get romantically involved with anyone. She was far too busy trying to do her dad proud with this spying business and not get sent home.

Today, the only fiery words she was likely to exchange with anyone would be with Sophy. But since the outcome of their training course might well depend on how they managed this special mission, she rather hoped they would work together smoothly and put aside their differences.

As she walked the short distance into town, the dawn light began to grow in intensity until she no longer had to pick her way carefully.

Dimly, she saw two figures up ahead, near the corner at the top of Belle Vue, sheltering from the wind in the porch of a closed shop, conversing in low voices.

With a jolt of surprise, she recognised one as Mr Gladly, one of the instructors on her course, though he was largely responsible for fronting the printing works and rarely spoke to the trainees. The other person was a white-haired old lady in a knitted hat with a large white embroidered flower on it, who had wrapped up against the cold in a saggy brown coat with deep pockets into which both her hands were pushed. Their voices had sunk to whispers, Alice realised, as she walked past, as though concerned they might be overheard.

Alice said nothing, for one of the key elements of her mission was to be 'unnoticeable'.

All the same, Mr Gladly lifted his head to stare at her as she passed, clearly recognising her too. The old lady glanced her way as well, sharp-eyed, and that was when Alice realised who she was. She couldn't remember the woman's name perfectly. Dora, perhaps? Or Doreen? She was an elderly lady who ran one of the smaller boarding houses on Downs View Road, a narrow-fronted building that was becoming a little scruffy and needed repainting, its yellow façade cracking in several places, though nobody bothered about such things now there was a war on. Painting and decorating was something that would happen once the war was over. If it was ever over, Alice thought drearily.

Mr Gladly wasn't a very chatty man and had never spoken to her much. Nor did he say anything now. Grateful for this, Alice hunched her shoulders in her coat and kept walking, looking straight ahead.

But she was confused. Why on earth were Mr Gladly and Doreen whispering together in a shop doorway before seven o'clock in the morning? It was bloomin' odd. Unless perhaps Doreen was Mr Gladly's gran, and they were discussing family matters, but it was still an unusual time and place to have a cheery natter. Well, it was none of her business.

Reaching the appointed rendezvous slightly ahead of time, she took up a place a little further down the street from the building they would be watching, pacing nervously up and down in the still-milky light of dawn. Soon she was joined by Patrick and, five minutes later, by a breathless Sophy, who had clearly overslept. Her blouse was buttoned wrongly and although her hair had been brushed, she had not set it as she usually did. Not that Alice cared about such things, but since Sophy regularly made disparaging remarks about her shabby appearance, it was difficult not to take some enjoyment out of the other girl's unkempt appearance.

'H-Have I missed anything?' Sophy gasped, checking her reflection in the shop window and straightening her crooked hat with an anguished expression.

'Not a dicky bird,' Patrick told her cheerfully.

The building they had been instructed to watch was situated right at the heart of the small town. According to the information they had been handed, three US Rangers had been billeted on a local family above a shop. It was an ironmonger's with a narrow alley to one side. The side door to the property lay at the end of this alleyway. Their 'special mission' was to follow one of those three soldiers as he went about his business today, the designated 'mark', without being suspected or preferably even noticed. This would take some coordination between the team members, such as not all following him at the same time, or following in ones or twos, to make their surveillance seem casual. At the end of the day, they would deliver a jointly written report to Rawlings to prove that they had never lost sight of their 'mark'.

'If our information is correct, they usually leave the billet just after seven o'clock. So they must be about ready to head off,' Sophy reminded them, glancing from Patrick to Alice. 'So, who's going first? Have we decided on a shift pattern? Because I haven't had a chance to eat anything and I'm famished.'

Patrick laughed. 'I grabbed something to eat before heading out, so I'm all right to take first shift.' He raised his brows at Alice. 'How about you?'

Alice shrugged. 'I haven't eaten either. But, to be honest, I'm not all that hungry. I can never eat when I'm excited.' She checked her watch for about the tenth time. 'This is pretty exciting, isn't it?'

Sophy looked at her as though she was barmy. 'Exciting? What if we get caught? Lord only knows what will happen to us. It's *terrifying*, if you ask me.'

'Oh, this chap must know he'll be followed at some point this week,' Patrick said easily, reassuring her. 'The Americans are our allies, so they'll be working together with our instructors, I'm sure.'

Alice wasn't quite as convinced but kept quiet. She knew the other two didn't rate her opinion very highly, not having been born with a silver spoon in her mouth like them. But she thought it would be just like Rawlings to make this mission as realistic as possible, to sort the wheat from the chaff, as her old gran might have said.

'I'll take first shift, then,' Patrick told them, then hushed as he noticed someone coming down the road towards them. 'Watch out. Civilian headed our way.'

All three of them immediately began doing something different. Alice took out her notebook and pretended to be studying it, head down, so her face couldn't be seen under the brim of her hat. Patrick crossed the road and headed off down the other side, whistling quietly, his hands in his pockets, staring into the shop windows. Sophy marched up to Alice and asked, rather too loudly in Alice's opinion, 'Excuse me, could you tell me the time?'

Alice looked at her drily, then checked her watch before saying, 'Nearly half past seven.' What a ridiculous thing to ask. And in such a wooden way too.

The man tapped his cap respectfully in passing, uninterested in them. Once he had gone, Sophy glared at Alice. 'You could have been more convincing.'

'You could have asked a less silly bleedin' question.'

Sophy's eyes flashed. 'And did you really expect that man to believe you were reading your notebook *when it's still so dark*?'

Patrick, crossing the road again, put a hand on Sophy's shoulder and propelled her gently away from Alice. 'Come on, Sophy. You promised. You heard Rawlings. We have to work together. We're being tested on teamwork as much as spy craft. So enough of the backbiting, all right?'

'Easy for you to say,' Sophy snapped back. 'She didn't break *your* nose, did she?'

'I didn't break yours either,' Alice pointed out mildly. 'There's no need to exaggerate.' But she was a little nettled by Sophy's bad temper.

Before the argument could continue, Patrick said swiftly, 'Hush, I hear them coming out.' He peered up and down the street. It was not quite full daylight yet. Everywhere was quiet, the road empty of traffic. 'You and me together, Alice,' he said. 'Sophy, run to the top of the street. We'll follow them first, and you follow *us*, ready to take over if they rumble us. Only keep your distance, for God's sake.'

'And what about my breakfast?'

'Nobody cares about your damn breakfast!' Patrick saw her hurt expression and sighed heavily. 'All right, if there's somewhere along the way where you can grab something to eat, do it, but *quickly*.'

With a nod, Sophy turned and fled.

They had discovered in their preliminary checks of the property that the three Rangers shared a room at the back of the house, so would be unlikely to see them on the street outside the property, especially before dawn. That was their hope, anyway. But they needed to be far more careful now that a soft, glimmering daylight was slowly filling the streets.

'Boyfriend, girlfriend?' Patrick muttered to Alice, who

felt frozen in place, her gaze flitting anxiously down the alleyway where they expected to see the soldiers emerge at any moment. She was more nervous than she'd expected.

She stared at him. 'Eh?'

'I thought that's how we ought to play it. As lovers . . .' Patrick gave her a wink. 'Perhaps we should make it look as though we've had an argument. Judging by your face, that shouldn't be too hard.'

Two men in Rangers uniform had emerged from the side door of the house opposite. As Alice watched, pretending to be deep in conversation with Patrick, the two soldiers began strolling along the alleyway towards the street. One was still combing his hair, uniform cap in hand, while the other rolled a cigarette.

'He's not there,' Alice whispered, turning away. They had each received a description of the man they were supposed to be following. No name, but a list of attributes. Approximate height and weight, hair and eye colour. The two men did not match the description given.

Patrick risked a quick glance. 'Yes, he is. See? He's just a bit behind them. The one with the red hair.'

Sure enough, Alice realised that the third man had left the house and caught up with his friends. The three Rangers walked down the street, talking and smoking, and seemed not to have noticed Patrick and Alice at all.

'Come on, get a move on,' Alice said, grabbing Patrick's hand and dragging him eagerly down the street in pursuit. 'We don't want to lose them.'

'No, that would be a wretched start to our mission.' Patrick's face was alight with excitement; he too seemed to be enjoying himself. 'But I wonder where they're going. I assumed they'd be going to the beach for more training exercises. I hope Sophy's seen which way they're going.'

Patrick glanced back over their shoulder as casually as he could manage. 'Good girl,' he murmured under his breath. 'She's following but at a discreet distance. Not making it too obvious.'

Alice, who had been watching the men intently, said, 'Look, they're turning to the right. How odd. They must be heading out of town. Towards the railway station, perhaps?'

But at the bottom of the hill, the three Rangers turned right and crossed the bridge, heading for the canal and the imposing Falcon Hotel. Patrick heaved a sigh of relief, for he'd been laboriously counting out his pocket change and had calculated they could only afford train tickets for two, which would mean leaving one of them behind. Hardly teamwork, he'd said ruefully.

Sophy was keeping a good distance behind them, as they had been taught during surveillance classes, dawdling with a bored expression on her face.

As the men slowed, going uphill, Patrick turned and nodded Sophy towards the Falcon, miming eating. Sophy nodded and ducked into the popular hotel, presumably to see if she could grab herself some breakfast, while Patrick and Alice continued walking.

But after a few hundred yards, the road they were on left the hotel and pretty cottages behind, turning into a wooded lane running almost parallel to the canal before sloping uphill. In the misty light, the trees loomed dark and sinister. Alice shivered, glancing frequently over her shoulder, her spine tingling at every odd rustle or cracking sound from deep among the trees. The narrow lane twisted and turned on its way uphill until they could barely see the three men ahead.

For the first time, she began to feel uneasy.

Patrick was frowning. 'I don't think they've spotted us yet. But if they do, this could become difficult. I mean, walking around town, looking in shop windows, that's one thing. But following them out here, where there's not much around . . . Well, it's going to look damn suspicious.'

Alice agreed, but said out loud, 'Boyfriends and girlfriends go to lonely places though, don't they? To get away from everyone else,' she added awkwardly, 'and . . . and to be private.'

Patrick grinned. 'You're a dark horse, Alice Fisher.'

Up ahead, in a gloomy clearing, the three men disappeared into a long, low hut. It looked newly built, and Alice guessed it must have been put up by the Americans since their arrival. Trees had been cleared to make room for it, and a few yards away was a US army jeep, standing still and silent on the rough ground, a faint bloom of condensation on the windscreen as though it had been parked there all night.

The two of them hung back, unsure what to do next.

'What are they up to in there, d'you think?' Alice eyed the hut and the jeep with mounting suspicion but couldn't put her finger on what was troubling her.

'I don't know, but let's wait out of sight,' Patrick told her, frowning. 'We're too obvious here. Maybe over there, in the trees?'

One after the other, they stepped as noiselessly as

possible through low, muddy undergrowth until they were hidden among the shrubs and trees that bordered the track.

Nearly ten minutes passed while they waited for the men to leave the hut again. Daylight grew steadily brighter, birds chirping and singing in the bare branches above them. Alice moved restlessly, rubbing and clapping her arms to keep warm. But she couldn't help shivering in the cold bite of January weather, having to stay still for so long.

'This is stupid. We need to take a look inside that hut,' Patrick said eventually, coming back from peering down the track. 'Though I wish I knew where Sophy has got to. I didn't expect her to take so long, just getting breakfast.' He looked chilly too, folding his arms and blowing out reddened cheeks. 'Maybe she couldn't find which way we went and has gone back to town.'

'Maybe.' Alice chewed on her lip. Their brief had been simple: tail the unnamed soldier without being seen, and keep tabs on what he was doing. She had assumed he would be with his unit all day and mainly visible. Already, this 'special mission' was turning out to be trickier than she'd expected. But they were here now and might as well get on with it. 'There's a window at the back of the hut,' she pointed out. 'Do you see? It's too high for me to look through. But could you reach it, do you think?'

Patrick's face brightened. 'Yes, I'm sure I could,' he told her, studying the hut with more excitement. 'I'll go take a peek inside. You wait here.'

'No,' Alice insisted, catching him by the sleeve as he set off. 'We have to work as a team, remember? I'll come and keep watch.'

Patrick looked uncertain but gave a reluctant nod. 'That makes sense, I suppose. But what if anyone comes along?'

'Then I . . . I'll make a bird call, like we were taught in class.' She demonstrated, copying a bird's fluting cry with her own whistle. 'But louder, of course.'

'Well, if you insist. But don't get seen, all right?'

She resisted a sharp retort, merely saying with careful restraint, 'Same goes for you.' She wasn't sure she liked him but they were a team now, and Rawlings had stressed how important it was to trust your team members and work with them, even if you couldn't be friends.

Cautiously, they edged out of the trees and crossed the narrow track into the clearing, trying to keep out of sight of the hut.

Patrick signalled her to hide behind part of a felled beech trunk that still lay uncut in the clearing. Then he tiptoed through tangled undergrowth to the back of the hut. Crouching low, Alice watched with her heart in her mouth. If they should be caught . . .

Patrick stood on tiptoe, pulling himself up to the windowsill to peer inside. He had only been there about thirty seconds when the door of the hut was flung open and all three men ran out, heading around the back.

Panicked, Alice tried several times to make the warning bird-call whistle. But her lips were dry and she was breathless, so it came out more like one of Joe's pigs squealing than any bird she'd ever heard.

One of the men glanced around at the odd sound, easily spotting her crouched in horror behind the felled beech. He threw out an arm, pointing straight at her, and shouted something. The other two men, meanwhile, had grabbed hold of Patrick as he attempted to flee and were dragging him back into the hut.

Turning to run, Alice got maybe fifty paces down the rough track before she tripped over a stone and went flying, landing face-down in cold, hard-ridged mud. Above the thud of her heart, she caught the alarmed clatter of birds rising all at once from wintry branches, a sound like clapped hands in the silence, and wondered if Sophy, perhaps heading towards them a little further down the track, might hear it too and guess something had happened.

Seconds later, hands plucked her up from the muddy ground, and the soldier began dragging her back towards the hut as well.

Furious with herself for getting caught, she kicked and struggled, and even swore. The American merely gave a laugh, saying, 'We've got a live one here, Sarge.'

One of the other soldiers had reappeared, the tall, dark-haired man she'd seen rolling a cigarette earlier. He had seemed relaxed and friendly before. Now his expression was harsh, his eyes snapping. 'Quick,' he told the man holding her, 'get her in the hut with the boy, and let's find out who they are and what exactly they know. Before we're seen.'

These words sent a chill through Alice's heart. She hadn't recognised any of the soldiers and, up until this point, she'd assumed this was a mutually arranged training mission, that the Americans knew one of them was a 'target' and were just playing along so they could practise their spy craft. War games, in other words. Not for real. Now, for the first time, she considered another, more sinister possibility. That Rawlings had deliberately sent his trainees after a genuine target, either a Nazi sympathiser working against the Allies or a member of a criminal gang within the military. Black-market racketeers, for instance, who could face a court martial and a long prison term if discovered, and who might be prepared to kill anyone they suspected of knowing about their illegal activities.

The interior of the hut was dim, lit only by greenish light from the back window. Patrick's arms had been bound behind his back and a Ranger was holding him forcibly seated on a chair. Alice too was thrown down onto a wooden seat next to him, glaring up at her attacker. She considered making a break for it, but the red-haired American – their 'target' – had taken up position in front of the only exit, and despite her hand-to-hand combat training, realistically she had no hope against even one of these big, strapping blokes, let alone three.

'I say, what are you doing?' Patrick demanded hotly as her own hands were bound behind her back. 'Let her go. She . . . She's my girlfriend.'

The red-haired soldier began rolling a cigarette. 'Liar,' he said easily before transferring his gaze to Alice. 'Okay, tell us who you are and what you're doing, and maybe we'll let you go. Both of you.'

'Dunno what you're talkin' about, guv,' Alice exclaimed, deliberately laying it on thick with her strongest East End accent, her eyes wide with shocked innocence. 'Me and him . . . We was just kissin'. No law against it, is there? And what's it got to do wiv you anyway, eh?'

There was a short silence. The three men exchanged glances.

Then the soldier who'd dragged her into the hut seized

her chin and dragged it up into the light, turning her head roughly from side to side as he examined her face. 'Yeah, this is the one, all right,' he told the others, striking a chill in Alice's heart. 'Okay, so we've got her. But what do we do with the boy? Let him go? Or get rid of him?'

CHAPTER TWENTY-THREE

As Penny left the shop for her lunch break, meaning to run down to John's cottage to call on him, a girl she had never seen before came dashing up, breathless. She was about Alice's age with glossy brown hair cut short and a curvy but trim figure that Penny would have killed to have. The girl had been crying – that was clear from her tear-stained cheeks and wet lashes – but she said in a surprisingly steady voice, 'Excuse me. Are you Penny? Do you live with Alice at Downs View Road?'

Taken aback, Penny's heart leapt in sudden fear. 'Yes, that's right. But what is it? Is Alice hurt?'

'I don't know.'

Penny stared, not understanding. 'I beg your pardon?'

'I can't tell you what's happened, exactly. But I need some help and I know Alice trusts you. Besides, Patrick may be in trouble too.' When Penny frowned, the girl made a dismissive gesture. 'He's one of the others who work with us.'

'At the print shop?' Penny was confused.

'Erm, yes, I suppose so.'

Passers-by were looking at them curiously, probably because they were blocking the pavement. Penny pulled the girl aside, saying impatiently, 'Look, I've only got forty-five minutes for lunch. Can you be a little clearer. Who are you? And what's wrong with Alice? If there's been an accident at the print shop—'

But the girl shook her head, repeating in a hoarse whisper, 'I can't tell you what's happened. I know it's awkward, but . . . I don't know where else to turn.' She added as an afterthought, 'I'm Sophy.'

Penny had the feeling she'd heard Alice muttering something once or twice about a 'Sophy' who worked at the printers with her. Nothing complimentary though.

'Alice is in trouble?' she asked. 'You're being awfully mysterious about this.'

The girl shrugged helplessly. 'I'm not allowed to . . . Loose lips sink ships.' A tear ran down her cheek as she gazed wildly about the busy shopping street. 'There's nobody at the workshop. It's all locked up. And I went to where the boys are lodging and they're not there, and nobody's seen them all day. You see, we had to go on a special m—' She stopped dead, blushing fiercely, and then said haltingly, 'A special job for the . . . the printer. Only I fell behind, and by the time I'd caught up with Patrick and Alice, they'd been . . .' Stopping again, she rolled her eyes. 'Oh, for Pete's sake, this is impossible to explain without . . .'

'Words?' Penny suggested wryly, thinking the girl seemed badly confused. Then a sudden thought struck her, and her eyes widened. 'Wait. You said, *loose lips* . . . The

293

printers' workshop . . .' She gasped, putting a hand to her mouth as she thought back over some of the odd things Alice had said and done since coming to Bude. 'The work you do there . . . Is it for the . . . the *government*?' The last word was only spoken in a whisper.

Sophy nodded, her tearful gaze locked on hers.

'Oh goodness.'

'We were sent out to follow someone, early this morning. In a team of three. Only we got separated, and Alice and Patrick have been . . . Well, someone's got them.'

Penny felt cold inside. '*Got them*?'

'They're being held prisoner in a hut in the woodlands beyond the canal.' Sophy heaved a worried sigh, adding ruefully, 'And I'll probably be shot for telling you that.'

'I'm sure you won't be,' Penny said sensibly.

'I've been running around town and I can't find anyone to help me. It's horrible. Then I ran past the dairy shop and remembered Alice telling me she had a friend working there. She'd described you and . . . Then you came out and I thought my luck was in.' Sophy grabbed her sleeve. 'You will help me, won't you?'

'But help you do what, exactly?' Penny was scared for Alice, but she was even more scared of the enemy. She certainly couldn't imagine tackling them herself, just her and this girl. 'These people who've taken them prisoner . . . Are they Germans? Is Cornwall being invaded?' Her voice rose in panic. 'Because we need to tell someone. Ring the church bells, mobilise the townsfolk, get the army here,' she continued, louder and louder, until interrupted by Sophy's frantic shushing.

'Not so loud!' The girl shook her head, glancing hurriedly

about. But nobody was passing at that moment. 'Whoever they are, they're not Germans. Though they may be enemy sympathisers.'

'How can you be sure? Did you get a look at them?'

Sophy bit her lip. 'Not close up. I was coming along the track, trying to find them, when I caught sight of two men dragging Alice into this hut. And I could hear Patrick's voice inside. He sounded really angry, shouting at someone to let him go.' The girl hugged herself, shivering in a particularly cold gust of wind. 'I hung about, hoping to see them come out again. But they never did.'

'Oh golly, that does sound bad.' Penny frowned. 'But who on earth are these men? Are they locals? Cornishmen?'

Sophy shook her head. 'Americans.'

Penny was stunned. 'No, you've made a mistake. The Americans came over here to help us. They would never do something horrid like this.'

Sophy shrugged. 'They looked and sounded American. And they were wearing US Ranger uniforms.'

'Good God.'

'Anyway, after I'd been watching for about an hour, one of the men came out and walked back into town. I thought they might let my friends go, then. But they didn't.' She looked pleadingly at Penny. 'I know I shouldn't have left them, but I couldn't do anything on my own. Not against armed men. So I ran back to the workshop to tell Mr Rawlings.' She looked embarrassed. 'That's the man who sent us out to follow the men. Please forget I said his name.'

'Whose name?' Penny gave her a wink.

Sophy gave a half-grin, continuing quickly, 'Only the

whole place is empty as the grave and I can't find a soul to tell. Please say you'll help me.'

Penny had been thinking hard. She nodded. 'I was about to call on my . . . Well, on a young man I know.' She blushed. 'He and I . . .'

'Your boyfriend?'

'I suppose so, yes.' Penny started to walk briskly downhill and the other girl fell in beside her. 'The thing is, John's a local. He may know someone who can help us.'

'Can he keep a secret?'

'I'd trust him with my life,' Penny said, nodding, and realised with a shock that it was no exaggeration. She really would trust John Pascoe with her life, while the young Americans she knew at the boarding house . . . Well, she liked them very much and they were all good soldiers, she was sure. But she simply didn't feel the same way about them as she did about John. He was a good man and solid as a brick, and if she needed to turn to one man for help, it would always be John. 'He won't say a word. And neither will any of his family.'

John was in the small back kitchen of the cottage with his father and grandfather. His mother was there too, kneading dough at the table, her hands and apron white with flour. She listened without comment, as did the three men, while Sophy explained the situation in an awkward, secretive manner, with occasional side remarks from Penny in case they weren't sure what the other girl meant. At the end, John looked at his father, who looked at his own father in turn.

'Well?' John asked them both, and jumped to his feet as though ready for action. 'What should we do?'

His father rubbed his bearded chin, frowning. 'Sounds like a rum deal to me,' he said at last. 'And a job for the Yanks too. Their men took 'em, they're the ones should sort it out.'

'But you heard the girl,' John cut in. 'It was all hush-hush. She can't go blabbing to the Americans how Alice and the boy were following one of their own. Wouldn't look good for the British.'

'Aye, that's right,' John's grandfather chipped in with his gravelly voice. 'But someone should help that girl in the woods, at any rate. I wouldn't mind going.' His eyes twinkled with excitement. 'I've an old axe in the shed, if it's weapons you're needing.'

'I'll go. You stay here,' John told the old man, shrugging into his heavy coat and fisherman's cap. 'Look after Penny and Sophy.' He touched his grandfather's arm. 'And thanks, but we won't need the axe. Just our wits.'

'That's right, no axes,' his mother agreed, still kneading energetically, her sharp gaze shifting to her husband's face. 'You'd best stay too, love. Let John go and fetch his friends to look for this "hut in the woods". Don't sound safe to me.'

'I don't need to be looked after,' Penny exclaimed, glaring indignantly at John, 'and I'm not staying here, like a piece of left luggage.'

'Nor am I,' Sophy agreed hotly. 'I'm going to help my friends.' Her wide, anguished gaze flew to the clock on the wall. 'Oh, I've been gone nearly an hour. Anything could have happened.'

John was frowning, but since Sophy was already halfway out of the door with Penny a few feet behind, he followed them, sighing heavily as he buttoned his coat. 'If you get yourself hurt, Penny Brown . . .' he began.

'Then it'll be my business, John Pascoe,' she interrupted fiercely. 'Alice is my best friend and I am *not* leaving her in the lurch.'

'Best come along, then,' he said mildly, and led them along the narrow lane in the direction of the canal. 'I've a good idea where this hut is. But Ma's right. We should drop by the pub first. Get a few extra hands on deck.'

'We're not crewing a ship, you know.' Penny felt giddy with relief now that John had agreed to go with them. 'Goodness, my heart's thumping so hard. I only hope nobody gets hurt.'

'If there's a fight, you'll not be anywhere near it,' John told her firmly, but there was a light in his eyes as they reached the canal towpath and quickened their pace. 'There's the pub.' He pointed across the water.

'No,' Sophy insisted. 'The fewer who know about this business, the better.'

'I'm not doing this alone,' John exclaimed.

'Then run back home,' Sophy told him sharply. 'You won't be alone. You'll have me.' John began to protest, but fell silent when she threw him another irritated backwards glance. 'Look, we're not completely unarmed. I've got a knife up my sleeve.' Briefly, she pulled it out to show him, the blade flashing evilly. 'And I've been trained in hand-to-hand combat. So, if we can take them by surprise, that will even the odds.'

John fell back a few paces, raising his brows at Penny. 'Friend of yours, is she?'

'Never seen her before in my life. But Alice has

mentioned her a few times.' She hesitated before adding in a whisper, 'I don't think they get on very well.'

'I wonder why,' he murmured.

The track into the woods grew quiet and lonely soon after they left the bustling hotel behind. Up ahead in the distance, they could see a row of buildings and some activity taking place. Vehicles turning in the narrow lane, men shouting and moving about. Nearer, squat and still in the dull January light, stood the solitary hut where Alice and Patrick had been taken prisoner earlier that day.

Sophy had pointed out the hut a few hundred yards back down the path and led them quietly into the trees, keeping low and out of sight.

For the first time, Penny began to feel scared. Perhaps she ought to have taken up John's offer to stay behind at the cottage with his mother and father. As it was, she was already hideously late back from her lunch break. But any concerns for her position at the dairy after yet another late return to work weighed next to nothing compared to her fear for her dear friend, Alice, who was in serious trouble.

Sophy held up a hand and pointed ahead, her gaze fixed on the hut.

A large car, which had been previously invisible to them, was parked under the trees behind the hut, out of sight of the road. Behind the wheel sat a large man in a dark, broad-brimmed hat, deep in conversation with another man who looked to be wearing an American uniform. As they watched, the American climbed out of the car, which then drove off slowly back along the lane towards town, passing close to their hiding place. The Ranger rolled a cigarette and stood smoking for a moment, head bowed, then strolled back into the hut.

Penny crept up behind Sophy and John. 'What was all that about, do you think? And who was the big man in the car?'

Sophy was looking strangely pale. 'That was Mr Rawlings,' she said with obvious difficulty after a moment's silence.

'Who?' John looked baffled.

'He's one of the men in charge of us at the . . . the printers.' Sophy peered down the lane but the car had long since gone. 'But I don't understand. Rawlings was the one who sent us here. He . . .' She closed her eyes for a moment, and then shook herself, squaring her shoulders resolutely. 'Well, that doesn't matter for now. First things first. We have to find out if Alice and Patrick are still in there. Until we know that for sure, we dare not do anything.'

'Agreed.' Penny turned to John, only to realise he had gone.

They both stared about the woodland, but the fisherman was nowhere in sight. Then Sophy gasped, pointing. John was at the back of the hut, standing tall to look through the window. After the briefest of peeks inside, he crouched and nodded at them, frantically jerking his thumb towards the hut as though to say, 'They're inside.'

Penny felt sick at the danger he'd put himself in, just to help her and Alice. If that soldier were to catch him, Lord alone knew what he'd do to a local man found snooping around. But if Alice was still being held prisoner by these men, it was clear she had to be rescued. Danger or no danger.

'All right, so what now?' she whispered.

'We need to get them out of there and safely back to town.' Sophy pulled a face. 'But how?' She frowned. 'Hold on, what's he saying?'

John was acting out some kind of dumb show, pointing to himself and then the hut, and then miming running away down the lane. Then he pointed at Sophy and Penny and the front of the hut, and nodded, looking at them questioningly.

'Good God.' Sophy sounded stunned.

'What is it? What does he mean?'

'I think he's planning to distract whoever's holding Alice and Patrick and then run away so they'll follow him. Meanwhile, we'll sneak around the front and get them out of the hut while nobody's guarding them.'

'No, no, he mustn't!' Penny was horrified by this insane plan. 'They probably have guns. He could be shot.'

Sophy didn't dismiss this as she'd feared but nodded. 'Yes, it's too risky,' she said slowly, and began miming, 'No,' back to him and indicating that he should return to their hiding place among the trees.

'Oh no,' Penny groaned, when it became clear that he was not going to stand down from his crazy plan. She waved her arms, but he was no longer looking. 'He'll be killed.'

'Let's hope not.' Sophy grabbed her arm, looking her straight in the eye. 'Do you want to get Alice back or leave her to the Americans? They could be torturing her right now in that hut. Hurting her badly . . . or worse.'

'*Worse*?' Penny shook her head when Sophy opened her mouth. 'No, don't . . . I get the idea.'

Sophy's eyes were piercing. 'If you don't feel brave enough, you can stay here while I try to get them both out *on my own*.'

Guilt pricked at Penny's conscience. 'Oh, well, when you put it like that,' she muttered, and took a deep breath. 'All right,' she agreed, swallowing hard and feeling very far from brave. 'What do you want me to do?'

'Just follow my lead and try not to get shot.'

Penny clutched her stomach, which was roiling with fear. 'Right,' she said faintly, and fell in behind Sophy as the other girl tiptoed through the trees to a better vantage point. 'Try not to get shot. That's good . . . good advice.'

At last, they were facing the front of the hut, but still hidden within the trees. John peered around the back of the hut, looking their way. After a long moment, during which Sophy seemed to be listening to the rumble of voices inside the hut, she gave a clear thumbs-up signal and nodded, telling him to put his plan into action. Penny watched, her breathing constricted, blood thudding in her temples, as the fisherman suddenly banged his fists on the back of the hut, yelling something like, 'Yankee dogs! I'm coming to get you, Yankees!' and then kicked the hut violently so the whole structure shook.

The door of the hut flew open and two US Rangers rushed out, armed menacingly with rifles and staring about the clearing in angry astonishment.

One of the men spotted John, now legging it as fast as he could down the track towards town, and shouted, 'Hey you, stop right there!' after him.

John slowed and then stopped, seeing they were not pursuing him. He cast about the dirt track briefly, picked up a few large stones, and began to lob them at the hut. He must have had good aim, for one audibly cracked the glass.

'What on earth . . . ?' One of the soldiers swung the rifle off his back. 'Right, he asked for this.' To Penny's horror, he leveled the rifle at John's chest.

'No!' the other soldier barked, knocking his arm. 'Just get after him.'

'On my own?'

The other soldier pulled a face, and then both began to run down the track towards John, who had zigzagged hurriedly into the trees at the first sight of that rifle.

'This is it,' Sophy hissed.

They dashed across the track. It was damp and gloomy inside the hut. Alice and Patrick were there, both tied to chairs. Patrick was gagged but Alice wasn't and she exclaimed in horror on seeing who had come to her rescue. Sophy dragged off Patrick's gag and bent to untie his bonds, nodding her towards Alice. 'Hurry, before they come back.'

'Penny? What are you doing here?' Alice looked furious rather than grateful. 'You shouldn't have come. It's dangerous.'

'Shut up,' Penny groaned, fumbling with the looped knots. 'Oh, these are impossible.' Dimly, she recalled something John had once told her about releasing knots when he'd been tying up the *Mary Jane*, tugged gently on the end that was sticking out and, almost miraculously, the knot slipped loose and the ropes came undone. 'Thank God,' she gasped, helping Alice to her feet. 'Now let's get out of here.'

Worryingly, there was no sign of John or the soldiers

outside. Penny stared down the lane, hoping to goodness they hadn't shot him.

'This way,' Patrick said hoarsely, leading them up the wooded slope beyond the clearing. 'We can't go back by the road.'

Sophy, scrambling up the slope after Alice, saw Penny's anxious, wide-eyed expression and said, 'I'm sure he's fine. He knows this terrain better than them, remember. And I didn't hear a shot.'

Realising she was right, Penny allowed herself to breathe at last. There had been no sound of gunfire, and in those quiet woodlands, it would have been audible for miles. But she knew she still wouldn't rest easy until she'd seen John with her own eyes again, safe and sound. She'd been so fearful back there when the soldier had turned his gun on John. She'd been ready to leap forward and have the horrid man take aim at her rather than see John killed.

What did that mean, though? Did it mean she was in love with John Pascoe? Because she'd never been in love with anyone before and had no idea what it might feel like. She'd certainly never thought about giving up her life for someone else in such a dramatic way. But then, she supposed people in love must have been doing that all across the continent as Hitler rolled inexorably forward with his tanks and troops, subduing towns and villages in country after country, and murdering thousands in the process. It ought to feel momentous, realising she was in love. But what did it matter how one woman felt for one man when so many had died and were still dying?

All she really knew was that she hoped John had escaped and that she would soon see him again. Her chaotic mind, still teeming with fear and confusion, simply refused to look beyond that moment.

'Traitors,' Patrick was saying to Sophy in an undertone. 'They must be traitors. Why else take us prisoner like that?'

In clipped tones, Sophy told the other two about Rawlings sitting with an American in his car outside the hut. Alice listened to this tale without comment. Several times, she stopped to give Penny a hand, who was finding the steep ascent difficult.

'Alice, do you think that man Rawlings is a traitor?' Penny asked quietly as they reached a well-worn path at the top of the hill, stopping there for a breather.

Alice was staring down at Bude, the beaches and harbour and river laid out below them, glinting prettily in the cold January light.

'That doesn't seem likely.' But she was frowning.

'How else do you explain him being there, then?' Sophy insisted, coming back towards them, her tone suddenly antagonistic. 'And why did the Americans want you so badly?' Her eyes narrowed in suspicion on Alice's face. 'You need to tell us the truth.'

'No, what I *need* is to find Rawlings,' Alice shot back at the girl, and turned, striding away on the path that led back to town. 'As soon as possible.'

'Rawlings? Are you mad?' Sophy stared after her. 'He can't be trusted. I saw him with my own eyes, talking to one of the Americans who were holding you. And then he just drove off,' she pointed out angrily, raising her voice, 'leaving you and Patrick to rot.'

But Alice made no response.

Penny hurried after her friend, glancing back every few

minutes in the hope of seeing John emerge at the top of the wooded hill. To her growing disquiet, there was still no sign of him.

It would be too dreadful if the Americans had taken him prisoner instead, after everything he'd done to help them. And she was so confused, her thoughts in a proper muddle. The US Rangers were meant to be on their side. The United States were allies with Britain against Germany, for goodness' sake. So why had those Americans treated Alice and Patrick so badly, tying them up in that hut, and then threatening to *shoot* John, of all people?

Something was deeply wrong here.

She only hoped that Alice, who was the smartest person she knew, could work it out before anything awful happened to John.

CHAPTER TWENTY-FOUR

To Florence's amazement, her sister remained true to her word. Ever since the awful night when she'd been caught with a young man in her room, Imogen had behaved impeccably. She had also taken on many of Florence's own household chores, a most welcome relief for Florence, who was feeling tired and rundown.

She knew her depressive mood was due in part to the horrifying realisation that she had fallen in love with Miles and knew those feelings to be wrong. The American officer was just passing through her life, while she was rooted here in Bude with her son. There could be no hope of a relationship with him. Even if by some miracle Miles managed to survive the war, and the Allied Forces won and peace was restored, the chances of them being able to forge a happy future together were low indeed. Not least because he lived in the United States, a place she knew nothing about.

Besides, his relatives would not look kindly on a marriage between them. She was a widow with a young child, for goodness' sake. Not exactly the romance of the century, was it?

She and Imogen were outside, struggling with the twice-weekly laundry in the backyard, their hands red and chapped in the cold January air, when her next-door neighbour called out to her over the wall, 'Mrs Pritchard, there's someone waiting at your front door.' There was a slight hesitation, then she continued unhappily, 'I'm afraid it looks like the telegram boy.'

Florence glanced at Imogen, her heart full of turmoil, not sure what to think. But they had no brother or husband at war, and their parents were fairly safe from bombing on the outskirts of Exeter, though the city centre had been hard hit. The telegram boy only ever brought bad news, and the last time she had received that horrid brown envelope, it had been with an official announcement of her own dear Percy's passing.

Thanking her neighbour, she dried her hands on her apron. 'I'd better go and see what it's about,' she said quietly. 'Are you able to finish the washing on your own, Imogen? I'll be back to help you put them through the mangle.'

'Of course.' Imogen was looking curious though. 'I wonder who the telegram is for. Maybe one of the soldiers who are billeted here. Though there's Alice too. Or maybe Penny?'

'Yes, it seems unlikely that it could be for one of us. After all, who would be sending us a telegram?'

Leaving her sister up to the elbows in a tub of cooling soapy water, Florence hurried into the empty house. The telegram boy, thankfully, was still on the doorstep when she opened the front door. No doubt her neighbour had told him to wait. The boy held out the brown envelope and Florence took it, not daring to meet his eyes.

'Telegram for Staff Sergeant Miles Miller.'

Her heart clenched hard at that familiar name but she thanked the boy without comment and watched as he turned away.

After he'd gone, she walked to the garden gate to peer up and down the road. But there was nobody else in sight. The rolling marshy downs stretched away towards the town, green and peaceful, and from the beach she could hear the familiar shouts of the American troops being put through their paces.

She looked down at the envelope in her hand. Was Miles at the beach? Ought she to walk down that way to hand him this telegram personally? It was early afternoon, and he might not be back until suppertime. Maybe not even then, for his work often kept him out late in the evenings. But if this was important enough to deliver as a telegram, rather than a letter, it really ought to be delivered by hand as soon as possible.

Going back into the house, she looked up to find Imogen, sleeves still rolled up to her elbows and her hands dripping, studying her nervously from the other end of the passageway.

'Well? Who was it for?' her sister asked.

With a surprisingly steady voice, Florence told her and saw her sister's face change. Fear fell away and sympathy took its place.

'Oh dear. I'm so sorry, Florence.'

Florence frowned. 'Why are you sorry? It's not for me.'

Her sister's brows arched up sharply. 'I'm neither blind

309

nor stupid,' she pointed out. 'I know there's something between you and Miles. If you want to pretend there isn't, that's fine too. But I'm still sorry.'

There didn't seem much point in denying it. All the same, Florence decided not to respond. There was something between her and Miles. But it was nobody else's business except their own.

She reached for her headscarf and knotted it under her chin. Then pushed her arms into the sleeves of her winter coat and fastened the buttons. 'It might be important, so I'm going to walk down to the beach and see if Miles is there. Or he may be up on Maer Cliff, training with the Rangers. Either way, I can't wait until he gets back. It's a telegram. It's meant to be delivered as quickly as possible.'

She didn't know why she was making all these excuses for a simple trip down the road to see if one of the men who lodged with her was available to take this telegram. Or rather, she did. But she didn't want her sister to know how deep her feelings went for Miles. It was all still so new and raw in her heart, and she was hugging that secret knowledge to herself for now. It couldn't go anywhere, could it? And now this telegram . . .

She dreaded its contents. But she knew she had to get it to Miles as soon as possible. 'I'll be back soon,' she told Imogen. 'Don't try and work the mangle on your own. You could lose a finger.'

On reaching Crooklets Beach, she was directed up a muddy and meandering path onto Maer Cliff where she could see row upon row of Rangers going through their routines.

She was not allowed to approach the soldiers directly, but one of the guards at the checkpoint, after asking her business, went to fetch Miles for her. She didn't explain her errand, merely told the soldier that it was urgent she speak to Sergeant Miller, assuming he could be spared.

At last, she saw Miles himself, a tall figure against the backdrop of a coldly glittering ocean, detaching himself from the ranks and heading in her direction.

'Mrs Pritchard,' he said with a formal nod. 'Is something the matter? How can I help you, ma'am?'

Trembling a little, Florence held out the telegram, folded over to form a sealed envelope. 'This came for you just now. I was worried it might be urgent. Otherwise I would never have disturbed you during training.'

Miles hesitated before taking the telegram from her. 'Yes, I see.' Without opening it, he slipped it inside a pocket of his jacket. 'Thank you for your trouble, Mrs Pritchard. That was very kind of you.'

With another nod, he returned to his men. Precisely as though they had been strangers.

Slowly, Florence retraced her steps back home, barely noting the soldiers scaling the cliff or the squad hurrying past her at a quick march, singing a jaunty song to help them keep rhythm. All she could focus on was his expression as she held out the telegram. Miles had shrunk from it even while accepting it from her hand. That was why he had not read it, but put the dreaded object away for later. He knew what the message was in that envelope. Or feared what it must be. He wished to be alone when he read it and his worst fears were confirmed.

Back at Ocean View Boarding House, she found Imogen

struggling with the savage machinery of the mangle, despite her advice not to touch it.

Sighing, she put her apron back on and showed her sister how to use it safely, threading each sodden garment through its vicious, hard-grinding rollers with a twist of the wheel and out the other side, squeezing out all the excess water. There, the garment would tumble into a basket, ready to be hung on the line for drying. Imogen was in charge of the shaking out and pegging up, which was not a problem for the sheets and pillowcases. Florence helped with the sheets, for those needed to be folded once before hanging. But her sister floundered with personal items, not knowing how to peg along the seam or hang trousers upside-down, and had to be shown how to do that too.

'You've never dealt with laundry before, have you?' Florence asked, unpegging one of Imogen's pretty blouses and demonstrating how to hang it up so the pegs wouldn't leave marks on the fine fabric as it dried.

'Well, I've never needed to,' Imogen said defensively, plucking another damp blouse from the basket and attempting to place the pegs correctly that time.

Watching her critically, Florence nodded when she stepped back, job done. 'Better.'

Imogen grinned. 'High praise indeed!'

She did not see Miles again until late afternoon when, tidying the front sitting room, she heard a thud of boots on the stairs and peered out to see him going up to his room. Putting away her duster, she hurried upstairs to knock at his door. 'Sergeant Miller?' she said uncertainly, then added more softly, 'Miles? It's Florence. Are . . . Are you all right? Do you want to talk?'

'No, thank you, ma'am,' came his muffled reply, then he jerked open the door. At a glance, she saw that his army rucksack lay on the bed, a stack of clothing beside it. His face was sombre, a look of strain in his eyes. 'I've been granted compassionate leave. I'll be shipping out first thing tomorrow.'

Compassionate leave . . .

'Why, whatever's happened?' she whispered, her heart tugging at the tremor in his voice.

He dashed a hand across his face. 'My . . . my pops . . . He . . .' The words were all but incoherent. Dragging a deep breath into his lungs, Miles straightened his back, standing as rigid as a pole, then said more clearly, 'The telegram was from my mother.' All emotion had been wiped from his face. 'My father has died.'

'Oh no! I'm so sorry, Miles.'

His hand on the door frame tightened at her sympathetic cry, the knuckles whitening, yet somehow he maintained his iron self-control.

'Thank you, ma'am. The funeral is in two days,' he pushed on grittily. 'I didn't expect to be allowed to attend, but I put a request in and my commanding officer has granted permission, so long as I carry a few of his dispatch boxes back with me to the States. There's a transport flying out from Cleave Camp first thing tomorrow and I intend to be on it. So if you'll forgive me . . .'

'What can I do to help?'

Her vision swam with tears, not only for this brave man, battling to hide his natural distress, but remembering how

313

it had felt to receive that awful telegram about her husband. The whole world had crumbled about her at that moment, and yet, life had had to continue, the intensity of her feelings concealed at all costs . . . Because if you let a crack show, the torrent of tears might flood out . . .

'Nothing.' His voice was gruff.

'Can I fetch you something to eat or drink, at least?' she offered, her voice trembling. 'A sandwich? A cup of coffee? Or a pot of tea, perhaps?'

Silently, Miles shook his head.

He was clearly impatient to close the door. To shut her out and get on with the gruelling business of grieving in private. But of course he was.

'Then I shall leave you to it,' Florence said, forcing a wan smile to her lips. 'Again, I'm so very sorry for your loss.'

Miles swallowed. 'Thank you,' he said, and his voice cracked.

She took a step towards him, every fibre in her body aching to draw this man close and show him how much she cared. 'Miles . . .' She gave him a quick hug, sensing how still he had become and hoping he did not resent her interference.

But to her amazement, as she began to draw back, he pulled her close again and kissed her full on the lips. For a moment, they stood locked together, his body pressed against hers. Then he jerked back, his face contorted. 'Florence, I beg your pardon . . . I don't know why I did that. Please forgive me.'

And he turned away, shutting himself in his bedroom.

Stunned and breathless, Florence walked slowly downstairs, her lips still tingling from his kiss.

Someone was knocking urgently at the front door. The noise broke through her daze and she jerked the door open to find Mrs Roskilly on the step, the farmer's wife who ran the dairy shop in town where Alice worked.

Mrs Roskilly glared at her angrily. 'Is Penny here?'

'I don't think so.' Surprised, Florence went to the foot of the stairs and called up to Penny's room. There was no response. Going back to the door, she told the woman coldly, 'No, I don't believe so,' for Penny had frequently reported mean treatment at the hands of her boss. 'Sorry.'

She began to close the door, but Mrs Roskilly stuck her foot in the way.

'She didn't come back to the shop after her lunch break,' she said shortly. 'For the umpteenth time. So, when you see Penny, you can tell her she's sacked. She's done this once too often for me to turn a blind eye.' Her chest heaved with indignation. 'I've had to leave my boy in charge while I've been running about the town, looking everywhere for that bloody irresponsible girl.'

'I'll thank you not to use bad language in my house,' Florence told her, thrusting out her chin. It wasn't right that Penny hadn't returned to work. But she could easily see why the girl would be reluctant to go back, having to put up with this horrid woman all day.

'I'm not *in* your house,' Mrs Roskilly pointed out with a snap. 'I'm on the doorstep.'

'The doorstep is still my property.' Florence pointed to the garden gate. 'So, if you wouldn't mind leaving . . .'

'Well, I never!' Mrs Roskilly exclaimed, but bustled away down the path, fury in every line of her body. 'I should have known better than to expect proper behaviour from you . . . A young widow, taking in a dozen or so soldiers? Don't think we don't know what's been going on here after dark.' On that outrageous remark, she flung open the garden gate. 'And Penny's just the same. I should have sacked the shameless girl when she started walking out with John Pascoe, and after making eyes at my own husband too.'

'I beg your pardon?' Florence was shocked by such a wild accusation.

'You can tell Penny, she'd better not come asking me for a reference, that's all. Or her wages for this week. Because she won't be allowed back in my shop. Enough is enough.'

'Penny is a good girl and I trust she'll be paid whatever she's due,' Florence threw down the street after her, incensed by the woman's attitude. 'Otherwise, you and I will have words, Mrs Roskilly.'

But, as her temper abated and reality struck home, Florence began to worry. She sometimes forgot, in the effort of caring for all the soldiers in her boarding house, that she also had two young women under her roof, who needed someone to consider their welfare too. Even after Mrs Roskilly had vanished out of sight, she still stood frowning at the gate, her gaze scouring the empty downs and road to the beach.

Where *was* Penny?

CHAPTER TWENTY-FIVE

Tied to a chair in that gloomy hut in the woods beyond Bude canal, Alice had never been so scared in all her born days. Yet she'd never felt so alive either. Something exciting had happened to her at last, after years of reading novels and wishing her own life could be as thrilling as the stories she devoured from bookstands or the lending library. Her fear had been largely for Patrick – and Sophy too if she happened to be caught. Her team members. But there was also a growing fear for her father. Since, as it turned out, that was who the Americans had wanted to know about.

The three men had interrogated Patrick first, who'd looked terrified when they started going at him hard. Perhaps the boy had feared they were planning to shoot him, though Alice had personally thought that unlikely. Why would their own allies shoot them? It would make no sense. Though none of this made much sense, she had to admit to herself.

Alice had expected Patrick to stand up to interrogation well, as he always had in their training sessions, boasting afterwards about how he could handle being tortured for hours without giving anything away. Yet he'd lost his cocky swagger early on and had soon begun stammering about how they were only on a training course and not real agents.

After being threatened with having his fingernails removed, he had quickly given up their instructors' names, urging them to, 'Go and find Rawlings, for God's sake. Don't hurt me. I'm nobody, I was only following orders by tailing you.' He'd even broken down in tears at one point, snivelling and begging the soldiers to let him go when they discussed breaking his kneecaps. 'You said it was her you wanted, not me. This isn't fair!'

After a while, one of the men untied Patrick and took him outside at gunpoint. Alice had watched this separation with concern at first, fearing they did mean to shoot him. But she'd rapidly guessed this was merely done to allow her own interrogation to be handled in private.

Alice had been left alone with the red-haired soldier and the other man, who then began interrogating her as they had done with Patrick. The ropes had cut deep into her wrists, its coarse fibres chafing against her skin. She had concentrated on the pain this caused, recalling how her father had told her once that pain could keep the mind focused during an interrogation. She'd been fascinated at the time, but never dreamt she would ever need to put that tip into practice herself.

The red-haired American had crouched beside her, staring into her face. 'We know who you are, Alice Fisher. And we know whose daughter you are.' Lighting a cigarette, he had blown smoke into her eyes. 'We don't want to hurt you, okay? But we will, if we must. So why not make it easier on yourself? Tell us what we want to know and we'll let you and your friend go. How does that sound?'

Tightening her lips, Alice had said nothing.

The two men had exchanged glances, then the red-headed soldier had turned away with a shrug, smoking his cigarette.

The other man had leant forward instead, his hands on her shoulders, pushing his face right up against hers. He was more aggressive, which she'd been told was often the case when an agent was interrogated by two people at the same time. One might offer an easy way out, while the other threatened punishment if she didn't talk. The trick, she'd been taught, was to treat them both equally and say nothing.

'Listen, you little fool,' he said harshly, 'I don't care what happens to you. I just need some information and I don't mind how we get it.' His eyes had run over her in a way she'd found distinctly uncomfortable. 'It would be better for you if you told us straightaway where we can find your father. Otherwise, things could get unpleasant here.' He had paused, studying her expression. His eyes narrowed, his voice more calculating as he'd added, 'For your friend as well as for you.'

That had told her they planned to use Patrick against her. Hurt him if she didn't speak, for instance. Some small comment had been required to delay that possibility.

'My father is dead,' she'd said flatly.

The man leaning over her had given a harsh laugh and slapped her face. 'Liar!'

It hadn't been a hard slap but her cheek had stung

afterwards and quick tears had sprung to her eyes too. A physical response, that was all. She wasn't *crying*, she had told herself, glaring up at him with her lips tightly sealed again. What a coward, she'd thought. Easy to hit a girl tied to a chair!

The red-haired man had elbowed his companion aside, still dragging on his cigarette. 'Sorry about that. My friend here isn't very civilised. He likes the rough stuff. But I have a softer touch, if you know what I mean.' He too had studied her figure with a look her aunt Violet would have described as impertinent. 'There's more than one way to skin a cat. I think you know what I'm talking about. Or maybe you don't . . .' Then he'd run his fingers down her cheek, watching closely for signs of a reaction. 'You want to find out or are you ready to talk?'

Alice had shuddered but still said nothing.

'Tough nut to crack, huh?' The other man had moved behind her and suddenly grabbed her hair, dragging her head back so he could stare down into her face, his face upside down. 'Okay, doll, where's your father? When did you last see him?' When she'd continued to say nothing, he'd pulled harder on her hair until she let out an involuntary cry of pain. 'Start talking, Alice, or I'll get the knife out. Slapping and pulling hair is fun. But I know better ways to make a girl talk.'

'What's your father's full name?' the red-haired soldier had demanded, taking over again. He too had slapped her face when she didn't respond and then grasped her chin, squeezing hard enough to hurt. 'Just tell us his name, for starters. Cooperate and we won't hurt you anymore.'

Alice had known there could be no harm in telling them

her father's name. That was hardly a state secret. Except that it could be the start of a dangerous conversation. If she buckled under pressure and told them his name, she might then be inclined to go on and tell them other things too. Such as what he was doing for this country and when he had last been on British soil.

Better to remain completely silent than risk any harm to her father.

Biting her lip so hard she'd been able to taste her own blood, Alice had sat trembling and in silence, determined not to say a single word, whatever they did to her . . .

After maybe half an hour of this interrogation, the men had given up and dragged Patrick back inside. She had studied the boy for signs of bruising or other hurts, but it hadn't looked to her as though he had been interrogated at all. They had tied him to the chair again and begun discussing among themselves how to proceed.

One of the soldiers had then left to return to town on foot, perhaps to make a report to some superior officer.

Maybe an hour later, someone had kicked the back of the hut, shouting insults at the Americans inside, and the two men left to guard them had stared at each other, amazed. Then they'd rushed out, leaving the door unguarded . . .

Now, striding back into town with Penny, Patrick and Sophy at her back, Alice found it impossible to answer any of the string of questions racing through her mind.

It had been Rawlings who had given them this special mission. Rawlings who had made it clear from the start he knew who her father was and that he worked for the

British government. Rawlings was the only one who could possibly have alerted the Americans to the fact that she was connected to an operative and might have useful information. Was he in fact a traitor?

Alice considered that, rubbing her sore wrists where the ropes had bitten into her skin. Her instincts told her that Rawlings was not a traitor. Yet the evidence was against him . . .

Her head spun and she pushed the questions away, impatiently. She needed to see Rawlings face to face. Only then would she be able to tell whether he was a traitor or not, and if he was the one who had deliberately set them up. Because that had been an ambush, no doubt about it. Those Americans had known they were being followed and, more importantly, who was following them. They hadn't been interested in Patrick. It was her, Alice Fisher, they'd been focused on right from the beginning.

Reaching the bridge that took them into the town, she whirled on Patrick. 'Did that man interrogate you when he took you out of the hut? What did he say? Did he ask about me?'

Blinking, Patrick ran a hand through his ruffled hair. 'He asked one or two questions about Rawlings, actually. I never trusted Rawlings, you know. Always struck me as a slippery type.' He glanced at Sophy and added, drawing himself up straighter, 'Though I did ask why they were so interested in you. But he refused to answer.'

'Hmm,' she said, not believing for a minute that he would have had the courage to ask such a question of his interrogator.

'Anyway, why did those men say *you* were the one they

wanted?' His gaze narrowed suspiciously on her face. 'What are you not telling us?'

But Alice simply shook her head. If she hadn't told those men in the hut about her father, who had been threatening her with every kind of torture, she certainly wasn't going to say a word to pimply Patrick.

Even more convinced now that it had been a set-up, Alice hurried on into town, the others running to keep up with her long, forceful strides. But when they finally reached the printers' workshop, she stopped and turned to Penny. 'You can't come in – it's not safe. You need to go back to the boarding house, understand?' There were tears in her eyes as she hugged her friend, for she knew how much Penny had risked to come and save her. 'I hope that man . . . John, was it? I hope he gets back safely, that they let him go. I'm sure they will. But if they don't, I'll bloomin' move heaven and earth to get him back. Because it weren't his fault, none of this,' Alice whispered in her ear before releasing her. 'The Americans were after me, you see.'

'After *you*?' Penny looked bewildered. 'But why? I don't understand.'

'Nor do I,' Alice admitted. 'But I intend to find out.'

'Oh, Alice, do be careful,' Penny warned her.

'Don't worry about me, love. I can take care of myself,' Alice told her stoutly, though she had to admit to some trepidation at what lay ahead. 'Thanks for everything you've done. You're the best friend in the world.' With a shaky laugh, she rubbed a fist over her damp cheeks. 'Blimey, look at me! Sobbing like a little baby. But you and John were smashing back there, Penny. Absolutely smashing and I won't forget it.' She glanced over her shoulder into the gloomy alleyway. 'All the same, you need to go home now. Go up to your bedroom and stay there until I come back. We'll talk then.'

Penny stared at her, amazed. 'You don't think they'll come after me too, surely?'

'I don't know but I'd hate to see you hurt.' Alice swallowed. 'I hope I will see you later, Penny. But if I don't, if something happens to me, will you tell my aunt Violet and my gran that I . . .' Words failed her and she gulped.

'Tell them what?' Penny searched her face, concern in her eyes.

'That I love them very much, that's all.' Alice hugged her friend one last time and then said goodbye.

Resolutely, not looking back, she marched down the alleyway to the printers' workshop, which looked empty and in darkness. The cold January afternoon was drawing in and it would soon be dusk. Patrick followed in silence, with Sophy bringing up the rear.

'Those men knew you were following them,' Sophy whispered as they crept into the unlocked workshop, looking nervously about. 'Which means someone must have tipped them off.'

'Yes,' a man's voice said from the shadows, and Rawlings stepped forward, his hands in his pockets. 'Someone tipped them off all right.'

Alice's heart thumped with shock. 'It were *you*, weren't it, Mr Rawlings?' she accused him directly, jabbing a finger in his direction. 'You might as well come clean about it. I may have trusted you once but I ain't stupid. Them Americans knew all about us. Which means you laid that trap and let us walk straight into it, didn't you?'

'I did,' he agreed smoothly.

Sophy was staring at him wide-eyed, amazement and horror in her face. 'But you're our instructor. Why would you do such a thing?'

'Because it was necessary,' Rawlings told her.

'*Necessary*?' Patrick echoed in disbelief. 'What on earth are you talking about?' His voice rose angrily. 'Those men hurt me. Alice too. They bloody well *tortured* us. Don't you care?'

Rawlings flicked a glance at him. 'Of course I care.'

'But we could have been killed.'

'I assure you, your lives were never in any danger.' There was a ghost of a smile about Rawling's mouth. 'It's all part of the training, I'm afraid. An unpleasant experience but not a dangerous one.'

Alice, who had been watching him in silence, burst out with, 'It was a test.'

'Yes, my dear, it was a test.'

'And the three Americans were in on it,' she said wonderingly. 'You told 'em our weak spots. Got 'em to prod us where it hurts.'

'Something like that, yes,' Rawlings nodded, an approving look in his eyes. 'I had a call a few minutes ago to let me know you were free and probably on your way back here.' He smiled at last. 'It seems you passed the test with flying colours, my dear. You refused to give up any information, regardless of the threats made to you.' His gaze moved to Sophy. 'As did you.'

Sophy's eyes grew round with surprise. 'Me? But I wasn't even interrogated.'

'No, but you found a way to rescue your team members, despite a lack of time and resources. That was also part of the test. To see whether you could think on your feet and find ways around difficulties. Deeply valuable skills in the field.'

'Oh.' Sophy looked pleased.

'And me, sir?' Patrick dug his hands into his trouser pockets. From his miserable look, it was clear he already knew the answer.

'We'll discuss your test results another time, I think,' Rawlings told him gently, looking the boy up and down. 'For now, I think all three of you should head back to your lodgings, have a bath and a hot meal, and try to get some sleep. Debriefing will take place tomorrow morning, and I'll accept no excuses for turning up late.'

'No, sir,' Alice agreed, but hesitated as the other two shuffled out of the workshop, looking at each other in trepidation. 'Sir?'

'Yes, Miss Fisher?'

'There was a man who helped us escape. A local fisherman. I don't suppose you know what—'

'Mr Pascoe was allowed to return to town unmolested, don't worry.' Mr Rawlings chuckled. 'I only hope he won't discuss what happened with anyone.'

'I'm sure he won't,' Alice said quickly.

'I'm glad to hear it.' He paused. 'Pascoe's clearly a brave man, if a little foolhardy. I shall recommend him to the Bude Invasion Committee. They're always looking for capable, quick-thinking citizens who are prepared to take the initiative . . . Our first line of defence against an invasion by Germany.' Rawlings nodded her towards the door. 'Go on home. You look exhausted. It's been a long day.' He smiled. 'We can talk more tomorrow.'

'Yes, but . . . *They knew about my dad*.' She couldn't hide the accusation in her voice.

'Not the truth. We gave them what we call a "script" about your father, that he was their fictional "target" during the interrogation. When you refused to answer, they would simply have assumed you were following the same script. Those men know nothing about your *real* father, Alice, believe me.' He paused. 'Besides, they form part of our intelligence unit while they're stationed in Bude. They can be trusted.'

'But Patrick's suspicious now,' she pointed out unhappily. 'He knows they were particularly interested in me, but not why.'

Rawlings frowned. 'I'll explain to him about the interrogation script. Though I doubt it will be a problem – Patrick will be moving on soon.'

Her eyes widened. 'He's leaving?'

'Let's call it a redeployment,' he said easily. 'Not everyone is cut out for this kind of work. And, between you and me, young Patrick has other skills worth developing. Listening skills, for instance.' And he winked. 'Something you know all about, I should imagine.'

Alice stared at him, amazed. Was Patrick being sent for further training at Eastern House, the government listening station where she and her family had worked as cleaners on first coming down to Cornwall? A mere stone's throw from Joe's farm at Porthcurno . . .

That would be a turn-up, all right. Though Patrick would hate it, being stranded for months out there in the sticks.

She laughed, feeling happier than she'd done all day. 'Well, you know best. Blimey though, I'm starving! This spy business don't 'alf give you an appetite.' Heading out, she turned at the door, saying, 'Goodnight, sir,' but Rawlings had already vanished into the shadows again.

'I swear, that man's like a bloomin' ghost,' Alice muttered, and began the short walk home through the freezing dusk, already dreaming of her supper.

CHAPTER TWENTY-SIX

Penny stood forlorn, watching Alice and her friends disappear inside the printers' workshop where, until today, she had thought Alice was undertaking war work as a printer. It was hard to come to terms with the knowledge that she had in fact been training to be . . . what? *A spy*? She wasn't sure, but she did know she couldn't talk about it to anyone. Or not anyone she hadn't been out with today.

It wasn't dark yet, but light was failing as the afternoon wore on and a few clouds had gathered overhead. A large-wheeled farm vehicle trundled by slowly, spitting mud clods, with a greengrocer's van following impatiently behind. Opposite, a woman was peering into the window of a shop, her headscarf flapping in the breeze blowing through the town centre. A man, hurrying past, touched his hat in greeting when Penny glanced at him, and she heard herself say, 'Good afternoon,' in response.

Life in Bude was going on as normal all around her. And yet, something quite amazing and breathtaking had just happened.

Now Alice had told her to get back to the boarding house and sit in her bedroom. Just in case . . . Well, she didn't know what. Would those Americans come looking for her too? The thought scared her. But it also made her angry because they were supposed to be Britain's allies and whatever risk they thought Alice and Patrick posed, there was no excuse for holding two young people against their will, not to mention frightening them half to death. As for pointing a rifle at John . . .

Her heart gave a sickening thud, and Penny turned impulsively, heading downhill. She wasn't going back to Ocean View Boarding House, but in the opposite direction, back the way they had come, in search of John.

Crossing the bridge at the bottom of the hill, she saw John heading her way. Relief flooded her and she ran to him. 'Oh, there you are! I've been out of mind . . .'

But her voice tailed off as John grabbed her and spun her around, her feet in the air, completely oblivious to passers-by staring at them.

Once her feet had touched down again, John led her inside the cottage and closed the door, laughing. His face was glowing as he turned and planted a kiss on Penny's lips. 'Thank you.'

'Whatever for?' she stammered.

'For today, of course. It was the most marvellous adventure I've ever had. Like going to war, except I never had to leave Bude. I wish I could do it all over again.' He was grinning. 'Tell me your friends got away, Penny . . . Tell me *that*, at least. That I wasn't wasting my time running about the woods with American soldiers armed with semi-automatics chasing after me.'

Penny had stood shocked after his kiss, listening in a daze to his exuberant speech, but now she came back to life, crying out, 'Yes, oh yes, they got away! You did brilliantly, John. I was so proud of you.' She looked up into his face shyly. 'When you threw those stones, even in the face of their guns . . . I've never seen anything so brave in my life.'

In response, John kissed her again, and for a long while there was silence in the small front room of the fisherman's cottage.

He drew back at last and smoothed a hand over her hair, the gesture tender. 'Look, I'm probably going to make a mess of this,' he said shakily, 'even though I've rehearsed it in my head, and I know it may seem sudden, but . . .' John paused, frowning. 'I knew before today, of course, but I only properly realised it when I was leading them soldiers away from you in the woods.'

'Realised what?' she asked, perplexed.

'How I feel about you.' His eyes were earnest and shining. 'I was risking my life but I didn't care. It didn't matter. All that mattered was *you*.' A smile burst on his lips, tremulous with joy. 'I knew then that I . . . I'd do anything for you, Penny. Maybe I'm making a hash of this after all, but the simple truth is, I think I'm in love with you, and I'd be honoured if you would agree to be my wife.'

Penny's jaw had dropped open. She hadn't expected to hear a proposal from him, and certainly not so suddenly, coming out of nowhere.

Carefully, not wanting to hurt his feelings, she asked, 'Are you sure you mean it, John? That is, thank you, I'm awfully flattered. But I'm sure you can't be serious.'

He looked surprised. 'Why not? I've never been more serious in my life.'

Penny thought back over his behaviour the last few times she'd seen him and realised that he had been more attentive than usual. And more interested in kissing her too. The signs had been there, but she had simply missed them. Perhaps because she'd long since given up hope of attracting the sort of man who was interested in marriage and was just taking each day at a time instead, trying to enjoy life while she could, war or no war.

'Goodness . . . Well, I don't know what to say.'

'Say yes,' he told her eagerly.

'The thing is, I don't know how I feel about the idea of getting married. I mean, it's an amazing offer and I'm very grateful to you for asking . . .' Abruptly, she stopped trying to be polite, both hands flying to her hot cheeks. 'But marriage is forever, John. *Till death do us part.* And I'm only twenty-two. It's very young to be getting wed. I need time to think about this.'

The excitement had faded from his face. John nodded, taking a step backwards. 'Of course,' he agreed more slowly, running a hand through his hair. 'You must take all the time you need. And remember, I don't mean we should marry next month or even next year. I'm happy to wait if you prefer a long engagement. I just wanted you to know how I feel.' His gaze sought hers, and his smile was the sweetest thing she had ever seen. 'So, here's me telling you . . . You're a smashing girl, Penny. And I'm in love with you. That's all.'

She couldn't help smiling in return. 'Thank you, John. Let me think about it and I'll give you an answer as soon as I can,' she promised, and saw the light return to his eyes. 'I'm sorry not to be saying yes at once. It's not because I don't like you very much indeed. Because I do, John Pascoe.' Her blush deepened at the words. 'Only it's such a big decision. I don't want to feel later that I was rushed into it.'

'Nor do I,' he admitted, nodding vehemently, and took her hands in his. 'I'll wait. Even if it takes you forever to make up your mind.'

'It won't take me that long,' she reassured him, and they grinned at each other.

A few minutes later, the door to the cottage opened and his mother came in from the shops, followed by his father and grandfather. John and Penny had been seated together on the settle but jumped up, awkwardly dropping hands.

'Now, what's been happening here?' John's father demanded in a jovial way, nudging his son. 'Alone with a girl? You'll be asking her to marry you next.'

To Penny's relief, John didn't tell his family that he had already asked and was waiting for an answer. He shot her a smiling glance though.

'How did you get on in the woods? You was gone a mighty long time, my boy,' his grandfather said, fixing him with a curious eye.

'Yes,' his father agreed. 'Your ma was worried, so me and your grandpa took a walk out past the canal, looking for you. Found that jerry-built hut the girl spoke of. But there weren't nobody about.'

John scratched his chin. 'Ah yes, well . . . We sorted it out. Got the boy and Penny's friend out of there. There was a bit of a scuffle, but nothing to write home about.' He grinned. 'I'm alive, least ways. So that's that.'

'Such goings-on in Bude,' his mother grumbled, tightening her clutch on the shopping basket. 'You ought to know, that Mrs Roskilly from the dairy is out looking for your girl. She be on the warpath, good and proper.' She shot a sharp look at Penny. 'You might want to go into the shop and apologise, my dear. If you want your job back, that is.'

'My job back?' Penny repeated, perplexed.

John stared at his mother, his eyes wide. 'Whatever do you mean, Ma?' He turned to Penny, frowning. 'You've not lost your job at the dairy, have you? Not that anyone would blame you for walking out . . . That woman's a fire-breathing dragon, you ask me. But you never mentioned it.'

'Because I didn't know,' Penny said blankly, also astonished.

She recalled with a start that she hadn't gone back to work after lunch, all because of that episode in the woods. Mrs Roskilly must have lost her temper for the last time and given her the sack.

'Oh dear . . . I clean forgot about work.' Wrapping her arms about her stomach, she hugged herself. 'Whatever shall I do?'

John's grandfather gave her a friendly nudge. 'No need to look so down in the dumps. We all lose a few jobs now and then. You'll soon find another. There's a war on. Plenty of work to go around. And John's right. That Mrs Roskilly is an old dragon. She had her eyes on our boy once, when he was young,' he remarked, nodding to his son, who threw back his head with a burst of laughter. 'That didn't prosper long, did it? And thank goodness. I'd not ha' had that

334

sour-faced woman as a daughter-in-law for all the tea in China.'

'Oh yes, I was the lucky one there,' John's mother said with a dry intonation that had the Pascoe men all laughing.

But Penny couldn't even smile, too worried about having to face Mrs Roskilly.

'Hey, Grandpa's right,' John said reassuringly, accurately guessing her thoughts. 'There's plenty of work if you know where to look. I've heard they're wanting more Land Girls up at Tregarry Farm on the road to Boscastle. It's a bit of a hike,' he admitted, 'but I'd come and visit you.'

'They're looking for help at the hospital in Stratton too,' his mother remarked, eyeing Penny. 'I know a few of the girls on the wards. I could put in a word.'

'Thank you, Mrs Pascoe,' Penny said shakily, though she couldn't imagine working in a hospital. Still, she hadn't been sure at first that she could stick working indoors after Joe's farm, yet had managed it all the same at the dairy.

'It's getting dark,' John said, lifting his mother's curtains to glance up at the sky. 'Let me walk you home, Penny. Unless you'd like to stay for supper?'

'I'd love to stay,' Penny admitted, 'but if I'm not at the boarding house when Alice gets back, she'll only panic.'

She said her goodbyes to the Pascoes on the doorstep. It was close to dusk and the sea breeze had become unpleasantly chill. Penny shivered, wishing she was more warmly dressed, and was glad when John drew her hand over his arm as they took the lane uphill from the river.

'How are you bearing up?' he asked softly.

'I'm all right,' she said with more bravado than truth, and smiled up at him shyly. Goodness, she thought, he'd offered to marry her. Even though she'd asked for time to think rather than saying yes straightaway, it still warmed her heart to think of it. And he'd helped Alice escape by bravely drawing those soldiers' fire . . . 'You're a good man, John Pascoe.'

John looked embarrassed but chuckled under his breath as the lane steepened. 'That's something, I suppose.'

It was dark by the time they reached Downs View Road, the wind whipping up gritty clouds of sand that blew into their eyes. At the garden gate, Penny turned to John and asked awkwardly, 'Would you like to come in? I'm sure Alice will want to speak to you if she's back. I just hope nothing bad has happened to her.'

But the door opened and John grinned. 'Here she is now, look. Safe and sound.'

Overjoyed, Penny gave a squeal of delight and hugged her friend tightly. 'Alice! Thank goodness! I was so worried in case . . .' She stopped short, aware that 'walls have ears' as the government posters were always warning them, and she ought to keep her secret conversations for later. 'Well, I'm glad to see you in one piece.'

'Ditto!' Alice exclaimed. 'Where in gawd's name have you been? I've been out of my mind . . .' Then shook her head, smiling faintly over her shoulder at John. 'Oh, as if I need ask.' She leant forward to shake John's hand, pumping it vigorously. ''Ere, thanks for everything what you did,' she said, lowering her voice. 'We'd never have got away without your help, I can tell you.'

John protested modestly, but asked, 'Did you find out what was going on? Are you in any trouble?'

Alice shook her head. 'Sorry, I ain't allowed to say anything about it. But no, I'm not in trouble.' She hesitated, her cheeks colouring. 'Look, can I ask you not to tell anyone what happened today? It's all a bit hush-hush.'

'I won't tell a soul – you can trust me,' John assured her.

'Ah, I knew you was a good 'un,' Alice told him with a wink. Inside the boarding house, she glanced down the passageway, and her face changed. 'By the way, Pen,' she whispered, 'you've got visitors. In the sitting room. Though you might want to tidy yourself up before you go in there.'

'Visitors?'

Baffled, Penny glanced at herself in the hall mirror and almost shrieked at her reflection. Her hair looked like she'd been dragged through a hedge backwards. All that nonsense in the woods, and then the dusty winds on the way home . . . She looked like a scarecrow.

Hurriedly, she dragged her fingers through her hair, saying, 'What do you mean? Someone to see me? But who on earth . . .'

At that moment, the door to the sitting room opened and out came Penny's father, followed by her mother, both of them looking smart and austere as ever, their expressions forbidding.

'Thank the Lord,' her mother said fervently, hurrying towards Penny. 'Your landlady told us you'd been gone ages. I was beginning to think you would never come back.' She embraced Penny, smelling of expensive perfume and peppermints. The familiar scents brought a wave of nostalgia tinged with uneasiness. 'How are you, my darling?'

Penny muttered, 'I'm fine,' confused that her parents should have travelled such a long way just to see her, especially given how strict fuel rationing and train travel had become. 'Whatever's wrong? Has somebody died?'

'Of course not.' Her father cleared his throat. 'We got your letter, that's all,' he said darkly, and thrust his chin into the air. 'We talked it over, then thought we'd better come and see you in person, even despite the expense.'

'Is this *him*?' her mother whispered in her ear, though loudly enough for everyone in the hallway to hear, including Alice, who was still loitering halfway up the stairs with a curious expression, listening to every word.

'Sorry?' Penny stared, perplexed. 'Him who?'

'You know very well who.' Her father strode forward, glaring at John but addressing Penny. 'What exactly do you mean by getting involved with this young man? A local fisherman, you wrote in your letter, for God's sake.' Before Penny could say a word, her father shook his head. 'I didn't pay for you to have a good education just to see you throw yourself away on some . . . *fishing person*.' He drew himself up, ignoring John's loud protests. 'Either you renounce this young man straightaway, or we're taking you home with us.'

Her mother nodded, putting a consoling arm about her shoulders. 'It will be for the best, darling. You won't see it now. But, in years to come, you'll thank us.'

Penny was astonished. And outraged. And awfully, wildly angry. 'You came here to tell me that I . . . I can't . . . ?' She shook her head. 'I don't believe it.'

'It's all right, Penny.' John put his cap back on that he'd whipped off at the first sight of her parents. 'Don't you go falling out with your folks over me. It ain't worth it. I'll take myself home, not to worry.'

'Oh no, you won't!' Penny said crossly, and grabbed his hand. 'My *folks*, as you put it, are the ones who are leaving. Aren't you, Mummy and Daddy?'

'Now, listen here,' her father began in a hectoring tone, but Penny interrupted him.

'No, Daddy, you can listen to me for once. I'm not a child anymore and you have no right to tell me who I can't be friends with. Anyway, as it happens, John and I are engaged to be married.'

John gave a groan, but kept hold of her hand, squeezing it encouragingly.

From the shadowy stairs, Alice exclaimed, 'Oh!' at this announcement, and then grinned broadly. 'Congratulations.'

'Thank you,' Penny and John chorused, and glanced at each other, also grinning.

'Engaged?' her mother repeated, wide-eyed.

'Don't be ridiculous,' her father insisted.

'It's time to say goodnight,' Penny told them coolly, and turned to open the front door for them. 'I'd like you to leave. I've nothing more to say to you. Not until you can behave in a more reasonable manner towards myself and my fiancé, that is.'

Her parents seemed dumbfounded by this ultimatum. Her mother said faintly, 'Oh no, darling,' but left the house meekly enough, followed with shuffling steps by Penny's father.

'I shall write to let you know our plans for the wedding,' Penny told them on the doorstep, rather grandly, she felt. 'Don't worry, you *will* be invited.' But she experienced a twinge of regret when her mother cast her a sorrowful last look before disappearing into the dark.

Once the door had shut behind them, John turned to her, searching her face. 'You sure about this, Penny?' he asked uncertainly. 'You weren't just telling me yes to get rid of your folks?'

'Not a bit of it,' Penny told him, her mind made up. 'Though that doesn't mean we have to set a date anytime soon,' she reminded him, and then staggered sideways, fending off Alice's fierce bear hug. 'I know,' she told her friend, laughing. 'You're very happy for us both. And yes, I shall be needing you for a bridesmaid at some point. Just not yet!'

'I'd love to do it,' Alice agreed promptly, and then gave her a wary look. 'So long as the dress ain't yellow or has flounces,' she added severely, 'or too much lace and whatnot. Because I might put up with that kind of malarkey for me old gran, but there are limits . . .'

'You can wear whatever you like,' Penny promised her, chuckling as she recalled what Alice had told her about the horrid bridesmaid's dress she would be expected to wear at her grandmother's wedding. 'Though you may need to carry a posy of flowers.'

'Gawd blimey,' Alice muttered, casting her eyes up to heaven.

CHAPTER TWENTY-SEVEN

Florence was putting the finishing touches to the evening meal when she heard raised voices in the hall and stopped, mystified and a little alarmed. Leaving Imogen to monitor the bubbling vegetables, she slipped out with Billy on her hip to investigate. Earlier, she had ushered a respectable-looking couple into the sitting room, who had introduced themselves as Penny's parents, and now hoped perhaps the missing girl had finally made her way home. But if so, why did there appear to be an argument going on?

Sure enough, she found Alice and Penny in the hall, hugging and talking excitedly by the front door, where a young local she recognised as John Pascoe stood listening, cap in hand. But nobody appeared to be angry and there was no sign of Penny's parents.

'Penny, you're back. Thank goodness! I was getting worried.' Florence noticed in passing that the front room was empty and was surprised, for she felt sure the couple could not have spoken for long to their daughter before leaving. 'You saw your parents, I take it?'

'Yes, thank you,' Penny agreed, adding in a strained voice, 'though I rather wish they hadn't bothered coming to see me. You see, John and I . . .' She paused and glanced at the young man, blushing. 'We're engaged to be married.'

Florence stared. 'Well, I'm blowed! Congratulations, that's marvellous news.' She hesitated. 'Though aren't you a little young to be tying the knot?'

'We don't plan to get married straightaway,' Penny explained. Then her smile faded. 'Though, to be honest, my parents said much the same thing. In fact, they weren't terribly happy about the news. It's all been a bit awkward.'

'I'm ever so sorry to hear that,' Florence told her with genuine feeling, for she recalled only too well how she and Percy had struggled to get her parents' blessing before they married. 'They wanted to see you, so I let them wait here until you came back. Was that the wrong thing to do? They seemed like nice people.'

'They're very nice, yes,' Penny agreed, but with a look of chagrin on her face. 'Only they didn't take to John and basically forbade us to get married. But it's none of their business, is it?' She was chewing on her lip now, a glimmer of tears in her eyes. 'I'm afraid I asked them to leave.'

'You poor thing.' Florence sighed, letting Billy get down, for he was fidgeting on her hip. Her son dashed back towards the kitchen and she called after him, 'Wait for me, Billy.' To her relief, he stopped and turned, but reluctantly, blowing what sounded like a raspberry at her, though she chose to ignore that rude noise. At least he had heeded her for once. 'Good boy.'

Glancing at the closed front door, a wild idea crept through her head . . .

'Penny, I know this is none of my business, but would you mind terribly,' she asked, 'if I were to go after your parents and speak to them myself? On your behalf, I mean?'

Penny gawped at her. 'Would you, Mrs P? That is . . . No, I wouldn't mind.' She looked at John Pascoe, who had been listening intently. 'Would that be all right with you, John?'

'I'm happy to go along with whatever you decide, Penny,' he said stoutly.

Imogen had wandered out of the kitchen and was gazing curiously at them. Billy tugged on her apron and her sister bent to scoop him up automatically, looking almost maternal with a wooden spoon in one hand and a child perched on her hip. 'Whatever's going on?' she asked Florence, frowning. 'Dinner's nearly ready, you know.'

'I'm sorry, Immi . . . Could you hold the fort a little while longer?' Florence grabbed her jacket off the coat stand and opened the front door, a whirl of cold night air greeting her. 'And look after Billy? Thanks ever so much, I'll be back in a few minutes.'

And she dashed outside into the dark.

At first, she thought it was hopeless and that Penny's parents must already have left. But then she saw a couple walking slowly away towards town. Perhaps they had been debating whether to try and speak to Penny again before leaving.

She soon caught up with them, saying breathlessly, 'I say, Mr and Mrs Brown? I'm sorry to disturb you but could I have a quick word?'

The couple turned, surprise on their faces that was

visible even though it was past dusk, a glimmer of light still flickering in the western clouds. They were well-dressed and stiff-backed, clearly still offended by what they had just been told. Their expressions of outrage reminded Florence of her own very correctly behaved parents, who had struggled with Imogen's antics for years, and her own decision to wed a man of whom they disapproved, having fixed views about how young women should behave. This strengthened her resolve to speak to them, knowing the pain of parents who considered the love of their child less important than adhering to convention.

'Penny told me what happened,' she began awkwardly, 'and I'm so sorry. Is there anything I can do to make things better between you?'

Mr Brown addressed her coldly, 'Yes, you can start by refusing admittance to that young man she's been seeing.'

'Penny's too young to be married, you see,' his wife added in a soothing tone, her gloved hands twisting together. 'Maybe in a few more years—'

'Never!' Mr Brown exploded. 'My daughter, a *fishwife*? I won't hear of it!'

His wife fell silent.

'I see how it is,' Florence said, taking a deep breath, 'and I understand perfectly. You don't want your daughter throwing herself away on a nobody.'

'Exactly right.' Mr Brown gave a savage nod.

'The thing is, John Pascoe isn't a nobody. He's a fisherman, and that means he's serving our community in time of war. He's providing us with food we wouldn't otherwise have. And he risks his life to do it, just like any soldier – his whole family do, in fact, like all the other fishing folk hereabouts. It's not safe out there.' She gestured behind her at the whispering sea in the distance. 'I don't just means storms and winter squalls, though they're terrifying enough. I mean German submarines and other enemy craft, who will take down a fishing vessel as soon as a navy boat because they know we need them and rely on them. But John and his father and grandfather still go out, in all weathers, to do their bit for King and country.' Her voice had risen, impassioned, and she forced herself to speak more quietly, aware of the couple staring at her. 'All I'm saying is that John is a brave, hard-working young man, and you should give your daughter a chance to be happy with him.'

'I beg your pardon?' Mr Brown demanded, sounding incensed.

'Isn't Penny's happiness your priority here?' She waited but the couple said nothing, glancing at each other in silence instead. 'It should be. And I appreciate this is none of my business. But I've got to know your daughter a little since she came to live here and Penny is a sensible, intelligent girl with her head screwed on. If she thinks John is the man for her, then he probably is. And, frankly, all you should be considering is how to love and support her in that decision. That's what parents do for their children.' She swallowed, thinking of her own parents, and how they had not always done that. 'Or what they ought to do, if they want their children to keep in touch and not drift away in adult life.'

Mrs Brown gave a muffled sob and shook her head, a gloved hand at her mouth. 'We do love Penny. We . . . That is . . .'

'Come along,' Mr Brown said curtly, taking his wife's arm. 'We'd better go. It's very late.' He nodded to Florence. 'Good evening, Mrs Pritchard.'

Florence shivered in the cold wind, her heart sinking as she watched them walk away. Had her words been in vain? Penny's father had been offended by her interference; that was obvious from the way he'd dismissed her. But she was heartened when Mrs Brown turned her head, calling back faintly, 'Thank you . . . Please would you tell Penny I'm very happy for her? And that I'll write.'

'Of course.'

Smiling, Florence hurried back to the warmth of the house. But her own words had given her much food for thought too. She had been so worried about allowing herself to love Miles, fearing the hurt that might follow if he too was taken away from her by a bullet or bomb, as Percy had been, but also concerned that Billy might not be happy, or that her more strait-laced neighbours might gossip if she were to cast off widowhood . . .

But whose damn business was it anyway, except her own, who she loved? She shouldn't allow such feeble considerations to hold any weight with her. The only thing she should consult were the feelings of her own heart. And she already knew what lay there . . .

She found the door wide open and John on the doorstep, cap in hand, talking earnestly to Penny, Alice sitting behind her on the bottom step of the stairs. Florence swept past him, saying hurriedly, 'Goodness, you're letting all the heat out of the house!' She smiled at him though. 'Come back inside, John, or else go home. But please don't stand there with the door wide open.'

'Sorry, Mrs Pritchard. I was born in a barn, my ma would say.' John replaced his cap, smiled broadly at her and the girls, and said, 'Goodnight, ladies. I'll be on my way, then.' He gave Penny a wink. 'I'll call on you tomorrow, if you're here, and we can take a walk.'

Penny nodded enthusiastically.

When she'd closed the front door behind him, Florence turned to Penny and gave her a quick hug. 'Don't look so worried. I spoke to your parents and your mother said to tell you she's very happy for you, and she'll write soon.'

'Oh, Mrs P, you're the best!' Penny exclaimed and hugged her back. 'I'll tell John tomorrow. He'll be so pleased.'

'I know his mother, Mrs Pascoe, from our sewing circle.' Seeing Penny bite her lip, she grinned. 'Yes, I found her a bit . . . quiet at first. But she soon thawed, and now she's always the first to offer help when I'm stuck with an embroidery project.' Florence patted her on the back. 'You couldn't have made a better choice. A polite young man from a good family. Congratulations.'

'What did Daddy . . . I mean, what did my father say?'

Florence thought it best not to lie. 'I'm sure he'll come around once he's had a chance to think about it properly,' she said soothingly, though she knew how prickly some fathers could be, especially over sensitive issues like a daughter's marriage. 'Meanwhile, dinner's almost ready. Why don't you go up and wash, and come down to eat in about ten minutes? Both of you,' she added, glancing at Alice in a meaningful way, hoping the girl would take the hint that Penny needed a friend right now.

To her relief, Alice grabbed Penny's hand and began dragging her up the stairs. 'Gawd, yes, I'm bloomin' starving! I hope there are potatoes tonight, Mrs P. I love potatoes. Come on, Penny, let's wash our hands and faces, and have a slap-up dinner to celebrate your engagement. You'll feel much better on a full stomach, trust me.' She winked at her friend. 'I always do, at any rate.'

While they were talking, the front door had been thrown open again, the young Rangers coming back home after a long day's training and no doubt a hearty supper too at the American 'chow house' on the beach. They tramped in from the dark in twos and threes, their cheeks glowing but their eyes tired, and trod heavily up the stairs, some calling out politely, 'Evening, Mrs P', and others, more cheekily, 'You're looking mighty fine tonight, Flo.'

She found herself blushing and shook her head, laughing at their boyish compliments. They really were incorrigible but so charming . . .

The last of the soldiers had left the front door open, letting in the cold night air again. She hurried to close it and, turning back, found Miles there, standing on the stairs, still in his uniform and looking directly at her.

Her breath sucked away, Florence clasped her hands at her waist, feeling dreadfully vulnerable and off-balance. She didn't know why, for he was the one in mourning. Her own feelings of loss were less painful these days, though her grief was ever-present. Once, it had been an all-pervading sadness that had tinged each waking moment since her husband's passing. But a new joy had begun to press against her heart, and it was growing stronger every day. For the first time, she felt . . . happy. Not that she wanted to *forget* her late husband, for that could never happen. But she would like to smile properly again, to throw back her head and laugh, without thinking of the emptiness of life without him . . .

'How are you?' she asked quietly, raising her gaze to his.

'Just dandy, thank you.' He said this glibly, without expression, and she knew he was lying.

Hurriedly, smoothing over the awkward silence between them, she said, 'You must have missed supper at the officers' mess, I expect. Why not come and join us in the dining room? The food is almost ready. We eat with Penny and Alice these days. They feel like part of the family now.' She hesitated, seeing his uncertainty. 'We'd welcome you at the dinner table tonight . . . If you're hungry, that is.'

Miles came towards her and held out his hands. She found herself taking them automatically, even though she knew she shouldn't. It was too intimate a gesture. Too much like a promise it was beyond her power to make. 'Florence,' he said huskily. 'I shouldn't have spoken to you like that earlier. Or behaved so badly. Can you forgive me?'

He was talking of their kiss as much as his curt tone when she'd gone upstairs to check how he was doing.

Her blush deepened. 'There's nothing to forgive. You were upset.'

'I was,' he agreed, his eyes sombre. 'But that's not why I kissed you.'

'Let's not talk about that. It's in the past. But dinner is in the future.' Florence smiled. 'Please come and eat. It's almost ready to put on the table.' Life was easier when she focused on practicalities. Cleaning, laundry, cooking, laying the table, seeing to her guests' comfort. Thinking about matters of the heart left her fragile and close to tears. And she had cried enough over the past few years. She

349

didn't want to cry ever again, if she could help it. 'Will you join us?'

His gaze warred with hers, then he nodded. 'That's very kind of you, ma'am,' he said, as formally as though they had only just been introduced, and released her hands. So they were back to *ma'am* again, were they? That was probably for the best, she decided, even though her heart felt hollow as she made her way back to the kitchen. It was better this way.

The dinner table was animated that evening, with Alice on sparkling form, telling wild anecdotes that Florence didn't quite understand, while Penny giggled and made sly comments about her new fiancé and the possibility that Alice might one day be a bridesmaid for her. Imogen fell into a conversation with them both about the best material for bridesmaids' dresses, and how to run them up easily on the sewing machine, assuming Alice didn't have a nice frock of her own to wear.

During all this, Billy rocked back and forth in his chair, chewing with his mouth wide open despite her remonstrances, and occasionally struck the table noisily with his child-sized fork.

Caught between listening to the girls' lively conversation and preventing Billy from throwing his dinner to the floor, Florence had little time to assess Miles's state of mind. But she could guess at it. He barely said a word throughout the entire meal, except to compliment her politely on the food and to congratulate Penny on her engagement. His usual good spirits seemed to have deserted him but that was hardly a surprise. The poor man had just learnt that his father had died, thousands of miles away across the

Atlantic, and now he had to return home for the funeral. Of course he was subdued and absorbed in his own thoughts.

All the same, she watched him with concern as he helped clear the plates before politely refusing a dessert bowl of tinned fruit and bidding them goodnight instead, insisting that he needed an early night. 'I need to be out of the house by five o'clock,' he said apologetically.

Once he had gone upstairs, Imogen came to find her in the kitchen, and asked, 'What's the matter with Miles? I've never seen him so down. And why is he leaving so early tomorrow?'

Since he had not asked her to keep it a secret, Florence told her sister briefly about Miles's father. 'He's been granted compassionate leave,' she explained, and returned to scraping the dirty plates. 'He was lucky to be allowed home to attend the funeral. One of the perks of his particular role as a liaison officer, perhaps. It's such a long way to travel. But how could he not say goodbye to his father?'

Imogen looked at her curiously. 'He looked lonely at dinner. You should go and talk to him.' When Florence protested about her chores, her sister touched her arm. 'I'll finish up here and put Billy to bed for you tonight. You should go and be with Miles. I've seen the way you two look at each other. Besides, I'm sure he could do with somebody to talk to. Someone who knows what he's going through,' she finished gently.

Florence was surprised by how well her sister, too often immune to other people's feelings, had read the situation. But the offer was tempting. She hesitated, glancing at Billy, who was yawning extravagantly, and then allowed her feelings to get the better of her. 'If you're sure? Though he may not wish to speak to me, of course.'

'Take him up some whisky.' Imogen fetched two glasses and their only bottle of whisky from the cabinet, putting them on a tray. 'Even if he returns to Bude after the funeral, he may not come back here. You realise that? This could be the last time you'll see him.'

Florence stared at her, floored by this awful possibility. Never see Miles again? Her stomach pitched at the thought and it was with difficulty that she nodded, saying huskily, 'Thank you, Immi. I'll take him up the whisky. But only because of his father.'

Imogen smiled, opening the kitchen door for her.

When Florence finally plucked up courage to knock on Miles's bedroom door, he took a painful long while to answer it, and then stared at the tray in her hands. 'What's this?'

He had changed into civvies, wearing casual trousers and a white shirt that was unbuttoned at the neck, showing a glimpse of tanned skin beneath with curling dark hairs. The intimacy of such a sight left her shocked and tingling, and she could barely summon the strength to speak.

'I . . . um . . . thought we could have a drink together before you go tomorrow.' She heard the tell-tale stammer in her voice and was glad that the young Rangers, who had trooped down to the sitting room en masse, were playing music and talking noisily. There was nobody to hear their conversation, for she had left Alice and Penny seated at the dinner table, enjoying a cup of tea while they played a few hands of cards. 'Unless you're too tired . . .'

Goodness, she thought, and blushed deeply. Said out loud, it had sounded far more like a sexual proposition than when Imogen had suggested it downstairs.

His eyes met hers, dark and unreadable, and then he stood aside stiffly to let her in. 'Thank you.'

She placed the tray carefully on top of his chest of drawers, the glasses rattling, and turned hesitantly to find him closing the door.

'Oh, you . . . you were packing,' she said, her voice trembling, glancing at the empty rucksack on the floor. 'I'm sorry if I've interrupted—'

But she got no further, for Miles had crossed the two or three strides between them in a matter of seconds and folded her in his arms, finding her mouth.

She did not resist but tilted her face to his. His hands stroked her hair and face, his body pressed ardently against hers, and her pulse began to thunder in her ears.

I shouldn't be here, she thought faintly, but said nothing when his fingers fell nimbly to the buttons of her blouse, helping him instead by unbuttoning his shirt. Below them, someone turned up the gramophone, the sound of laughter and chatter rising with the music. But none of it was loud enough to drown out the wild, insistent beat of her heart as Miles led her to his bed, murmuring her name over and over . . .

CHAPTER TWENTY-EIGHT

Alice could not quite believe what Mr Rawlings had just told her. She chewed nervously on a few strands of her hair, going back over his mystifying words, and then shook her head. 'No, sorry, I . . . I don't understand. Can you say that again?'

But Rawlings merely smiled.

Her instructors had summoned her to a private meeting at the back of the workshop, closed the door, and begun telling her what they'd decided in the wake of the 'test' they'd performed, sending her, Patrick and Sophy to tail that red-haired American. But she hadn't been able to take it in.

'As Rawlings said, it's a simple choice,' Sidney told her, looking uncomfortable on his wooden stool. 'You can be sent to Porthcurno on completion of your training, like Patrick has been, and spend a few months at Eastern House, learning more about codes and ciphers.' He cleared his throat. 'Or you can go to London for further training in the kinds of skills you've developed during your time here in Bude. Later, depending on your skills and aptitude, you might be deployed overseas.'

'*London*,' she repeated, concentrating on that magical word rather than any of the more dangerous and unfamiliar stuff he'd said, and took a deep breath, still not quite sure this was happening. 'Go back to London . . .'

She'd been born in Dagenham, to the east of London, but her grandmother's family had all come from the city and it was in her blood. Besides which, a bus ride from the capital would soon take her home to see all her old haunts – or what remained of them after the Germans had flattened the place – and maybe some of the people she'd known as a girl. A bitter-sweet nostalgia filled her heart as she contemplated making that journey back home, seeing the old streets again and the neighbourhood where she'd grown up.

Mr Rawlings was studying her thoughtfully. 'You like the idea of London?'

'Yes, but I don't know what to say to that offer. To be honest, I thought you was going to throw me out,' she admitted, 'after that unholy mess we made of following the Americans. I mean, I understand now. It was a test, to see how quickly we would break. Give up important information, and all that.' She frowned, rubbing her forehead. 'Though I didn't like my dad getting dragged into it. That gave me the frights.'

'I'm sorry, but as I said before, it was all part of the test.' He grinned. 'I spoke to Patrick, by the way. He's convinced they targeted you because you're female, and as a man he might have felt obliged to cooperate with them, purely in order to save *you*. So far as I could tell, he has no idea

355

about your father's existence. We saw to that by insisting the Americans separate the two of you during questioning.'

'Blimey, you lot really are quite . . .' Alice, astonished, struggled for the right word, then came up with: '. . . *devious*. Ain't yer?'

Sidney bared his teeth. 'What did you expect? This is our job.' He paused. 'But that was just a game. The real enemy is still out there. Both here in England, often hiding among us in plain sight, and out there in the world, wherever the Nazis hold sway. And we constantly need new operatives. New agents with strong nerves and high levels of training who can work to defeat Germany's efforts against this country.'

Rawlings nodded his agreement. 'And we believe you may have the makings of just such an agent, Alice. But we've taken you as far as we can here. Now you need to move up a level. And that means specialising at Porthcurno, or going to London for a wider brief.'

'Oh gawd,' Alice muttered, chewing on her hair again, excited but scared at the same time. 'I don't know which one to choose, Mr Rawlings, honest to God.' She was deeply, horribly, conflicted. Going back to Porthcurno, being trained in codes and ciphers at the secret listening station in Eastern House, would mean relative safety and living on her aunt's doorstep, seeing Violet and Joe and her dear old gran any time she wanted. But London represented an enormous step up in her training, and she knew it. Her father had told her, at their last meeting, that he'd been trained in London before going behind enemy lines. So there could be no hope of 'safety' going down that route. But was staying safe and around family what was really important to her? Or was she ready for something bigger?

'Do you want to serve your country, Alice?' Mr Rawlings asked, as though he could read her mind.

'Of course I do.'

'I'm glad to hear it. But how do you think you would serve England best? By becoming an expert in codes? Or following in your father's footsteps?' There was a short silence while she considered that question, then Rawlings added softly, 'We know you already speak pretty good German. Learnt at your father's knee, I should imagine. He is a native speaker, after all. But wouldn't you like a chance to take proper lessons with a top-notch tutor? Really brush up on your language skills, both written and oral?'

'Doesn't sound too bad,' she agreed in German, and saw both men exchange glances before smiling at her.

'I take it you're choosing London, then?' Sidney asked.

Alice came to a decision. 'Yes, but I need a chance to tell my family before I go.'

'You can't put any of this in a letter, I'm afraid,' Mr Rawlings reminded her. 'And, strictly, you can't tell them the whole story.'

'Even if they already know about your father, you'll still need to be discreet,' Sidney warned her, nodding. 'Think up a story and stick to it.'

'I know, and I'll only tell them what they need to know,' she agreed, thinking back to how her father had kept quiet about his true business, even when it meant they wrongly thought he was dead for several years. 'I meant face to face, anyway. Which means waiting until my gran's wedding, when everyone will be together again. So, maybe another month or two?' She looked from one to the other, crossing her fingers behind her back. It was important that she told her sister in person, for with Lily expecting a baby soon, the shock might make her unwell. 'Is that possible, d'you think?'

'More than possible,' Mr Rawlings said smoothly, getting up. 'Your training here isn't finished, don't forget. We still have things to teach you. Plus, there's a series of written tests to complete the training, and you won't be sitting them for another few weeks yet.'

'*Written* tests?' Alice's eyes widened. 'You never mentioned *them* before.'

Sidney laughed. 'I don't know why you're looking so worried,' he said, also getting up and coming across with his hand outstretched. 'You'll sail through them. Unlike Sophy. Congratulations, by the way.'

'Thank you.' Alice grinned, shaking his hand. It was true; Sophy's written work was awful, barely legible and full of spelling mistakes, despite her 'good' education at a posh school. Alice secretly thought Sophy ought to have spent more time reading books at school, like she'd done, and then maybe her standard of English would be better. But she'd never said that out loud. Not everyone could be good at reading and writing, as she knew well, being about the only one in her family to enjoy a good book.

Mr Rawlings also shook her hand. 'Congratulations,' he said deeply. 'Your father will be proud when he hears of this.'

'*Will* he hear of this?' Alice asked curiously.

But Rawlings ignored her question as usual, his face

358

cool. 'I'll put the paperwork in motion straightaway. Then everything should be ready by the time your London travel permit comes through.' He inclined his head. 'I must say, I'll miss your funny little ways, Alice . . . One of our more entertaining students. Wouldn't you agree, Sidney?'

'Oh, that's for certain,' Sidney said, his normally dour face lighting up with a rare smile. 'But you've not gone yet, Missy,' he added, reminding her sternly, 'we'll be doing advanced hand-to-hand combat training for the rest of this week. And this time, try not to punch your fellow trainees' lights out, all right?'

'I'll do me best,' Alice said cheekily, and gave them a wink on her way out.

Her step was light and almost giddy as Alice headed back to the boarding house, though her insides were churning too. She was going back to London to finish her training as a spy. And then . . . Who knew where she might end up? It was beyond exciting. And ever so slightly terrifying, she thought with a shiver, remembering how it had felt to be in fear of her life when those Americans had been questioning her in the woods. But she had known what to do and how to respond, and it had all felt so . . . right.

But one thing was for certain. She was going to make her father proud, following in his footsteps like this, and that meant the world to her.

But she still had her family to tell. That would be a difficult conversation and no mistake. Aunty Vi would be frightened for her, and Gran would probably be livid and say she couldn't go, and Lily . . . Well, Lily would understand, but might be worried all the same. And then there was Penny, who might not be very happy to learn that her best friend was about to abandon her in Bude for a glamorous London posting.

Though given that Penny's head was full of nothing but John, John, John at the moment, she might not even notice that her would-be bridesmaid had gone missing, she thought wryly, chuckling to herself.

'Oh, hello,' she called out, spotting Imogen crossing the road. But Florence's younger sister didn't respond, holding both sides of her coat closed against the wind, her face hidden beneath the brim of her hat. Perhaps she hadn't heard.

As she watched, Imogen slipped down the alleyway towards the printers' workshop. Surprised, Alice hesitated a moment, and then continued on her way with a shrug. Whatever Imogen was doing at the printers, it was none of her business. Perhaps having some business cards printed for the boarding house, as the workshop genuinely took orders from the public in order to disguise its double purpose as a training location.

And she had plenty of other more exciting things to think about without worrying her head over something so unimportant. Like how it would feel to be back in the Big Smoke at last . . .

CHAPTER TWENTY-NINE

On the other side of town, Penny was hurrying to the Pascoes' cottage for dinner after a long first day as an orderly at the cottage hospital in Stratton. Her new job was a demanding one and she'd been run off her feet for hours on end, assisting nurses with mopping floors and washing windows, moving beds and other furniture about, and generally preparing the hospital for an expected influx of new patients, though the place was not particularly busy at the moment.

'What new patients?' she'd asked the nurses several times, but nobody had really had an answer for her. It was all very mysterious and a little worrying too. It was as though something important was about to happen, and everyone but Penny knew about it and was keeping quiet.

Yes, it had been a long day and it wasn't over yet. But she'd enjoyed the new challenge as much as all the physical activity, after weeks standing idly about in Mrs Roskilly's dairy shop, tidying shelves of canned or boxed produce or cutting slabs of cheese. Plus, her new working companions were so lovely and friendly, she couldn't be happier. There was Nancy and Patricia and Carole, all of them wonderful young women who loved to gossip over a cuppa but who always got their work done in good time too. And if her immediate superiors were a bit stuffy, well, she didn't have to spend much time talking to them, as a hospital orderly.

Though someone must have spotted her good secretarial skills on her résumé, learnt at school, for she'd already been suggested as a possible temporary assistant to Cecily, the hospital receptionist, a sweet old lady but a bit dotty, who didn't seem very good at keeping track of the dozen or so patients in the hospital. 'Cecily retired about five years ago, but they dragged her back in to lend a hand after all the men went to war. Goodness knows how the poor dear will cope once we're full to bursting,' Carole had whispered, shaking her head. And again, Penny had frowned and wondered why such a quiet country hospital would suddenly be *full to bursting*? But right now, she had other things to occupy her thoughts . . . such as tonight's exquisite torment.

When she walked into the cottage to find John's mother busily cooking a special dinner, her nerves, kept at bay during her working hours, finally roiled in her stomach and refused to be ignored. For tonight, her parents had been invited to dinner with the Pascoes, so they could all sit down together and discuss Penny and John's wedding, 'like civilised people,' as John's father had put it gruffly.

Her parents had written back a few lines in response to this invitation, rather baldly agreeing to turn up, and Penny had tried not to think about seeing them again . . . until now, that was, finding the Pascoes' modest dinner table laid with unaccustomed splendour, with wine and beer glasses laid out, along with the best cutlery and plates, and even embroidered cloth napkins.

'Goodness, how marvellous the table looks,' Penny exclaimed, and then burst into tears. 'Oh, I'm so sorry, Mrs Pascoe. I don't know what's the matter with me . . .'

John's mother, who had been busy chopping vegetables, hurried through to put a reassuring arm about her shoulders. 'There, there, child,' she said, looking flustered. 'Your parents can't stop you marrying our John. And we won't let them bully you under our own roof. All right, my love?'

Penny nodded, rubbing her damp cheeks and feeling awfully embarrassed. 'Yes, Mrs Pascoe,' she agreed.

'Call me Mum,' John's mother said, giving her a quick hug. 'Now, take a breath and let's have no more tears. You don't want a red nose, do you?' And she bustled back into the kitchen. Seconds later, Penny could hear her chopping vegetables again. 'John's washing upstairs. The others will be home soon. You sit down and wait.'

Sure enough, John came thundering down the stairs a short while later and embraced her. 'Feeling strong and up to seeing your parents tonight?' he asked cheerily, and she nodded, glad he hadn't seen her crying earlier. 'That's my girl. How was your first day at the hospital?'

'I've never done so many jobs in so few hours,' Penny admitted with a shaky laugh. 'The place is practically empty and yet they're taking on new staff and cleaning the whole place from top to bottom. I don't understand it.'

He gave her an odd look. 'Don't you?'

'Oh, won't you please explain if you know what's going on? It's driving me mad . . . All this talk of "new patients" yet nobody seems to want to say where they're coming from, or when.'

John kissed her on the cheek. 'You're a darling, Penny, but sometimes . . .' He shook his head. 'Do you remember the Pathé newsreels we saw last week? About all the troops in readiness and how high morale is at the moment?' He'd taken her to the pictures again, several times, though the whole place had been packed with US Rangers on each occasion and they'd been lucky to get a seat. 'It's been going on for weeks. I mean, everyone's being very discreet about it, but it's as plain as the nose on your face.'

'What is?' she demanded, perplexed.

'Why, the *big push*, of course.' John took her hands in his and squeezed them reassuringly, his gaze warm and loving on her face. 'Churchill's getting ready to give the order.'

Finally, she began to understand. 'The order to invade France, you mean?'

'To *liberate* France,' he corrected her gently.

'Oh, my goodness! Are you serious?' Penny thought back to the pristine hospital with its wards full of rows of empty beds, just standing vacant, waiting for patients. And she shuddered. 'But that's terrible. I mean, yes, it's wonderful to think we may nearly be at the end of this awful war. But what about all those young men they'll be sending to France? The Americans and our own troops, and all the other Allies? All the deaths and horrific injuries . . .' She gave a cry. 'Oh, John, I don't think I can bear it.'

'We must bear it,' he told her sombrely. 'It's the only way.'

She swallowed hard. 'I suppose you're right. It's either that or . . . or Hitler comes here, isn't it? And he'd take us over the way he's taken over everywhere. Turning England's green and pleasant land into a . . . a torture chamber.' Penny felt like weeping again, yet somehow the steadfast look in his eyes forced her to be brave. 'No, you're right. It has to happen. I just wish it didn't, that's all. That we could somehow win this war without any more bloodshed.'

He held her close and stroked her hair. 'I know, love. But we're all doing our bit to help out. And you'll do a fine job at the hospital when the time comes.'

Pushing that grim thought away, Penny nodded her agreement. 'When the time comes,' she repeated faintly. 'We're going to win this war, aren't we?'

'I hope so,' John said, 'because the alternative doesn't bear thinking about.' Then he straightened, looking towards the door with a grin. 'That sounds like Pa home at last, and Grandpa with him. They'll need to wash up too. Blow, it's almost five o'clock already. Your parents will arrive any minute.'

His father and grandfather came stamping into the cottage, jovial as ever, shaking her hand and again wishing her congratulations and every luck tonight dealing with her 'prickly parents'. Not surprisingly, they had been a little offended when she'd explained how her parents felt about her marrying John. They thought she and John too young to be married themselves, not because of any problem with John, only that the times were so precarious for them to be setting up home together.

Anxiously, wanting to do *something*, Penny dove into the kitchen, asking, 'Are you sure I can't help, Mrs Pascoe?'

Swathed in white clouds of steam, John's mother turned to her, brandishing a ladle, and said sharply, 'Thank you, no need. I know what I'm doing.'

John came and propelled her out of the kitchen with the gentlest of touches. 'My mother guards her territory like a dragon guards his hoard of gold. Good rule of thumb: never go in the kitchen while Ma's cooking. Not unless she's called you in to eat, that is.' A gale of laughter from his dad and grandfather accompanied this advice, with much sage nodding, and Penny found herself laughing too. It was hard not to be jolly with the Pascoes. They were so very different from her own family.

Before long, the dreaded knock on the door came and John's father welcomed in her parents. They all shook hands and exchanged a little small talk about the weather. John's mother came in, minus her ladle, to check if her husband had offered them a drink yet. He had not, so while John was summoned to assist his mother with serving the food, John's father doled out a small sherry to everyone.

Penny, who had only drunk sherry once or twice in her life, hated the taste, but dutifully sipped at her glass, not wanting to seem immature. She had embraced her parents warmly but could still sense a distance between them.

They had not forgiven her for that embarrassing scene at the boarding house, that was clear.

Dinner went surprisingly well, with everyone being very polite about the food, even though the meat was a trifle burnt and the vegetables soggy. John's mother had the air of a woman who knew she had not done herself justice. 'It's a small kitchen to be cooking in for seven people,' she commented, 'but I done my best.'

John's father touched her shoulder. 'That's all anyone can ask, love.'

After dinner, they moved to the sofa and armchairs while a pot of coffee was served. The Pascoe men stood by the hearth, where a good fire was burning, for there were not enough seats to go around. There was a long silence. The mantel clock ticked oppressively. Penny glanced up at John, who shuffled his feet and cleared his throat.

'Eh, we should have toasted them young people at dinner,' John's grandfather said at last in his thick Cornish accent, indicating his coffee cup, 'and now all we have is this foreign muck. Shall we drink a toast to them, anywise?'

'Now, there's a thought, Poppa!' John's father cried, jumping up with his coffee cup raised on high. 'To John and his Penny, and their engagement. We wish them both very happy.'

Penny thought his toast had been well done, for it had not mentioned the controversial wedding. All the same, she saw her parents looking uncomfortable and knew something had to be said.

After the toast, she stood up in her turn, though horribly nervous, and said in a strained voice, 'Mummy, Daddy, I know you think we shouldn't be doing this. But John and I are not as stupid as you think. We've talked it over and we're content to wait a while before tying the knot. There's war work to be done, and I'd much rather wait until the war's over, frankly. I want a nice dress that's not bought on ration coupons, and for us to live together without fear of being bombed or invaded. Or the whole world going to rack and ruin about us.' She paused, drawing a sharp breath. 'I wish you could be happy for us. I mean, *truly* happy, not just pretending like you are now. Because it hurts when you do that.' Her voice shook as she tapped her chest. 'Deep down in here, it hurts. I'd rather not see you at all, to be honest, than listen to you pretending.'

John strode across to stand behind her, putting a hand on her shoulder. 'I agree with Penny,' he told her parents gruffly. 'If she's unhappy, then I'm unhappy. Not but what you're welcome here, Mr and Mrs Brown, and it was handsome of you to come tonight. But we'd rather have honesty as we start our life together. I hope you understand.'

Penny looked round at him gratefully, and a warmth stole into her heart. She had made the right decision in choosing John and accepting his proposal. It wasn't the mistake her parents believed it to be. Sometimes, she thought, you had to take a risk on gut instinct, rather than know for sure whether something would work out. She had taken that risk with John, and now she knew in her heart that everything was going to be all right.

But to her horror, her mother put down her cup and saucer, and burst into tears. Even her father took out a handkerchief and noisily blew his nose.

'I'm sorry if I've upset you,' John added, consternation in his face.

'No,' her mother told him, through her tears. 'It's not about you, John. You seem like a nice young man, and your parents have done a fine job bringing you up. It's just . . .' Her voice quivered and fresh tears came. 'We live so far away from Cornwall. We thought she'd be coming home to Surrey after the war, and we've been so looking forward to that day, even redecorating her bedroom . . . But now it will never come. She'll live here with you instead, as a married woman, and never think of her parents growing old miles away.'

Gasping, Penny cried out, 'What? Of course I'll come and visit you after we're married.' She hugged her parents and found that she too was crying. She shook her head. 'How could you think that I'd *forget* about you?'

John spoke up again. 'I shan't stop her visiting you,' he insisted, looking equally amazed. 'I'm not an ogre. And Penny has a mind of her own, you know.'

'Aye, that she do!' his grandfather agreed, chuckling.

'But if you're so worried about us losing touch, why don't you two move down to Cornwall to be nearer me?' Penny suggested, smiling through her tears and still holding her mother's hand tightly. 'Bude's a lovely place to live. And, Daddy, you've often spoken about moving to the countryside once you reach retirement age. I'm sure John's father would be glad to help you find a place. He knows everyone here.' She glanced over her shoulder. 'Wouldn't you, Mr Pascoe?'

'More than glad,' John's father agreed, beaming.

Her parents looked at each other uncertainly, and then her mother gave a tremulous smile. 'That's not such a bad idea, Geoff,' she said softly. 'What do you think?'

Penny's father scratched his head. 'Well, Pen's right. I've often had a hankering for a little cottage close to the sea. But I'm not at retirement age yet. And we'd need to wait until the war was over, that's for certain.'

'I think everybody's waiting until the war is over, so we can start living again. We're all just holding our breath, aren't we?' Penny dabbed at her wet cheeks, glancing at her fiancé and thinking of the happy times that might lie ahead, if the universe should smile on them. 'I only hope that day comes soon, and that it brings *us* victory, not Germany.'

'To England winning the war,' John's father said with a nod, raising his cup to the room again, even though their coffee was just cold dregs now.

'To England,' they all chorused, smiling mistily at each other.

Her parents went back to their lodgings for the night with the promise of a nice walk and picnic up on the cliffs in the morning, and John offered to walk Penny home, as he always did whenever she visited them for a spot of supper.

As they walked back together, they held hands and talked expansively of their plans for an unknown future. The moon rose in a clear, velvety-black sky, its cold bright light shimmering on the ocean that stretched out before them in the distance. They stopped for a little kiss and cuddle on the lonely stretch between town and Downs View Road, and then walked on, grinning foolishly at each other.

'It seems impossible there could be a war on when we're so ridiculously happy,' Penny murmured.

'Aye,' John agreed, a tinge of sadness to his voice. 'Monstrously unfair too.'

As they approached the boarding house, they heard a commotion in one of the neighbouring houses, with thuds and raised voices, and stopped instinctively. There were no lights showing, for it was long past curfew, but it was clear something untoward was going on. Men's deep voices could be heard at the door and a frightened woman replying, then a scuffle.

'That's old Doreen's boarding house,' Penny whispered, afraid. 'Oh, John, it sounds as though she needs help.'

'Wait here, I'm on it,' he said fearlessly and dropped her hand to stride forward. But a man appeared out of nowhere to block his path, his face unseen in the darkness.

'None of your business, son,' the man said in an authoritative voice. A Cornishman, by his accent. 'Best be on your way.'

To Penny's shock, John fell back without a word and then escorted her hurriedly along the road to Florence's house. She stared up at him, and then over her shoulder at Doreen's place, where the moonlight showed two shadowy figures escorting what looked like Doreen herself down the road to a parked vehicle, where the engine was now running.

'Why did you let them take her?' she demanded, angry for the old lady's sake.

'Because one of those men was our local constable. He's been policeman here in Bude for years.' He pulled a face. 'Used to terrify the life out of us kids when I was young, and even my father wouldn't dare cross him.' Seeing her expression, he gave her hand a comforting squeeze. 'Trust me, love, if he's taking Doreen away, there'll be a good reason for it.'

Penny looked back but could no longer see or hear anything, and could only hope that John wasn't mistaken. 'Poor Doreen. I hope she'll be all right.'

John stopped at the front door and kissed her, his arms warm about her in the darkness. 'I'm glad it's all worked out between you and your parents.' There was relief in his voice. 'Seems like they're coming around to this marriage lark, any rate.'

Penny laughed. 'A lark is precisely what our marriage is going to be,' she told him, with an impetuous grin. 'If I know you at all, John Pascoe.' And she let him kiss her again.

CHAPTER THIRTY

It was a sunny morning, and Florence was playing a game of tag with Billy and Emily in the backyard while her friend Charlotte looked on and laughed uproariously. A plane approached from the sea, and they all looked up, instantly silent and wary, only to see the now-familiar markings of a large US army troop carrier. Florence wasn't sure exactly which type it was, for she wasn't very interested in aeroplanes, but to Billy, all friendly planes deserved to be celebrated, so he sped about the yard with his thin arms outstretched, mimicking the sound of its engines, while Emily ran to hide behind her mother's skirt.

The plane swung briefly overhead, the deep note throbbing in the quiet air, and then continued higher up the coast.

'Heading for Camp Cleave, I expect,' Charlotte said, watching it from behind a raised hand. She shot Florence a knowing glance. 'Bringing that nice Sergeant Miller back from the United States, perhaps?'

'I wouldn't know,' Florence said primly, though her own

gaze followed the plane until it was out of sight. She hadn't told Charlotte that she and Miles had become more than mere friends in those last few days before he left Bude. It was a secret she preferred to keep locked in her heart. But she'd probably mentioned his name more often than was to be expected of a casual acquaintance. 'Well, time for lunch?'

'I have to take Emily home,' Charlotte said quickly, 'but thanks for the offer. Another time, perhaps? Once Peter's gone back.' Her husband was due home on official leave in a few days, and she'd been happily tidying the cottage ready for his return.

As Charlotte gathered up Emily's things, she added quietly, out of earshot of the two little ones, 'Did you hear about Doreen, by the way?'

Florence hesitated. She'd heard some unsettling rumours about her elderly neighbour about the town and wouldn't have been able to believe them if Penny hadn't mentioned seeing her being bundled into a car by a policeman at the dead of night, and if Alice herself hadn't come home a few days ago and told her the stories were all true. And Alice seemed to know so much about things like that, Florence had accepted it without argument.

'About her being arrested, you mean?' She nodded sorrowfully. 'Though I still can't believe that, all this time, right under our noses, our lovely old Doreen was a *spy* for the Germans. It's simply incredible.'

Except it wasn't incredible, for Imogen had already told her there were German informants dotted all around the country, hiding in plain sight, and seeming so ordinary and British, nobody would ever suspect them . . . Though somebody must have suspected Doreen in the end, mustn't they? Otherwise, she would never have been caught.

Charlotte agreed with her, helping Emily into her coat. 'I know, it seems so crazy . . . Doreen, of all people. Though now they've carted her away, everyone seems to be saying they always thought she was dodgy. Young Joseph at the butcher's shop says he saw her sneaking around the back alleys several times, peering into people's windows. And Sally the postie says Doreen used to get some very odd foreign letters, and she wished she'd reported them now.'

'Well, my sister did have a spat with her once . . .' Florence's voice tailed off, as she realised with a start that Imogen must have known about Doreen back then. She'd almost called her a spy, hadn't she? Something about her being *nosy* . . . But how on earth had her sister known that? And was Imogen the one who'd tipped off the authorities?

'Hmm?'

'Oh, nothing. Have a lovely day.'

Florence waved them off at the front door, fed Billy a simple lunch of bread and cheese with stewed apples, and then put him down in his cot for a quick nap, since their morning's fun and games with Emily had tired the little man out.

Washing up their lunch dishes, she heard the front door bang but didn't think anything of it until the kitchen door opened. She turned, expecting to see Imogen there, for her sister had walked into town earlier to post some letters and run a few errands. But it wasn't Imogen standing there. It was Miles, with his army bag slung over his shoulder and an intense look in his dark eyes.

'Oh!' Her heart leapt, but she stayed where she was, hands dripping with soap suds, her gaze locked to his face.

She had woken in the cold dark of early morning after their night together to find him gone, his drawers emptied of clothes, and had wept bitterly, wishing she had not gone to his room. For she had known he might never return and thought she could never bear the loss . . .

Now he was back. And she couldn't be sure what would happen next. Perhaps he had regretted the night they'd spent together and simply wanted to forget her.

Then he dropped his bag and ran to embrace her, and she closed her eyes, sobbing with joy, tucked into his chest.

'You came back,' she said unnecessarily, and then forced herself to ask, as gently as she could, 'How are you? How did it go?'

She meant his father's funeral. Miles understood, nodding and drawing her to a kitchen chair, where he sat and pulled her onto his knee, cradling her there with strong arms.

'We laid Pops to rest and held a wake in his memory. It was a nice ceremony, and all his friends came, and dozens of my aunts and uncles and cousins.' He sounded sad but he was smiling. 'I stayed that night and travelled back to the base in the morning. Momma wanted me to stay longer, but it was impossible. Rules are rules.' His voice broke. 'She's got my sisters staying with her, and her grandchildren, and a few cousins too. She isn't alone. But it was hard having to leave her, all the same.'

Florence shaped his face between her hands, looking deep into his eyes. 'But you were there for the funeral. That's what counts. You went back.'

'And now I'm here again.'

'But for how long?' she whispered, trying to read his expression.

His face closed up. 'I can't say. Not long though. The order's come through from the top, so the Rangers will be moving on soon. As for me, I'll be sent ahead again to organise the transition, make sure transportation and billets are in place for the whole unit, and everything happens smoothly.' His arms tightened about her. 'I don't want to leave. But I have no choice.'

'I understand,' she said as calmly as she could, though her heart was breaking.

'I'm not sure you do.' He put her down and stood up, staring restlessly out of the kitchen window into the sunlit backyard, where washing was still billowing on the line, white sheets snapping and blowing back and forth in a brisk wind. 'I had plenty of time to think on the flight back. And I realised that, in leaving Bude forever, I'd be leaving my heart behind.' He turned, looking at her strangely. 'Only I don't need to do that.'

Her eyes widened. 'You're not thinking of leaving the Rangers?' she asked, horrified, for she guessed that would surely mean a court martial for him.

To her relief, Miles chuckled. 'Nothing so drastic. Besides, I love the Rangers. I'd never leave them until forced to,' he admitted, 'by death or perhaps the end of the war.' His voice had dropped. 'Given the right motivation, I'd happily leave military service if we won the war.'

She waited, not understanding.

'*You* would be the right motivation,' he continued slowly, and came back to hold her hands. 'A woman like you could make me settle down at last, Florence.' He hesitated, searching her face. 'If you can stomach a hard-boiled American soldier like me, that is.'

She blinked, confused and breathless. 'Wait . . . What are you saying?'

'I didn't do that too well, did I? Let me start again.' Miles looked down at their linked hands, his brows knotting in a frown. 'You told me you about your husband, and I listened real hard, believe me. You said Percy was the love of your life. Now, I know there's no way I could ever compete with that, and I'd never try to.' He swallowed. 'But what I'm offering instead is a chance at second love. Second happiness. Maybe even a second child for you, if we were so blessed. But I'd settle for happiness.'

She held a hand to her mouth, trembling. 'Oh, Miles.' There was anticipated pain as well as love in his eyes, and she wanted to throw her arms about him, pull him close and explain that she felt the same, that his wishes were her wishes. But she also knew that he was very much a man on his dignity in this moment, and that allowing him to finish was the better choice.

She waited. With her eyes, she encouraged him to go on, to say the words she could feel behind that speech, fretting to be heard . . .

In the silence that followed, he dropped to one knee before her, still holding her hands. His eyes met hers, deep with emotion. 'Florence Pritchard, I love you. Is there any chance that you'd consent to be my wife, and allow me to keep you safe and warm all the days of your life?'

It was the most romantic thing in the world, looking down at this man she had fallen in love with and listening to his proposal of marriage. She was overjoyed and giddy and ecstatic, all at once. But then common sense kicked in and she bit her lip. 'Are you sure about this? You've just lost your father, Miles . . . You may not be thinking clearly. And you live in Texas and I live in Cornwall, and—'

'I'll see about moving to Cornwall after the war if you won't come to Texas,' he said stoutly, though she could see how much it cost him to make that offer. 'You Brits will owe us big time if we win, so I'm sure it could be done. Though I'd still like you to go and see where I was born and brought up, the farm back in Texas, and to meet my mother.' He winked. 'I told her all about you while I was there.'

'You . . . You told your mother about me?' Florence was astonished and curious too. 'And what did she say?'

'Momma told me she can't wait to meet you . . . and young Billy too, of course.' His eyes twinkled. 'She's got a big personality, my mother. Folks say she's an acquired taste but I'm guessing you'll love her straight out of the gate.'

She was smiling, but then sobered as the reality of their situation struck her. 'Oh, Miles, it's a lovely dream . . . But it's impossible. You'll need to leave soon, you said. And we both know the Rangers have been training for the front line. For . . . For the liberation of France.' She swallowed, her voice cracking with sudden tears. 'We may never see each other again.'

'I know,' he said, still on his knees. 'That's why I want us to be married here in Bude, straightaway, before the battalion leaves. I've already made enquiries, and there's a chapel where we can marry if I'm granted a special licence.'

His eyes locked with hers. 'I love you, sweetheart. Let's be together for as long as we can now, and if I get through the war alive, I'll come and find you once it's all over.' Emotion was throbbing in his voice as he added, 'Take a chance on me, Florence, and say yes. I swear I'll stay true to you for as long as I live, so help me, God.'

She wondered what Percy would say if he was looking down on them. She felt sure he would understand. That he would not have stayed single forever if she'd been the one to die. But regardless of that, Percy was gone, and while she still loved him, there was room in her heart to love Miles as well. Because she *did* love him and she knew it for certain. So what was she waiting for? The rest of her life still lay ahead, if she was brave enough to choose a new path . . .

'Yes,' she said, crying for joy. 'Yes, Miles.' And laughed through her tears. 'Billy's going to love Texas, I promise you.'

Rising to his feet with a wondrous smile on his face, Miles kissed her and they held each other for a long while.

'So, you want to move to Texas after the war, then?' he asked, his arms about her waist. 'Are you sure?'

'I want to be wherever you are,' she told him. 'And I know you'll want to stay close to your mother.'

He closed his eyes briefly, and then smiled. 'That first day I came to Bude, I knew as soon as I clapped eyes on you, stuck up a ladder washing that sign, that you were the perfect woman for me. You were so feisty and determined . . . Only you clearly still loved your husband, so I thought I had no chance with you.'

'You didn't,' she said bluntly. 'Not at first. But then you

grew on me. And I saw how you were with Billy, and that started me thinking what a good father you'd make.' She blushed at his intent expression, remembering what he'd said about a second child. 'Not that I'm suggesting . . . Not before the war's over, at least.'

'Heck, why shouldn't you suggest it? We can be married as soon as I can get that special licence. Your sister can be your bridesmaid and we'll be granted a guard of honour from the Rangers. Mother Nature will take care of the rest.' He cuddled her, and she listened contentedly to his strong heartbeat, knowing herself genuinely happy for the first time in a long while. 'Whatever else happens, I'll be a good father to Billy, I swear it. And just to prove it, before I leave, I'll teach him to play baseball.'

'Baseball? But he's only three!'

'First thing you'll discover when you come with me to Texas is, you're never too young to learn baseball,' Miles told her with a mock-serious expression, and they both laughed and held each other tight, while Florence wondered what on earth she was going to tell her parents, without really caring what they thought.

It was her life and she was going to live it to the full, no matter what. She and Billy and Miles together . . .

They were married at the small chapel near the river in a quiet ceremony – if by 'quiet' one included an honour guard of US Rangers, making a steepled tunnel for them with their rifles hoisted in the air; a small crowd of locals who had gathered to throw rice and cheer them into a waiting car; and Imogen upstaging the bride in a figure-hugging green dress, attracting no little attention from the two dozen or so soldiers who had also come along to wish them well.

Despite all that, for Florence it was indeed a quiet ceremony, for she had eyes for nobody but her handsome American bridegroom.

They murmured their vows and he slipped a heavy gold band onto her finger, where once she had worn another man's ring, and her throat ached with tears at that old memory, tears that she refused to shed. For this was her and Miles's wedding day, and she had no room left in her heart for regrets. Though she wasn't a fool, of course. She knew that the next two days and nights might be all the time they would ever spend together. For her new husband was due to leave Bude soon, in advance of the Rangers moving on to a new town, somewhere hush-hush on the other side of the country, and they might never see each other again. Not this side of heaven, at any rate.

But she smiled bravely and took his hand, and laughed with him as they bowed their heads to run through the steeple of rifles, and dodged handfuls of rice from the crowd, and greeted their many friends who had come to witness their wedding, all without any hint of the sadness she knew might lie ahead. The sun shone brilliantly for them and the clouds stayed away, and if the sea breeze was a little stiff that day, it only served to flap her cream wedding dress prettily and tug at her headdress of silk flowers, and cause a ripple of scandalised laughter when Imogen's skirt blew up before she was able to smooth it down again with a flirtatious giggle. And Billy ran about throwing rice indiscriminately at all the wedding guests in the officers' mess later, before Miles scooped him up, laughing heartily, and set the boy on his knee to tell him extravagant tales of life in Texas . . .

Charlotte, her husband having left again after his short leave of absence, kindly moved into the boarding house with her daughter Emily to look after Billy, at least for the two nights the newly-weds had been allotted before Miles had to leave. This allowed Florence to spend her wedding night in her friend's cosy cottage instead, with its cheerful fire and deep comfortable armchairs, and one rather creaky mattress made up with crisp white linen that smelt of Cornish sunshine and happiness.

Not that happiness was a smell, she had to admit. Yet happiness was what she felt when she woke the morning after her wedding, hearing birdsong as well as traffic in the street outside, and turned over on those now-crumpled sheets to find Miles awake too and smiling at her, so that they reached for each other quite naturally and began to kiss again.

'Whatever happens,' he told her softly, a little later, 'however our story ends, I shall love you for ever, Florence Miller.'

And she knew it for the truth.

EPILOGUE

Porthcurno, West Cornwall, February 1944

The church was so silent, Alice could have heard a pin drop. Everyone looked at each other, suddenly wary and questioning as the vicar's voice died away into echoes . . .

The three evacuee children sitting on Alice's left in the front pew began to shudder with silent giggles they dared not share with the congregation, not unless they wanted to face Sheila Hopkins' wrath later. In a pew on the other side of the aisle, Alice caught Aunty Violet's deeply ironic eye, and almost giggled herself. Beside Violet sat Uncle Joe, dressed smartly for the occasion and as usual looking mighty uncomfortable in a jacket and tie, his back straight, his face sombre. In the pew just behind them sat Hazel and George Cotterill. Baby Lily, red-cheeked due to teething, was moaning and whimpering, so that Hazel had to keep bouncing her up and down on her knee to stop her ruining the service with piercing cries.

George saw Alice glance his way and winked, nodding

to her bridesmaid's dress. Alice felt ridiculous in the foaming yellow frock that Gran had run up for her on the old Singer sewing machine, having even more flounces and lace frills on it since the day she'd tried it on in Bude. But Violet had insisted she wear the dratted thing and not kick up a fuss, not on Gran's big day. So she was wearing it with a good grace, because no one and nothing was more important to her than her gran.

She looked away, hearing a cough. Behind the evacuees, sat her still heavily pregnant sister Lily and her handsome, ginger-haired husband, Tristan, who had driven all the way from St Ives for this special occasion. Lily was rubbing her enormous bump and smiling, while Tristan studied a blue-backed hymnal with apparent fascination.

The reason for the stillness in the old church at Porthcurno on this sunny February afternoon was that the vicar, the Reverend Clewson, had just addressed the congregation, his hands spread wide in urgent supplication, saying loudly, 'If any man can show just cause or impediment why they may not be lawfully joined together, let him now speak or else forever hold his peace.'

Nobody said a word. Everyone held their breath.

After what felt like an eternity, the vicar smiled benignly at the couple facing him and opened his mouth to continue with the ceremony.

Except that Arnold Newton, the white-haired bridegroom, interrupted him by glancing over his shoulder at the congregation. 'Looks like nobody knows about my other ten wives, then,' he quipped, tipping a wink to the three evacuees in the front pew.

Two seconds later, his bride also turned to the

congregation, eyeing them with a steely look, and said loudly, 'Oh good, nobody was stupid enough to open their mouths. I should bloomin' well hope not.'

The church erupted into gales, snorts and guffaws of laughter, and even Alice grinned, despite her discomfort at being dressed like a Victorian debutante.

While Gran and her beloved Arnie exchanged vows and rings, for Gran had purchased a man's gold wedding ring in Penzance for her new husband, Alice played with her bouquet of spring flowers. It was lovely and fragrant, all whites, pinks and yellows, a delicate mix of snowdrops, crocuses and elegant narcissi, mostly culled that morning from the Cornish hedgerows along the farm track.

In her mind, she was rehearsing what she would tell everyone later that evening, once all the other wedding guests had gone and it was only family left up at Postbridge Farm. For she hadn't yet shared with them the startling news that she would be returning to London to complete her training, too terrified of what Auntie Vi would say to the matter.

Gran would be off on her honeymoon straight after the wedding reception – five days at a posh seafront hotel in Penzance, where thankfully the bombing had lessened in recent months – and Alice had decided she shouldn't be told until after she got back, in case it spoiled her holiday.

Lily, she was sure, would be pleased for her, if a little concerned for her safety, all alone in the big smoke at what would soon be the tender age of nineteen.

All the same, Alice wasn't looking forward to spilling the beans . . . But her train ticket to London was for the day after tomorrow, and she couldn't put off the awful moment any longer. She had brought all her luggage back to the farm, much to Gran's bemusement, pretending she needed a break from Bude. But as soon as she could, she would pack a smaller bag to take to London and leave everything else behind for whenever she might return. Which she hoped would not be too far in the future, though Mr Rawlings had suggested she could be gone for as long as six months without being permitted a visit home.

At last, Sheila and Arnold were man and wife. After the service, everyone streamed from the church and up the steep hill out of Porthcurno to Joe's farm, where sandwiches, cake and copious amounts of tea and beer were being laid on for the many guests. The bride and groom travelled in style, of course, for the Land Girls had rigged up Joe's old tractor for them with green garlands and a clattering tail of tin cans – 'Well, he is a shopkeeper!' Lily had pointed out with a chuckle – while the guests followed on foot, except for a lucky few with cars.

She spotted Penny walking ahead with the Land Girls, seemingly back on speaking terms with Caroline and Selina, and chatting happily enough to the soft-spoken new girl who had replaced her, Joan. No doubt Penny was telling them all about her fiancé John, who was out at sea this week on the *Mary Jane*. There'd been no date set for their wedding, but Alice had the impression they were planning to tie the knot that summer. Penny had been unhappy when Alice first admitted she was leaving Bude, but since she was such good friends with Imogen and Mrs Pritchard – who was now Mrs Miller, in fact – Alice suspected she wouldn't be too lonely, even though the Second Battalion US Rangers had finally left Bude.

'Hop in, Alice,' a deep male voice called merrily as she began the familiar trudge uphill in her flouncy yellow dress, and Alice turned to find a car pulled up beside her, the driver a man with short dark hair and twinkling blue eyes. 'See, we saved you a seat.' He had an American accent too, which no longer sounded so strange to her ears after spending so much time with the Rangers.

Her eyes opened wide. 'Hello, stranger!'

It was Flight Lieutenant Max Carmichael, husband to Eva, whom Alice had got to know when they first started work at Eastern House back in 1941.

Eva's dad, a colonel, had been overseeing the military in Porthcurno in those days, but although his daughter was a posh girl who spoke English like she had a mouth full of marbles, she'd mucked in with the rest of them like a proper trouper. Then Eva had gone off to the sanitorium in St Ives to nurse Max, who'd been caught up in a London bombing with her, and the two of them had eventually married, though only after Eva had persuaded Max he could walk again if he put his mind to it.

Eva, seated in the rear of his car, was cradling their new baby and waving cheerfully. Beside her, Hazel Cotterill sat with her own child, beaming, while Lily was crammed into the window seat.

Max nodded for her to jump into the front. She supposed his permanent leg injury must not affect his ability to drive. At least, she hoped so.

'Come on, Alice, shake a leg!' he called out, as the car behind beeped its horn at them to move, for they were blocking the narrow lane. 'We're holding everyone up. Unless you *want* to walk?'

'Yes, do hurry up, Alice,' Lily complained from the back seat. 'We're packed in like bloomin' sardines here.' She chuckled at Hazel and Eva's protests. 'No offence, ladies. But I am rather *large* these days.'

George Cotterill was behind the wheel of the vehicle behind, with various elderly villagers crammed into his large car, no doubt to save them from having to scale the near-vertical hill out of Porthcurno, simply in hope of a bloater sandwich and a slice of wedding cake. And following George were several more cars, all packed with wedding guests, some of them also waving and beeping their horns. She wondered if anyone in Porthcurno had *not* been invited, except for those in the listening station at Eastern House, for Gran knew nobody there these days except George Cotterill, and perhaps a few ladies on the cleaning staff.

Below them all was the heavily camouflaged façade of Eastern House, tucked discreetly into the valley bottom. As she opened the car door, Alice glanced that way, wondering if Patrick was down there right now, diligently working on his codes and ciphers.

She'd learnt, after his departure, that it was Mr Gladly who Patrick had been set to watch, one of their own instructors. Apparently, he'd seen Gladly meet an elderly neighbour of Florence's several times, a woman called Doreen, in suspicious circumstances, and had taken the information to Rawlings. Later, both Gladly and Doreen had been arrested as spies, for working against Britain's interests by passing information to Germany. It had all been a big shock, but no doubt all that close observational work had earned spotty Patrick a place at Eastern House, despite his shortcomings in the field . . .

With a grin, she climbed into the front seat. 'Thanks, Max, that's saved me a climb,' she admitted, and turned to say a proper hello to her old friends in the back. 'Hazel, you've cut your hair! It suits you. I hope you and Baby Lily are both well?' When Hazel agreed cheerfully, Alice turned to the other woman. 'But what's this? Eva Ryder . . . Sorry, Eva *Carmichael* . . . back in Porthcurno at last? And this must be your baby. Congratulations! What's his name?'

'Hello, Alice, I swear it's been absolute yonks since we last saw each other. You look so grown up!' Eva looked as pretty as ever, and was very smartly dressed in a pale green dress with matching cardigan. She tucked a wayward strand of lustrous blonde hair behind one ear, cuddling her baby son with a doting smile. 'We're calling him Edward after my uncle who passed away last year. Had a stroke, poor old soul. But little Teddy looks so like him, it's uncanny.'

'That nose . . .' Max murmured ironically. 'Unfortunate child.' The former ace pilot, who now trained younger men to fly fighter planes, flashed Alice a sideways smile as he drove. 'Eva's right though,' he drawled, 'you were a child in short socks when we last saw you. Now you look . . . well, ready for anything.' And he winked.

Seeing Lily's amusement at this remark, Alice smiled too, though she couldn't agree. She was too uncertain about what London was about to throw at her. But she thanked him anyway and rattled on for a while about Bude, never once admitting to the secret training she'd undergone there. This was family, not work, and she was fast learning to keep the two separate.

The wedding party at the farm seemed to go on forever, though in reality it was only a few hours, as gatherings of that size were strictly meant to be kept to a minimum, according to wartime regulations. There was a fiddler and a boy with a drum in the field beyond the farm gate, where people were dancing and a beer tent had been set up. One of the other farmers, with a nod and a wink, had brought a pig that was being roasted on a spit, and the local constable was carefully pretending he hadn't noticed this flouting of rationing protocols.

Alice surprised herself by dancing, first with a village boy who grinned throughout, and later with George Cotterill, who used the opportunity to ask discreetly how her training was going. She also had a wonderful natter with Lily, catching up with everything her energetic sister had been doing to keep herself busy since leaving work in preparation for the birth of her baby. She was a midwife, so knew what to expect at the birth, but as Lily herself admitted, 'It's one thing bringin' the little darlings into the world, and quite another to look after 'em and worry about 'em for the next two decades.' But Alice had reassured her that she would be a fabulous mum, with Tristan nodding, holding his wife's hand and smiling.

At last, the time came for the bride and groom to depart for their honeymoon. Arnie shook a few hands and then climbed into the car, exchanging banter with Joe and Max about the old engine while Gran went about hugging all the guests, thanking everybody for coming and for their lovely wedding gifts, and tearfully promising to send each and every one of them a postcard from her honeymoon.

'You're only away five days, Mum,' Aunty Vi reminded her, shaking her head, but she too was crying as she kissed her mum on the cheek and stood back to watch the white-haired newly-weds climb into the car Arnold had borrowed to take them to Penzance. 'Oh, bless you both, have a lovely time on your honeymoon, and try not to crash into a tree, Arnie.' Violet dragged an already damp hanky from her sleeve. 'I swear, all these weddings . . . One of these days I'll get through one without weepin' for Britain.'

Joe put an arm about his wife, his mouth quirking in a smile. 'I doubt it, love. But you've plenty of hankies, so I wouldn't worry.'

After Gran and Arnie had driven away, the wedding party began to break up. Beer-befuddled guests disappeared back down to the village in groups, some of them a little unsteadily. Cars slipped away at intervals, hopefully being driven by non-drinkers. It was early afternoon and the light was still sharp and crisp, for Gran hadn't trusted Arnie to drive safely after dark, unable to use his lights during curfew.

At last, only close family and friends remained at the farm, plus the Land Girls and the three evacuee kids – though Janice had disappeared up to her bedroom to read a stack of old women's magazines that Eva had brought her specially, as the girl was keen to train as a hairdresser one day. Aunty Vi gathered together the remains of their wedding feast onto the kitchen table, made a fresh pot of tea, and grudgingly allowed Joe to broach the last crate of beer, which they'd apparently been hoarding for months in anticipation of this event. There wasn't much room for young Eustace and Timothy, so they grabbed a sandwich each and ran out to play in the farmyard.

The women sat at the table while the men stood about or lounged against the wall or, in Joe and Max's cases, leant on their walking sticks. Eva and Hazel were talking babies while Violet listened with undisguised fascination, having already told everyone she was expecting and been widely congratulated, with lots of back slaps for Joe too. Lily was quietly knitting a pretty yellow baby cardigan that would be fine for either a boy or a girl, while Joe and Max talked cars, George chatted amiably with Tristan about Cornish politics, and the three Land Girls said their goodbyes and went back up to their attic rooms, each with a slice of homemade fruity wedding cake.

Sitting opposite, Penny sipped her tea and waggled her eyebrows meaningfully over the rim of the cup. She alone of those present knew about London but had agreed not to say anything until Alice felt ready.

It was time, Alice thought, and stood up with a scrape of her chair. The conversation died away and everyone looked at her in surprise. She cleared her throat, her heart thumping violently. It was just like when she'd told the family she was off to Bude, she thought, her nerves jumping. Only this time it was far worse. This time she would be out of easy reach of her family, and that would be difficult to explain without giving away government secrets.

'I've something important to tell you all,' she said, looking mostly at Aunty Violet and Lily, and already her voice was shaking. 'I expect you all know I've been doing this war work at a printers' workshop in Bude. Well, it's gone all right, and now the printer is sending me on a . . . a more advanced course. So as I can be better at doin' me job.'

'Congratulations,' Joe said in his slow, measured way, but she knew there was more to come when he paused, studying her. 'And where's this "more advanced course" taking place?'

'London,' she said faintly.

'What? *London*?' Violet put down her cup and saucer and stared at her as though Alice had sprouted two heads. 'Are you pullin' my leg, Alice Fisher? I hope you've told him no.'

'Erm . . .'

'I won't have you going into danger, my girl. You ain't forgot, I 'ope, why we left Dagenham in the first place? Because of all the bloomin' bombs!'

'It . . . It ain't so bad now, honest,' Alice said, her cheeks hot as everyone's stare seemed to be fixed on her face. 'I'd be in the centre of London too, where there's loads of shelters. Besides, it's a good opportunity to get proper training. And that'll prepare me for a trade,' she added hurriedly, 'for when the war's over.'

'A *trade*?' Lily seemed astonished. 'You've never wanted a trade before. I thought you was happy helping out at the school in Penzance. Teachin' them kiddies to read and write. That's more your thing, ain't it?'

'I was happy doing that, yes,' Alice admitted. 'Only this special printing work . . . It's different to what I expected. *Better*.'

'But when the war's over,' Joe said, frowning now, 'the men will come home and take over those printing jobs again. The jobs men have always done. Printers have guilds and they'll protect their profession. The women will go back to keeping house and . . . well, whatever women do.' He pulled a face, looking troubled. 'It's not what you want to hear, I know. And, speaking for myself, I think women can work just as hard as a man and at all the same jobs too. But we don't get to make that decision, and that's the reality of it, love.'

'I'm afraid Joe's right,' Eva agreed softly, her face sympathetic. 'It's a man's world, no doubt about it. Though for what it's worth, it's brave of you to try, Alice. But would you be happy in London without anyone you knew to call on if you got into trouble or needed a shoulder to cry on?'

'We don't live close to London anymore,' Max added apologetically before she could respond, nodding at his wife, 'or we would have offered to put you up during your stay. How long is this course?'

'About a . . . a year,' Alice stammered.

'*A year*?' Violet jumped up, her eyes flashing. 'Oh, not a bloomin' chance! Tell her, Joe. I've had enough. She's to forget this printing nonsense at once and come home to us.'

Alice shot Penny an anguished look, but her friend merely gave her an encouraging smile and a thumbs-up, nodding her to continue. *Oh blimey*, Alice thought, wringing her hands and wishing she knew what to say to make her family and friends understand why she had to go, without giving the game away.

'Aunty Vi, Uncle Joe, Lily . . .' Alice struggled for the

right words, and then told them in a strangled voice, 'It's all been decided. I . . . I've got the train ticket in my bag. It's too late to say no.' Her aunt shrieked, Lily muttered something disapproving, and Joe banged his stick on the floor in exasperation. Desperately, Alice looked around at them all, the people she loved best in the world, and wished that her dad was there to smooth things over, as he always did. But he was far away and the only person she could rely on was herself. Picking her words carefully, she added, 'Dad would understand, if . . . if he was still alive.'

She had to be cautious with what she said. Not everyone there knew that Ernest Fisher was not missing presumed dead, but still alive. At least, he had been last summer when he'd come to visit them briefly in Cornwall. They had been sworn to secrecy though, just as she had been in Bude, and she couldn't break that oath. Not even to avoid parting from her family and friends in this wretched, unhappy way.

'Dad?' Lily looked puzzled. 'But—'

Tristan put a hand on his wife's arm. 'I think what Alice is trying to say is that your father Ernest, God rest his soul, would have wanted her to do this.' His clever gaze met Alice's. 'Am I right?'

'Yes,' she said, nodding eagerly. 'That's exactly right.'

'*Ernest*?' Violet sat back down, staring at her.

'Your dad would have wanted you to go to London?' Joe asked slowly, and then caught Tristan's frowning look. 'Oh . . . I see. *London*.' He blinked. 'Well, I never.'

Violet shook her head, but the fire had gone out of her eyes. 'I don't like it. Though I suppose you're a grown woman now and I can't stop you. Especially if your heart's

397

set on it. But what's your gran going to say, eh? She'll blame me for letting you go. I won't hear the last of it.'

'I'll write Gran a letter,' Alice promised, 'and leave it for her to read when she gets back.'

That seemed to settle Violet's mind. But later, when the others had gone and the farm was quietening down for the night, Lily came to find Alice in the old attic room they'd shared before her sister's marriage to Tristan.

'Are you learning to be a spy, Alice?' she asked bluntly, lowering her voice so the Land Girls in the next room wouldn't overhear their conversation.

'I can't tell you that,' Alice whispered.

'Good grief. That's a yes, then.' Her sister stared at her, then gave her a hug. 'For gawd's sake, don't risk your life. Do you hear me? It would kill Gran if anything happened to you. Aunty Vi would never be the same either.' Her eyes filled with tears. 'And as for me—' Her voice broke in a sob. 'You'll always be my little sister. Promise me, Alice, that you'll look after yourself and not do anything dangerous. Swear it on our mother's life.'

Alice held her sister close, and then whispered, 'I swear it.'

But her heart ached, because she might not be able to keep that promise. For the first time in her life, she understood why her dad had always seemed a little distant from the rest of them. Not because he didn't love his daughters, but because his work was dangerous and not something he could ever really discuss. He had kept quiet and stayed away in order to protect them.

Now she must do the same with her own loved ones. For their sake and the sake of her country.

Though she would do it her own way.

'I'm hoping Dad would be proud of me though, following in his footsteps like this.' She patted her sister's hand. 'And I'll be back before you know it. I'll send you my new address so we can keep in touch. I'll expect letters every single week, mind. Very long letters, at least four pages, and photographs of everyone too, and . . . and a lock of the baby's hair when it arrives.'

'Blimey,' Lily said with a gasp of laughter. 'Is that all?' She smiled through her tears. 'You never do things by halves, do you, Alice Fisher?'

Acknowledgements

Hooray, another novel in my Cornish Girls saga series completed, and first and foremost, I am so grateful to my fabulous readers for coming with me on this wonderful journey! From those who have picked this up as their very first Betty Walker saga to those who have shared every moment of the Cornish Girls series unfolding on Twitter, Instagram, TikTok and my Facebook author page over the past few years, I thank you all from the bottom of my heart. Without you, without readers, a story cannot come to life. Thank you.

On the work side of things, I am also deeply grateful to many people. My thanks as ever go to my agent Alison Bonomi for her unstintingly kind support and advice, and everyone at LBA for their hard work on my behalf. A huge shout of thanks also to my wonderful editor, Rachel Hart, who has been a steady pair of hands and a friendly voice throughout the birth of this latest saga. Many thanks too to the fab Thorne Ryan, and also to Helen Huthwaite, Raphaella Demetris, Gaby Drinkald, Ella Young, Elisha

Lundin, Maddie Dunne Kirby, and the whole team at Avon Books and HarperCollins. It's often been said that every book is a team effort, and my team is absolutely marvellous, book after book!

Also, a kiss to my husband Steve, who after more than two decades still puts up with my odd writerly behaviour without complaint (mostly), and thanks to my youngest three, Dylan, Morris and Indigo, who have all flown the nest for university now, but whose weekly phone calls are always fun and supportive. Thank you, and please come back soon. I miss my noisy team of washer-uppers and tea-makers!

Lastly, I couldn't end this without acknowledging the help of my lovely and miraculous characters. My Cornish Girls – and all their mothers and fathers and siblings and friends and lovers – have been my faithful companions throughout this saga series. Thank you, and I hope to see you all again soon and find out what you've been up to – something brave and breathtaking as usual, I have no doubt!

Betty x

Go back to where it all began – don't miss the first book in the glorious Cornish Girls series . . .

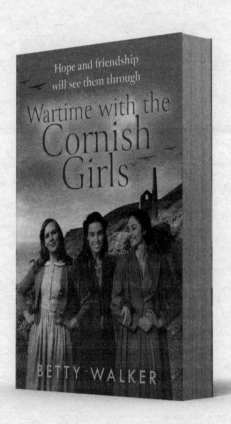

Follow up with some festive fun for
the Cornish Girls . . .

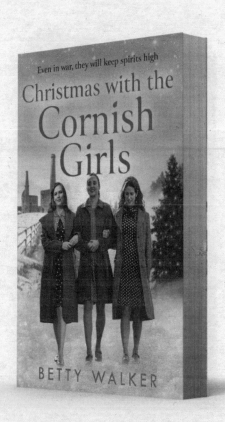

Available now in paperback, eBook
and audiobook.

Enemy gunfire on Penzance beach
brings the Cornish Girls rushing to
the rescue . . .

Available now in paperback, eBook
and audiobook.

Can the bonds of motherhood give them the strength they'll need to get through the war? . . .

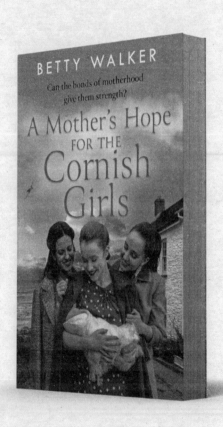

Available now in paperback, eBook and audiobook.